# WHIRLIGIG

A PARALLEL WORLD OF FANTASTIC CREATURES

JOHN BROUGHTON

# PREFACE

"I thought we were supposed to be best friends," Jayne complained.

"We are," Emily's tone was anything but friendly, "but that's got nothing to do with it."

"You're already in the long-jump and the sprint; now you want to take the high-jump from me!"

Emily, trying not to show the glee welling up inside her, put on her concerned face. "I'm only trying to do my best for the school. You want us to win the cup, don't you?"

"But I'm taller than you!"

"What's that got to do with anything? I'm more determined than you are. Miss Harrington knows it! You knocked the bar off in trials, and I cleared it by a mile."

"I told you, I had a tummy ache that morning."

"Any excuse, Janey beanpole. Admit it, I'm the better athlete."

Jayne's naturally pallid face blanched and she glared right into those taunting blue eyes. "You can find yourself another friend, Emily Gasbag!"

Jayne stormed out of her former friend's bedroom and out of her life. Gasbag was the nickname her classmates whispered behind her back: Emily knew it. She threw herself on her bed and fought back tears. That band of failures spoke out of envy because she was better than them, not just at sport, either. They hated that she was brilliant clarinettist and the maths teacher's favourite pupil. Wasn't she entitled to show off a little? Most of all, they were jealous because she was protective of her gorgeous younger brother, Adam. If any of them tried to chat with him, they'd unmuzzle the spiteful, cutting tongue they all dreaded.

Angrily wiping her tears with her sleeve, she reflected on the last twenty minutes. Jayne had no idea what went on in her head. All she saw was her friend's blustering. What did she know about feeling unloved and inferior? She didn't have a father who only wanted a son, did she? Emily had watched Jayne's father cuddle her and stroke her long straight hair. She thought that her long, corn-coloured hair was much more attractive than *Plain Jayne*'s. Well, she could live without her friendship—or anybody's for that matter. She would just live in her own perfect world and show daddy whose daughter was the best in town.

Not far from their home lay an extensive woodland where she and her brother played at explorers or simple games like hide-and-seek. To-morrow, the weekend was theirs. She would go there with Adam and to hell with Jayne!

In the middle of the woods, a green meadow opened out from an overgrown track. The hidden green, with a slight dome, had a copse at its crown. And, a secret within a secret, sticks barricaded a hole where two bushes met and touched the ground. The sticks formed a door dressed with twigs and grasses, so only the sharpest eye might notice them. This entry led to a space at the very centre of the copse sur-rounded by bushes and trees. Inside was a den made of branches and scraps of wood put to-gether over time to form a shelter. A board was nailed above the door with a warning: KEEP OUT OR ELSE.

Little light penetrated the thick bushes, so two electric torches lay next to an old book on a wooden table. Without them, the posters and pictures pinned to the walls could not be seen, and the book could not be read. The book lay open at a new chapter with the title *Gateway to the Other World,* written in strange flowing letters. Below the title was a set of instructions explaining how to enter this world. The book belonged to the joint owner of the den, and she'd learned the instructions by heart. Today was the *real* Midsummer's Day, not June 21 as most people believed, but St. John's Day – June 24; it was now midday, and on the green beyond the copse, the barefoot girl was carrying out the instructions to the letter.

The short grass was spattered with daisies, dandelions and other common field flowers. But it also had a strange feature, a place where the grass grew longer, darker and thicker. This curious grass formed a perfect circle: a ring that stood out clearly from the rest of the grass. The local people called these *fairy rings,* but nobody remembered why. The young girl paced her way around it, never stepping off the thicker grass. Her concentration was so fierce that she didn't notice the tickly sensation of springy grass under her feet. Her eyes were fixed one step ahead on the ring, and her lips moved as she recited the copied verse she held in her hand. Around her blonde hair, she wore a band of flowers, mainly St. John's Wort, but woven into the base were exactly 33 harebells, 17 cowslips, and 10 buttercups. The girl had bound them together before midday as instructed by the writer of the book. In her left hand, she held a rowan twig and, in her right, an ash wand. Emily was about to complete her third and last circling of the ring.

Lying face down in the centre of the ring, reading a football magazine – and truth be told, sulking – was a boy two years younger. He was fifteen. Adam ignored his sister; that is, he tried to ignore her and get on with his reading. But how can you ignore a girl who believes in fairies! And while he thought this *ritual* was *nonsense for girls*, he had to admit to being bothered. It troubled him that the ritual was written down in a book, and worse, it was written in a book with strange ancient-style handwriting.

They had just argued. Emily insisted that Adam's world of football, computers, television and cinema wasn't real, but made of illusions. She would show him that the natural world, *her* world, was real and that there was more to it than met the eye.

Last weekend Emily had found the *Book of Country Lore* buried under many others at an antiques fair. Their parents enjoyed hunting for bargains and rummaging around among old furniture and jewellery, and last time out, their mother had found a lovely Edwardian brooch and Emily had found the book. It was battered and unattractive, and she didn't pay much for it. At first, she let Adam look at its faded ink sketches and strange writing when he asked, but then she'd become secretive and possessive with it. And now she was supposed to be taking them into another world on Midsummer's Day! Ridiculous! In any case, he told her she'd got the wrong date, but she wouldn't have it. *Girls!* Adam snorted, in the age of satellites and video calls, nobody believed in superstitious nonsense any more: only Emily. Sometimes, he thought, she behaved like his *younger* sister. He glanced at her with a superior smile and went back to reading about his favourite team.

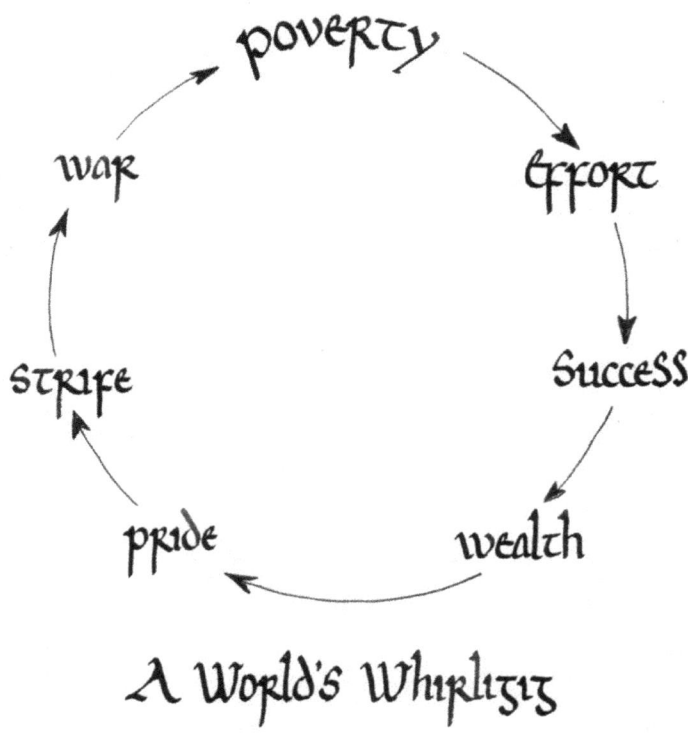

A World's Whirligig

*Dawn Burgoyne*

# I

# IN THE LAND OF POVERTY

# 1

---

*A*dam and Emily saw themselves as if from the outside. The girl watched one of her hands take her brother's and the other point to a dragonfly, circling their heads so that its wings almost touched Adam's nose. Emily gasped as she saw something impossible: a woman dressed in white sitting on the dragonfly. Tiny and perfectly formed with a golden crown above her long, silver hair, she smiled at the girl. Emily clutched Adam's hand tightly and wanted to tell him that fairies exist after all and that she'd been right all along, but her words misbehaved. They came from the world of her imagination. Her words were spoken in another tongue: a lovely sound like tinkling Tibetan bells. Adam understood her perfectly; but as he replied, the air vibrated and whirled. It felt as though they would be swept off their feet and into the air while Emily's grip on his hand became increasingly painful.

The trees behind them blurred green as they spun, and the air became opaque like a steamed-up mirror. Then the mirror cracked across, so the gap created widened while all else spun and whirled around it. But the scene within the crack was firm and well-defined, while the outer, opaque part, swirled like an impenetrable fog. Adam and Emily found themselves inside the gap as if sucked in, but she swore she hadn't taken a step. There was no sign of the dragonfly; instead, all around them, a chilling mist covered the land, cloaking a wilderness of filthy pools dotted among patches of gorse. Bad gasses mingled with the damp air and Adam held his nose and complained. He asked, "What happened to that weird little woman? Where are we?"

Emily looked around with frightened eyes. This wasn't what she'd intended to happen when she began her recital. She had no idea and said so in words of a strange, sweet language. Adam stared at his sister, blinked hard and rubbed his eyes. Her long, blonde hair, like her blue eyes, were now shining silver. Above all, she was very pretty indeed; she was still their Emily but like a film star from one of the posters in their den. Of course, he couldn't see himself, or he would have been amazed. Despite the strangeness of everything around him, Adam had a sense that all was as it should be. He really should be terrified, but he wasn't. He felt puzzled and curious, but *brave* as well.

He asked himself what had happened to the middle of June: it seemed like the end of February. For that matter, where were the woods and their den? As for Emily, her toes were numb and she curled them against the cold. She folded her arms across her chest and, her breath wreathing upwards, told Adam to follow her through the gorse. It snagged their jeans and scratched their arms even when they were being careful so that they cried out several times. The barbed bushes seemed to be waiting, watching and then lunging spitefully at them. Soon Emily was limping and crying from the thorns that pierced her bare feet. Luckily, she was just tall enough to see over the spiny bushes to a track.

The track was kinder to her feet; determined, they continued along until it forked in three directions. One way led off through the gorse; another wandered discouragingly downhill through puddles and swamp; the last, broadest and best worn, led uphill. They took the easiest path without a word. Twisting slowly, it gave a view from the top over a wilderness stretching as far as the eye could see. And they saw rough, marshy grassland with stagnant pools, broken by mazes of gorse and tangled briar.

"It's hateful!" Emily sobbed, "We're lost and I'm so cold. I'm sorry, Adam, I didn't mean to. I just wanted to see what the *Other World* was like." She shivered and looked so wretched that Adam put an arm around her and told her not to worry.

"Well, you've seen it! And it's horrible! I don't suppose you could get us back to *Our World* now, could you? Please?"

Emily gasped; she'd been so keen to visit the *Other World* that she hadn't thought about finding out how to get back. She fought back tears, looked crestfallen at her brother, then her expression changed to wonder. She'd been so occupied with the pain in her feet and how cold she felt that she hadn't really looked at him until now. How he'd changed! He seemed taller and older and more handsome, and his blond hair was silver! His eyes were silver, too! Emily looked down at her long hair falling over her chest and gaped. She grabbed it and felt it. It was silver, but very fine and soft like silk. "Adam," she said in her strange new language, "what colour are my eyes? Am I ...am I ...pretty?"

"Silver. You're not pretty, Em, you're beautiful like a princess! Have I changed too?" he asked hopefully.

"Well, yes, you're handsome!" and tears filled her eyes, "but it isn't *us* and we don't *belong* here, it isn't *Our World*," and her voice broke into a wail, "and—*I don't know how to get us back home again!*" Emily buried her face in her hands; her body was wracked with sobs as she thought of home and her mother and father and her cat, Jasmine. "And I'm so cold!"

Again, Adam felt brave, like he could overcome anything or anybody. Definite action was needed, so he plunged down into the briar and gorse and began untangling dead stems. Although the thorns scratched his hands, he ignored the pain and carried an armful back to his sister, who was stamping her feet and wiping her eyes. Adam tossed the thorns down beside her at the top of the hill, where he pulled a matchbox from his pocket with a smile. He was glad he always carried a penknife, magnifying glass, string, ballpoint pen, bottle-opener, and so on—you never knew when they'd be needed. Soon, a flame was crackling and dancing across the thorns, sending a thin plume of smoke skywards.

Emily leant forward, holding her hands grate-fully near the fire.

"I'll build it up ..." Adam's words died on his lips.

All about him on the hill were little people. Thin, hungry-looking, ragged people, standing no higher than his waist. They had long, pointed ears and greenish skin. Their tattered green and brown clothing blended so well with their sur-roundings that they could hardly be seen. In fact, Adam blinked and rubbed his eyes, thinking that it was a trick of the light. But the strangers were still there, fixing him with yellow eyes dull with defeat and fatigue.

"Who are you? Who has dared release the Hag's spell?" One, with a squint, asked in a fluting voice. These curious beings spoke in the same tinkling language Adam and Emily were using.

Emily moved towards Adam and whispered fearfully, "They're pixies, aren't they?"

Brother and sister were shocked when the creature replied, even though these beings were small, they had powerful hearing!

"Ay, we are," the same pixy said, "but who are you, tall as trolls, but fair as elves? You will not harm us?"

"He heard me!" Emily gasped and, remembering her manners, added: "I'm Emily, and this is my brother, Adam. Of course, we won't harm you. You see, we are lost—" She stopped because the pixy had taken off his hat and was bowing to them.

"I am Lar, Leader of the Lostlings. At your service."

"At my service...?"

"Of course, you, who have broken the spell binding us to the Hag."

"B-but ... we haven't done anything!"

"You have burnt thorns on a fairy hill."

"Well – er – yes, but—"

Emily looked at Adam and then stared at the eager faces around them. Moments passed, and slowly the look of defeat returned. The pixies murmured among themselves and shook their heads.

"Look at the confusion you have caused," Lar accused them, his face growing ever more wrinkled as he frowned. "Strange fate, indeed, it is to be led by one ignorant of fairy lore!"

"He's got a queer way of talking," Adam whispered to Emily. He was startled to see that Lar had heard his words, judging from the severe squint he received. She ignored her brother and burst out: "I know *lots* about fairies." Adam looked at her doubtfully. "I *do*," she insisted, "you're the one who's never believed in fairies and pixies, and now you're talking to pixies and I've read books about them, so there!"

There was shocked silence at Emily's outburst. Then Lar said firmly: "Good! Then you must lead us, Emily."

"Lead you? Lead you where?"

"Out of this accursed land. Away from the clutches of the Hag. You must! You have released her spell, now lead us!"

"But I don't even know where this land is! I told you, we're lost—"

These words had a startling effect upon the band of pixies. Heads dropped and shoulders sagged under the weight of misery.

"No, wait!" Adam said. "Who's this Hag you keep talking about? Tell us everything!"

"Everything? Everything would take many moon-risings," Lar replied gloomily, "but I'll tell what I can."

The pixies immediately sat cross-legged on the ground and Adam and Emily copied them.

"This is the Land of Poverty. It is the land," he lowered his voice to a whisper, "of the Hag, the Ill-Favoured One, the Wicked Fairy. She is a witch whose will is winter and whose heart is ice." Lar's yellow eyes fixed Emily, and he waved an arm around him. "She has created all this. It is a land of suffering, a doomed land."

"It's horrible," Emily nodded and added, "but why are you all here?"

"Her will. Even from afar the Hag's power is great. Whomsoever her will settles upon is weakened, brought low and finally falls under her spell. Lar pointed to the smallest pixy, a child who was sitting in his mother's lap and his face became sadder still and more wrinkled. He squinted hard at Adam: *"It's an unhappy bird that's born in an unlucky nest,* is it not so, Master?"

Adam nodded thoughtfully, wondering at being called *Master*.

"And this land is very unlucky, very bad," Emily agreed.

"Once under the Hag's spell," Lar went on, "forever a Lostling."

"What does that mean?" Emily asked, brushing her hair out of her face.

As his sister questioned the pixy, Adam studied the curious creature with his squint, who spoke so piteously, yet so wisely, and who had called him Master. The pixy's next words bothered him even more.

"We are doomed, condemned to a life of misery, to wander these wastes in search of scraps of

11

comfort," Lar said with bitterness in his voice. He looked hard at Adam again: *"He who has food eats and he who has not, bites his nails,* is it not so, Master?" It seemed that the pixy had a saying for every situation. Lar continued without waiting for Adam's reply. "Even so, we are tormented by the Hag's spriggans—"

"Spriggans?" Adam asked.

Emily seized her chance to impress the pixy company with her knowledge of fairy lore. "Spriggans are wicked creatures," she informed her brother.

"Ay, *wicked*," Lar paused upon the word and repeated it as if the word itself could do harm. "Oh yes, wicked. They torment those who disobey or resist the Hag in any way. They vex anyone who crosses their path," he sighed, "and as if that's not enough, we're at the mercy of the trolls too..."

"Trolls!" Adam and Emily cried out together.

"They're giants, aren't they?" Adam gasped.

Lar eyed the boy from head to toe. "Ay, almost as tall as you..." he said gravely, but his words trailed away as his gaze followed those of the other pixies over to the east. There, the sky had lowered into a dark swathe such as Adam and Emily had never seen before. Beneath low clouds, in the distance, a snowstorm flailed towards them. Already the odd snowflake swirled about them, a forerunner of what was about to break.

"What's happening, Lar?" Emily asked nervously.

The pixies were on their feet now, waiting for orders. Lar, like the others, clutched his hat, to prevent the whistling wind from whipping it away.

"It's the fury of the Hag, Mistress. The Ill-favoured One has missed us but doesn't yet know where we are. The snow is Hagspite. It's full of her wickedness. What is your will, Mistress?"

Twenty pairs of eyes turned, scrutinising Emily's face. She tried not to show her doubts and fears, after all. She had not asked to be called 'Mistress' but, in this matter. she didn't seem to have any choice. Evidently, these pixies saw her as their only hope, but everything seemed so unreal to her. She thought of home, her garden and her cat, Jasmine, those were real. What on earth was happening to her and Adam? For a moment, she had the strange sensation of being in a film, then it passed.

"Oh, it's cold," she said out loud and shivered. She wasn't dreaming this chill.

She glanced at the track, which by now was

only a scar across the cloak of snow among the bushes. Further along, other scars crossed it or branched from it. Emily snapped out of her trance. "There's no point in staying here," she shouted above the wind, "though, as I said, I don't know my way in this land."

"Nor do we, Mistress," Lar answered, shivering even more as the snow thickened, "at least, not these parts." He turned to the others: "Who among you has tramped these by-ways?"

Adam smiled to himself at the pixy's peculiar way of speaking and looked around the little band. At first, nobody moved, but, at last, one made her hesitant way forward. She made an old-fashioned curtsy in front of Emily.

"This is Lenya from the Land of Halewood," Lar introduced Lenya, who now spoke in a sing-song voice: "I was this way two moons ago, Mistress, seeking berries; I know," she lowered her voice, "where this track leads."

"Where?"

"It leads to the troll's lair—the troll known as Nabgrasp! I was fortunate to escape with my life!" Even though Lenya had kept her voice low in the wind, pixy hearing is very sharp, so at the troll's name, groans broke from the snow-shrouded company.

"Nabgrasp?" Emily repeated the name.

"Ay," Lar nodded. "The Snatcher. The troll who takes what little one has. The Hag only unbinds broken-spirited pixies who agree to obey her every command. She sends them into the wider world to steal for her and to bring her coins, jewels or trinkets of value, which she then flings down a bottomless pit into the earth—"

"That's stupid, isn't it?" Adam butted in.

"Because the more she takes out of the world, the poorer it becomes and the happier she is. It is poverty she craves most of all."

"...And none of you has agreed to obey her," Adam said. It wasn't a question, but Lar looked hard at the boy, who by now half-expected some wise saying to follow.

He was right: *"Even if the rings have gone, the fingers still remain,"* Lar declared in a squeaky voice that was meant to sound noble, "is it not so, Master?"

"Ay," Adam imitated the pixy.

"But where does this troll Grabnam fit in?" Emily asked quickly.

"Nabgrasp...*Nabgrasp!*" Lar repeated impatiently. "He steals what little any Hag-ridden pixy might have, should he chance upon him or her. Or if he catches one of us carrying treasure to the Hag, he will take the lot!" Lar's brow darkened and a look of hatred burned behind his squint. "But any poor pixy who falls empty-handed into his clutches..." Lar didn't finish the sentence but sighed and, catching Adam's eye, added: *"It rains only on the person who's already soaked,* is it not so, Master?"

"Ay, it is so," Adam nodded, but Emily nudged him and the grin vanished from his face.

Adam and Emily were full of questions, despite the snow which was piling on their clothing while the wind slashed across their faces.

"Why does the Hag allow the troll to get away with her treasure?" Emily frowned.

"Trolls are far older creatures than fairies and therefore resistant to fairy magic. The Hag is too lazy to rid her land of them. There are four of them; she finds it easier to leave them. Besides, the more Nabgrasp has in his hoard, the less there is in the world outside. Though, I dare say if his hoard grew too great, she'd turn her spite on him...but, Mistress, I beg you," Lar shivered, "lead us from this place before we all freeze to death."

## 2

---

$\mathscr{E}$mily looked at the pixies' thin clothing. "This way," she shouted into the wind and led them off downhill. At least she could look determined, even if she hadn't a clue what to do. Anyway, walking would warm them a little. Meanwhile, she hoped to think up a plan. The small folks followed her in a dejected column, their poor, half-starved bodies were defenceless against the spite-laden wind. Lar knew that they couldn't last long like this, so he joined Emily up front.

"Mistress, the Hag intends to kill us with her spite, with this wind." Lar raised his voice to make himself heard: "Besides, I think I told you, the troll's lair lies this way."

"Yes, Lar, I know—" Emily's words were half-lost in the storm, "I have a plan; you must trust me!"

Whipping out of the sky, the snow began to settle thickly, making their progress very difficult. Since Adam was so much bigger than the pixies, Emily ordered him to make a pathway for them by dragging his feet. As she pointed out, he had shoes whereas she didn't. At first, he grumbled about not taking orders from a girl, but the pixies looked so upset at his words that he agreed quickly and got on with it. He decided he'd sort out his arrogant sister later. Even though he was big and strong compared to the rest of the band, it was tiring work for him. At last, they came to their destination, where he and Emily were the only ones relieved by the sight of the troll's cave lying at the foot of the hill.

"The lair of the troll," Lar muttered darkly.

"Listen, Lar," Emily said, "you and the others must work hard. You must each build a snowman as tall as Adam and I. We'll help—"

"No, Mistress! Think of the danger!" Lar cried; his yellow eyes opened wide with fear. To the pixy, this was an invitation far worse than being snapped and crushed in the troll's heavy jaws. But the Mistress seemed to know what she was doing.

"What's dangerous about making snow-men?" Emily grumbled, "Come on, it's an important part of my plan!"

Lar shrugged and looked as if he wanted to say much more, but he bit his lip and stared at the snow as if it were a deadly creature. After a short silence, he began to organise his followers. Emily took Adam aside and explained her plan. He resented her bossing him about, but Emily stamped a bare foot and hissed that it was hard enough to get the pixies to do anything and did he want to freeze to death out in the cold? So, he nodded his head and swallowed his pride. Reluctantly, muttering all the while, the pixies began to build snowmen. They worked so unwillingly that Emily had to threaten to leave them several times to make them hurry. At last, there was a snowman for each pixy and five each for the children, so it seemed that a silent army was standing before the troll's cave.

"We're ready, Adam!" Emily shouted. "Be brave, Lar, hide with your pixies behind that snowdrift."

"Willingly!" Lar looked relieved. In an instant, all the pixies seemed to have melted into the snow.

Heart pounding, Adam strolled down to the troll's cave, comforted that the pixies had told him he was taller than the troll. In his mind, trolls were enormous, massive giants that gobbled up children. That was in fairy tales and, after all, fairies were tiny—trolls were sure to be giants in their eyes. Half-persuaded, Adam stood in the cavemouth and shouted: "Oi! Where are you, Nabgrasp? Come out, horrid old troll!" His voice echoed in the cave although he tried to make it deep, it still sounded boyish. Adam took a step back into the snowstorm. A few frantic heartbeats later, heavy footsteps thumped deep inside the cave. A voice rumbled and echoed: "Rrrr, rrr, Old Grasper don't smell pixies! He don't smell spriggans! Who's outside his Bone-Mill? Grrind to powderrr! Grrind to dust!"

In the gloom of the cavemouth, Adam could not make out the creature's form. The stomping steps and deep voice scared him. It came closer. He could hear its breath rasping. The troll stopped suddenly a few paces from the boy. He was incredibly ugly and stank. The troll's heavy cheeks, like a bloodhound's, and his glum face, the whole topped by a shock of spiky hair, suggested stupidity. But above his warty nose, two small eyes full of malice and cunning warned Adam to take care. The troll was too sturdy for Adam's taste, even if he wasn't so tall. His knotted arms, too long for his short, hairy legs and body, drooping and swinging from a leather jerkin, looked capable of snapping the boy in half. Nabgrasp's red rheumy eyes glared at the boy, but his jaw dropped. He'd never seen a human, a boy, before and he was puzzled and doubtful.

"'Ere, what'rrre you then?" he growled, showing his dirty yellow teeth. He was used to terrifying pixies much smaller than himself, not a stranger standing straight and fearless in front of him. Adam was terrified, but he wasn't going to let the troll know. If anything, he felt oddly inventive.

"You don't know, do you, Nabgrasp? I am Lord of the Trolls. I've come to claim my tribute. I've travelled for days with my army—" He swept an arm towards the snowmen and watched Nabgrasp's eyes widen. The snow, falling heavily now, made it hard to see the shapes clearly, convincing the slow-thinking troll of his danger. Adam's voice grew bolder: "I am here to claim tribute and to make sure you aren't being wicked."

The troll scratched his spiky hair uneasily, puzzled. He peered anxiously through the thickening snow towards the ranked army at the stranger's back. Trolls are not quick thinkers. Entire seconds passed in which there was no sign of movement. Finally, Nabgrasp's small eyes narrowed to slits, and his huge hands clenched into fists and slowly unclenched again. He took a step forward and, baring his yellow teeth, growled: "Old Grasper knows no Lord and Master!"

Adam's stomach, already knotted tight, heaved as the troll's breath hit him. It stank of rotten fish. He felt weak and frightened. He wanted to run away as the troll stepped forward, but he couldn't abandon the pixies to this monster. He straightened up to his full height and drew on unexpected reserves of courage. Fixing the troll with a menacing stare, he pointed into the distance and cried: "Nabgrasp, leave now or it'll be the worse for you!" He held his breath, hoping that his bluff would work. Nabgrasp hesitated. Confusion, fear and hatred battled in his red eyes, but like all trolls, he was stubborn. The loss of his cave and treasure was too much to bear. He stood his ground and swung his long arms like a wrestler about to fight. Adam's heart sank. Their plan wasn't going to work. Well, he decided, he'd better carry the bluff through to the end. "Right men," he called, "forward, attack! Drive the troll away!"

Adam didn't bother to turn; there was no point. He was just hoping that the troll's nerve would break first and that Nabgrasp would panic and run off. The troll's face turned dirty white, and he *did* take off! Adam watched in disbelief as he ran down the path, downhill, as fast as his stumpy legs could carry him. Adam's eyes opened wider still, as the first snowman rushed past him. The rest followed, brushing him aside. The snowmen only had two holes for eyes, where the pixies had poked their long fingers, but they all chased after Nabgrasp as if they could see. *"Alive...?"* Adam gasped. He stared at the snow where they left no trail behind them. Adam watched them disappear at high speed, close on the troll's heels, over the hill and into the next valley. He closed his mouth and not for the first time that day, rubbed his eyes. He had to be dreaming! What kind of place was this *Other World*? Pixies! Trolls! *Animated snowmen!*

"Hooray! Come on!" Emily called to the excited pixies to come out from behind the snowdrift.

Completely confused, Adam led the way into the troll's cave.

The place stank of troll. Firelight reflected from the dripping walls and glowed deep inside the cave, where smoke was swirling up and away through a natural rock chimney. Behind the fire, at the back of the cave, a small pile of gold and jewellery sparkled and along with them were scattered many more small coins of base metal. "Pixy wages," Lar muttered, "stolen along with the rest."

Most of the pixies huddled around the fire, grateful for warmth at last. Others raided the troll's larder, which was stuffed with hams and cheeses, along with other, more revolting meat, which everyone avoided. The pixies ate as if they hadn't eaten for a lifetime and, soon, tinkling laughter echoed in the high cave.

Adam, brooding, suddenly said, "What I don't understand is how the snowmen came to life—"

"Me neither," Emily admitted between mouthfuls of ham. There was a sudden silence as the laughter died away.

"Was that not your plan?" Lar asked, accusation in his voice. "A wild and dangerous plan, to be sure, but one upon which you gambled successfully? The snow was Hagspite and therefore enchanted. You made effigies out of it and commanded them with spite, and because the troll is evil and wealthy, they obeyed you and went after him."

Red-faced, Emily coughed uncomfortably, then asked: "What will happen to Nabgrasp now?"

"He will be chased back to the Hag. Then

she will learn from the troll who it was that set her spite onto him. Therefore, we must leave soon before she turns her face towards this place."

"That's good," Adam laughed, "she'll hear some garbled tale about the Lord of the Trolls."

"Well, at least, let's take some of this treasure," Emily said, fingering a sapphire which flashed entrancingly in the firelight.

Lar shook his head. "Far better to travel without wealth in this Land, for in the Land of Poverty, all wealth is ill-gained and can only bring misfortune."

"What about this, Lar?" Adam asked suddenly, picking up a silver sphere from among the coins. Lar joined the boy. His dull yellow eyes shone for the first time. "This is an elven orb, Master, sealed with a binding spell. I cannot imagine how the troll was able to lay his filthy hands on it."

"A binding spell?"

"Ay, can you not read the runes?"

"Runes...?"

"Here." Lar's long forefinger traced the lines carved into its surface. "See, its name is *Cari*, which in Elfish means 'Charity'. The spell binds the orb to serve only one who fights evil with a pure heart. This elven orb certainly

25

could have been of no service to the wicked Grasper."

"I'll put *Cari* in my pocket," Adam said. "It might come in useful."

"Beware," Lar warned, "that orb could be of great harm if the bearer be unworthy."

"Don't worry," Adam said softly, "it'll be all right with me until someone worthier comes along." Indeed, *Cari* seemed to shine even more in his hand.

Leaving the gems with reluctance, Emily ordered the pixies to gather as much food as they could carry for their journey. She didn't want to leave the warmth of the cave, but she knew that Lar was right. It would be dangerous for them to remain any longer in a place where they could be so easily trapped.

They hurried through the passage back to the cave mouth. To their amazement, the land outside was clear of snow and, though not warm, at least free of mist and rain.

"That's better!" Adam said.

"Nay!" Lar shook his head.

"Why not?"

"The Hag has not cleared the snow for our benefit. It can only mean one thing—she has sent her spriggans after us. We must flee!"

At the word *spriggan*, the pixies scattered in

all directions. Most of them were used to roaming the wilderness singly.

"Wait!" Emily shouted. "Nobody will escape the Hag unless we stick together. You can't give up for fear of spriggans. We'll think of another plan!" Emily was very determined. Since she had been chosen to lead the pixies to freedom, that was exactly what she intended to do. Emily hadn't seen the Hag, but she could sense her wickedness everywhere around her. She felt it was her duty to defeat the witch. Emily liked the pixies, and it made her angry to see them looking like whipped dogs.

The pixies made their way back and gathered around her, watching her from under lowered eyes.

"Are spriggans as big as trolls?" Adam asked.

Several pixies tried to answer at the same time, each shouting louder in their high voices and each making spriggans sound worse than the other. Lar calmed them with difficulty and took over the explanation: "Spriggans are no bigger than us, but are given by nature to malice and harm." He looked hard at Adam from under bushy eyebrows: *"The wildcat never spares the sparrow,* is it not so, Master?"

"Ay," Adam laughed.

Lar stared even harder at Adam, and his

squint became even more noticeable. "Have I amused you, Master?"

"*Er*...no, it's just a thought I had, Lar," Adam said quickly, not wishing to offend.

"We must make haste," Lar urged Emily. "Many of them will be coming this way even as we talk. The spriggans carry slings and their stones, when they strike, burn like fire coals. Above all, the spriggans are savages and they pinch, scratch and bite and pull hair out by the roots. Look!" Lar took off his brown hat and pointed to a patch of scalp without hair. "They are wiry and slippery, and we have no weapons against them," Lar ended lamely.

Emily looked thoughtful and said, "Well, if we haven't got weapons, we'll have to use trickery. Lar, I remember reading that folks can be *pixy-led*, isn't that some kind of trick?"

"Ay!" Lar curled his lip, "I should say so!"

"Well, then, we mustn't go so far from here," Emily ordered. "The spriggans will come here first. They're going to find us!"

3

_enya_ showed she understood by crying out excitedly: "I know just the place! Come on!"

The delicate pixy ran ahead, laughter tinkling, leading them along a valley until they came to a hillside. It was lined with a patchwork of collapsing stone walls. Lenya turned and grinned at Emily and Lar, who exchanged knowing looks. Only Adam looked puzzled and cross at being left out. The old pixy noticed the boy's frown, so he began to explain patiently: "They are pixy fields from the _Old Days_, Master, from a time before the Hag ruled. There's no farming or honest work done in this land now. It's cursed." A look of great sadness passed over Lar's face. He sighed. Then, curling his lip, just as before, he added: "This field will be perfect. There's a tuft of grass in the gateway."

Emily took over the explanation so that Adam's face brightened. The pixies were more cheerful, too, and their mood seemed to lighten the gloomy surroundings.

Lar chose five of the older pixies to go with Adam and another five to stay with him. The rest followed Emily to a safe hiding place.

Lar and his five pixies joined hands and danced in a circle around the tuft of grass in the gateway. The words they chanted were strange and made Adam think of years ago as an infant when all the world was a mystery. Satisfied, Lar and the others gathered stones to narrow the gateway until the opening contained only the tuft that they had danced around. Nobody could enter the field without stepping on it. Their work finished, Lar and his companions joined Emily's group in hiding. Instead, Adam and his pixies waited in the open field for the spriggans to come. They took up position on the other side of the wall opposite the enchanted gateway.

Time passed while they exchanged tales

about their different lands. Adam's first discovery was that all pixy names begin with 'L' and are easy to say. They sounded sweet in his new tongue: Lex, Lygg, Loy, Lajx and Lupp. Sleepy-eyed Loy, under his strange, pointed hat, explained how he had fallen into the Hag's clutches.

He had been unlucky when freshly cured of Rainbow Sickness. The complicated cure left him weak and unable to work, vulnerable to the Hag's spell.

"What's Rainbow Sickness?" Adam asked.

The pixies looked at each other, and their mocking laughter made him more curious. Loy began: "It was my own fault. I saw a rainbow and it was so pretty. You must never point at a rainbow with your first finger. I forgot and that's how I got ill."

"What's the illness like?"

"First of all, your skin turns pink...like yours! That's why we laughed just now!" Adam looked about him at the five grinning, greenish faces and smiled too. "Worse," Loy continued, "you lose all your energy and spend all your time looking at waterfalls and fountains."

"How do you cure it?"

"Wait until the Moon wanes, because the

illness has to slip away from you. Get you to a stream when the sun is half-set. Wade into the stream, holding a gold object in one hand and a silver one in the other. Bend forward with your fists just in the water. Then the healer asks you a question. *What have you got in your hands?* she says. *Gold, silver and water*, you reply. Then the healer commands, *Go away to the sea, Rainbow Sickness!* and she says some magic words, which only healers know. For the next three mornings, the healer takes you under some arches, when the sun's half-risen...and this is the worst part, she makes you drink three silver spoonfuls of a horrible concoction. *Bleah!*"

"What?"

"It's a mixture of twitch grass and saltpetre," Loy shuddered at the memory.

"And did it cure you?"

"The cure always works," Loy said firmly. "On the third morning, I turned back from sickly pink to this healthy green colour."

Adam smiled.

"But I didn't have chance to get my strength back," he added, "when the Hag's spell latched on to me—that's how I left Halewood for the Land of Poverty."

"Listen!" Lex interrupted; his head cocked to

one side. Lygg spoke for the first time in a calm, low voice: "They're coming!"

"The spriggans?" Adam asked. He couldn't hear a thing.

Instead, he saw them first, in the distance, before the sound of chanting and of pounding feet reached him. Standing up, he clutched *Cari* in his pocket. In some way, the orb comforted him with its presence. Even so, he felt very tense, but the pixy faces were even tenser.

"You'd better stand up and be seen," he said grimly.

The spriggan force advanced at a trot, but when their leader saw Adam, he halted the column. There were about forty of them. They weren't taller than pixies; however, their ugliness was revolting. They wore no clothes, revealing their leathery bodies covered in rough brown hair. Their eyes were horrible. Even though the small, enchanted field lay between Adam's band and the spriggans, those black-slatted, grey eyes still chilled his heart. They spanned the short distance in a blaze of cruelty and hatred. Adam could sense terror hammering in the pixy hearts at his side and understood what fear the evil nature of these creatures induced. He shuddered as the spriggan chief's eyes passed over him from head to foot.

Adam saw the malign creature sneer and his long-nailed fingers close around his sling. Even so, he wasn't ready for such speed of arm. Before he could move, a stone struck him viciously under the right eye. It burnt horribly and left a painful mark on his face.

"Quick, run!" Adam shouted urgently, shaking the tears from his eyes with a toss of his head, relieved that he hadn't lost an eye. As they turned, fiery stones hailed down, burning their shoulders and backs, and the strange battle cry of the spriggans rang in their ears: *Pruk, pruk, pruk!* It sounded like some kind of horrible croak.

Everything went to plan as the spriggans sprang forward in pursuit. They were forced to enter the field through the narrow gateway prepared for them. So, their clawed feet trampled the tuft of grass as they squeezed through one at a time. Once inside the field, they began to run about most oddly. First, they ran in a column to the middle of the field where they stopped, looking around in confusion. Then they ran aimlessly again. This sequence of actions was repeated many times.

"It's working!" Emily cried joyfully as she led the main band of pixies to re-join Adam's group. "They're well and truly *pixy-led!*"

"Of course," Lar smiled. *"Where Nature fails, art obtains,* is it not so, Master?"

"Ay," Adam nodded doubtfully because he didn't really understand.

"Quick, look!" Lupp cried, jumping up and down with excitement.

The spriggans were beginning to argue among themselves. Every time they rushed forward, the illusion of a way out changed position. Since spriggans are too spiteful to put up with frustration for long, they began screaming, pulling hair, scratching and biting among themselves. Before long, burning stones were flying, causing their screams to become more piercing and pain-filled.

"Serves them right!" Emily laughed. "Let's go!"

"But won't they know how to break the spell?" Adam asked anxiously, touching his face tenderly where it still hurt.

"They might know if it comes to that," Lex chuckled, "but they can't do anything about it! The way to break the spell is to turn your coat inside-out and, as you can see, they don't wear coats. They will be there until the Hag chooses to release them."

"Why did they make that strange croaking

noise?" Adam asked. It had made an impression on him.

"When they go into battle," Lex explained, "they imitate the raven call, *pruk, pruk,* because the raven is the *bird of death* and a favourite of the Hag."

Adam was silent. He didn't feel like asking any more questions.

# 4

*A* worried discussion soon replaced their joy at tricking the spriggans. They had to get out of the Land of Poverty, but where should they go? Nobody knew how to break the Hag's boundary spell. The only point of agreement was that she must be avoided at all costs. The wasteland looked the same everywhere and, in the end, all tracks led to her hovel.

Emily, meanwhile, had been thinking hard about fairy lore, suddenly remembering something important. There was the flower called St. John's Wort – the one she had worn in her Midsummer Crown in...what she now called...*My Own World*. She knew this pretty, yellow-coloured flower was a sun-symbol and powerful protection against fairy magic. It flowered in June, July and August: the warm months. What chance was there of such a flower blooming in this cold wilderness? The pixies shook their heads. The only flowers they had seen were hardy flowers which grew on mountainsides, flowers which could survive the cold.

Lupp cleared his throat; everyone stared, for Lupp spoke so rarely that it was considered an event. Twice in one day, after many moon-risings of complete silence, startled them. Maybe his quiet voice was so gruff owing to lack of practice.

"I know a place where the earth is hot," he growled, "there are underground springs." He paused as if embarrassed at such a flood of words.

"Ay? Ay?"

"It's a fearful, dangerous place—"

"Why, Lupp?"

"Because the wild beasts that live in this cursed Land gather there for warmth."

"How do you know about this place?"

Lupp, stressed with talking, sighed heavily: "I got lost and only just escaped the fangs of a white-coated fox."

"You never told me that!" Lex's tone was hurt because he was Lupp's best friend.

"You didn't ask."

Emily interrupted impatiently: "Did you see wildflowers there, Lupp?"

"Yes, Mistress, many."

She got no more out of him because he had used a year's ration of words in a couple of minutes. He nodded when Emily asked him if he could lead them to the place, convinced in her heart that if they could find St. John's Wort, they would escape from the Hag's power.

They set off cheerfully, heartened by having a plan. Lupp strode on wordlessly, seeming to know where he was going. For the first time, the pixies chatted happily, their stomachs full, buoyed by two quick victories over the Hag. Everyone felt hopeful that the Mistress would overcome the witch. Meanwhile, the weather held with no sign of spriggans. Even so, Lar's anxious eyes darted backwards and forwards all the time.

A sudden tug at her sleeve and Emily gazed down into the eyes of Lajx, one of the older pixies. His leathery face was full of wrinkles and concern.

"Mistress, we should go no further this way."

"Why not?"

"The troll, Blunderbore, lives over the next hill."

"Are you sure?"

"Ay, quite sure."

"Wait!" Emily called to Lupp, her cry halting the little band.

It was true. Although the land all looked horribly the same to Emily, other pixies recognised the place. At that moment a black kite screeched high above them. Adam and Emily saw the dismay on the pixies faces at the hawk's call. Adam looked at Lar: "What's up? It's only a bird."

"See! Even now it's winging away to warn its mistress of our whereabouts."

"The Hag?"

"Ay."

Gloomily, they realised that they had lost the element of surprise, which was the only advantage they had. To avoid Blunderbore meant going far out of their way and losing their one chance to outwit the foe.

Loy and Lupp volunteered to scout ahead with Adam, hoping that Blunderbore wouldn't be at home. They proceeded carefully, without taking risks because, as Loy explained in a high-pitched anxious voice, Blunderbore was known as the *Crusher*. He was the simplest and the strongest of the four trolls, with big, hairy feet which he used to trample down pixy homes. There was no point in putting up anything but the crudest shelter or trying to live in a cave, because otherwise, no sooner did a pixy build a home than the Crusher would come along and trample it down again. It was a kind of game for him. His feet were so big that the pixies could, at least, hear him coming; so, they could always escape outdoors in time.

They crept on hands and knees towards Blunderbore's cave, hiding behind gorse wherever possible. Blunderbore was at home in the company of three other trolls. Adam recognised Nabgrasp and Blunderbore by a glance at his big, hairy feet. Trembling at the sight of the four trolls together, Loy managed to whimper: "That's Thundell, the fat one. He steals our food; the other one is Rickett, the hunchback troll with runny eyes. He's the foul troll, you mustn't go near him, because if he breathes on you, you can catch all sorts of horrible diseases."

The four trolls were arguing; bellowing at each other, as trolls do. Adam and the pixies kept their heads down and listened.

Adam had no need to envy pixy hearing on this occasion because every word came loud and clear and they were all about *him*.

"...and I tell you," roared Nabgrasp, "I saw him, he drove me out of my cave. He's Lord of the Trolls!" He said so! Rrrr! He stole my cave and all my trrreasure!"

"Nonsense!" Blunderbore growled. "There's no Lord of the Trolls!" He turned to the other two trolls and scowled menacingly. "I've never heard of him, have you?"

They didn't answer at once, for trolls are very slow thinkers. Rickett scratched his patchy hair and shook his head slowly, while Thundell rubbed the stubble on his chin and frowned.

"But I *saw* him, I tell you! I even spoke to him!" Nabgrasp roared so loudly that his voice boomed among the rocks. "He is a mighty war-rrrior, tallerr than me, with fierrrce silver eyes and silverr hairr, I've neverr seen one like him beforrre!"

Feeling tall and strong, Adam smiled behind the gorse. "But I've got blue eyes," he whispered. Lupp looked at Loy and shook his head; the boy's eyes were obviously silver.

"I can soon settle this *Prince-o'-the-Trolls* business!" Blunderbore boomed. "An' pixies might fly!" he chuckled. "I've got a book o' troll lore in my cave. Just hang on a minute." He moved with a flat-footed stomp which rocked the ground way beyond Adam and the hidden pixies.

Rickett scratched his head, and Thundell,

who was sitting on a rock, began to pick his toe-nails, but it wasn't long before the ground trembled at Blunderbore's return.

"Look at Old Crusher!" Loy whispered, amazed.

Blunderbore was staggering under the weight of an enormous leather-bound book, as thick as Adam's leg and as big as a pixy dinner table. Blunderbore dropped it in front of Nabgrasp, sending up a cloud of dust. "There!" he challenged the Grasper. "Go on then! Find a *Prince-o'-the-Trolls* in that!"

"'S not fair!" Nabgrasp sulked. "You know I can't rrread!"

"Can you read, Rickett?" the Crusher growled anxiously. He couldn't read himself; he just owned the book.

"Try reading with cross-eyes," Rickett snarled unpleasantly, one eye challenging Blunderbore and the other on Nabgrasp.

"Lucky for you dimwits that I'm here," Thundell boomed importantly, his stomach wobbling. "Fancy having a bloomin' *Book of Lore* and not being able to read!"

"Watch it!" Blunderbore growled, "or I'll trample your fat head!"

Thundell ignored Blunderbore, who limited

himself to grinding a stone menacingly into powder under his hairy foot.

Trolls by nature are very impatient but can go deeply into something which interests them. Troll lore interests them. Trolls rarely study troll lore from one century to another, but when they do, they are fascinated. So, Thundell pored over the *Book of Lore*, never skipping a word and sometimes reading a page three times, while the other trolls sat down and stared into space. Perhaps they were thinking, or they were just staring into space.

A boring wait for Adam and his companions followed. Some of them passed the time by eating food from Nabgrasp's lair.

Thundell suddenly looked up. His face was troubled. "Listen to this!" He began to read slowly, stumbling and hesitating over many words, especially if they were longer than four or five letters: "...in the beginning, the King of the Trolls, King Mou...Mou...Mount...e...bank banished the wicked trolls from the Great Cave and con-condemn...ed them to roam in Poverty. They were only...to return" Thundell coughed nervously, "if they led good and noble lives."

"That's daft!" Blunderbore boomed. "Everyone knows that trolls are bad and wild and *'orrible* ..." he spat the last word out with relish.

"It gets worse," Thundell's voice dropped from a roar to almost a whisper. "In order to check on their be-hav...haviour, Prince Rockell, Lord of the Trolls, was to visit them every five hundred years..." The trolls looked at each other. Trolls have excellent memories, so good that they can remember everything; but only for two hundred years at a time. Then their memories fill up. None of them could remember anything about King Mountebank or Prince Rockell.

Nabgrasp's brain was working slowly, but very slightly faster than the others. "There y'are then! He's due ain't he? The *Lord o' the Trolls* is here—I told you so!" He looked very nervous and fidgety.

Blunderbore rubbed his nose. "You might be right," he conceded. "Go on, Thundell, what else does it say?"

After double-checking, Thundell found his place again and read slowly: "Should he find them unchanged—that is, wicked—Rockell was charged to cut off their heads with his golden sword. There has never been, nor will there ever be, a w-w-warrior so great or fierce as he." Thundell almost wailed, "If he should find them worthy, he was to lead them out of Poverty and back to the land, *er,* to the land of their birth—back to the Great Cavern of Comfort."

"Gor! 'Eck. What'rrr we to do?" Nabgrasp was tenderly feeling his head; he knew he had been wicked—he liked his head where it was.

Behind the gorse, Adam couldn't believe his luck. Without stopping to think, or speaking to the others, he pulled out the orb, *Cari,* and bounded towards the horror-stricken trolls. "I am Rockell!" he boomed, in a voice taken from the trolls themselves, "the fiercest troll that has ever lived! I have come to check your worthiness! By all the magic of my silver sphere!" To Adam's surprise, the elven orb sent four flashes of brilliant light over the trolls' heads. "Why are you cringing? You haven't been wicked, have you?" He took advantage of the orb's help.

"Nooooooooo!" they chorused. From the way they were trembling, troll lore had made a deep impression upon them.

"Mmm! We shall see." Adam frowned, looking around. "Aha! There are some passing pixies. Do not be afraid, little fellows, come and join us!" Reluctantly, very slowly indeed, Loy and Lupp came from behind the gorse. They came a certain way but would come no further.

"Well," Adam said, tossing back his silver

hair, "let's ask whether you've been kind, help-ful, good-natured trolls—"

"Nooooo!" Nabgrasp wailed. "Don't ask those two! I know them, they're liars and cheats and—"

"My, my, that's not very polite, is it?"

Nabgrasp was hopping from foot to foot in terror. Adam turned to the pixies and asked them to describe the trolls' behaviour. As the pixies spoke, fearfully at first, but growing bolder, the trolls became white-faced and began to plead and argue.

"Enough!" Adam cried. "I, Rockell, have de-cided—" Blunderbore gulped and Nabgrasp held his head in place with his hands. Thundell fainted and fell with a tremendous, earth-shaking thump at Rickett's feet.

"I have decided that you are to be —forgiven!"

"Aaaaaaahhh!" Nabgrasp screamed because he was expecting to have his head chopped off and his brain hadn't yet caught up with Adam's words. Slowly, the word *forgiven* sank into the trolls' consciousness and they began to smile, hoping to gain Prince Rockell's favour.

"Be silent!" Adam commanded. "Forgiven... on condition that—"

"Anything," Nabgrasp pleaded as Thundell sat up dizzily.

"On condition that you solemnly swear on the *Book of Lore* to be kind to pixies; fight spriggans on sight and confuse the Hag." Adam had to repeat the conditions slowly several times until the trolls had grasped them all. Then, one by one, he made them swear an oath on the Book. He vowed that any troll who broke the oath would be beheaded at once if he didn't first die of Black Troll Fever.

"Black Troll Fever?" Thundell repeated the words fearfully. He'd never heard of it, but it sounded terrifying. He didn't want to catch Black Troll Fever and, judging by the faces of the other trolls, nor did they.

"Take good care of your heads. I shall be watching you, but you won't see me. Farewell!"

He led the pixies over the hill without a backward glance.

Emily's silver eyes flashed. "Brilliant Adam! We should have no more trouble with those four. There's only one thing though—"

"Yes?"

"What happens if the real Lord Rockell shows up?"

"He won't," Loy said.

"Oh, why not?"

"Because trolls can only remember for two hundred years at a time, and we've just heard that Rockell was supposed to visit every five hundred. Well, Rockell's a troll too, so naturally, he'll have forgotten.'

"Trolls are odd creatures!" Adam shook his head.

It was time to move on. Adam ordered Lupp to lead on past the troll's lair, while he and Emily watched from a hiding place. The pixies marched in a nervous state down the valley towards Blunderbore's cave. There wasn't one among them who felt brave. Now, however, they trusted Adam completely and obeyed even this terrifying command. The four trolls were still there. Each was staring into space, thinking slowly. Thinking about what they had been told. Nabgrasp noticed the pixy column first and spoke to the other trolls. The pixies looked straight ahead and hurried their step a little.

"Yoo-hoo! Nice pixies!" Nabgrasp waved.

"Lovely day!" Rickett called, showing his black and rotting teeth in what was supposed to be a friendly smile.

"Great!" Adam whispered to Emily. "They're stupid, aren't they?"

"Stupid, yes, but very dangerous and difficult to beat," Emily warned. "Stay out of sight!"

# 5

After the trolls had returned to their thinking, Adam and Emily rejoined the pixies. Lupp led them on until they came to a barrier of gorse. On either side, stagnant pools blocked the way. The stench from them reminded Adam of Nabgrasp's breath. The troop halted. "What now, Lupp?" Adam asked. It seemed to him that there was no way through.

"There's a way through; there's a narrow opening that leads into a maze of gorse."

"A real maze?" Emily asked.

"Ay, Mistress, it's very difficult to get through."

"Is it the only way?"

"It is. The Hag turned the gorse into a maze to stop anyone reaching the hot springs. Since they come from deep within the earth, the Hag cannot control them with magic."

They found an entrance and squeezed painfully into the maze. By standing on tiptoe, Emily, the tallest of them all, could see over the gorse. Because of this and because the pathways were well-beaten, they made good progress towards the centre. Suddenly the gorse began to grow and the paths to widen. The pixies stopped, terrified.

"It's Hag magic," Lar explained. "We've been lured into the maze; she's making it grow so that the Mistress cannot guide us."

"How does she know?" Adam asked.

"Her will is everywhere in this land," Lar's voice sounded beaten as his squint followed the gorse growth upwards.

"Never mind, Lupp can lead us, he's been here before, remember?"

There was no way of telling the difference between one track and another except for a knuckle of gorse branch or a broken spiky twig. The band plodded on, twisting and turning through the maze for ages. Finally, Emily called a halt.

"This is no good, Lupp. We've been past this knuckle of gorse three times now. Admit that you're lost."

Lupp looked anxiously at Lar and nodded.

"Right," Emily said, "I'll sort this out." She tore her cotton handkerchief into narrow ribbons, fastening one to a gorse stem. "Now we'll know if we've been this way before. I seem to remember reading somewhere that you should always turn right in a maze till you get to the middle. Honestly, Lupp, I don't know how you ever got through the maze last time."

Lupp hung his head and looked miserable.

Pausing only to tie more ribbons to gorse, they made progress, until, as Emily had foreseen, they came to the middle of the maze.

There they found a stone with runes carved on it. Lar read:

*'LEAVE? EASIER TO MAKE HOLES IN WATER!'*

"It's a message from the Hag, Mistress."

"We'll see about that." Emily pursed her lips.

They pressed on, away from the centre, always turning left. But the plan didn't work. The Hag was too clever. Their efforts always brought them back to read the same hateful message on the stone.

Eventually, Lar said, "Mistress, I fear the Hag has a sealing spell upon the maze. We shall wander till we drop." The pixies' shoulders sagged, even Adam hung his head.

"We don't give up that easily," Emily muttered and set off again blindly. She began mixing right and left turns, wondering whether or not the absence of ribbons was an improvement. Deep down, she knew that without a system, the words on the stone were destined to come true. But she couldn't think of a plan. They pressed further into the maze until they came upon a hole in the ground in one corner. It was a rabbit hole. Emily stared at it and then at Adam. Since the maze had grown about twenty times, so had the hole.

"What about it?" Emily asked.

"I'm game if you are," Adam nodded.

There was no doubt that the pixies could pass through the tunnel, but it would be risky for Adam and Emily. They couldn't know where the tunnel led. It might simply take them deeper into the maze, or as they hoped, there might be an exit outside. There wouldn't be much air down there and what if the Hag shrank the maze back to normal? They would be buried alive. What's more, they weren't sure it was a rabbit hole.

Whatever had dug the hole could be twenty times bigger down there.

"'*He who hesitates is lost!*' That's one of our sayings, Lar." Adam smiled at the little pixy as he slowly repeated these words while he pulled *Cari* from his pocket. Holding the orb for courage, he squirmed head-first into the tunnel. He felt as if he couldn't breathe with the darkness pressing in on him. Pushing to the back of his mind the frightening thought that the Hag could shrink the maze at any moment, he squirmed forward. For the moment, it was enough to wriggle on, despite the soreness caused to his elbows and knees.

A dim light began to glow in his right hand. Adam stopped for a moment, causing Emily to crash into his shoe with her arm. The glow was getting brighter until the tunnel ahead was lit by a silver beam: the elven orb was working its magic. Encouraged, Adam began to struggle on again.

On its own, the orb's beam was not enough to calm Emily. She couldn't stand being in the dark, in closed spaces. This tunnel was airless while soil filled her hair and entered her mouth and nose. The only way to keep from screaming and losing control was to stare at Adam's shoes and not to think of anything except her grazed knees. She suddenly felt a horrible tickling on her left hand. Emily screamed. A millipede twenty times its natural size was running its thousand legs across her hand. This moment seemed to last forever, then the creature was gone past the column of pixies who were advancing comfortably through the tunnel behind her. The only discomfort for the pixies was that they had to walk with their heads slightly bowed, so not to scrape their caps against the tunnel roof. Heart still pounding from the shock of the millipede, Emily heard Adam mutter something and then move off to the right. Emily saw that the track forked and Adam had chosen the right fork. This was a decision he made five more times; perhaps because he was right-handed, thought Emily, who was left-handed.

Adam's heart leapt because he saw a chink of light ahead. Maybe they were getting near the end of their ordeal. Wondering where the tunnel would bring them, he knelt on a bone and gasped in pain. At that moment, *Cari's* beam faded away until there was only the dimmest spark at its centre. Adam looked at the sphere, thinking that the spark was like a heart. *Cari* seemed like a living creature to him. As he thought this, he felt around him with his left-hand and discovered several more bones littered on the ground. These

remains were leftovers from some beast's dinner.
Just as this idea occurred to him, Adam saw two
huge greenish-yellow eyes glowing in the gloom
ahead.

Once more, Emily crashed into Adam's shoes
as he stopped dead. She was suffering too much
to protest and unaware of the danger ahead.
Adam clutched *Cari* tighter. He couldn't make
out the shape of the creature, but he could feel
its hostility. All he could see were the eyes. Its
attack began with a low growl, a throaty rumble
before the eyes launched towards Adam. All the
creature's strength was channelled into its hind
legs. It sprang as if fired from a catapult. Again,
Adam smelt revolting breath. He just had time to
glimpse a mouth full of vicious teeth, which
seemed to go on forever. The darkness that half-
hid the beast from the boy's terrified eyes saved
him. He had enough courage left to react. Even
as he threw himself backwards into Emily, Adam
instinctively thrust *Cari* forward. The dull spark
suddenly ignited so that the orb blazed out a
blinding beam of white light, keener than a
blade. It seared the creature's eyes, causing its
shaggy body to twist in mid-air and crash to the
ground. The shaken pixies covered their sensitive ears from the creature's agonised wails filling
the crowded space. The creature scuffed a cloud

of dust as it turned and fled out of the tunnel. Emily, ears ringing, stared disbelievingly at the orb, *Cari*. "What was that...thing?" she asked with shaking voice.

"A weasel, I think, but a monster-sized one!"

"It's the Hag's spell, Mistress, everything here except ourselves has grown. We have the elven orb to thank for our lives," Lar explained. Adam puffed out his cheeks in relief; he'd never imagined himself as weasel lunch, not even in his worst nightmare.

They pressed on upwards towards the crack of light, where the air slowly became sweeter and lighter until Adam was able to wriggle out of the tunnel and breathe in clean air. The sensation was so good that he didn't even notice where he was. It was Lupp who cried out: "Mistress, what fortune! We are out of the maze and not far from the hot springs!"

The pixy set off, sure of his direction this time. Lar looked anxiously high into the sky, where two black kites were wheeling and screeching. As if alerted by Lar's gaze, they flew like arrows over the hills and away. "We haven't long to find the flowers, Mistress. The Foul One's messengers even now are on the wing."

Picking their way past stinking ponds and tangled briar, they had gone some distance when

Lupp looked round. "Look!" he growled. The maze was shrinking back to normal size, and as Lar squinted behind him, he could see the hills beyond quite clearly.

"The Hag knows we have outwitted her," Lar said grimly. "Her fury will know no bounds."

# 6

They hurried on; meanwhile, the air grew still until their voices seemed to ring in hollowness. Emily recognised the feeling that made her so uneasy: the silence before a storm. Before long, it burst. The wind began to whip dust into their eyes so that their steps became exhausted against its force. Soon, the clouds lowered, dimming the light almost to darkness. Hailstones began to thrash down on them, each one as big as a pixy hand. Hurled by the gale, they struck with a painful bruising force.

"Quickly!" Emily shouted. "Turn your backs to the wind and gather hailstones, we'll build an ice wall."

Labouring through a painful beating, the pixies built a wall. Adam and Emily, so much bigger, gathered great freezing armfuls of hail and built ten times faster than their companions.

"The Great Wall of China!" Emily shouted.

But Adam's eyes were full of tears, he couldn't manage a brave smile, because he'd been hit a painful blow by a large hailstone on the forehead.

"Shelter behind the wall," Emily ordered. The plan was simple, but it worked. The huge stones cannoned harmlessly into the ice wall.

"I wonder how long she'll keep this up?" Emily murmured.

"Not long, Mistress," Lar replied, "because she's using a lot of energy. I believe she means to weaken us before her next attack."

"I hope she doesn't suspect what we're up to."

"If she does," Adam tentatively fingering the lump on his forehead, looked at his sister, "she'll find a way of stopping us."

As he spoke, the wind dropped as suddenly as it had started and the last few hailstones thumped to the ground.

"She's resting, we must move on while there's time," Lar warned.

They slipped and slithered along the trail as quickly as possible. Lupp didn't waste any time but led them directly to a gorse barrier with a gap through which the footpath passed.

The opening which served as a gateway for the pixies was too narrow for Adam and Emily, so they were scratched and snagged as they forced their way through. Their attention was concentrated on this struggle, so they were even more astonished at the scene before them when they finally broke through.

They found soft grassland surrounding a small brook that bubbled from a spring. Patches and swathes of wildflowers were dotted among the green grasses as if from an artist's brush, while startled birds and wild animals scattered and flurried away in all directions at this invasion. After the wilderness, the little clearing seemed the most beautiful place they had ever seen. Everyone ran towards the spring. The sparkling water was clear, tempting some of the pixies to kneel for a drink.

"Listen!" Adam gasped in amazement, "the stream is speaking."

"*Welcome to my waters. Drink and be refreshed,*" the brook babbled repeatedly.

"Of course," Lar looked curiously at Adam

and Emily, "is it possible that you have never heard a stream?"

"I've heard lots of streams," Adam grinned, "but I've never heard one talk before."

"*All* streams speak, Master," Lar said in a matter-of-fact voice, turning away to examine their surroundings.

"It's just that we can understand now," Emily whispered to her brother. "And doesn't it have a lovely melody?"

"Ay," several pixies muttered at the same time so that everybody laughed.

"I wish I had their hearing," Adam said in a normal voice.

"I would have stayed," Lupp suddenly announced, sighing heavily and startling everyone by speaking again, "if it hadn't been for the wild beasts that gather here."

"It reminds me of home," Lar said sadly. Emily thought she saw a tear in his squinting yellow eyes.

Adam's eyes, instead, were searching the air for black kites. There was sign of neither bird nor beast. Lar wiped an eye and nodded at Adam: "I, too, am worried. There is no sign of life, which means that the creatures are afraid of what is about to happen." Lar raised his voice: "Quickly, search for the flower!"

Lex tugged at Emily's sleeve. "Where's China, Mistress?"

"Not just now, Lex! Search for St John's Wort."

As quickly as possible, she described the flower to the pixies. They must search for a long spindly plant, with branches ending in small yellow petals like little stars.

Before long, there was a high-pitched cry of joy. Lenya had found the flower. There were several of the plants scattered around.

"Pick them all," Emily urged, "every last one." Breaking each stem carefully, she began to plait the flowers into twenty-two bracelets, twenty small ones and two big ones. She eased her bracelet over her wrist; the others did the same.

"Now, if I'm right, we are proof against fairy magic."

Emily looked around her at a circle of up-turned greenish faces, each one trustful and expectant. The pixies were waiting for orders. Again, Emily felt responsible for the little band of pixies. It was a strange feeling. In all her young life, nobody had ever depended on her. She, like Adam, had always relied on her parents for help and advice. She loved these gentle pixies, and she felt that they admired her. If she were honest with herself, she enjoyed the power of command. She felt it was natural. Nothing must harm them, not if *she* could prevent it. She was determined to defeat the Hag.

The pixies waited for orders. Now they were protected from fairy magic, but they still didn't know where to go to escape from this land.

"We'll only get out of the Land of Poverty with courage and determination," Emily said, thinking aloud. "We must find the Hag, face up to her and make her show us the way out of here."

Fired by her successes up to now, Emily felt sure that this was the answer. The pixies, on the other hand, knew the Hag. Lenya began to cry softly, making Lex put his arm around her. Emily looked at the tense fearful faces, but she had no other solution to offer.

Four black crows flew towards them, circled the clearing twice, cawing harshly, before winging quickly away. The crows were the only visible creatures in the eerie stillness.

"They're from the Hag, aren't they?" Adam asked.

"Ay, Master."

"Why not the black kites?"

"The Hag has many foul servants all a part

of the same vile design," Lar said in his peculiar way.

Emily led the pixies back to the maze, entering confidently, sure that their bracelets would prevent the gorse walls from growing. Indeed, it seemed to be the case. Emily could see over the top easily, so they passed through the maze quickly. All the time, they had the feeling of being watched. Adam noticed several black dots in the grey sky. They were flying in tight circles so high above them that they were almost invisible.

"The kites are back," Adam said to Lar. "Look, they're as fast as lightning." Every so often, a kite streaked away, only to be replaced by another. The Hag obviously knew their every move.

"Ay, like lightning," Lar nodded slowly and added grimly, *"after the lightning comes the thunder,* is it not so, Master?"

Lar had many intriguing sayings, but this one seemed too obvious to Adam. Suddenly, his brow furrowed as he understood the meaning of their perilous situation. The threat of the Hag hung over the little group. They marched on without another word in the ominous silence of the wilderness.

Leaving the maze behind, they came to Blunderbore's cave. There was no sign of the trolls. But before long, there was plenty of evidence of their activity. Here and there lay the bloodied bodies of slaughtered spriggans. There must have been a dreadful battle. "It looks like the trolls have taken me very seriously," Adam muttered, turning away from the terrible sight.

"That has solved one serious problem," Emily said with relief, "because our bracelets are no defence against spriggans."

"We should take this track if we are to find the Hag," Lar said with a quaver in his voice. It was clear that he wanted to say more. His new Mistress had never seen the Hag. How could she imagine the danger involved in this encounter? He wanted to explain how his heart seemed to be beating at the back of his throat. How his stomach felt in an icy grip and how the Hag was pure *evil*. How it was better to be, like the spriggans, broken and lifeless in the wilderness. The Hag's vengeance, spurred by her recent defeats, would be without pity or mercy.

Not only Lar was terrified; Adam too felt the weight of fear. With every step, he felt his heart beat faster. What wouldn't he give to avoid the Hag? Something nagging at the back of his mind wanted to break to the fore, to grab his attention.

This numbing fear wouldn't let it. What was it? They needn't meet the Hag, they could escape! But how? He knew they could escape, if only— fear closed in again. His hands were sweating and his knees trembled as he walked.

## 7

They continued along the track, Lar dwelling in gloomy thought, searching for the right words to dissuade his Mistress from this meeting when he was interrupted by caws. Once more, four large, black crows flew along the track and circled around their heads.

"The Hag's guides!" Lar's voice held a note of panic.

The little band halted.

Emily stared down the trail, but there was nobody there. Her gaze passed along the path into the wilderness towards the horizon. Her gaze lingered on the distance, so they weren't focused on the figure who was standing in front of her, where there had been no-one a moment before. The Hag! Emily's eyes and mind fought a private battle. Her stare fixed on a malign creature leaning on a blackthorn staff, ten paces away. Her mind told her this apparition was impossible.

She stared at the malign creature: her heart and stomach suddenly felt like Lar's. This was no ordinary being, but one so wicked that she could feel the harm projected pass over her body like an evil caress. Behind Emily, three or four pixies began to cry.

Under a crown of nettles, the Hag's hair was wintry white and fell straight to her shoulders. Her eyes were colourless like slivers of ice: two hollow slits peering from a Haggard face as worn as the fading year. Draped around her bony shoulders was a woven cloak of wilted weeds, which fell aside as she raised an arm and pointed a long-nailed finger at Emily.

"I'm going to turn you into a ghoul," she hissed through yellow pointed teeth. "You'll be more dead than alive, my pretty one...and *not* so pretty," the Hag cackled and her voice rose menacingly, "not much flesh, only bones bound in skin! *Bound in skin!*" The black kites swooped around the trembling little band, screeching in unison with the Hag's laughter as if sharing the cruel joke. The Hag's eyes fixed Emily's yellow bracelet. Emily wasn't sure, but perhaps there was a hint of fear in the Hag's voice. "What happens when I rip them off your wrists, my lovely?" Emily's knees shook, but she forced herself to take a step forward. She raised her arm, displaying the flowers to the Hag, her voice weaker than before.

"Horrible old witch. You daren't come near them!"

"Look out!" Adam yelled, just in time.

Emily snatched her arm away as a swooping kite, vicious talons fully extended, failed by a hair's breadth to tear the bracelet from her wrist. Adam wasn't so lucky because a second kite swooped, its talons gouging his cheek. He cried out in pain and blood coursed down his face. Mopping it with his shirt sleeve, he held it there to stop the flow.

Another kite caught Lajx unawares as he was staring open-mouthed at Adam. Its talons hooked around his fragile bracelet and snatched it away. The Hag's laugh, more like a shriek of glee, almost pierced their eardrums. The witch raised her finger again and pointed at Lajx. The small band of pixies, Emily, and Adam watched in horror as the elderly pixy began to shrink before their eyes. To begin with, he didn't have much spare flesh, but now his cheeks sank inwards, he seemed all eyes; his arms and legs dwindled until they were little more than skin and bone, and what little grey hair he had fell out. The Hag lowered her hand; she preferred to leave the pixy just enough life to suffer and serve as an example to the rest. Lajx bent slowly with great difficulty and picked up a stone. He wanted to make a valiant attempt at defiance, but his poor body was too weak. He only succeeded in throwing it a few feet towards the Hag, whose evil face contorted in rage. She raised her finger again, and Lajx staggered. Under the rags that passed for his clothes lay a crumpled heap of bones without flesh.

Emily managed another step towards the Hag, who screamed and stepped backwards, her face twisted in fear, fury and confusion. While her eyes were still fixed on the flowery band at Emily's wrist, her lips moved rapidly trying to chant a spell to ensnare them. Like a spider trying to trap its victim, but for whom the web wouldn't spin, the frustrated Hag realised that her magic had no effect against the bracelets. She bared her teeth and hissed: "Only Ancient Lore saves you from my will. If I ever find you bare of the cursed weed, I shall change your fate, my lovely! I promise you—it will not be a happy end for you!"

They stood there, glaring at each other, the Hag in thwarted fury and Emily in fearful doubt. She wanted to be as brave as Lajx and defy the witch, but in the face of such evil, she couldn't find the words. Behind her, Adam and the pixies trembled and clutched their bracelets to their chests for fear of the circling kites. Even without her powers, the Hag was so malign that to look at her was enough to drain away anyone's courage. For the first time in this wilderness, Adam was bereft of his unexpected bravery, facing the Hag was too much. Her hollow eyes terrified him, leaving him as weak as a pixy. In future, those eyes would give him nightmares. He kept thinking that only a few fragile flowers protected him from a horrible fate.

At last, Emily steeled herself. Her silver eyes flashing, she took her third step towards the Hag. But the moment was lost—

"Hello, dear pixies! Greetings, Lord Rockell, we've seen to the spriggans!" The ground shook as the four trolls, waving and grinning, appeared over the hill. The Hag spun around and glared at the trolls. With indescribable hatred, she spat: "Dear pixies! Idiots! Have you lost what little reason you have? Where are my spriggans?" She pointed at hunchbacked Rickett whose satisfied smirk made him look more grotesque.

"Dead, that's what!" Blunderbore growled, looking at Lord Rockell for approval.

"Just as Lord Rockell commanded," Thundell boomed, pleased with himself.

"Lord Rockell! *Lord Rockell!*" the Hag shrieked. "That's not Lord Rockell, that's just a boy, a human boy! You could eat him! You could boil him! You could drink his blood! Fools!" she hissed.

The trolls looked at each other.

"Not Lord Rockell?" Rickett said slowly, his brain struggling to cope.

"Not Lorrrd Rrrrockell?" the Grasper gasped.

"No! No! *No!*" the Hag reproached.

"Run!" Adam yelled. Emily and the pixies ran, but Adam stood his ground. His courage had returned; it troubled the trolls, who hesitated.

"Savage him!" screeched the Hag, whose magic was useless against the boy's bracelet. "There are four of you and one of him!" She was beside herself with fury. "Rip the bracelet off him! Then he'll be worse than dead!"

Blunderbore rushed forward and raised a foot. *Cari* flashed, and the Crusher howled in pain. Not a single hair remained on the giant foot that glowed red and painful.

"Elven magic! *Elven magic!* Another curse!"

The Hag's fingers clawed in frustration at the air above her head.

The trolls cowered as Adam looked at them. "It's true, I'm not Rockell," he shouted triumphantly, "but if you follow me, you'll pay dearly!" The tiny eyes of the other three trolls were on Blunderbore, who was sitting on a rock, nursing his glowing foot and howling like a wounded wolf.

"I'll seek you out! Wherever you go, I'll find you, then you'll wish you'd never been born!" the Hag screeched, sounding like her kites swooping about Adam's head, their talons flashing past his bloodied face. The great hawks could easily have torn off his bracelet or gouged out an eye, but Adam guessed the birds were also afraid of the orb.

He joined the others at a five-barred gate where a wonderful sight awaited him. The gate separated wilderness from sown land. A golden field of grain shone beneath a sun such as never penetrated the clouds over the Land of Poverty.

"Look!" Emily cried happily. "Our bracelets have cancelled the Hag's binding spell. We have found the borders of her land—we are free to leave."

"Let's get through then! Quickly, while our luck holds," Adam urged.

The company slipped through the gate, Adam last, closing it carefully as if to shut the Hag out of his life forever. But her shrill words rang in his ears, "I'll seek you out!" Adam shivered. The pixies were shivering, too, only because this land was warm and their thin bodies were adjusting to the change. Adam looked back over the gate and saw the trolls. He held the elven orb high, but he needn't have bothered. The trolls knew where Adam was and that they couldn't follow him there. Beaten, they hung their heads and three of them plodded and one limped back deep into the wilderness.

Adam pocketed the orb and turned just in time to see a stranger who had been staring at the sphere. A dwarf! Emily was staring open-mouthed at the dwarf too. The pixies, instead, were smiling at him. The dwarf, however, did not return their smiles. Under bushy eyebrows, his solemn, dark eyes studied each of the band in turn. The curiosity and suspicion were plain to see there.

"You cannot come through the gate," his voice rumbled from deep in his barrel-chest "unless you mean to work very hard."

Emily and Lar looked at each other and smiled. "We'll work as hard as you like," Emily said earnestly, "just as long as we don't have to go back into the Land of Poverty!"

Lar took off his hat and bowed low: "My name is Lar, leader of the Lostlings. These are my people." He waved his arm at the other pixies. "We are a hard-working race, and we seek only the opportunity to live and work in peace. In this way, we shall be able to return to Elmdale and Halewood," Lar smiled encouragingly at Lenya, who was standing at his elbow, "our homelands."

Lar followed the dwarf's eyes to Adam. "This is our Master, and this is our Mistress," his fluting voice was full of gratitude. "They have saved us from the Hag and have led us here. They are..." Lar hesitated, "...*humans*." He glanced anxiously at Emily, having repeated the Hag's word, now he hoped it was not offensive. Emily smiled and copied Lar's bow. Adam, from whose face the dwarf's suspicious eyes had never moved, suddenly realised that he should do the same. Embarrassed, he bowed awkwardly.

Straightening up, Adam said, "About this hard work, I've always done well at school, will that do?"

The dwarf half-smiled and looked at Emily, who didn't say anything. The truth was, she preferred daydreaming to schoolwork.

At last, the dwarf spoke again in his deep voice. "The *humans* come with me. Pixies, follow this track which will lead you to a village on the road for Elm-dale. Once in the village, you may find work to earn enough for your journey." The dwarf folded his arms and waited.

Lar spoke first, turning to Lex. "Lex, you must lead the Lostlings back to our homeland. My fate is different. I must remain with our Master, for he needs me."

Adam looked at Lar, but Emily replied, "No, Lar, you are the leader of the Lostlings, and you must lead your people home."

"Mistress," Lar's squinting, yellow eyes studied the girl's beautiful face, "pixies do not know their destiny, but they have a strong sense of where Fate will lead them." Lar turned and embraced the pixies one by one. "Be careful," he warned, "never to return to that cursed place."

Not that such a warning was necessary, the little band of pixies departed, some with tears in their eyes, strangely sad and quiet for people who had just escaped the Hag. Adam smiled at Lar. "Well, Lar, it looks like we are friends." He held out a hand clumsily. Lar stretched on tiptoe to put his little hand into Adam's much larger one. *"A good friend is worth more than treasure,* is it not so, Master?"

"Ay, it is so," Adam laughed, but his laugh was forced. His head was spinning, his cheek was throbbing, and he didn't feel at all well.

"Follow me," the dwarf boomed. "We shall see what the future holds for you."

# II

## TRIALS AND EFFORT

## 8

The *Most Serene Council of Dwarves* was forty strong; its members were known as the Grisly-beards because their combined age was six thousand four hundred and twenty-eight. Despite their venerable years, not a dwarf among them had wrestled with a problem such as that now under consideration. What to do with the pixy and the girl was no problem: The Constitution of the Dwarfish Lands was clear on that point; so was the Dwarfish Code of Hospitality, known by heart even to dwarflings. What to do with the boy Adam was another matter.

First, there was a problem since he was seriously ill—worse, he was hovering between life and death. He'd lain in a fever for many days, his skin had a deathly pallor under the beads of sweat, and the girl and the pixy had refused to leave his side. Balom, having found the companions, felt a responsibility for them, so it was he who called the best doctors in the land to Adam's bedside. It was clear that the gash to the boy's face was infected. He'd learnt from the girl that the slash had come from a foul black kite. Those birds were worse than carrion crows: one never knew what their talons might have ripped through.

Emily was distraught. She couldn't get the three dwarves that passed as doctors to make a decision. Dwarves love taking their time and are prone to argument, so while Adam, gripped by fever, struggled for his life, the three dwarves spent their time quarrelling. It was when she threatened to get rid of two of them that they reluctantly reached a decision. Their fear of not being the chosen one was greater than the antipathy among them. Dwarves hate to lose face, so they agreed (with astonishing speed) to clean the wound and to mix up a medicine made of the third part of sesame oil, the third, grated beeswax and the third, honey.

Some dwarves were ordered to carry a brazier to place by the bedside where the doctors (not without angry discussion first) melted the ingredients over a gentle heat in a double boiler. Then they argued again about what to add to the liquid. It was only when Emily, who'd been bathing Adam's forehead with a cool, wet cloth, screamed and threatened them with the scalpel she'd confiscated (when they wanted to bleed her brother) that they decided (with astonishing speed) to add five drops of peppermint oil. They removed the liquid from the heat, and when they'd finished arguing about how cool it should be, they applied it to Adam's wound.

The fever broke the next day; Adam woke to find his sister's silver eyes, full of grateful tears, peering down at him. He felt as weak as a female pixy, but as Emily said, he should be grateful to be alive—and he was. Now he must get his strength back. For this, the doctors recommended a diet of bread and honey. Honey, they said, was the best remedy. On this, all three agreed immediately, which convinced Emily that honey really was the best remedy!

Meanwhile, the meeting of the *Most Serene Council of Dwarves* had lasted only seventy-three days, a short time by Dwarfish standards, when they reached a decision about Emily and Lar. "It is clear," Balom the Black announced, "that the girl and the pixy are not a problem.

They may stay, always provided that they agree to work hard."

"They will have to be apprenticed to a craft or a trade," Torobin, the oldest and most wizened of the dwarves, cautioned. Once Torobin agreed to anything, a decision soon followed, as he was by far the most difficult of the dwarves. The vote allowing them to stay was taken; so, the quickest decision in the entire history of the Dwarf Council – a mere seventy-three days – was recorded.

The problem of the boy was certainly a knotty one. It took four hundred and eleven more days, during which time Emily and Lar had served their first year of apprenticeship before the dwarves reached a decision. Even then, they wouldn't have done so had Torobin not been suddenly stricken by Dwarfish Lock-tongue. This ailment (which can afflict over-talkative elderly dwarves) forced him to take to his bed. A circumstance which enabled a decision, urged by the most forceful of the councillors, Balom the Black, to be hurried through.

"The boy is clearly a problem," he summed up. "If he had come here without the orb, that would have been a different matter. But to come from that foul place with a stolen orb—" the dwarf knitted his imposing black eyebrows, "why, it is a *grievous* matter." He paused and looked around the gathering, which, after four hundred and eighty-four days, was just beginning to warm to the case. Some stroked grey beards, others nodded sagely or rested a forefinger wisely against a lip.

"While it's true that boy was not the original thief, he must still be put to the test," Balom's deep voice rumbled from his barrel-chest.

"Ay, put him to the test!" others agreed eagerly.

"We don't really know where the boy comes from. He, least of all, seems able to explain. Yet, he must have some good in him," Balom argued, "or else the orb would have punished him by now. We all know about the elven magic sealed in the sphere and how only one who is worthy may safely bear it."

"Ay, but *how* worthy?" Strutt the Stammerer was so interested in the case that he didn't stammer.

"Put him to the test!" various Grisly-beards shouted.

"Should agreement be reached without Torobin?" someone asked.

"It would never be reached *with* him, that's for sure," Balom grumbled. Later, after his tongue was freed, and to the end of his very long life, Torobin always swore that the decision was taken with unseemly haste. In the high-vaulted Council Cave, the decision was taken to put Adam the Stranger to the test. It was to be no ordinary test. For, to tell the truth, Balom was more cunning than the average dwarf, who is generally simple and honest (if stubborn). Balom was aware of the powerful elven magic in the orb. He saw an opportunity here for all the Dwarfish race.

The boy was to seek the lost Key of Ingenuity. Once the suggestion left Balom's lips, there was no restraining the enthusiasm of the assembled Grisly-beards. What did it matter that the Key was with Lentor the Dragon? It had been so for a thousand years. Should the boy prove worthy, the elven orb would protect him; if not, he would simply be devoured. In either case, the problem of Adam the Stranger had been most ably resolved.

Balom the Black decided to carry the news to the Stranger himself. He left the high cave mouth behind him and wandered deep in thought through neat fields of oats and barley to the village. It had been many generations, he reflected, since the dwarves had left the caves and turned to farming. Long ago, before the Key had been lost, dwarves worked on the crafts dwarves had always worked on. Magic blades, beautiful jewellery, fine armour, all these had been the everyday skills of even the simplest dwarf. Now, almost all these skills had been lost. What art was left, was practised by few, such as Bella the Fair. Well, she had been fair in her younger days. Balom smiled at the memory. Now Bella the Wrinkly would be more apt. Bella, alone among them, retained some of the old skill for fashioning beautiful objects.

They chose the girl, Emily, to be apprenticed to Bella. Balom wondered how she was getting on. Four hundred eighty-four days she had been with Bella: no time at all, really.

Balom turned down the main street of the village and almost fell over three dwarf children playing hop-dwarf. One of them had succeeded in rolling his stone onto number 754 and had hopped straight into Balom. "Look out, young rascal!" Balom the Black growled fiercely. "Haven't you anything better to do with your time, like work, for instance?"

"Oh yes, sir," the dwarfling answered politely – for dwarflings love work – "but we've only been playing this game for three weeks, sir." This reply satisfied Balom, who headed for Bella's workshop, after patting the dwarfling on his head.

Bella was almost three hundred years old. Quite an age, even for a dwarf. Her hair was completely white and her skin was terribly wrinkled. It was a source of general amusement that she bought expensive herbal anti-wrinkle cream at the market. She still had a twinkling eye, but it was difficult to imagine that she had once been a beautiful dwarf. The joke doing the rounds was that Bella's wrinkles were so deep that she needed mortar rather than anti-wrinkle cream. Balom smiled to himself but, for all his gruffness, was very fond of Bella.

He looked around the workshop. All sorts of tools with the tackle that goldsmiths use for their work were hanging from the low, beamed ceiling. Likewise, tools and half-completed pieces of jewellery covered the benches.

"Bella!" Balom boomed, startling the old dwarf and the girl, who was sitting on a stool in a corner of the workshop.

"Balom, you oaf!" the goldsmith snapped. "You've made me solder the wrong joint! I shall have to start again!" She tutted crossly and removed her magnifying glass from her eye. "What do you want, anyway?"

"Thought I'd call in and see how the girl is coming on."

"Oh, her!" Bella snapped. "She's driving me

mad," the goldsmith screwed up her wrinkled face until it looked like a large raisin.

"Oh?"

"Well, she's only been here two minutes; now, she wants to make things. *Make things!* I ask you! As if it's that easy. Just look at all these unfinished things. I can't finish them. Things used to be different in the Old Days. And this little minx thinks she can just swan in here and make jewellery in two minutes without any snags. I ask you!" Bella paused for breath and unwrinkled her face a little. Emily had been listening to all this from her stool in the corner, where she sat with an enormous book on her knees. She had kept quiet because their visitor looked fierce. Now she looked up again.

She took a deep breath, and all her resentment flooded out. "Well, in the first place, I've been here for more than a year. All I ever do is read this book." She struggled to hold up the leather-bound volume so that Balom could read the title, *The Dwarfish Art of Jewellification*. At least, he would have read it if it hadn't been wobbling so much at Emily's effort to hold it up. "And I'm sick of reading it!" She heaved the book dramatically onto the bench, sending up a cloud of dust, and jumped off her stool.

"But a year is no time at all," Balom smiled

patiently as Emily's silver eyes flashed angrily. "Why, apprentices are bound for seventy years before they become masters of their craft," he explained.

"Dwarves maybe!" Emily burst out angrily. "But I'll be dead by then! Humans don't live as long as dwarves. In any case," she added boldly, "how do you know that humans don't learn faster than dwarves?" She smiled sweetly as she said this and was relieved to see the thunderous look disappear from Balom's brow. Balom had a weakness for a pretty face.

"Now you see what I have to put up with!" Bella grumbled.

"Well, Bella, let's face it," Balom said slowly, "*Success* hasn't passed through these doors for many, many years. Let the girl try her hand, eh?"

"But she's got another twenty-nine years' reading yet! The idea's preposterous!"

"The girl is right, Bella. She is not a dwarf. Let's see what a fine mess she makes!" He laughed and winked at Bella, who slowly changed expression, too, finally agreeing to the joke with a laugh. Why not see what a fool the little minx made of herself? She could start immediately. Emily bit her lip and looked very determined. She'd show them a thing or two!

# 9

The next day towards nightfall, Mangey Yellow-fang, half-starved with hunger, led his pack of wolves in a headlong charge towards the boy, the pixy and the dwarf. Their empty bellies drove them forward at breathtaking speed for the kill. The dwarf barely had time to leap to his feet and shout a warning and the boy scarcely time to snatch out his orb—but what an orb! At the sight of it, old Yellow-fang dug in his front paws and skidded to a halt. The pursuing wolves tumbled and barged into him, but his wary eyes never left the orb. He did not approach, for the creature that held the orb was content to stand its ground, and Yellow-fang sensed danger. The pain in his belly grew sharper in the knowledge that he would have to go hungry a while yet. The pack-leader didn't know why he was so afraid of the orb. Something about it flashed a warning to his savage heart; better to slink away with his miserable pack.

"Phew! That was close!" Adam thrust *Cari* back in his pocket.

"We must learn from it, friend Adam," Palustric the Dwarf cautioned. "Nothing is gained in this Land without toil. Here were we, thinking that the first day of our adventure had gone well, carelessly settling down for the night without making the proper effort. From now on, we must take the trouble to build a stockade at night, no matter how tired we are." Adam was too tired to build a stockade. Just the thought of it made him sway with weariness.

"Palustric is right, Master." Lar looked into the young dwarf's sincere brown eyes and nodded his approval. *"The tail is the most difficult part of the beast to skin,* is it not so, Master?"

"I don't *know,* Lar," Adam snapped. "I'm too tired tonight to think about what your riddles mean."

Palustric looked sternly at Adam. He folded his muscular arms across his broad chest and took a deep breath. "What Lar means is that towards the end of any task is the hardest part because that's when you're tired and you hurry to get finished, then you spoil everything."

"Well, I'm glad that you understand that I'm tired after all this walking," Adam grumbled.

After a tedious argument with Palustric (dwarves love arguing), they climbed a tree near the forest's edge. Adam settled into a hollow between two branches and unhitched his belt, which he fastened around a branch and through a loop in his trouser-band. He didn't like the idea of rolling out into space in his sleep.

Palustric didn't get to sleep, he was too uncomfortable in the tree. Elves, not dwarves, are suited to trees. As he dozed fitfully, he thought over what had happened the day before. His uncle Balom had always favoured him among his nephews. He was his uncle's sister's youngest son, still too young to wear a beard. Dwarves may only grow a beard after they reach fifty—the age of majority. Perhaps it was because he was still only forty-four that Uncle Balom continued to treat him like a child. Yesterday, Balom had made it clear that it was unthinkable to send one's nephew up Mount Ember, especially with a stranger. Palustric thought of Adam and smiled. Adam was a friend, and Palustric was proud that he had defied his uncle and come along, whatever fate lay in store for them. Balom

had also tried to persuade Lar to return to Elm-
dale, but Lar insisted that he would never
abandon his *Master*.

Still, something bothered Palustric; it would
give him no peace. Balom had made him swear
upon the Sacred Anvil and Bellows of the dis-
used Smithy, where the Key had been forged,
that he would go no further than the foot of
Mount Ember. In other words, thought Palustric,
easing his poor uncomfortable back into a better
position on his branch, he had promised to
abandon his friend just when he would be most
needed.

Palustric turned and squirmed in the tree.
He yawned and rubbed his eyes, turned and
wriggled and fell out of the tree, landing on a
perfectly soft cushion of leaves, where he fell
asleep, wolves or no wolves.

Adam woke feeling refreshed to find Lar and
Palustric already up and about. He yawned and
scratched his head before unhitching his belt and
climbing down to join them. Another yawn:
"What's for breakfast?" Continuing his conversation with Lar, without looking round, Palustric
pointed towards the heavy pack which he alone
had carried the previous day.

Adam stepped over to the pack and began to
unlace it. As he did so, he saw that the pack con-

tained at least ten big glass jars. He took out the first jar and examined it. Palustric and Lar were still talking. He held the jar up to the sunlight. It had a translucent golden colour. "Honey," Adam murmured, and a sour expression crossed his handsome but scarred face. He liked honey, but he'd eaten nothing else throughout his convalescence. He took out another jar: honey! All the other jars contained honey. Adam groaned. Just honey! No wonder the pack was so bulky. There were also three or four loaves of bread and some spoons. Adam raised his voice, "Only honey?"

Palustric and Lar stopped chatting and looked around.

"Don't you like honey?" Palustric asked, surprised.

"Well, yes, but we've *only* got honey."

"When there's honey, you don't need anything else. It is the product of endless toil by bees." Palustric looked at Lar for support.

"Ay, honey is full of energy, Master," the little pixy smiled.

Adam blew out his cheeks and said nothing. He replaced the jars, grumbling to himself, before biting into a hefty chunk of bread coated with honey. Palustric smiled as Adam ate because this was Uncle Balom's best honey. But when the boy had finished, he refused to admit how much he had enjoyed it. "It's all right, I suppose," he muttered, and Lar and Palustric smiled knowingly at each other.

They had a rough map which Balom had drawn for them. Judging by yesterday's progress, from the map, Adam calculated that they would be at the foot of Mount Ember in five days. An owl screamed twice, interrupting his thoughts. Adam looked around and found the bird perched in a nearby tree. Pleased, he called to Lar and Palustric: "Have you seen the owl?" He pointed it out.

"It's a barn owl," Palustric said, but his voice held a strange note.

Adam noticed at once. "What's wrong, they're supposed to be wise, aren't they?"

Palustric shook his head. "It's not the *barn* owl which is wise."

"Which owl is it, then?"

The dwarf shook his head again and seemed distracted. "I don't know, I can't remember."

"Lar, do you know?"

The pixy squinted hard and shrugged. "I thought all owls were wise, Master."

"No, they're not!" Palustric's irritability surprised Adam.

"Well, it doesn't really matter," he said. "Let's go!"

"No!" Palustric's deep voice boomed. "We cannot."

"Why not?"

"Because the owl is looking at you."

"Well?"

Dwarves are stubborn and very superstitious. *"Blessed where it sits, bitter where it looks,"* Palustric recited ominously. "Today we cannot move, or we'll surely meet with misfortune." He planted his feet apart and folded his arms.

"But it's only a bird!"

Lar's yellow, slightly squinting eyes moved from one to the other. Adam turned to him in frustration: "Tell him it's only a bird, Lar."

"The owl's call is a sign of misadventure, Master. Anyway, it's Tuesday."

"So what?"

"On Tuesdays and Fridays, one should never set off, Master."

"Oh no!" Adam looked from the earnest yellow eyes to the stubborn brown ones and back again. What nonsense! With pixies and dwarves, it was impossible to move. What would they do all day stuck at the edge of the forest? Just because an owl had hooted. He looked round for a stone to scare off the ill-fated bird, but seeing Palustric's fierce frown, thought better of it. The spot where he wanted to throw a stone was supposed to be blessed. Adam sighed heavily and recalculated the days to the foot of Mount Ember.

At the blessed spot, they built a sturdy stockade, where they passed the night. They set off on Wednesday morning, trudging along forest tracks until the trees on either side became dense. Here the trees were younger, and as the track ran down into a hollow with brakes of hazel on the rising slopes at either side, a strange sound struck their ears. That is, it struck Lar and Adam's ears, for dwarves are dull of hearing.

"Hush!" Adam said, beckoning Palustric to listen. "Can you hear it?"

Palustric shook his head.

"Surely, you can?" Adam pressed him as the beautiful melody grew stronger. Palustric had just heard it as a figure leapt out of the trees and stood before them. Taller and slimmer than a dwarf and fairer by far, the golden-haired person greeted them with a happy smile of welcome.

"Greetings, travellers." He spoke in a clear, sweet voice, lower than a pixy's but higher than a dwarf's.

"An elf!" Palustric whispered excitely to Adam. In the old days, dwarves and elves met regularly, but no more. This was Palustric's first encounter with the *Forgotten Folks*, just as it was Adam's.

Several golden-haired people, almost as tall as Adam, flitted from the trees. They moved with such ease and silence that Adam felt as clumsy as a bear. There was no doubt that if they hadn't wanted to meet them, the travellers would never have known of the elves' presence. Adam studied their clothes and tried to understand the colour. Their doublets, shirts and hose shimmered and changed colour as they moved, but the changes never varied from woodland colours: shades of green, tints of brown, and russet and yellows. It was bewildering to the human eye, at least. Adam wondered if his companions were having the same problem focusing on the elves. Elfin laughter tinkled and rippled around them because the companions' wide eyes and open mouths made them look amusing. The elf waved a green-yellow-brown sleeve towards the trees: "Come, be our guests! The day grows old; it is time to rest!" So sweet was his smile and, indeed, those of the other elves, that the idea of refusing didn't enter their heads.

The elves led them quickly through the hazel trees along a half-hidden pathway. Whether it was hidden by elven magic or by Nature, Adam wasn't really sure. In any case, before long, they were standing in front of a huge turf-roofed hall in a clearing. Once through its wooden doors, they found it surprisingly well-lit from long, narrow windows, which seemed to let in more light than their size suggested. The wooden walls were covered by tapestries of such fine needlecraft and shimmering colours that they sparkled and danced before the friends' wondering eyes. Some scenes of running elves seemed to be alive so that Adam half-expected the stitched figures to leap out of the tapestry in front of them, as their hosts had done in the forest.

"Welcome! Welcome, my friends," repeated the elf who had first greeted them. "Welcome to Spinney-hall." He led them towards a throne at the end of the hall, raised on a low dais. The elf bowed towards a lady seated there. The travellers copied him without a second thought since her presence inspired admiration. They were all charmed by this Beauty, whose golden hair spilt over her pale green gown. Her eyes held them spellbound, greeting them as softly as a violet sunset.

"My name is Inertia, Elfin Queen of the Woodlands and these are my sisters Linga and Supinia; my counsellors," she waved a hand lightly, "Langor, Torpor, Lollop and Tarry...oh, but *so* many names, you will never remember them all!" She smiled sweetly and clapped her hands. A long table was brought before her. At her command, her guests were seated either side of her as the table was loaded with all kinds of delicious foods, the very smell of which, made Adam feel as hungry as the forest wolves.

"We heard you coming," Inertia said.

"I'm not surprised," Adam said humbly. "I expect we sound like lumbering great rhinoceroses to you!" It took Adam a very long time to explain the rhinoceros to the patient company. He ended up by saying: "I expect an old rhino must seem as fanciful as a unicorn to you! They both have one horn, but the rhino *really* exists!"

Inertia laughed and waved a hand at a servant, who nodded and slipped out of the hall. He soon returned, leading a white creature by a silver chain, its coat shimmered in the light of the hall.

Adam, forgetting about good manners and his meal, leapt to his feet. His chair fell backwards to the floor as he gazed open-mouthed at the unicorn. Larger than a goat, but smaller than a pony, the unicorn stared back, timid as a deer, at Adam's approach. The two elves at either side of the unicorn held the animal steady. The beast's deep, blue eyes lost their fear as Adam gently stroked its wondrous soft coat. To his joy, the lovely creature pressed its head against his chest. Its horn, as long as Adam's arm, curled and tapered to a point.

Adam's eyes moved from the unicorn to the wall-hangings. "You are right, Adam," said Inertia, as if she could read his thoughts, "unicorns are much-prized by our people for their wool, which we dye and spin into yarn for needlecraft. This tapestry is half-stitched and indeed made of unicorn wool."

Just wait till he told Emily! She would never believe this—his joy gave way to sudden sadness and he frowned. *If ever he got back to her in one piece.* There was the small matter of the dragon ahead of him. Inertia's violet eyes studied the boy's face. Again, she seemed to read his thoughts: "You are troubled by your quest, but there is time for such things. Set your troubles aside here and rest. I was telling you that I heard you coming. We all did! But it was not the weight of your step, nor even that of the dwarf," (Palustric looked hurt), "which first told us of your coming, but the elven orb you bear."

Adam's hand went down to his pocket, where it closed around *Cari*. He looked guilty and confused. "I don't understand," Adam said. "How can an orb announce an arrival?"

"It's an *elven* orb," Inertia replied with a smile, "and it began to sing as it drew near to elves after so long away."

"So that was the music we heard..." Adam took *Cari* from his pocket with a sad look on his face. He turned the orb in his hand, admiring it for the last time, before handing it to Inertia. "Take the orb," he said unhappily. "It doesn't belong to me, I'm not an elf. It's better with the Elfin Queen of the Woodlands, isn't it?"

Inertia smiled even more sweetly, causing Adam's heart to beat faster. This elf was truly beautiful. "The orb, its true owner, and yourself have destinies entwined. You bear the orb without harm and must, therefore, continue to do so until the day comes when you deliver *Cari* to the one who awaits it."

"But who is the owner?" Adam asked.

Inertia smiled mysteriously. "Come back to the table and tell us how you came by the sphere, for we elves love a good tale."

The evening passed pleasantly with plentiful food and drink as Adam, with a little help from Lar, amused the elves with the tale of how he and Emily had fooled the trolls and beaten the Hag in the Land of Poverty. But it was the tale of their present quest which seemed to interest Inertia most.

Palustric explained how the Key of Ingenuity had been forged in the Old Days with all the art of his forefathers. While the Key had remained among them, it had been easy for any dwarf to turn his hand to the finest jewellery or armour. However, when the Key was stolen by the Ever-cursed Outsider, the wisdom of the Council was called into question. With the inspiration given by the Key, people had neglected to learn the old skills properly. Why bother when the Key provided inspiration without effort? The folly of this behaviour was now clear to everyone. Whatever the Ever-cursed Outsider had intended to do with the Key would never be known, because he was gobbled up by Lentor the Dragon, whose greed had been aroused by the beautiful Key. Lentor held the Key, along with all the other gold and jewels that he'd accumulated over the centuries. Palustric's face bore that great sadness, common to all his people when he spoke of the Key. Now, he explained, his people could not finish work of the finer kind. Regaining the Key would enable them to recover their old skills. Meanwhile, dwarves had been forced to become farmers and fishermen. Several brave or foolhardy dwarves had climbed Mount Ember, but none had ever returned. Palustric looked with troubled eyes at his friend. "I suppose I'm lucky really," he ended, sighing heavily. "At least I'm apprenticed to a blacksmith."

"Come, Palustric," Inertia said, "this is not the moment to be sad, and the task before you will keep for a while. Stay here with us and be merry for as long as you like!" There was something so oddly beguiling about the way Inertia spoke, as though she wanted them to stay forever. She clapped her bejewelled little hands and called for music and dancing, tumbling and juggling, wrestling and elf-magicking.

# 10

---

*B*ella the Goldsmith put down her eyeglass slowly, so as not to disturb the girl. Emily was in a kind of trance. Yet her hands were moving in a skilful way that Bella envied. She had not seen the like of this since she was a girl. Vague memories of her great-grandfather returned to her. What a goldsmith he was! And even he had admitted to being only a poor copy of his great forefathers. He had remembered some of the old skills. True enough, much of the knowledge was in the *Book of Jewellification*; that volume took years to read, and, of course, reading was not the same thing as actually doing. But this girl, this out-sider, had read the Book in a short time—in *no* time, you might say. Now, what was emerging under her hands?

Ever since coming to the workshop, Emily had wanted to make a brooch, a brooch which she could see now in a kind of vision, a brooch which told of how she had left her own world: a dragonfly brooch with a fairy upon its back, just like the dragonfly and the Fairy Queen that she had seen. In a trance, her silver eyes glazed like two mirrors; Emily's hands worked of their own accord. They fashioned gold plate, set with amber and enamel and embellished with moonstone, until the most beautiful complete brooch that Bella the Goldsmith had ever seen lay upon the bench. Even as old Bella hurried away to fetch Balom as fast as her short, dwarf legs could carry her, Emily began collecting materials for another similar brooch. Still in a trance, she pumped the bellows of the small forge, whipping the flames about the red coals.

Not even Balom's booming voice could make her look up or distract her for a moment from her task. Bella shrugged and pointed to the brooch: "The child has made this brooch." Bella sounded as if she couldn't believe her own words. "You and I, Balom, thought we would laugh at her efforts, but *this*...this is magnificent!" She turned the lovely object admiringly in front of Balom's face. "Work to compare can only be seen if it was forged in the *Old Days*."

Balom turned to Emily and spoke a few words, but the girl seemed not to hear him. Her fingers were flying about her second brooch. Balom caught her arm, but she shrugged him off, her eyes never moving from the work on which they were fixed.

"She won't even stop for meals," Bella said grimly. "It's as if the girl has lost the power of reason."

The two dwarves discussed the matter as they watched Emily create another, equally beautiful brooch. Only a dwarf could truly appreciate such work for its craftsmanship and skill. Bella and Balom gazed and gasped as Emily's hands flew backwards and forwards from the forge to the bench, to the pincers and to the hammer and then back again. They watched in awe as the girl plied and twisted, smoothed and cut the heated metals. It was late in the evening before Emily finished. Balom was still there; he watched as she blinked and looked at the jewels with normal eyes.

A slow, mysterious smile spread across her face. "I'll be here early in the morning, Bella," she said. "I've such a lot of work to do." Emily left Bella and Balom bending over two perfect brooches.

The weeks ran together in Bella's workshop. They were all the same to Emily. Glazed eyes and sweated brow, she laboured over her brooches. She didn't care if her hands were dirty and her face smeared with soot. Although Bella begged her to make something different, she would not—or could not. To please Bella, from time to time, she changed the design, though the subject was always the same: a fairy astride a dragonfly.

"Why do you do it, child?" Bella asked, but only received stubborn silence or a mysterious smile in reply. On the other hand, Bella's workshop was building up a beautiful collection of jewelled brooches, each subtly different, but of one basic design.

Before long, word spread; at first, rich dwarves came to buy Emily's brooches. As news travels quickly, people from further afield began to arrive. If Emily hadn't been in a trance, she would have marvelled at the pixies, brownies, and occasional ugly goblin who came to buy. All of them were rich and prepared to pay well for Emily's work. Many asked for other designs, but Bella told them that to appreciate the beauty of jewellery, one had to have *the eye*. The kind of eye, she explained, which could distinguish the subtle difference between one fairy-mounted dragonfly and another. Everyone believed her and bought all the more eagerly. Of course, Bella knew that her strange apprentice wouldn't, or couldn't, make any other type of jewellery; however, by now, Bella had become an excellent salesdwarf.

Bella became ever more anxious as the business prospered. "You should be careful, Emily," she warned one day when the girl had finished her work and the glazed expression had passed. "The way things are going, *Success* could come to you any time. Be ready, that's all!"

Emily just smiled and looked at the brooches that she had made that day. She was so fast and skilled that she could turn out three superb brooches in one day—she had no idea how. All she knew was that when she was busy, everything was blotted out. This meant that she didn't have to worry about Adam; she tried not to think about him now and blinked away tears. What would happen to him? What would happen to *them?* She tried to push the thought out of her mind, but she had a feeling that things were not as they should be. She often had this feeling, especially when she thought of her brother or home. They had been away a long time now. At first, she thought, it had been exciting meeting pixies and dwarves, seeing real magic and witch-craft. Now she longed for the comfort of home, her father's whiskery kiss, her mother's cookery, Jasmine's purring—a tear rolled down her cheek. She wiped it angrily with the back of her hand and left a long black smear across her cheek. She tried to work out why that strange feeling was so important, but she couldn't.

*a*dam was uneasy. He wasn't sure what was bothering him: a feeling that wouldn't go away, but it wouldn't come to the front of his mind, either. He, Lar and Palustric were having a wonderful time. They had been in Spinney-hall for many months now, but none of them was worried about the time passing. Adam had never felt so contented anywhere: so cheerful, comfortable, well-fed and pleasantly entertained. He felt permanently drowsy and lethargic. In fact, the three friends barely gave their perilous quest a thought these days. When he occasionally thought of Emily, or home or dragons, Adam just shrugged. It was as if that kind of thought didn't belong in this place. On such occasions, Adam would pick another bunch of dark, juicy grapes—one of the reasons why he was putting on weight—and try to forget his uneasiness.

Lately, he had spent a lot of time in front of the mirror, something he'd never done before. Sometimes he spent hours adjusting his silver hair or admiring his profile from various angles and worrying that his scar spoiled his good looks. He certainly was good-looking, he would tell himself in these quiet moments, staring into his reflected silver eyes. Maybe the scar made him more rugged. He sighed deeply. He knew he was in love, but could an elfin lady love a human boy? In any case, this was no ordinary elfin lady.

One morning, having decided to roll slowly out of his cosy bed, Adam bumped into Lar outside the hall. He yawned and grinned at the pixy, who squinted sleepily back at him. Perhaps it was the air of laziness and luxury about Lar that finally brought Adam's worries to mind. Suddenly, everything fell into place.

"Lar!" Adam cried. "We've got to get away from here!"

The little pixy's mouth dropped open. "What for?" he yawned again.

"We must! Find Palustric now!" Adam was shouting in his anxiety.

Lar could not understand. What was wrong with his Master? Everything here was magnificent. There was no need to go elsewhere. Why should they move? Everything he had ever wanted was here in Spinney-hall, as far as he was concerned. He said as much to Adam.

"That's just it, Lar. Don't you see? Inertia—" he struggled for names, trying to remember, "Tarry, Lollop...all those names! Don't you see? We've been blind! Why didn't I see it before? All those names mean the same thing. Don't you see, Lar?" Lar shook his head sleepily and looked confused.

"They mean *hanging about, doing nothing* —just what we're doing! The idle life has tempted us: temptation has got the better of us. Don't you see, now? We'll never complete our task if we linger here!" He waved his arm towards the door of the hall; his gaze followed his gesture, as did Lar's. But instead of seeing Spinney-hall, they saw Palustric standing alone in pyjamas. Otherwise, the glade was empty and silent.

"W-what's happened?" Palustric said pathetically.

"The illusion's gone, Palustric," Adam said gently. "We've seen through it, that's what! Come on, my friend, get dressed. Mount Ember awaits us, along with the quest which we have set aside for so long."

Palustric looked back over his shoulder, where Spinney-hall should have been. His expression was unhappy, and he hesitated. The little pixy broke the spell: *"The horse can die of hunger waiting for the grass to grow,* is it not so, Master?" Lar's wrinkled face spread into a broad grin.

"Ay!" Adam and Palustric said in the same instant, and laughing, Palustric pulled off his pyjama jacket and pulled on his leather jerkin. Soon, the three of them were on their travels again.

The days that followed seemed never-ending —forest, more forest and more forest. At last, four days out of Spinney-hall, they came to the farthest edge of the forest. They were glad to see open plain before them, but a brooding peak beyond the grasslands tempered their joy: Mount Ember. Even from a distance, it looked a forbidding place. Sombre and sullen, its grey form peaking icily into clouds of the same colour.

"It's an evil place," Palustric shuddered, "wrapped in legend and superstition and none of it pleasant. Its other name is Mount of the Dead, you know, because—"

"Shut up, Palustric!" Adam snapped. He

didn't want to go there one bit. Every step seemed to be heavier than his last as he drew nearer to the sinister mountain. Palustric was making matters worse. He didn't have to go there and become a dragon's dinner. Adam didn't know why he was going through with this. The dwarves had said that he would have to go back to the Land of Poverty if he didn't make this effort. Then again, there didn't seem much to choose between the Dragon and the Hag. What a mess! Adam sighed heavily; noticing this, Lar was about to come out with another of his wise sayings. Adam's silver eyes flashed fiercely, and Lar thought better of it.

They marched on in heavy silence, Adam thinking about Emily or the dangers ahead; Palustric thinking about Spinney-hall which had been snatched from him; Lar wondering whether he'd be able to slip in his wise saying later on.

By the end of the fourth day, they had crossed the rough grasslands, where the blades of grass towered overhead and silent snakes slithered sneakily out of sight. They stood at the foot of Mount Ember.

"Well, this is where we part."

He handed Adam a smaller backpack. "I've put you two jars of honey and bread in there."

He smiled sadly. "You'll need to keep your energy levels up!"

Palustric looked ashamed at Adam's words and in a low voice said, "I have sworn to stay at the foot of the mountain. Good luck though." He took Adam's arm and pointed to a cave a long way up the mountainside. "See, there dwells Lentor the Dragon. Mind that you never gaze into his eyes. Even the slightest glance is fatal. They say that looking in a dragon's eye numbs the spirit and steals the will to live. Take care, Adam!"

"Thanks, Palustric, you're a true friend. In any case, I wouldn't have let you come with me—this is my affair."

He turned to Lar and held out his hand. "See you later, Lar," but his thoughts were far less certain than his words.

"Master, I shall come with you!"

Adam looked into Lar's faithful, squinting yellow eyes and put his hand on the pixy's shoulder. "No, Lar, I'm going alone. If I don't come back, I want you to find Emily and help her to get back home." Adam turned quickly; his voice felt thick and he fought back the tears prickling in his eyes. He set off up the mountain track. As he climbed, he felt better. He decided to turn and wave to his friends. When he did so, he found Lar right behind him. "What...? Lar! I told you! Go back at once!" Adam had to be firm and insist for Emily's sake before Lar unwillingly rejoined Palustric.

Lar stood for a long time and watched his Master go up the mountainside. Slowly and sadly, he returned to Palustric who was waiting and also watching below.

"Adam will be back," Lar said to Palustric, but his eyes begged the dwarf to agree with him.

Palustric shook his head; his eyes were shining too much. "I fear not, dear friend." Then in a booming voice, he called up the mountainside: "We'll wait here two full days, Adam..." his voice dying away at the shameful thought of the unspoken part: *then we'll go home and tell them you died bravely...*

*"Troubles and burdens are like shadows that follow you everywhere,* is it not so, Palustric?" Lar muttered, his eyes never leaving Adam's back as the boy disappeared up the mountain.

Palustric stiffened. Lar sensed his friend's tension. The pixy's squinting eyes followed the dwarf's gaze. Wheeling high, near the craggy summit, were five black dots in the sky.

"Kites!" Palustric spat out the word.

"The Hag!" Lar trembled.

"It's a bad omen for all our people," Palustric

muttered. "With the Key, there's no danger of dwarves ever falling into Poverty, without it...is another matter. Much is riding on Adam's success."

The two friends anxiously scanned the sky until their eyes hurt and their necks ached with the effort.

Adam's legs felt as if they had been hollowed out and the space filled with lead. They were on fire with the effort of climbing. The path was steep and winding with the constant danger of loose rocks, and he was soon tired with the effort of concentration. If his legs had ruled his mind, Adam would have been back in the forest, his mission unfulfilled. For that matter, if his mind had ruled his legs, he would be going downwards not upwards. He paused to catch his breath and wondered, so if his legs and his mind weren't in charge, what was? Heart! *Heart*, he decided was in charge. *So that's what it means to be heartened.* Adam set off again. This thought drove him on. He felt as brave as he did in the Land of Poverty —well, at least until he looked the Hag in the face. He must remember not to look the dragon in the eye, he told himself.

Lost in thought, Adam failed to hear the screeching kites' approach. So, he wasn't prepared for the swooping attack. The first he knew of it was a black streak which flashed past his face and the talon which ripped his shirt at the shoulder. He wasn't hurt, but the power of the predator pulled him off balance. The other black kites swooped at his face, wicked talons lunging towards him. The path was narrow and full of loose stones. Just as the Hag wished, trying to escape from the onslaught of the great hawks, Adam lost his balance and fell down the mountainside.

It would have finished him, but luck was on his side. A solitary mountain shrub broke his tumbling, bruising fall. Adam lay stunned, caught in the thorny bush. Dazed, a screech brought him round. A kite had settled on a crag not far away, its head turned sideways so the yellow eye could consider the state of its prey. Adam could hear the others screeching and wheeling above him, and he was sure that they had been sent to ensure his death on this mountain. The hunter raised its wings slowly. Painfully, Adam reached into his pocket, gratefully realising that no bones were broken. He pulled *Cari* from his pocket, and a fiery spear of energy from the orb left the kite a smouldering bundle of black feathers on the mountainside. The boy didn't see the other kites arrow away.

He realised that they had gone by the lack of screeching. He lost consciousness again.

When he came around, his body was cold and he shivered uncontrollably. He raised himself with an elbow into a sitting position, and it seemed that every bone in his body hurt. Slowly, head spinning, his body full of aches, bruises and grazes, Adam got to his feet. He thanked his luck and hoped that the elven orb would continue to save him, but he wondered what it could do against a dragon. Dragons were more ancient creatures than elves, and elfin magic would not affect them.

As he dragged his body up Mount Ember, Adam reflected. He should always be on guard against the Hag, who wanted his life. His mission must be even more important than he had thought if the witch wanted to stop him. This Key must be more valuable than he imagined. Rubbing a badly bruised arm, he struggled on.

He spent a starless night on the mountainside, aching and unable to sleep, chilled more by fear than the coldness of the night. He felt doomed. What chance did he have of getting the Key? He would not be allowed back without it, and the Dragon wasn't going to hand it over with a friendly wink. Even with *Cari*, he didn't fancy his chances. For a dragon, he needed a bazooka. He reckoned that his young life had come to an end here in this desolate place. Well, what did he care in the end? It was no life without his mother and father and his sister. The only consolation was that he wouldn't have to put up with his sister's bossiness and her pesky cat; he smiled wryly. Jasmine had the habit of jumping up behind his head when he was sitting on the sofa and massaging his scalp with her paws when he was trying to watch his favourite TV series. Emily said she did it as a sign of affection, but Adam hated having his scalp massaged by a feline.

He shrugged his shoulders, managing to doze fitfully after he'd given up hope of sleeping. He was awakened at dawn by the loud shrieking of a circling hawk, which was not a black kite. Nevertheless, he took it to be a bad sign. Adam opened the pack and spooned honey onto his bread. Back to bread and honey again after all the delicious food with the elves, he sighed and munched without appetite.

He stood up shakily and set off. His body felt even worse than the evening before, but he groaned and gritted his teeth. The cave mouth gaped above him. He hoped for a moment that the dragon would not be at home. He would sneak in, silent as the slithering snakes below, then help himself to the Key. Adam took a last look at the rubble-strewn mountain below and knew that there was no such thing as good luck in this place: only doom. He took a deep breath and, murmuring a prayer, climbed up into the gaping entry.

He didn't have to go into a deep, dark hole in the mountain. Lentor was right there in the opening, sprawled upon a pile of treasure. The dragon was huge. Its dull, purple-grey scales, heavy as armour, contrasted with the diamonds, rubies, sapphires and gold which sparkled and winked under its belly. Adam's amazement at seeing a legendary creature almost betrayed him. He stared at the dragon, his mouth agape. The creature seemed to be asleep. Just in time, he remembered Palustric's advice. It was as well. The oldest trick a dragon knows is to feign sleep and then to flick open an eyelid, catching the victim checking on whether one is asleep. This time Lentor was disappointed. His eyelid sprang open, baring a huge reptilian eye, but Adam was staring at the floor in front of the dragon's nose.

The dragon spoke in a low, hissing voice and a strange tongue, but stranger still, Adam could understand it: "I thought I could smell a human. I'm never wrong, you know. But to tell the truth, I prefer the aroma of roast human!" He flicked out a tongue of flame, which on purpose, fell just short of Adam. The dragon chuckled. He chuckled again as he watched Adam pull out *Cari*. "An elven pin-prick for dragon armour, tch, tch! I thought humans were more intelligent."

Adam thrust the orb back into his pocket. "You're right, Lentor, it doesn't help."

"Come, come, it's not polite to talk like this. You should always look someone in the eye when you speak, you know."

"Oh no, you won't catch me like that," Adam said bravely, hardly believing that he was having a conversation with a real dragon.

"Plucky little fellow, aren't you?" Smoke poured out of Lentor's nostrils as he hissed. "First you come in here, bold as dwarf brass, then draw your orblet; next, bandy words with me! You know I could finish you with a flick of my tail, don't you?"

"Yes, but you won't," Adam said boldly, forcing his quaking voice not to betray his terror. Since he had given up hope the day before, desperation had taken the place of fear.

"Oh, why not, eh?"

"Because you're curious..." Adam said, holding his breath and hoping.

The dragon looked at the boy slyly and, with a great creaking and groaning of armour plating, sat upright, towering above Adam, his head almost touching the high cave roof. His hind leg slipped on his pile of gems and pieces of gold, starting a dazzling cascade.

"You're dead...right, of course!" Lentor laughed wickedly. A trail of smoke was snatched from his mouth by the gentle breeze passing the cave mouth. "It's not every day, no, not every four or five centuries even, that I have the pleasure of eating...er...I mean, *meeting*...a human. Especially a young, juicy one like you." Lentor lingered lovingly over the word *juicy*.

Adam shuddered and waited.

"So, what do you want, eh?"

"Just one thing," Adam said quietly.

"Oh, oh, just one thing, eh?"

"Ay, if you give it to me, I'll go and never bother you again."

"Oh, you will, will you? And what makes you think you can go, a juicy morsel like you? Why should I give you anything? Things have to be earned or bought. Why should they be given?"

"They shouldn't, I agree," Adam said, "things ought to be earned or bought. That's why I've come to ask for the Key of Ingenuity. It was not earned or bought. It was stolen by an unknown thief. You ate that thief and took the Key. Now I've come to ask for it back."

"Nothing less!" Lentor roared, sending a cloud of acrid smoke from his nostrils down over Adam, who coughed and spluttered. His voice revealed that he was angry for the first time.

"Clever with words, aren't you, boy! Twisting what Old Lentor says in that way...but no match for a dragon, I'll bet! We shall have a little sport, you and I. Everyone knows that the dragon is the cleverest creature in Creation. Let's see, then! We'll have a contest. Yes, a contest—a battle of wits! Your puny wits against my massive ones. Quite unfair, I know, but I'll make it worth your while. First prize for you will be the Key of Ingenuity, and for me..." Lentor's voice dropped to a menacing hiss, "...dinner. *You!* Roast boy! What do you say, boy? D'you agree, eh?"

Adam cringed against the wall. What should he say? He could only agree. There was nothing to stop Lentor roasting him there and then if he so desired. So, he spoke up bravely, "It's a deal, Lentor. My wits against yours, it is!"

"Ho, ho! Wonderful! I love a little sport before dinner," the dragon rumbled. "Riddles! That's it! *Riddles.*" Lentor announced this as if working out riddles was a sudden, brilliant inspiration. But, of course, all dragons love riddling and cannot resist any opportunity to pit their wits. "I love a riddle, don't you?" he chuckled, a little flame licking from the corner of his mouth.

"Good, well we'll start," he hissed. "Listen carefully, boy, because you have to solve this riddle." Lentor's voice took on the pompous ritual tone that dragons use when riddling:

*A moth ate words.*
*Strange that such a creature*
*Should swallow a man's song.*
*A thief fed in the darkness*
*On a great man's speech.*
*The thief was none the wiser*
*For having swallowed the words."*

"There," Lentor chuckled smokily, "got you straight away. Admit it, boy; so that I can roast you without delay! Go on!"

"How long have I got to solve it?" Adam asked nervously, looking fixedly at the floor.

"Five minutes, even if five centuries aren't enough for a human brain," the dragon sneered. "Shall I repeat it?"

"Not really." Adam smiled because he'd heard that one before: "The answer is a *bookworm!*" He grinned and stopped himself, just in time, from staring triumphantly in the dragon's eye.

"You've heard it before!" Lentor accused menacingly.

"So what?" Adam shrugged.

"It doesn't count," Lentor snorted, sending twin plumes of smoke coiling out of the cave. "Right, see if you can get this one...!"

"Hey, just a minute, isn't it my turn?"

"All in good time, all in good time. I can see I didn't take you seriously enough. It's always a mistake to underestimate the opposition!" Lentor was enjoying himself at his favourite pastime, and he wasn't going to let a little matter of fairness spoil his fun or his appetite. Dragons rarely get the opportunity to riddle; there are so few of them. Whenever they meet, they riddle. It might be by chance, out on a foray, or officially, at the Septennial Dragon Reunion. Six years and six months had passed since the last reunion, so it was due soon. That was why Lentor was delighted to get in a little practice. "What about this one then?"

> My breast puffed up and my neck
>     swollen,
> I've a fine head and a high waving tail,
> Also, eyes and ears, but only one leg.

*Long-necked, strong-beaked,*
*With a back and two sides*
*A rod through my middle,*
*My home is high above men.*
*Whipped by the lash of rain I stand*
     *alone;*
*Bruised by hailstones, attacked by frost,*
*Half-hidden by snow, I put up with*
     *all this*
*Without a word."*


"There, you can't have heard this one. I've just made it up! Got you this time! Want to hear it again?" Lentor was happy and repeated the riddle without being asked.

Adam closed his eyes and thought feverishly. What had a puffed-up chest and only one leg? He couldn't think of anything with only one leg. Lentor's chuckling didn't help, nor did his taunts: "Go on, admit it, I've got you this time! Yummy-yum, roast boy!"

Suddenly, Adam thought of the rod right through the middle and the home high above men.

"I know!" he yelled triumphantly. "A *weathercock!*"

"Harrumph!" Lentor snorted. "Nearly had you, try this one then."

"That's not fair! It's my turn now. I've solved two of your riddles, after all."

"Whose cave is this?" The dragon stared stonily at the boy whose eyes were firmly fixed on the floor. "I could always roast you now." The dragon's voice lowered to a menacing hiss: "We play to my rules! Now, pay attention...

*The breeze carries little creatures*
*High over the hill slopes.*
*They are very dark, dressed in black coats.*
*They travel in groups, here and there,*
*Singing lots of loud songs.*
*They live by wooded cliffs,*
*Yet they sometimes come to men's houses.*

"Hee, hee, hee, hee!" Lentor chuckled, lying down noisily again on his treasure hoard and closing his eyes. "Just taking a gentle before-dinner nap!" he mocked.

Adam closed his eyes, too, and thought about the little creatures. There seemed to be several possibilities. They could be crows, no—too big—whining gnats? That was the idea he liked best and was about to announce this solution when something stopped him. *Cari* began to hum at his side. Adam glanced out of the corner of his eye at Lentor. But the dragon's eyes were firmly closed.

He didn't seem to hear the orb humming. The hum grew louder. Still, Lentor didn't move. It occurred to Adam that perhaps the dragon couldn't hear the sound. The hum filled his ears and formed into two words: the answer to the riddle.

Adam clutched the orb gratefully in his pocket. "Thanks, *Cari*," he said out loud.

Lentor opened one lazy eyelid. "Eh? Give in?"

"Of course not. The answer is *house martins*."

Where Lentor had snorted before, this time he bellowed: "Harrumph!" Adam threw himself against the cave wall as a tongue of flame roared past him.

Below at the foot of the mountain, Palustric and Lar heard the rumble and saw the flame blast out of the cave mouth. "Poor Adam," the young dwarf mumbled and, sobbing, sat down on a boulder. Lar said nothing but put his arm around his friend's shoulder.

Inside the cave, Lentor hissed, "What sort of boy are you, a genius?"

"No, an ordinary boy. It's just that dragons aren't as clever as they think they are."

Lentor roared again, sending an even longer spurt of flame out of the cave. A wheeling falcon had to use all its aerial skills to avoid being a roast hawk.

"Not clever enough...not *clever enough!*" Lentor couldn't believe this impertinence. He spluttered smoke, which slowly spread like fog in the cave. Adam's eyes began to sting.

"No," Adam coughed. "If you were clever, you wouldn't be so afraid to let me set you a riddle."

"Afraid?" Lentor snorted more smoke. Adam could only just make out the dragon's shape in the thickening smoke. "Dragons fear nothing. Go on then! Solving it will give me a better appetite."

"Won't you give me more tries, as you had?"

"No."

"I'd better make it a hard one, then."

"Just a minute," Lentor growled from behind his smokescreen. "No cheating. I don't trust humans. It has to be something you've *seen*, right?"

"Ri...*cough*...right." Adam could hardly speak for the smoke. He was squatting on the floor where there was a little air. "Listen...*cough*...carefully, Lentor." And using the same pompous tone that the dragon had used, recited:

> *"I lived in water...cough...when I was*
>    *young,*

*But...cough...grew up to fly faster than*
*others...*
Cough...*I take my food on the*
*wing...cough...*
*And though my life is short,*
*I bear on my back the long-lived one:*
*Wings on wings...cough...*
*And a crown to top it all.* Cough, cough,
cough."

Adam finished with a long coughing fit.

"Say it again, say it again!" Lentor snapped. "And this time without coughing!"

"How can I," Adam choked, "with all this smoke?"

Lentor took a deep breath and this time blew fiercely, without flame or smoke, and a black bank of smoke rolled out of the cave. Adam gulped in air gratefully; his head was spinning.

"That's better," he said and repeated the riddle without interruptions.

Lentor sat up suddenly on his treasure heap. Coins and jewels scattered here and there. From high above the boy's head, the dragon's voice hissed flatly: "I shall have to take my time, of course."

"Take all the time you need," Adam replied. "I'll just sit in the cave mouth, for a breath of fresh air." His clothes reeked of smoke. "I'll be leaving first thing in the morning, *with the Key*," he called over his shoulder.

"Unless you've been gobbled up and thoroughly digested. Now, what was that riddle? Fly faster than others? Mmm."

Lentor closed his eyes and looked as if he were asleep. Now and then a smoky sigh and hiss or the odd word slipped out: "food on the wing, mmm..." ... "the long-lived one..."

Time passed slowly for Adam. He sat cross-legged in the cave mouth and watched the shadows lengthen over the dreary landscape. Below, he fancied he could see the tiny figures of Palustric and Lar moving about. He wasn't sure until he saw a wisp of smoke from their evening fire. How he wished he was safe with his friends now. Adam looked back at the dragon in the evening gloom of his cave. "For such a clever creature, you're taking your time, Lentor."

The old dragon's eyes seemed to set even closer together. The strain of trying to solve this riddle was beginning to get to him. "You're not cheating me, are you? I'll find out," he hissed, "then you'll be done to a turn. Is it really something you've *seen*? What has wings and carries something else with wings on its back? Nothing! That's what! Admit it, eh? Admit it!"

"I've seen it with my own two eyes. I swear, I give you my word. So has my sister. Dragons aren't too bright at riddling, are they?"

Lentor sat up suddenly again with his scales clanking. He tried, rather unsuccessfully, to turn the anger in his voice into a polite wheedling hiss: "Give me a clue. Go on, just one, be a nice boy...!"

"A clue? To help you gobble me up, you must be joking!"

"Go on! Just one. And I promise to keep my word about the Key. I wasn't going to. I'll make an exception this time and be trustworthy. Go on, just one clue!"

Lentor was desperate. Dragons pride themselves on their riddling prowess. They boast that they can solve any riddle in the end. Dragons can become ill. It's rare because they are almost immortal. However, one of the few things that can make a dragon ill is struggling with a difficult riddle. Lentor already had an awful headache and was beginning to feel listless and depressed.

"All right, I'll make you a deal," Adam said, staring at one of Lentor's front claws. "I get to hold the Key of Ingenuity, and you get a clue; only a little clue, though, because I don't want to end up as your main course."

Lentor struggled inwardly, wrestling with his

natural greed in his misery at being baffled by this riddle. At last, his desperation got the upper hand. "Oh, all right," he snapped, curling a talon beneath the bulk of his body. His claw rummaged about among the glittering, priceless objects he brooded over until it grasped the Key.

"Here," Lentor growled, his claw slowly held out the beautiful object. His eyes sought Adam's, hoping to trick the boy into meeting his gaze. Adam's eyes stayed fixed to the floor. "Don't try to run away with it, either. I can fly faster than any bird...once I get going, that is. Not to mention the fact that I can launch a flame sixteen oak-tree-lengths without trying." The claw slowly released its grip on the Key, which dropped into the boy's outstretched hand. Adam turned it over several times, and it flashed and shimmered even in the fading light of the gloomy cave. He gasped at its beauty. The old dwarves had put all the pride of their craft into its creation. The wrought gold was studded with sapphire and ruby, giving a violet sparkle to the whole. Lentor eyed the Key with sorrow similar to a mother giving away her child.

"Now, what about the clue?" he hissed spitefully.

"All right." Adam wrenched his eyes away

from the Key. "For the first part of the riddle, think about yourself, Lentor."

Lentor waited for more, but it didn't come. "Call that a clue? I already know that!" he hissed savagely, sending two curls of smoke towards the cave roof. "It's a *dragon*fly. I know that! But what kind of dragonfly? It's the second part that's got me puzzled. Dragonflies live in water when they're young, and they become the fastest insect. I've got that! That's no help at all! Give me another clue." The dragon's voice betrayed his desperation.

Adam grew bolder: "No, a deal's a deal. That's your lot!"

Adam settled down against the wall, near the cave-mouth and waited. He was too afraid to sleep or even to doze. Night drew on. Lentor was lost in thought and feeling dizzy. Time passed. Adam thought of his friends below, and then he thought of Emily. Was she still with Bella? Was she in danger? He stared out at the starry sky and thought of nothing in particular.

He stared up at the twinkling stars and yawned. He jerked himself awake; it was no use nodding off because he didn't trust the dragon one bit. He held *Cari* in one hand and the Key of Ingenuity in the other. It was a long night. The longest Adam had ever experienced.

Lentor began to feel poorly. His flame died down to a spark and just before dawn, died out altogether: a clear sign this, of an ailing dragon. His short legs felt heavy and numb; there wasn't any spare energy for take-off—not even for grasping with his talons. His massive brain had used up all its energy: a bad case of *Dragon Riddling-Sickness*. There was only one cure, and Adam possessed that—the answer to the riddle. Without it, Lentor was doomed. He would simply fade away and die. Apart from a blade in the soft skin under the armpit, it was the only way a dragon could be killed. Not many people had the chance to drive a blade into that unarmoured part of a dragon. But absolutely no-one (apart from another dragon) had ever managed to make a dragon ill from Riddling-Sickness. Dragons were always doing it to each other, which is why the world isn't overrun by elderly dragons. Lentor, for instance, was now as weak as an eagle-chick. But the boy didn't know that.

Dawn broke at last. With the first light, Adam stood up.

"Well, Lentor," he said, and his heart was pounding, fit to burst, "I'll have to be going. You've lost! You haven't solved my riddle, have you?"

Lentor shook his head weakly. There wasn't a trace of smoke.

"I expect I'll have to tell you the answer, then."

"Oh yes, please," Lentor croaked weakly, knowing that his life depended on it.

"Well, it's the Fairy Queen mounted on her dragonfly."

Had Lentor had the strength to roar, he would have. He would also have roasted Adam on the spot. Instead, he could only hiss faintly, his feeble hiss loaded with hatred: "We agreed it should be something you have *seen*. You are more treacherous than a dragon!"

"That's not true!" Adam protested. "I've been quite honest. I *did see* her" He explained just how he and his sister had come to the Land of Poverty. "The trouble is, we don't know how to get back home," he ended lamely.

The dragon's voice was weak and low and full of self-pity. "I couldn't be expected to solve the riddle," he moaned. "Who'd believe that a human boy had seen *Aeshna*, the Fairy Queen? But I *do* know how you can get back home," he hissed craftily. "You see, dragons are pretty clever, after all."

"Tell me, Lentor."

"I will if you give me back my Key."

"It's not your Key, nor mine, and I can't give it back."

"You'd better go then before I change my mind and roast you." The dragon regretted his words at once. He knew he was weak, but the boy didn't. He changed to a coaxing tone. "Excuse me," he wheedled, "I'm forgetting my manners. I'd like to get to know you better. It's not often that a dragon gets to meet a human—a genius at that. Why don't you stay for..." Lentor calculated quickly, he needed a week to get his strength back, "for a week's holiday before you set off. During your stay, I'd be pleased to tell you how to get back to your world."

Adam didn't look in the dragon's eye. He didn't know why the scaly creature was feigning friendliness, and he didn't care. He had no idea why betrayal and death hadn't come his way. For some reason, the dragon seemed unable to kill him. Was it the orb? In any case, he had to fulfil his mission.

"I'm sorry, I must go."

"Curse you!" Lentor hissed. "When I feel well again, I'll come for the Key. I'll have my treasure back, and I'll roast you ever so slowly and your tasty sister!"

"I don't think so, Lentor," Adam said. "With the Key, the dwarves will be able to make armour to resist any dragon. You'd only be wasting your time. So long!"

As he made his way down the mountainside, Adam couldn't believe his luck. With help from *Cari* and, above all, with his wits and courage, he had triumphed and succeeded in his quest. Once only, he looked back at Lentor's cave. The dragon had dragged himself weakly to the mouth and was peering gloomily after the boy who was taking *his* Key away. Luckily, Adam was far enough away, and it didn't matter that he had gazed at the dragon's face. What he saw there was a mixture of hatred and sorrow. Adam laughed out loud and held up the key for Lentor to see better.

"He'll never get the key past the elves. Then I'll get it from *them*!" Lentor hissed spitefully before dragging his listless bulk back onto his comforting treasure pile.

At the foot of the mountain, the three friends were joyously reunited. Adam's triumph was told and retold, while the pixy's admiring squinting eyes never moved from the boy's face and the dwarf's eyes never moved from his people's magnificent, legendary Key. It was at the foot of Mount Ember that Adam learned of *Dragon Riddling-Sickness* for the first time from his pixy friend.

## 12

---

*B*ella the Goldsmith had become a wealthy dwarf. She could afford to buy expensive food and clothes. She had given up her gold-smithing and had become a shopkeeper: a jeweller. Like most jewellers, Bella was rich. The reason for Bella's change of fortune was the beauty of Emily's work. The girl was turning out three masterpieces a day. Whenever Bella worried that her good luck, in the form of Emily's work, would run out, she had only to mention Adam, and the girl would immerse herself in her task. It seemed that working was the only way for her to blot out her worries. Now the only real concern was when *Success* would decide to arrive.

Pixies, goblins, brownies and even different types of elves came to Bella's workshop to buy dragonfly brooches of exquisitely haunting beauty. Elves: the dwarves hadn't seen them in living memory, but beauty drew those ethereal creatures. They are beautiful themselves, and Emily's brooches attracted them as butterflies are attracted to a nectar-laden flower.

Bella feared that one elf, in particular, would come—her fears proved correct. When she came, she wore a blue gown woven with stars that shone like those in the night sky: matching her golden hair. Her turquoise eyes were more beautiful than any Emily had ever seen. When those eyes looked into hers, the girl felt as if she wanted to be the elfin maiden's slave. Indeed, only those whom her eyes beckoned dared to approach this awesome elf.

These seductive eyes fixed on Emily at her workbench. Bella hurried over to a hatch in the wall, which gave from the shop into the workshop. From there, in dismay, she watched the beguiling stranger smile sweetly at the girl. Up to now, nothing and nobody had succeeded in interrupting the girl at her work. But this elf with her alluring eyes and mischievous smile was taking Emily by the hand.

"No!" Bella wailed. Between her fingers in

front of her eyes, she watched the elfin maiden lead the girl out of the little beamed workshop and off down the high road. As if to herself, Bella muttered: "It had to happen, sooner or later, I knew *Success* would take Emily away from me."

## 13

———————————

*A*dam and his companions camped in the grasslands that night. Until now, none of them had shown any real ability for building a stockade. This time, whatever they attempted to create was a brilliant success. Simple ideas like making a fence from woven stems went so well that the fence ended up surprisingly well-designed and strong, in no time. When they had finished, they admired their work. Palustric insisted that with the Key of Ingenuity dwarves, more skilful than he, would be able to work miracles. There was no doubt that the Key was responsible for their new-found skill, he explained. He went on for hours, long after Adam had fallen asleep, describing what life with the Key would be like for the dwarves. Lar, whose hearing was so much more sensitive than Adam's, couldn't get to sleep until Palustric's enthusiasm had run its course.

Palustric told how Fate had punished the dwarves in the Old Days because instead of working hard to learn the secrets of their skills, they had only relied on the inspiration given by the Key. Once the key was stolen, the dwarves' ignorance of their traditional crafts was laid bare. Now, with the precious Key safely returned, the dwarves could re-learn their skills, but never again would they make the mistake of relying on inspiration without the necessary solid base of learning and labour.

Lar had used at least fifty *Ay-s* and a dozen wise sayings before the eager dwarf finally closed his eyes.

The three friends made good progress the next day until they came to the place of tall grass once more. Lar caught Palustric by the jerkin. "Listen!" Lar whispered, "We are not alone." Adam and Palustric strained to catch any sound other than the rustling of the tall grass or the buzz of a bee.

"I can't hear anything."

"Me, neither."

"And yet, we are not alone! Let us hope that no-one means us harm."

They continued forcing their way through grass which was slightly taller than the top of Adam's head. Occasionally a small yellow snake would slither away; otherwise, there was no sign of movement. At last, they came to a clearing in the grass, where the ground was rockier.

"Let's have lunch here," Adam suggested and, sitting on one of the flat rocks, unslung the pack from his back. He reached into the pack, his fingers passing over the jewelled surface of the Key of Ingenuity to the bread and jars of honey lying under it. There were six jars of honey left. Just as well, it was the best honey he had ever eaten. At least when you got it in your mouth, the taste took away the thought that it was honey again. He spooned out another dollop of honey onto a wedge of bread and began eating. Lar and Palustric did the same.

Before long, there was a noisy buzzing. Two or three fierce-looking bees began to fly around their hands and faces, attracted by the sweetness of the honey. The friends swatted at the bees or darted across the clearing, while desperately trying to gobble up their lunch before more bees arrived. Lar cried out in pain, dropping his bread and honey. His hand began to swell and change from a greenish tinge to an angry dark green.

"There must be a nest nearby," Palustric mumbled with his mouth full. Adam threw his piece of bread and honey into the grass and walked over to re-lace the pack. Lar joined him and sat unhappily on the rock, looking from two or three bees buzzing around his abandoned lunch to his throbbing hand. Palustric, who had managed to eat (in wolf-like gulps), joined them to sit on the rock.

"Perhaps we should find another place for lunch?" Palustric was never tired of bread and honey.

Suddenly, Lar stopped rubbing his swollen hand and pointed it across the clearing. Silently, as if by magic, several golden-haired elves slipped out from the long grasses. Dressed in green, they were pointing bows, drawn with sil-ver-headed arrows, at the three companions. Adam swallowed a half-chewed piece of bread and almost choked. Like Palustric and Lar, he looked behind him, only to see more of the same elves, all with their arrows trained upon them. They were surrounded.

Adam stood up slowly and cleared his throat.

"We mean you no harm," he said. "We are

peaceful travellers, we have no arms." He raised his hands slowly to prove his words.

An elf stepped lightly forward, lowering his bow and signalling to the other elves to do likewise. Lar stood up too and whispered to Adam: "They are Elves of Adversity. Don't trust them, Master." Palustric remained seated.

The elf smiled, but his eyes did not. "My name is Bane," he said, with a slight, arrogant nod of his head. "It is your misfortune that we meet today."

"Why?" Adam looked the elf in the eye.

"These are our lands." The elf never stopped smiling, but his tone was cold. "You have come among us with objects which we prize greatly. I ask you to surrender them without loss of time." As one, the elves raised their bows again, while Bane stepped towards Adam.

Adam looked into the unsmiling, golden eyes of this Elf of Adversity, where he saw no mercy whatsoever.

"I have an elven orb whilst you are an elf. For some time, I've been looking for an elf to give it to." There was something in Adam's voice that surprised his friends. They were even more surprised when Adam reached into his pocket and passed the orb to Bane. The elf's lip curled into a mocking smile as he gazed at the orb in his hand.

In that instant, *Cari* glowed red, and the elf threw the orb to the ground with a cry. He wrung his hand as if it had been badly burnt and glared at the sphere at his feet. It was no longer glowing, just shining silver in the sunlight.

"Perhaps you aren't worthy of the orb," Adam said quietly. "Maybe one of the others could claim it?"

Bane stared hard at Adam for a long moment. He was judging the boy's sincerity. Finally, he turned and pointing at the sphere, called: "Travail, pick it up!" An elf left the group and crossed the clearing to Bane.

"Why me?" There was fear in his eye.

"Because, dear Travail, I have ordered you. And because you are the worthiest of this worthless band—apart from myself. Pick it up!" Bane's lip curled even more.

"Wait!" Adam said. "The person who possesses the orb must be pure and noble. Remember that!"

Travail hesitated and looked at Bane. "I'm not worthy," he said, angrily, "and you know it!"

Bane sneered unpleasantly, "You've always challenged my leadership; let's see what kind of elf you are now!" He drew a wicked-looking knife from his belt. "Pick it up!" he commanded again. Travail glared at Bane and, bending slowly, obeyed. All eyes were on the orb, from which flashed a blue flame in the instant that the elf touched it with his fingertips. Travail howled with pain and Bane laughed spitefully. Then he turned to Adam. "It seems you must keep your orb, Stranger, but not the other inestimable object. Hand me the Key!"

"The Key doesn't belong to you. It doesn't belong to any elf. You have no right to it. It belongs to the dw—"

"The dwarf! He's gone!" Travail cried. "After him!"

All the elves rushed forward, leaving Adam and Lar alone in the clearing.

"He must have sneaked away while Bane was making the other one touch *Cari*." Adam bent to pick up the orb and, marvelling at its coolness, replaced it in his pocket.

"Ay," Lar nodded, "and he has the pack with him. But a clumsy dwarf is no match for a band of fleet-footed elves; I fear that Palustric must surrender the Key. We must hope that they do not slay him, Master."

"After them, then," Adam said grimly. They both plunged into the tall swaying grass.

Palustric calculated that he had, at most, a two-minute start. He knew that the elves were faster than him and that they were armed. Moreover, the Elves of Adversity had a bad reputation. Of all the elven races, they were the only ones capable of harming travellers. Palustric was desperate. Adam had only just regained the Key after it had been lost for centuries, and it was unthinkable that it should be lost again, so soon. Once it was in the hands of Bane and his elves, there would be no recovering it. Like all elves, they could disappear without a trace. Palustric was prepared to give his life in an attempt to save the Key from this doom.

The young dwarf tried not to panic. There was no point in running blindly through the grass. In this way, the elves would soon be on him. Palustric squatted in the grass and thought.

For Bane, Travail, and the others, it was easy to follow the dwarf. His heavy frame had left a trail of broken and trampled grasses; they could hear him crashing ahead through the whippy stems. Suddenly there was silence. Bane halted his band and listened. Silence: broken only by the occasional buzz of an insect or a bird's call and by Adam and Lar following. Bane ordered his elves to advance slowly. He was puzzled by the silence: either the dwarf had fallen or he was planning something. But what could one dwarf do against twelve elves?

Palustric followed a bee. Soon there were

several, all flying in the same direction. He followed them to a hole in the ground which they
entered one by one. He had found their nest.
Now he had to move quickly. He unslung the
heavy pack and laid it nearby. He took a knife
from his belt and feverishly began cutting the
long, whippy grass stems. He didn't have much
time. When he had a sizeable pile, he unlaced
the pack and touched the Key of Ingenuity.
Palustric closed his eyes and concentrated.
Turning to the grass stems with a strange smile
on his face, now he set to work, his fingers flying.

Bane and the elves could hear movement
ahead of them. Warily, they nocked their arrows.
When they came to a small clearing, they parted
the grass silently. They could see the dwarf's
capped and jerkin-ed figure sitting motionless
among some grasses at the other side of the clearing. His pack was on his back. Bane smiled
grimly. The dwarf was hiding, but he hadn't escaped them. Without a word, Bane pointed to
his bow and nodded. The Elves of Adversity
stepped lightly from the grasses, and eleven
deadly arrows sped across the clearing. Each one
thumped into the dwarf's body; Palustric
slumped lifeless to the ground.

The elves stepped forward and, in that instant, a net crafted from whippy stems fell over

their heads. The elves struggled to free themselves, but the more they struggled, the more
they became enmeshed. It was impossible to
break such a skilfully woven net, so Bane struggled and shouted angrily, trying to make room to
draw his knife.

Palustric had to hurry. He rushed over to the
pack, kicking aside the jerkin-ed grass dummy
pierced with arrows. Pausing only to snatch back
his cap and to ram it on his head, Palustric hurriedly unlaced the pack. He pulled out the six
jars of honey and placed them in a line by the
pack. Taking the first jar, Palustric dashed over
to the netted heap of elves. He trampled heavily
over their struggling bodies, without worrying
that his boot squashed an elfin nose here and
there. He found Bane first and, with great pleasure, unscrewed the lid of his jar and half-emp-
tied it, pouring the sweet sticky liquid into
Bane's face and hair. Defenceless, with his arms
pinned in the pile of elves, Bane's curses became
muffled as the honey spread slowly over his face
into his eyes and mouth. Palustric emptied the
other half of the jar over the elf next to Bane.
The dwarf ran backwards and forwards until all
the jars were empty and every elfin head was a
sticky mess.

Adam and Lar crashed into the clearing.

"Quick!" Palustric shouted at his companions, who were trying to take in the scene. "Pull the arrows out of my jerkin! Get the pack, Adam! The Key's inside." Palustric disappeared into the tall grass.

He arrived at the hole in the ground. A bee was approaching. Palustric drew his knife and plunged it into the ground again and again. He ruined the entrance to the nest. Crying out in pain when three bees took immediate revenge on the offending hand, Palustric ran back into the clearing followed by an entire swarm of enraged bees. He ran straight towards the sticky, netted elves. The dwarf ran past them, but the bees didn't follow their tormentor. Instead, as one, and as Palustric had foreseen, they headed straight for the struggling elves. Palustric kept running and snatched his jerkin from Adam. "Let's get away from here!" he cried as the first screams came from the netted pile. "As fast as we can."

They hurried away, hearing screams for some time. After a while, Adam, who could not contain his curiosity any more, burst out: "How did you manage to make that dummy and the net so quickly? It's impossible!"

"Ingenious, eh?" Palustric laughed and suddenly looked glum. "But I made a bad mistake!"

"What?"

"I should have kept back half a jar of honey. We haven't got any lunch now."

"I'm fed up with honey. Far better that Bane and his elves enjoy it! They tried to kill you, Palustric."

"Well, luckily, I'm none the worse for wear, which is more than can be said for my jerkin! The Council of Dwarves can buy me a new one. This one's full of holes; hardly fit for a hero!"

The three friends laughed whilst Lar added, "The Elves of Adversity have become Elves *in* Adversity, is it not so, Master?"

Adam groaned before bursting out in the happiest laughter since he'd left his *Own World*.

They reached the forest's edge by late afternoon and decided to press on along a track which led into it. Lar was exhausted. The journey was more tiring for him because he had to take three steps for Adam's every one and Palustric's every two.

"We'll have to stop soon." Adam was aware of his friend's tiredness. "What'll we do for food?"

"I shouldn't have used that honey," Palustric blamed himself again.

Just then, as from nowhere, four figures appeared ahead of them on the track. There was no mistaking the beauty in the middle. Adam's heart leapt. Deep violet eyes looked into his and a smile lit up the lovely face.

"Welcome back, Adam, Hero of the Dwarfish Race! Come!" She held out her tiny hand. "Here you may refresh yourselves. Rest with me a while! Spinney-hall awaits you!"

Lar was already walking as if in a dream towards the elf. Tears pricked in Adam's eyes, but they were tears of anger with himself. How could he have been so foolish? How could anyone fall in love with a mirage? His voice had a very harsh tone: "I'm sorry, Inertia, we're far too busy to stay with you."

It was enough. A look of pain passed across the beautiful face, and Inertia and her elves vanished like mist in the evening air.

Adam put his hand on Lar's shoulder. "We'll stop here for the night anyway. But," he repeated, "what'll we do for food...?"

"Food's no problem, Adam," Palustric said. "Pass me the pack a moment."

The dwarf opened the pack, placed his hand inside, closed his eyes as if in deep concentration and then stood up with a strange smile on his face. He disappeared into the forest without a word to his friends.

He was gone for about twenty minutes, but

when he came back, he was carrying a dead hare. "I made a clever rabbit trap—" he proceeded to tell them all about his ingenuity.

There was plenty of wood around and, of course, Adam had matches. He struck one and was about to light a fire when a thought struck him. "Last time I lit a fire, Lar appeared with a band of...*ouch!*" The match burnt his fingers.

"Don't worry, Adam," Palustric laughed. "We're not on a fairy hill now and, anyway, there's only one Lar, thank goodness!"

Lar did an impersonation of a green raisin as he frowned at the dwarf. Then he smiled hugely and said: "Good men like me *are like white crows,* is it not so, Master?"

"Ay, Lar," Adam smiled, "that is if we consider pixies to be men!"

"Pass the matches, Adam," Palustric said quickly, fearing that a lengthy discussion might come between him and his stomach.

They ate well and slept better that night.

The next morning, they set off at dawn. The early morning sun filtered through the trees and the three companions shivered and tried to walk off the aches and pains that come from sleeping on the ground.

They had tramped along the forest track for

more than two hours when they came to a mist lying low at about Lar's chest height.

"Look," Adam pointed, "how strange! A rose-coloured mist."

They walked cautiously towards it, Lar sniffing the air like a wild animal.

"There's no smell, Master."

"It's only mist with a trick of the light," Palustric said and stepped forward confidently. "In any case, we have to go this way." He couldn't wait to get the legendary Key home and, so, take his place in Dwarfish history.

The mist suddenly enshrouded them. Instead of penetrating coldly to the bone, as mists generally do, this one was strangely warming and relaxing. They felt fine and continued walking cheerfully along the track. There was no need even to cover their mouths and noses from the misty air. Lar began singing in his high-pitched voice: a strange song from Halewood. Adam wasn't listening; he had wandered off the track and was bending over something.

"What have you found, Adam?" Palustric asked.

"It's an onion-shaped mushroom with green and yellow stripes. I wonder if there are any more?" Adam wandered deeper into the forest.

"Adam! Where are you? Lar!"

Lar was climbing a nearby tree. The dwarf was worried. "What are you doing?"

"There's a very strange nest in the tree, look!" Lar pointed to a round, woven nest hanging from one of the branches.

"We haven't got time for—" Palustric began but broke off when he saw some interesting paw prints in the soft ground. He followed them deep into the forest.

Adam walked alone, lost, for three days. In this time, he had given only a passing thought to his two missing friends. The mist continued unbroken, making the boy feel warm and relaxed, too relaxed to bother about anything else. His head spun with hunger and tiredness, but he ignored this, driven on by curiosity. There were so many fascinating creatures in the forest. Among other things, in three days he had observed a colony of yellow ants which spun webs like spiders; a pool of toads that sang in chorus by night; and best of all, he had watched a lone red woodpecker fell a sturdy beech. Afterwards, the same bird had settled on his shoulder for a few minutes, without pecking his head.

Towards the end of the third day, Adam emerged from the mist. Suddenly, the air was clear, and the boy had a familiar feeling. He felt as if he had just got up and was trying to shake the sleep from his body. Yet, it was evening. Adam yawned and stretched. Then he shivered in the cool air, wide awake and hungry. Where were Palustric and Lar? He looked round and called their names. The only answer was a bird's startled call and the crash of an animal in the undergrowth. The last few days seemed hazy to him, like a dream. He remembered the mist, which must have drugged them, lulling them into wandering off into the forest. He had lost his friends and a lot of time.

Suddenly, he remembered the Key. Quickly, he checked the pack on his shoulders. Everything was in order. What a relief! He could easily have left the pack lying around, deep in the forest, given that he had been in some kind of misty dream. Adam set off again along the track, wondering uneasily whether he was going in the right direction. Unfortunately, there was no moon and it was getting dark. Before long, he would be forced to stop walking. A wolf howled in the distance, and from another direction, others answered.

As he moved forward in the fading light, Adam's uneasiness grew into a sense of oppression. He felt as if there was an unseen evil presence watching him. Several times, he stopped and looked behind him, and even though he saw and heard nothing, the feeling would not leave him. Suddenly, in front of him, a shadowy form in the half-light, a black shape, hovered over the path, not quite touching the ground. His heart missed a beat as he recognised the dark outline of the Hag. Surely, he had seen the shade of the Hag. Although she could not reach him in this Land, her evil spirit was monitoring his progress. Adam shuddered, leant against a tree where he tried to calm down: better dead, he thought, than to fall into the Hag's clutches.

An owl screamed, and he jumped, looked around and sniffed the air. No, it wasn't his imagination; he could smell smoke. He hurried off, hearing the owl again and made his way towards the sound and the smoky smell, which was getting stronger. Cautiously, Adam approached a clearing and placed himself behind a bushy fern. He had the Elves of Adversity in mind and wouldn't risk losing the Key. He peered into the clearing and recognised the stockade they had built two Tuesdays ago. So, this was the same owl which had cost them a day's travelling time.

In the half-light, Adam could just make out the small, capped head that was peering over the wooden stakes. Lar's sharp hearing had alerted him to an intruder.

"Lar! Palustric!" Adam called happily. "It's me!"

"Master!"

"Adam, have you got the Key?"

A gate opened in the fence.

While they hungrily devoured a roasted wood pigeon that Palustric had prepared, they exchanged tales of what they had seen in the forest in the past three days. Adam particularly liked Lar's account of deer with antlers that glowed in the dark. But it was Palustric who explained what had happened to them.

"It's the Key," he said, "it attracted the mist. I had forgotten about the legend. You see, that was the Mist of Distraction. In the *Old Days*, when things were going particularly well, our forefathers had to be especially careful. The mist would come from nowhere. It has the power to make you lose your concentration and causes hallucinations. As its name suggests, it distracts..."

"Ay, but it was very warm and pleasant and we found lots of interes—"

"But, Lar," interrupted Palustric impatiently, "we didn't get on with our real task of getting the Key back to the Council of Dwarves. We were lucky the mist didn't last any longer, probably because we hadn't used the Key much. Also, none of us knows how to fight distraction."

"It's not difficult," Adam said. "We'll be ready for it next time." He'd rather face the mist a thousand times than the Hag even once; but he kept this thought to himself—no point in worrying his companions over a shade.

## 14

Towards the end of the next day, the tired travellers began to meet with dwarves. The news of Adam's success spread quickly, faster even than the mist of Distraction. When they arrived, just before sunset, the streets were lined with cheering dwarves, who showered them with celandine and primrose petals, the traditional *Dwarfish Heroes Welcome*.

The three travellers were taken before the Council, where they had to listen to long speeches about what heroes they were. The Key lay on a specially prepared velvet-covered oak table and none of the councillors took his eye off it for a minute, not even when making his speech. Palustric seemed to enjoy all this, but Adam and Lar were impatient.

To the collective horror of the Most Serene Council of Dwarves, Adam interrupted Balom the Black, mid-speech: "Look, sorry to butt in, but I'm very tired and I haven't seen my sister yet."

Balom looked sternly at Adam in bleak and offended silence. The swarthy dwarf cleared his throat importantly and declared: "You are part of Dwarfish history now, and I name you 'The Dragonteaser'." His fierce eyebrows seemed to leap out at Adam, and his severe eyes left no room for argument. Adam shrugged. "We haven't heard the complete and detailed tale of how you outwitted Lentor the Dragon. There are still twenty-four councillors to make their praising speeches. Then there is Palustric – my nephew's – tale...and the little fellow's, not to mention meals in between...and I wouldn't be surprised if there are popular ballads to be heard and processions to be made...presentations...awards..."

Adam groaned. It wasn't much fun being a hero. Balom's ferocious stare swept slowly around the Most Serene gathering, collecting solemn nods and claps of approval. There was no escape.

Ten days of fulsome praise passed agonisingly slowly for Adam. Ten days were only a start, but Adam brought it all to a premature end in a fit of rage. When, by chance, he learnt of his sister's disappearance, he was furious and refused to co-operate in the celebrations any more.

Even so, the dwarves would not discuss what had happened to Emily until they had taken a decision about the Key of Ingenuity. Adam was helpless, prisoner of this decision. He couldn't move until he had some facts. Since the dwarves were all agreed in principle, the discussion was brief (by dwarfish standards): just twenty-four weeks passed. In the end, Torobin accepted that a special stronghold, of construction inspired by the Key itself, should be built to house and protect the sacred object.

At last, the subject of Emily's disappearance could be dealt with.

"You see," Balom the Black explained, "*Success* led her off. Bella and I warned her that it might happen. I just hope that Emily was prepared for *Success* when she came."

"What do you mean?"

"I mean that *Success* often leads the unwary or unwise astray. You know, many people would like to go with her, but in truth, not many know how to cope with her. She's a real beauty, you see. An enchanting elfin maiden, one of the kind that makes you lose your head. The trouble is, she's got a hidden elfin side to her nature. You know what elves are like..."

"No, not really..."

"Mmmm." Balom nodded wisely, tugging at his thick, black beard. "Elves are very charming creatures, they're good-looking, whatever you like...but...but..."

"Yes?"

"What I mean is, take *Success* for example, she leads you to believe goodness knows what, then just when you're feeling at your most confident...she lets you down. And that's it, you're in a right mess!"

Adam nodded his understanding, thinking about Inertia. Then he had a worrying thought. "In danger?" he asked.

"Possibly that too," Balom nodded. "Mind you, some know how to handle her. Those who keep their feet on the ground and their eyes open. For those whom she befriends, there can be wealth and happiness ahead. You see, no-one can resist sweet *Success*, and her friends are always favoured. Let's hope Emily knows how to deal with *Success*...or else..."

"Or else what?" Adam was anxious now.

But Balom didn't answer; he just shook his great head.

Adam looked around the Council Chamber at the dwarves' serious faces.

"I must go after her," he said firmly.

"You, of all people, have a chance of finding her," Balom smiled encouragingly. "There are different ways of finding *Success*." Balom raised his voice and boomed: "Good luck, Adam, Hero of the Dwarfish People, Restorer of the Key and *Dragonteaser!*"

"Adam the Dragonteaser!" the councillors cheered and clapped. When the cheering died away, Balom vowed: "You shall not leave without a gift from the Dwarfish People."

Two weeks later, Balom found Adam chatting with his nephew. The dark dwarf had worked tirelessly, with the Key in his workshop, under heavy guard all the time. Now he beamed at Adam. He was holding a magnificent horn in his hand. Made of dull blue metal, the horn was inlaid with white and red gold. Adam smiled as Balom turned it in his hand to let him read the word 'Dragonteaser' worked in golden letters.

Balom looked at Adam with a stare so severe that the boy's smile vanished. "Listen carefully, Adam," Balom said. "This is no ordinary horn, and you must promise *never* to blow it, or to let anyone blow it. This horn must not be sounded by anyone but yourself. And only then if you are in the gravest peril and there is no other solution. Do you understand?"

"Well...er...yes, but what does the horn do?"

"Better not to know," Balom said gently. "Indeed, I sincerely hope you never have to blow it. But guard the horn with your life, for it may do the same for you!" He passed the horn to Adam, who turned it admiringly in his hands.

"It's beautiful, Balom, tha..."

"No!" Balom boomed, startling the boy. "The *Dragonteaser* must never thank a dwarf. Dwarves are eternally in his debt. Now," he frowned fiercely and growled: "Promise!"

"I promise," Adam said, and he knew that he would keep his word. He turned the horn again in his hands, admiring his workmanship. Its rim was not the usual smooth band of metal but was broken by the sharp, pointed ears of six owls, whose flat, disk-like faces stared out from the body of the horn. The masterpiece was suspended from a tooled leather belt, and the tooling told the story of a boy who outwitted a dragon on a mountainside.

"What lovely owls," Adam traced a finger over their feathers which seemed almost real.

"They are the symbol of wisdom," Balom smiled, "but for we dwarves, they also symbolise friendship and fortune. We have lots of legends about them...but anyway, we'd be here for another few days if I told them all. The important thing is that eagle owls are the dwarves' oldest allies. They fought alongside us long ago in the First and Second Goblin Wars."

"What were the wars fought about?" Adam wondered.

Balom the Black nodded, pleased at the boy's interest. "Because goblins are wicked by nature and in the *Old Days*, when the world was young, the wise old eagle owls were always there to chastise them. Tormented by their hooting, the goblins began their great owl hunts, determined to rid their lands of the tiresome birds that continually pricked what little conscience they had. But in their lust to kill, they chased a fleeing flock of owls into our lands and innocent dwarves fell to goblin swords. The First Goblin War soon followed, and that's how the alliance began." Balom's large, hairy hand took Adam's arm. "Anyway, back to the present, you'd better begin the preparations for your departure."

In the days before his departure, from the hard-working dwarves, no dwarf could tell Adam how to find *Success*. In fact, they looked at him as if he hadn't understood something obvious. Adam was puzzled and a little annoyed by their attitude. He decided, therefore, to take whichever road he fancied away from the Dwarfish lands. Both Lar and Palustric insisted on coming with him, and this time, Balom encouraged his nephew, whose place in Dwarfish history was already assured.

Adam chose the rocky mountain road away from the dwarves because it looked the most discouraging. Even if he didn't know how to find *Success*, he had learned one important thing in the land of the dwarves. He turned to Lar just outside the town and, looking up at the mountain track, uttered the first wise saying of his life: *"Little effort little gains,* is it not so, Lar?"

"Ay, Master, 'tis so!" the little pixy nodded slowly, unhurriedly considering the wisdom of these words and determined to add the saying to his extensive collection.

# III

# THE QUEST FOR SUCCESS

# 15

Just visible in the distance, sheltered in the lee of a hill, was a roof. This meant that there was life in the moorlands, which Palustric had likened to the *top of the world,* stretching as barren as anywhere in the Hag's land. The only company for the three travellers had been the occasional hunting hawk, a bird which Adam and Lar no longer trusted. However, so far, nothing had hindered their progress. All they needed was a rest and a break from the wind that chapped their hands and faces. They slept wherever they could huddle in hollows and crannies, and their packs contained, apart from honey, meats, cheeses and fruit (thanks to Adam). The sight of that distant roof brought thoughts of hot food, a welcome fire and a warm bed and a quickening of their step.

As they drew near to the building, they could see a sign over the door. It read: THE TRAVELLER'S REST. The T had slipped and was resting vertically on a narrow ledge at a slightly lower level. "We're in luck! It's an inn." Adam cried. Even as he shouted, a portly figure in a leather apron detached himself from the door-frame where he was leaning and began to wipe his hands on a cloth. Goblins have a special ugliness all of their own. Even if this one was friendly, judging by his smile, Adam and Lar were uneasy.

*"The host at the door is a sign of poor fare,* is it not so, Master?" whispered Lar.

"It's a goblin, isn't it?" Adam's tone was worried.

"It's all right," Palustric encouraged them. "Highland Goblins are friendly enough: always have been."

As if to prove Palustric's words, the goblin bowed low although such elegant behaviour seemed oddly out of keeping with the goblin's ugliness. His bow gave the travellers a close-up of his head. Tufts of spiky, black hair sprouted from his scalp, giving the effect of a worn brush which had lost more than half its bristles. When he straightened up, Adam noticed that similar spiky tufts also sprouted from the goblin's nostrils and pointed ears. His over-wide mouth spread in a broad smile; he spoke politely, "Welcome, welcome to The Traveller's Rest. It's not often we have visitors these days, especially not from the Dwarfish race."

"I'm not a dwarf," Adam said coldly.

"Quite so, sir," the goblin was still bowing. "I'm sure we haven't had a fine gentleman such as your lordship, for many a year. Mind you, we had a young lady not so long ago, ay, indeed!"

Adam raised an eyebrow and asked, "Was she slim, with silver hair and silver eyes?"

At last, the innkeeper came out of his bow and looked meekly at Adam. "Ay, now you mention it, she was, sir. But why don't you come inside where it's warm? You must need a rest."

The inn was old-fashioned, with a large fireplace and a chimney-nook, where people could sit on benches next to a log fire. There, Adam and Palustric warmed themselves, hungrily eating the hot soup and fresh bread rolls that the goblin had prepared for them. Adam asked the landlord for more information about Emily. It seemed that she had passed that way a few weeks before. She was with the most beautiful elf their host had ever seen. What's more, they had paid handsomely for their stay, way above the normal price: such generosity!

The goblin reached up to the mantelpiece over the fire. He carefully took down a small brass key and hurried off. A few moments later, he was back, holding something in the palms of his hairy, cupped hands, which he held out before opening them suddenly. The three friends gasped, as the firelight cast flashes of colour from the sparkling jewel. "They paid me with this!" he beamed. "It's *Aeshna*, you see, the Fairy Queen, riding her dragonfly. Isn't it beautiful? Must be worth a fortune! Oh, ay, those two are welcome whenever they like!" No, he didn't know where they had gone, they hadn't said.

The three friends felt happier that night as they slipped into warm, comfortable beds. Even Adam went straight to sleep, despite his feet sticking out through the bars of the bed frame. They had taken the correct road out of the Dwarfish lands, so they could relax. Each of them felt that their luck would hold and that they would soon find Emily, so they slept well, long into the morning.

After a hearty midday breakfast, they took their leave of the friendly innkeeper.

"Goblins are not as bad as they're made out

to be," Adam said in a low voice as they waved farewell. "Quite ugly, but friendly and kind."

"The Highland ones may be," Palustric sounded doubtful, "but then, there's goblins and goblins...and then again, there're *hobgoblins*." His voice trailed away as if he were unwilling to talk any more. "Anyway," he resumed in a more cheerful voice, "we're heading into Elven lands; so, we won't meet any hobgoblins."

They trudged across the moors all day, stopping only for a brief, late lunch, but owing to their late start, the evening was soon upon them. Even in the twilight, Adam thought the scenery looked familiar. As the weak sun began to set and the evening wind to strengthen, he spotted a roof in the distance. "There!" he said to Palustric. "What luck! Another building! The first we've seen all day. Just at the right time, too!"

His satisfaction died as they drew nearer. He saw the sign above the door: THE TRAVELLER'S REST. Out came the portly figure in his leather apron. "Well, well, I never! I wasn't expecting you back, sirs! Come in, do!"

"Blow my leg off!" Adam exclaimed. "We've come back in a complete circle, but I don't remember doubling back."

Lar made his raisin face, trying to come to terms with his Master's strange exclamation.

Confused and tired, the travellers ate and slept well once more before rising early and saying their farewells again. They travelled all day, this time being careful to mark their route from time to time with small wayside cairns of stones. Since they didn't pass any of these, it was safe to assume that they hadn't retrodden their path. Since it was well on into the long day's march, Adam pointed out that if they were going to circle back to The Traveller's Rest, they would have done so by now.

No sooner were the words out of his mouth than the well-known scene presented itself. First, the shape of the hillside, then the curve of the track, then the all-too-familiar rooftop. Palustric groaned while Adam put his head in his hands. As they drew nearer, their disbelieving eyes read: THE TRAVELLER'S REST.

*"We are drawing water with a sieve,* are we not, Master?" Lar sighed.

Out came the landlord, as usual, wiping his hands on a cloth. "My, my," he said, "if you were to ask me, I'd say, you three gentlemen were lost." He shook his ugly head solemnly. "Well, come in, do!"

Inside, Adam politely turned down the offer of food. He was much more interested in discovering why they were lost.

"Well, I could give you a map and a compass," the landlord's whiskery eyebrows knitted together, "but there'd be no point. The compass would just keep spinning round and round. Those are Elven lands and, what's more, you're after *Success*, an' those as are meant to find her do so, and the rest, well—"

"I'm not giving in!" Adam said hotly. "Hand me the map! We'll find her, you'll see."

Despite the comfortable beds, the companions didn't sleep well that night. Restless thoughts kept disturbing Adam. He wouldn't be happy till he found Emily.

On the doorstep next morning, their goblin host cheerily said: "Well, I won't say goodbye, because I'll be seeing you again soon!"

"You might as well say goodbye to me, I'm going to find *Success* and my sister," the boy said through gritted teeth.

The goblin smiled smugly as he handed Adam a compass and a map. There was no doubt that he expected the three travellers back before nightfall.

"If at first, you don't succeed..." Adam said to Palustric when they were out of earshot, finished the saying with a weary sigh, and continued, "Now, let's look at this map!" A few minutes with the map were enough to tell Adam that they needed to move in a south-easterly direction if they wanted to come to the nearest town in the Elven lands. He took the compass in his hand and held it steady so that the needle could settle. He waited patiently for a minute, but the needle swung wildly as if it had no idea where North was.

"Just as the goblin warned!" Lar squeaked.

Adam shook the compass, tapped the back of it, but nothing made any difference. He put the compass in his pocket and shrugged, the only thing to do, he decided, was to use the sun. The sun rose in the east, so that gave him a rough idea.

They plodded for two hours before Palustric, feeling tired, hungry and thirsty, called for a lunch break. They settled down under a gnarled elder tree, one of few blasted trees on the moorlands. Adam pulled *Cari* from his pocket so that he could sit more comfortably and ate a good meal, thanks to the goblin landlord, who prepared generous packed lunches.

Palustric suddenly pointed. "Look!" *Cari* was spinning round and round on the ground, reminding Adam of something he had seen recently.

"That's it!" he cried. "A compass needle! Are you trying to tell us something, *Cari*?"

As if in answer, the orb stopped spinning round and began rolling in the direction of a track which ran off the route they had been following up to now. "It wants us to go that way. We'll be all right with *Cari*, all we have to do is put it down whenever we don't know which way to go. There! Mr Goblin Landlord." Adam laughed defiantly. "We'll see who can find his way in these unknown lands."

They took the road down the valley, walking with a lighter step. Whenever they came to a parting of ways or a cross-track, Adam simply took out the orb, laid it on the ground and waited for it to roll away. In this fashion, they made steady progress until, by nightfall, they spotted a rooftop in the distance. It lay in a familiar fold of land, and Adam's heart sank. Was it possible that following *Cari* had made no difference? Weren't they back at The Traveller's Rest, yet again? After all, *Cari* was an elven orb; maybe it had betrayed them in the elven lands, perhaps feeling greater loyalty to the elves, who were well-known for their habit of misleading travellers.

"It's *not* The Traveller's Rest," Palustric said, relieved. "Look, there's a copse of trees we haven't seen before."

Adam unfolded the map, trying to work out the route they had taken. He struggled and pursed his lips, trying to make sense of their position. At last, he looked up. "I think we must be here." He jabbed a finger at the map: "*Sleight Valley*. Anyway, let's hope the owner welcomes travellers."

The cottage had a well-kept look about it, and on the smartly-painted gatepost was a brass plaque. They stopped and read: *I. Gloze, F.E.P.P.* and underneath, *Portrait Painter to the Famous*.

"How many famous people will you find in this wild spot?" Palustric muttered and shrugged.

Adam shrugged, too, and led the way down the garden path to a heavy oak door where a brass bell hung from a brass chain. Adam eyed it doubtfully before giving it a vigorous shake.

Shortly, an elf wearing a paint-splattered, green smock and holding a paintbrush in one hand answered the door.

"Sorry to disturb you," Adam said, "but we are travellers seeking shelter for the night. I wonder whether you take in visitors? We'd pay our keep, of course," he added quickly.

The elf eyed them mischievously, and Palustric, who (like most dwarves) didn't trust elves, would have turned away right then if the elf hadn't surprised him with: "Come in, I've been waiting for you!"

"You have...?" Adam stared.

"Do you find that strange," the elf asked, "in this land?"

Adam frowned and looked at the walls in the hallway, which were lined with portraits of elves mainly, but also pixies, dwarves and goblins. Lar gazed at one portrait in particular and smiled.

"Yes," said the artist, "you're right, it's Lucky Liix of Elm-dale. I painted him many moon-risings ago...I've quite lost count. You know him, of course!"

"Ay," Lar nodded. "Liix had been the most successful harebell farmer in Elm-dale, before disappearing without trace..." The pixy looked curiously at the painter, who put his forefinger to his nose and smiled oddly.

The painter led them into a large room where an open fire blazed near an inviting armchair. In the middle of the room was an easel and on the easel was a blank canvas, as if the elf were about to paint a new portrait. But it wasn't this that caught Adam's eye. At the other end of the room were several newly finished works. In the middle was a portrait of a breathtakingly beautiful elfin maiden. In the portrait, she was wearing a blue satin gown with golden stars and her long hair curled down her shoulders like poured honey. Her turquoise eyes held him.

They almost seemed alive, watching him from the other side of the room, from where they beckoned invitingly as if promising anything his heart set on.

"I can see you have eyes only for *Success!*" the artist laughed.

"*Success!* So that's Success," Adam whispered; he looked at the painting for several minutes without speaking. When he finally dragged his eyes away, he had a shock. Next to the portrait of *Success*, staring out at him, was his sister. She gazed out so life-like that Adam gasped: "Emily!" He looked at the elf. "So, my sister has been here! How long ago? Where is she now? Is she all right?"

"So many questions!" the elf laughed impishly. "All the famous come here, sooner or later."

"But my sister isn't famous!" Adam exclaimed.

The elf looked at him. "Oh no? What's this then?" he reached to the mantelpiece and held out a magnificent dragonfly brooch, enamelled and studded with jewels. "She left me this. Beautiful, is it not? Have you ever seen such workmanship? Miss Emily is undoubtedly the greatest living goldsmith!" The artist's eyes twinkled; his lip curled mischievously. Adam gazed in wonder at his sister's brooch. Only Emily and he had seen the Fairy Queen on her dragonfly, so Adam knew it was her work. The elf's smile broadened as he studied Adam's reaction. "Time for answers later," he chuckled. "First, I must paint your friends' portraits." He gathered together palette and paints and began to make sweeping strokes across the canvas, glancing at Palustric with that peculiar smile, his eyes sparkling with unshared amusement.

"But I'm not famous," Palustric protested.

"Of course, you are!" the elf chuckled.

Suddenly, Palustric's right arm began to fade away, then his left leg. The dwarf seemed to be petrified while Adam was rooted to the spot with horror. Palustric's right leg vanished, then his left arm. The elfin artist giggled out loud at the sight of just the dwarf's head looking down in shock at his missing body. Suddenly, the head disappeared too.

Adam leapt forward. "Fiend! What have you done? Where's Palustric? Where's Emily?"

The elf took a step backwards. "Now, is that the way to address I. Gloze— a Fellow of the Elfin Portrait Painters? I must get on with my work if no harm is to come to your dwarf friend." He eyed Lar. Before Adam could stop him, Lar's little greenish head, eyes even more squinting with surprise, had appeared on the canvas and disappeared from his body.

Adam sprang across the room as Lar disappeared limb by limb without a sound. The elf held up a warning hand. "Let me concentrate!" He began to create a familiar scene on the canvas around the dwarf and the pixy. The elf had painted every detail, including the slipped 'T'. The sign THE TRAVELLER'S REST was unmistakable, Adam would have recognised the building the elf had painted even without it. Just for a moment, Adam fancied that he saw the puzzled dwarf ring the bell of the inn, but when he blinked, the painting was quite still before him. He rubbed his eyes and turned to the elf, who laughed.

"Oh yes, they're back at The Traveller's Rest all right, where they'll be perfectly comfortable."

Back at The Traveller's Rest, the friendly goblin had a few welcoming words for Palustric and Lar. "Welcome back, my friends. Well, well, well, one less, I see! I must say, I was expecting all three of you, but it seems your friend has found *Success*."

"I don't think so." Palustric shook his head. "We met some sort of crazy portrait painter—I'm not sure what happened after that."

"I shouldn't worry." The goblin put an arm

around the dwarf's shoulder. "You're all right here. After all, some people spend all their lives seeking *Success* and never finding her. I'm afraid, my friend, you are one such person. Far better to put your feet up by my fire and consider what else you want from life, eh?"

As if to prove the point, the goblin fetched Palustric and Lar a steaming jug full of punch and began to chatter. "Take young Eror the elf, for example." The goblin landlord grinned. "He's famous everywhere in these lands. You might say he's the perfect example: Success would never come to him! Yet he's loveable and makes everyone laugh. Worth his weight in gold, I'd say."

"Who is this Eror?" Palustric asked, helping himself to another glass of punch before settling back comfortably on to the cushions in the corner of the chimney nook and thinking that maybe life here wasn't so bad.

"Eror isn't like the other elfin children," the goblin laughed a wheezing laugh. "He's a bit simple, you see. Do you know what he did last month? Ha! ha! His mother sent him to buy some salt and some pepper. *Be careful to keep them apart, Eror*, she said, giving him a large plate. *I don't want salt and pepper all mixed when you come home.*

"As he walked to the salt works, *ha! ha!* Eror hatched a cunning plan. Very cunning, oh yes! *Ha!* wheeze *ha!* He bought the salt and carried it very carefully on the plate to the pepper-grinder's shop. There, he asked for a certain weight of ground pepper! *And where shall I put it, Eror?* the pepper-grinder asked. *Here,* said Eror, turning the plate over. *Ha! ha!* wheeze *ha!*" The goblin wiped his eye. "As he hurried home, he thought how cunningly he'd kept the salt and pepper apart. Salt *under* the plate and pepper *on* it!! *Ha! Ha!*" The goblin wiped his eyes again, and Lar and Palustric smiled. "When he got home, said he: *Here's the salt and pepper, Ma! I haven't mixed them!*

"*But where's the salt?* his mother asked. *Here,* he said, turning the plate over!! *Ha! ha! ha!* wheeze Pepper everywhere! When they'd fin-ished sneezing...spilt pepper, you see...his mother chased him right down the High Street with her broom. *Ha! ha!*" The goblin slapped his knee and wiped his eye once more. "So, you see," he added, "you can be famous and content enough, without seeking *Success.*" The goblin took out a blue, spotted handkerchief and blew his large nose noisily.

"I don't know," Palustric shook his head

doubtfully. "Perhaps it's better to chase after *Success* than to be as simple as Eror!"

"But Eror's very much loved hereabouts—"

"Ay, that may be," Lar said, *"but the swineherd, even if he dresses in silk, still smells of the sty,* is it not so?"

The goblin and Palustric looked at each other. They fell silent and stared into the fire, thinking on Lar's words (which the goblin never fully understood).

They stayed until late, chatting and drinking by the fireside.

Adam sat down in the artist's armchair, also by a log fire, and accepted a hot drink. He felt more relaxed now he knew that his trusty companions were safe. The elf interrupted his thoughts, "So, you still want to find *Success*?"

Adam nodded absently.

"Very well, I'd better paint you, too!"

# 16

The elf dipped his brush in his palette and began with broad sweeps on a fresh canvas which he had placed upon the easel. After a hard day's march and with drowsiness sweeping over him as he sat in front of the fire, Adam hadn't paid attention to the elf's activities. He raised an arm to take another sip of his drink and was startled to see that the cup wasn't there, nor was his right hand! As he stared, his entire arm disappeared to the artist's chuckling. He looked down to see his right leg vanishing. He was about to protest when, dizzily, he saw the elf dissipate: not so, *he* had disappeared, not the artist.

He found himself tucked up in a warm bed;

the curtains were drawn, the valiant stub of a candle by the bed feebly lit the room. Adam was about to sit up, get out of bed and discover his whereabouts when a wave of sleep swept over him. He couldn't fight it, so, long after Palustric and Lar had set off from The Traveller's Rest the next day in search of I. Gloze, Adam awoke refreshed.

He dressed quickly and, to his relief, found that even if he had been painted, he still possessed the map, horn and *Cari*. Adam looked around him to see a tidy if barely furnished room. He moved across to the window and threw open the shutters. The landscape was always the same; he could easily have been near The Traveller's Rest or near the artist's home. He had never known land with fewer landmarks than this; ever since they set off, the feeling of being lost had never left him.

Adam walked across the room to the door and opened it. Standing at the top of some broad stairs, he heard sweet voices drifting up from below. One step at a time, he slowly went downstairs. There, a small room contained four elves dressed in yellow-brown and wearing small, pointed caps above their pointed ears, who turned to smile at him as if they expected his arrival.

"Have you slept well?" a bright-eyed, youthful elf asked.

"Ay, thank you, but I'm rather confused."

The elf smiled, adding to his dazzling good looks.

"Don't be. You came from I. Gloze, didn't you?"

"Ay, but I'm looking for *Success*...and my sister."

The elves smiled at each other as if sharing a joke which only they understood.

"Well, I'm afraid you've just missed them."

"What! They were here, then?" Adam shot a worried glance out of the window.

"The night before last. I like Miss Emily," the elf said in his lilting voice. "She gave me this." He opened a silk-lined box lying on the table; on the emerald green lining lay another beautiful brooch. It was subtly different from the ones he'd seen in the last two days but equally as beautiful. Emily certainly was a fine craftsperson. The elf smiled. "She's one of the greatest goldsmiths who has ever lived, did you know that?"

Despite its beauty, Adam hardly gave the brooch a second glance.

"I'd better be going if I'm going to catch

them. Did they say where they were headed next?"

"Just a minute," another elf said. She smiled at Adam in a way that he felt was mocking him gently. "I think you should have a plan, don't you? You seem to be chasing after *Success* without too much thought. Apart from anything else, eat a meal before you rush off. You don't know where your next one's coming from, do you?"

Adam shook his head. "My plan is to find *Success* as soon as possible," he said and was surprised when all four elves laughed their tinkling laughter until the tears shone in their beautiful eyes.

When they had finished, they didn't offer any explanation, irritating him.

"Why did you laugh at me?"

The elves glanced at each other, and he feared that they were about to burst out laughing at his expense again, but the girl replied with the same mocking smile, "You must work out a way of finding *Success*. We can't help, I'm afraid, but we can make you breakfast. Mayhap you should think about *Success* coming to you!"

Afterwards, the elves waved Adam good-bye. They had been kind, giving him a packed lunch to take but no advice, which he felt he needed more. Neither had they wanted to tell him who they were, insisting that they were ordinary elves.

As soon as he was out of sight of the elves' home, Adam took out *Cari*, which to his delight, spun around like a compass and rolled decisively towards a track which led over the hills towards a little cluster of buildings on a hillside in the distance. Adam sighed. He missed his friends and was tired of all this marching, but if it was the only way to find *Success*, he would have to put up with it. He replaced *Cari* in his pocket and set off.

Meanwhile, Lar was trying to stop Palustric from jumping up and down furiously on his hat. They had tramped all day and come back to The Traveller's Rest.

"Don't do that!" The goblin landlord rushed out, fastening his leather apron behind his back. "Good hats are hard to come by these days! I've got a joint roasting over the fire, that'll cheer you up— not everyone can find *Success*, you know."

Adam tramped on into the elven village towards the end of the day, only to find that *Success* had been there the day before and had left with Emily and one of the young elves who was a wonderful singer. The singer's parents were very proud that *Success* had come to their child, who practised singing for several hours each day. They told Adam that their child fully deserved to go with *Success*.

"But where will she take her?" Adam asked.

The elves shrugged. It depended, they told him; she might take her to find Fame or even Wealth, but if she were unlucky or even silly, *Success* would lead her astray. They had warned their daughter to be on her guard. The elves would not tell Adam more. Sometimes when he asked questions, they smiled that mocking smile as if sharing a joke that he couldn't understand. He had seen that smile too many times before, and now it annoyed him. On the other hand, the elves were hospitable and gave him a bed and food.

The next day, Adam, and Lar and Palustric, set off at about the same time from their separate starting points. This time, Palustric was determined not to arrive back at The Traveller's Rest. The moorland wind had a keener edge that day. Lar, who was thinner and weaker than Palustric, shivered. His greenish face was very pale and his teeth chattered with the cold. Twice, he asked Palustric to turn back to the warmth of The Traveller's Rest, but the stubborn dwarf wouldn't hear of it.

As they sheltered in a hollow for lunch,

Palustric realised just how much Lar was suffering. When he unlaced their pack, he noticed the pixy's damp brow and the fever in his squint. When Lar refused his honey, Palustric knew that the matter was serious.

Palustric had only his leather jerkin, so he couldn't even wrap a coat around his friend. What seemed certain was that a night on the moors would be the end of Lar. So Palustric told the pixy to move, promising that they would go back to the inn. But when Lar tried to stand up, he fell back in a faint. Alarmed, Palustric picked up his little friend, hoisted him onto his shoulders and began to run, stumbling and cursing over the rough ground, back towards the inn. Ignoring his tiredness, the dwarf ran for more than two hours, knowing that his friend's life was in danger. All this time, the pixy lay unconscious like a sack over the dwarf's sturdy shoulders.

At last, over a rise, he sighted The Traveller's Rest. Stopping for a moment, Palustric gasped in relief, gulping in huge breaths of air. The bitter afternoon wind blew across his face, and Palustric shivered violently with the feeling that the wind was especially keen. He mustn't stand still soaked with sweat, or he'd finish up in the same condition as Lar. He set off again, as fast as his remaining strength would allow and, at last, he came to the door of The Traveller's Rest. The door and the window shutters were closed as if no-one was at home. Palustric's heart sank, and he hammered frantically on the door with his fist. He needn't have worried because bolts slid back and the ugly, but friendly face of the goblin landlord appeared in the half-opened door. At that moment, the goblin seemed the best-looking person Palustric had ever seen.

"Well, bless me!" the landlord threw open the door. "I was expecting—" He broke off suddenly as his eyes moved from Palustric's anxious face to his shoulder draped with Lar's motionless body.

They hurried inside where the goblin threw more logs on the fire. "He's got the Moorbane," the innkeeper muttered. "It's all my fault, I should have warned you, but you've done well to bring your friend back here."

Palustric gently laid Lar on the rug in front of the fire. The pixy's eyes were closed, his skin had a ghastly pallor, and he was shivering uncontrollably.

"Moorbane?" Palustric asked.

"Ay, in the *Old Days*, the elves cast a curse into the wind. They reckoned that this, along with the misleading spell laid on the land, would confound any intruders."

"I don't understand."

"Well, you've seen how easy it is for the traveller to lose his way on the moors? That's the misleading spell. Moorbane's the curse borne on the wind every fourth day. That's why I had the door and windows closed just now. The Old Elves reckoned that anyone lost on the moors for more than three days could not possibly be an elf or a Highland goblin and must, therefore, be an outsider. Outsiders to them, at the time, meant danger. Had you not run back here, you too would have been stricken just like your friend and both of you would have died on the open moor. Fortunately, you are stronger than he!"

"Will he die?" Palustric panicked.

"Bless me, no! I should think not!" The goblin smiled broadly. "Not now you're back at The Traveller's Rest. You see, we innkeepers hand down the cure from father to son."

"Well, let's get started! We're wasting time —" Palustric urged.

The goblin scowled, his ugly expression reminding Palustric that goblins were strange-tempered creatures. Better be careful. "I'm sorry, I didn't mean to be rude. It's that I'm so worried about my friend."

The goblin's face softened into gentle ugliness as he smiled. He reached up to the mantelpiece and took down a white earthenware fire-pot with two curved handles at its collar. "There mustn't be any flower design on it," the landlord whispered mysteriously to Palustric. "Come into the kitchen." They left Lar trembling in front of the hearth.

"Take a knife, cut me three garlic tails and three branches of rosemary." Meanwhile, he poured red wine into the pot. "Done that? Good! Now slip outside and cut me three elder florets from the tree, but don't hang about in that wind," he warned as he reached up to a shelf. Palustric hurried out to find an elder tree. The goblin took down a jar with a yellowing label containing dried red rosebuds. *Buds of the Fairy Rose,* the label read. Whistling busily, the goblin threw them in the pot. "I collect them on Midsummer's Day, or it doesn't work," he told Palustric, forgetting that he had sent the dwarf outside. He threw three bay leaves into the pot after them and then added the ingredients Palustric had prepared.

"We're almost ready now," the goblin said, just as the dwarf came back indoors. He took the elder florets and broke the small flowers into the receptacle. He looked at Palustric's clothing. "First, we must change," he said.

"Why?"

"No black allowed," the goblin said, pointing

to the dwarf's trousers. "We have to wear red and white, you know, or else the magic doesn't work."

He led the way upstairs into a magnificent bedroom full of carved furniture where he opened a drawer and, taking out a white shirt, tossed it to Palustric. "Put this on and these," he said, throwing a pair of red pants onto the bed. They changed quickly and, in red and white, passed by the kitchen to collect the pot before hurrying through to the fireplace.

"Lift your friend and hold him in a kneeling position in front of the hearth," the goblin instructed. To Palustric, it seemed that Lar was a lifeless sack, except that the sack was trembling.

The goblin solemnly placed the prepared fire-pot on the hearth and, turning to Lar, touched him lightly on the head. At the same time, he said three or four magic words that Palustric couldn't understand, then spat noisily into the pot. They waited silently. Suddenly, to Palustric's amazement, the fire-pot began to tremble and jump, as if it were on the boil, except that, it had been in front of the fire for only two minutes. In that instant, Lar stopped trembling and opened his eyes.

"What's happening?" he asked. "And why are you wearing those strange clothes, Palustric? They're too big for you!"

Palustric hugged his little friend and then kissed the startled goblin on the nose. After a detailed explanation around the fire, the two friends agreed to abandon the search for *Success* and to wait, instead, here at The Traveller's Rest for news of Adam. As the goblin said, "*Who leaves the old road for the new, knows what he is leaving, but not what he'll find.*"

"I'll add that to my collection of sayings," Lar said, cheerfully.

"One thing's for sure, we're very comfortable here." Palustric smiled widely and took another bite out of his gigantic roast pheasant roll.

Adam tramped all day in the direction indicated by his orb. By evening, he arrived at the lonely farmhouse of an elfin butterfly breeder who made evening gowns for elfin ladies from butterfly wings. His gowns were very costly and fashionable in elfin high-society. He proudly showed Adam his latest creation, whose wonderful sheen changed colours as the elf moved it lovingly in the light. But it was not so much the gown which held Adam's eye as the splendid brooch pinned upon it. The Fairy Queen's crown flashed as brightly as the glittering eye of her dragonfly steed.

Adam discovered that Emily had been there the day before with *Success*. The brooch was, in fact, a present from the beautiful girl. The farmer had asked for a butterfly brooch, if possible, but the goldsmith didn't make butterfly brooches, he told Adam sadly. He wasn't sure why the goldsmith was so famous. True, the brooch was magnificent, but butterflies were far showier than dragonflies, didn't he think?

The elf chattered away over dinner about how *Success* had promised to come soon for him since she too liked his popular gowns. Adam struggled to follow his host's conversation, as it is difficult to eat soup with a butterfly perching on your nose or fluttering in front of your eyes.

It was always the same for Adam wherever he went: he had just missed *Success* with his sister by a few hours or a day—chasing after Success and never finding her.

## 17

It came as a shock to Emily to be abandoned by *Success*. The fickle elf disappeared one morning without a word. Emily searched for her and pleaded with the elves where they had been staying for help or information. They only conceded a curious smile as if they knew something that she didn't; yet, they would not tell her. She discovered that the elves were not surprised that *Success* had upped and left her.

She went out into the orchard of the house where she had spent the night. Under a pear tree, she sat with her chin on her knee, thinking. What would she do now? She had given away her last brooch the night before. She hadn't thought it mattered, supposing it was all right while she was with *Success*. Indeed, it seemed to please *Success* that Emily was so popular and famous. Was that why the elf had gone? Emily thought for a moment and groaned. Now, she understood her foolishness. All her jewellery had gone, so *Success* had vanished. The elfin maiden didn't want to know her now that she had nothing to offer. All Emily could vaunt now was that she had *once* been a famous goldsmith, but the point was she couldn't prove it. Without a single brooch, with nothing to offer but her reputation, *Success* had left her behind.

It was no good feeling sorry for herself, she thought sharply. She had been lured away from her brother and friends by *Success,* and now she had nothing and was alone and unimportant. While she had been with *Success*, she hadn't given Adam a thought, which made her feel ashamed and worried. The last she knew of her brother was that he had gone off to face a dragon. He could be dead, for all she knew. She tried to push this out of her mind by dwelling on *Success*.

She swore that if ever the elfin maiden came her way again, she would know exactly how to behave. In future, it wouldn't be so easy for the beguiling elf to make her lose her head—she'd keep her feet on the ground. Absent-mindedly, she crushed a dead pear leaf to powder and blew the dust away. "That leaf represents the past," she said, standing. "It's gone. I'm going to make a new start." She went back into the house and asked the elves the way to the nearest big town. They no longer smiled that knowing smile. Instead, they packed her a meal and drew her a map to follow so that if she hurried, she would arrive before nightfall.

About the time Emily was sitting under the pear tree, Adam was resting on a rock with similar thoughts passing through his mind. Ever since he had arrived in the Elven lands, he had chased after *Success* in vain, arriving too late. No wonder the elves had laughed at his questions. What a fool he'd been! It was no good chasing after *Success*, he could see that now. She had to come to you. At last, he had understood how Emily had met the elf and why. It wasn't a coincidence: *Success* had come to Emily because of her efforts and achievements.

Adam scratched his head and reflected. What had he achieved? Nothing! He groaned. He wasn't good at anything, except perhaps at catching newts, but that didn't lead to anything much. He drummed his fingers on his head; it always helped him think. What had he ever done well at? Was there anything that he might do well again to attract *Success*? He thought and thought, but the only thing he could come up with was the time he had outwitted the dragon on Mount Ember. He didn't fancy making a hobby out of dragon-tricking. He didn't know a single successful dragon-tricker, which proved what a difficult job it was. He was probably the only one who had lived to tell the tale.

Adam sat up with a start—*To tell the tale*—of course! Why hadn't he thought of that before? It was obvious! He didn't have to keep on tricking Lentor the Dragon, only to tell people about how he'd done it. After all, who had outwitted a dragon and lived to tell the tale? "Nobody!" Adam shouted and leapt from the rock. *That's what I'll do*, he thought. *I'll tell people all about it, as funnily and cleverly as I know how. We'll see if that doesn't attract Success!*

He spread out the map the landlord had given him. "Let's see!" he murmured. "Mmm, yes, under Herestar Fell," (the highest moor) lay Aldebaran, the capital of the Elven lands. "It looks quite far," he murmured to himself, "so I'd better get started." He put the map away in his pack and set off down the lane.

Two days later, on a street corner in Aldebaran, two elves were talking:

"My cousin went last night. She said he was fabulous!"

"Well, what sort of things does he do?"

"I'm not really sure," the smaller elf said. "Tells stories and teases people. Look at the poster, see?" She read out—ADAM THE TRICKSTER—"There, what did I tell you? He tricks people!"

The other elf shrugged, puzzled. "I don't see what's so good about that; my dad's always tricking me!"

"Well, I'm going to get a ticket, our Nova said he was brilliant!"

"You can't," the taller elf said smugly, pointing to the poster's big black letters.

Her friend studied the poster:

## ADAM THE TRICKSTER
## SEE
## THE ONLY LIVING DRAGONTEASER
### at
## THE STARLIT ROOMS

Then it gave dates and times, but as the taller elf pointed out with satisfaction, a sticker had been pasted over with bright red letters announcing, SOLD OUT.

"It's not fair!" The small elf stamped her foot

and, tossing back her golden hair, walked off in a huff.

That night in the Starlit Rooms, the Dragonteaser was performing his act on stage. Wearing the bold Cross of St George (as all good dragon-slayers should) over his clothes, he commanded the complete attention of his audience, who were hanging on his every word. With a magic lantern show, he had told the Saga of Lentor the Dragon to have them laughing till tears rolled down their cheeks. Now he had come to the highlight of the evening. Every evening, he issued a challenge for money. The Dragonteaser was so inventive that each night the riddle challenge was different. The brain-teasers seemed obvious afterwards, but at the time, they were so tricky. Rich elves flocked to pit their wits and their money against the Trickster. They always lost. Each night their money was put into a big pot so that the prize grew richer. The audiences kept coming to see if anyone could outwit the Trickster and take away his fortune. Up to now, no-one had won the challenge.

"So," the Dragonteaser announced, "who will take up my challenge tonight?" He stepped to the front of the stage, and everyone held his breath. No-one moved, and the Trickster's silver eyes seemed to twinkle brighter than elfin eyes.

"Tonight," he boomed, "I throw open my challenge to every one of you." He pointed to the pot overflowing with elven coins. "Solve my riddle, and the money is yours. Anyone can try tonight, free! You don't have to be rich to try—listen carefully to my words, then tell me the solution to the riddle. If you are right, it is yours; if you are wrong, we'll all have a good laugh!" The audience giggled as the Trickster sat down, but their eyes never left his face.

"Are you ready?" he asked quietly.

The elfin audience sighed and nodded silently, sitting on the edges of their seats. The Trickster recited his riddle in ringing tones:

'Four companions travelled together
Leaving tracks behind them.
The bird's support moved swiftly,
Diving into the blue pool,
Letting the struggling man work on,
Pointing out the path to all four
Over the snowy, white landscape.'

The Trickster smiled a twisted smile at his baffled-looking audience. "Work that one out, and my name isn't Adam," he muttered under his breath.

The audience began to murmur as everyone

whispered half-ideas to everyone else. There was much head-scratching, golden lock-tugging, nail-biting and tutting. At last, one young elf leapt to his feet.

"I know, I know!" he yelled.

"Well, come up here, then." Adam hauled the elf on to the stage. "Tell everyone the answer."

The elf, trembling with excitement and eyeing the pot of coins which he felt sure would be his. "It's four wolves in a snowdrift!" he announced triumphantly.

"Four wolves in a snowdrift!" Adam the Trickster snorted. "Rubbish! *The bird's support moved swiftly,* where's that in your snowdrift? Honestly!"

Elves hate nothing more than being laughed at and love nothing more than laughing at others.

The Rooms echoed to tinkling elfin laughter. The poor youth went back to his seat with a bright red face and his head bowed. Nobody else dared say anything; the hall went very quiet. The elves were puzzled. One elf on the back row got up silently and positioned himself by the exit.

"It's not four swans on a frozen pond, is it?" he shouted.

Adam pulled a face, and the audience burst

out laughing. Everyone turned to see who had spoken, but the crafty elf had already dodged out of the door.

It went terribly quiet again. So, Adam repeated the riddle, in case anyone had forgotten the words, then he pointed temptingly at the overflowing pot—a wonderful prize. Slowly, an elfin maiden stood up and walked towards the stage. An awed whisper winged around the audience. They knew her. A peculiar smile played upon the Trickster's lips as he watched the beautiful creature in a dark blue gown with golden stars climb onto the stage.

He had seen her before, but only in a portrait: her entrancing turquoise eyes held his and seemed to offer him anything in the world that he might desire. At last, the enchantress spoke: "I know the answer to your riddle. And to many others besides," she smiled seductively.

Adam snapped out of his trance. "Very well," he spoke out loudly, "tell us," but he knew she had the answer.

"A quill pen and fingers," she smiled confidently, keeping her back to the audience. "The four companions are the pen, the thumb and two fingers. The quill is the feather that once supported the swift bird. The blue pool is the inkwell, the tracks are the letters in ink, while the struggling man is the arm. The snowy white landscape," she smiled enchantingly, "is the paper. Am I right?"

"You know you are," Adam smiled. "Take the money, it's yours."

"It's not the money I want," the elfin maiden spoke softly, "but your company." She held out her hand to him, irresistibly. Before taking it, Adam picked up the pot and flung some of its contents in a golden arc into the audience. As they scrambled for the coins, the Trickster left silently, one hand clasping the pot and the other holding the maiden's hand.

"At last," he muttered, "even if my name isn't Adam anymore!" and *Success* smiled sweetly on him.

## 18

$\mathcal{E}$mily spent a chilly night under a bridge that provided little shelter, so she spent a lot of time thinking instead of sleeping. If she could have done things again, she would have done them differently. It was no use brooding over her mistakes—she would have to be determined and start over again. Her only regret was that she had lost her brother. If only he had half of her intelligence, she consoled herself that whatever had happened to him wasn't her fault. How could it be?

Emily set off again, sure that she looked a mess after her night sleeping rough. She felt sorry for herself and lonely as she arrived in the outskirts of the elfin city of Aldebaran. Elves were rushing about, looking as if they had something important or urgent on hand; not like her. Despite her high-opinion of herself, she didn't know what to do.

Now and again, an elf gave her a curious look, but mostly they ignored her. Feeling friendless, Emily walked into the main street of quaint shops with twisted roofs and wooden beams. She admired them, so neat, like the elves themselves, whereas she felt dirty and scruffy. She looked in the shop windows with their bright display of clothes or of musical instruments, some of which she had never seen before. Passing a greengrocer's, she suddenly felt hungry. A mouth-watering pile of apples caused her stomach to remind her that she hadn't eaten. She moved on, feeling sorrier for herself, when a sign caught her attention. Over a shop door in neat letters: SPARKLA & DAUGHTER; FINE GOLD-SMITHS & JEWELLERS.

Hope stirred in Emily's breast; she tried to smooth her hair as she studied her reflection in the window. Frowning at her untidiness, she plucked up courage and went inside. An elderly elf behind a counter, head over some tiny mechanism, ignored her as she came in. Emily stood waiting politely with her hands behind her back.

The elf continued to ignore her. *Ahem,* she coughed gently.

"Mmm? Ay, ay, what is it?" the elf grumbled. "Don't suppose you've come to buy anything, have you? Nobody ever does! Repairs, repairs, repairs! That's what they all want! What do you want repairing?" He looked up suddenly, studying Emily with the eye that wasn't occupied by an eyeglass. The girl wasn't what he was expecting. At least, his surprise stopped the flood of grumbling.

She seized her chance. "Hello, I'm Emily."

The old elf studied her with one magnified and one normal blue eye. Despite her scruffy appearance, his eyes filled with recognition and admiration.

"Not *the* Emily? Emily Dragonfly—the greatest living goldsmith?"

Emily's chest puffed up at this appellation. So, her fame had travelled before her. That could only help. She told the elf her story and ended up asking for a job. The elf hung his head. "How can I offer you a job?" he said, sadly. "My daughter has had to find work as a maid in a hotel. You must have noticed, all the time you were telling me your story, we didn't have a single customer. Times are hard. Gold doesn't grow on trees, you know! Only Golden Delicious! *Ha! ha!* Sorry, not very funny, eh?"

She looked unhappy. Emily's stomach rumbled again at the thought of apples. The old elf could see she was desperate and felt sorry for her. "Look, I'd love to help, of course, I would," he said sincerely, "but you can see how I'm fixed. If you can get the materials together, you can use my forge any time, free of charge..." his voice trailed away.

"That doesn't help," Emily shook her head. "I need a job. How can I get materials without money?" She shrugged helplessly and inwardly cursed her stupidity for having shown off when she knew *Success*. She had basked in glory and frittered away all her beautiful, costly jewellery. Now she couldn't scrape together even the essentials to begin again. She fought back a tear of anger.

"Perhaps I *can* help," the goldsmith said, kindly. "Come and have something to eat and leave things to me." He hobbled over to the door and turned the sign to CLOSED.

Through his daughter, Nova, Sparkla found Emily a job in the Starlit Hotel as a chambermaid. The manager wasn't sure at first because Emily had no experience in this work. Since she was so eager to start and as he was a shrewd elf, he saw that Emily was slightly taller and stronger than the other maids, so she would probably get through more work. He gave her the job.

Nova and Emily became friends. She was fun to be with, and as elves, in general, are good-natured, Emily found her work pleasant and to her liking. She saved all the money she could and, on her days off, she visited the market stalls where she looked for cheap jewellery from which she could make her own. Of course, it would be impossible to make jewellery like that in Bella's workshop. However, she occasionally got a bargain, when the stall-keeper didn't realise the value of a piece, so her hopes grew of beginning on a single beautiful brooch.

It was on a visit to the market that Emily bumped into Adam. She was sifting through some cheap brooches when he spotted her. He was surprised to see her in a chambermaid's uniform, and since she hadn't noticed him, he watched her for a moment or two, revelling in the joy of having found her.

He crept up behind her and put his hands over her eyes. "Guess who?"

"Adam!" She thrilled at his voice, and they stood beaming at one another. So, he hadn't finished up as a dragon's dinner! She was so happy!

Emily was about to ask her brother lots of

questions when the smile vanished from his face. His eyes strayed over her shoulder, and she saw them glaze over. She turned quickly to follow the direction of his gaze, but it was then that he gave her a hefty push. As she fell, Emily glimpsed familiar turquoise eyes mocking her from under a nearby market awning. Emily sprawled across the brooches, demolishing the stall.

By the time she had apologised and helped the angry elf sort out his stall, Adam had disappeared. Emily was shocked and upset. She searched the market for her brother, but there was no sign of him or of the mischievous elfin maiden. She couldn't understand why *Success* should treat her like this. No doubt it was the elf's influence that had made Adam behave so strangely.

Emily shrugged and set off back to the hotel. For the moment, there was nothing she could do. At least, she knew that Adam was alive and well, even if *Success* had somehow turned his head. As Emily left the Market Square, a peeling poster on a wall caught her eye. It was faded and out of date, but announced a performance by Adam the Trickster, the *Dragonteaser*. It had to be her brother, she thought, even if she hadn't had the chance to ask him about his meeting with the dragon. Perhaps she could find him, where did it say? She made out the words *Starlit Rooms* with difficulty. Wasn't that the theatre behind the hotel? She'd never been that way, even if it was close to work, maybe she'd pay a visit. She had to find Adam and warn him of the danger of *Success*. The elfin maiden was capable of taking you over and, after having led you astray, abandoning you without hesitation.

As she hurried off to the theatre, Emily thought about Adam. Judging by the Sold-Out sticker, he had been very popular, drawing big crowds. Why else would *Success* have sought him out?

At the theatre, she asked about her brother, but everyone from the Manager to the Cleaning Elf agreed that *Success* had led off Adam. "And where will I find *Success*?" Emily asked impatiently, but the elves just shrugged and smiled knowingly. It was the same smile that Adam had received when he was looking for *Success* and the same she had received at the house with the orchard. Emily knew what it meant now and what to do about it. She wouldn't chase after *Success*; she would attract her because now she was ready to start.

She went to see Sparkla the Goldsmith where she struck a deal. Emily could use his forge on her days off. Whatever she made, he would put in his window and, if they sold it, he would take one-third of the profit.

She came in on Wednesday morning, whereupon the jeweller lit the forge for the first time in many years. Sparkla was looking forward to seeing Emily Dragonfly in action, but even he, with all his years, had never seen anything like this. From unpromising bits of brooches and necklaces, bracelets and rings, Emily melted, hammered, twisted and soldered together an exquisitely beautiful brooch. Not her quicksilver hands, but her eyes startled the elf. He leaned forward and tugged at his pointed ear as he watched her with interest. She was like a person possessed in a feverish trance. When he spoke to her, she did not hear him; he might as well have been invisible. Her work engrossed Emily—and what work! What beauty! The old elf admired the delicate filigree wings in perfect proportion to the dragonfly's body and the silver fairy mounted on its back, wearing a sublime golden crown. Sparkla had lived one hundred forty-four elfyears, an advanced age for an elf, but in all that time, he had never seen craftsmanship to compare. Not since the days of the *Old Dwarves* had there been such workmanship, he was sure of that. The girl was a genius, and he took his hat off to her. But he put it on again because his hair was thin and his head soon got cold.

When she had finished, Sparkla took the brooch and laid it on a velvet cushion in his window. He placed a ticket next to it with the words *By EMILY DRAGONFLY* printed on it, but he didn't mark a price. Emily asked him why not, but the old elf smiled slyly, put a finger against his nose and winked. "Come back next Wednesday, and you'll find out," he said mysteriously.

If Emily had gone straight back into the shop, she would have seen the peculiar sight of a one hundred-and-forty-four-year-old elf skipping, whooping and chanting, "I'm going to be rich!" over and over again.

On Wednesday, as Emily neared the goldsmith's shop, Sparkla was already peering around the door up the street. When he saw her, the goldsmith waved excitedly and beamed. Emily quickened her pace, sensing that something was in the air. As she entered the shop, the elderly elf greeted her with two bulging bags of coins, one in each hand. "For the brooch," he grinned.

"That much!" Emily cried, taken aback.

"It comes from not putting a price on the goods," the wily elf smiled. "You see, all the posh elves have been bidding for the right to buy the brooch. It went to Lady Elgiva from the High Woodlands. And, to think, we have a waiting list of thirty-four takers at about the same price!" The elf dropped the bags of gold and grabbed the startled girl, leading her off in a wild jig around the shop. What a strange sight, a one-hundred-and-forty-four-year-old elf jigging with a human girl almost twice his height!

"You must give up your job at the hotel at once. So must Nova! She can be your assistant," Sparkla declared, excitedly. "There's no time to lose. Work to do, my girl! Now we have the money, we can buy the materials. We'll be rich, rich, RICH!"

Within a month, word spread that Emily Dragonfly was making brooches again. Beautiful, wealthy elfin maidens would not go out in public unless a dragonfly brooch clasped their robes. Elfin high-society was in a state. Fathers and husbands, boyfriends and would-be-boyfriends went to desperate lengths to obtain a brooch: elves offered others enormous sums for the brooches they had, whilst even more offered huge bribes for a place on the waiting list. All this time, Emily and Nova worked feverishly to keep up with demand. Emily always refused to change her design, but she altered the materials and tiny details so cleverly that no two brooches were ever alike. This made them even more collectable. The word spread that wealthy elves had bought several of the brooches and the waiting list never grew shorter.

Sparkla took care of money matters. His bank account grew. Indeed, he was so busy taking money and orders for Emily's work that he had no time for his repairs. He became tetchy with elves who reasonably pointed out that he had had their watches and damaged brooches for months. He suggested that they should buy a fine new golden one, like his own, which he'd purchased from his old rival, Ticka, whose shop was two doors away. Sparkla became very unpopular, but while the money was pouring in and the girls were working hard, he didn't care.

Therefore, it came as a severe blow when a beautiful elfin maiden came into his shop one morning. Sparkla had never, not in his wildest dreams, expected *her* to walk into his shop. Oh, he recognised her, all right. There was no mistaking those eyes, those beautiful turquoise eyes, so beguiling, promising the world and everything in it. Those eyes held him now. "No," Sparkla croaked, "go away! Please! Please, she's not here!" he lied, uselessly.

The maiden smiled. "Oh, but she *is*, Sparkla. I'm never wrong about these things."

"Please, please leave us alone!" the old elf begged.

"That's what I want to do," the temptress smiled.

"It is?"

"Yes, leave you alone, *quite* alone," she said with a malicious honeyed tone.

"No!" Sparkla wailed.

"Now, now, old elf, don't be so upset! Perhaps I'll leave you Nova, after all."

"Nova? No! Take Nova, if you like, but leave me Emily!"

The elfin maiden smiled and walked into the workshop, her long, blonde hair falling around her shoulder as she moved. A moment later, she returned, holding Emily's hand.

"It's all right, Sparkla," Emily said. "I have been waiting for *Success* to come to me. I expected it and I will go with her, but this time, with my feet on the ground. Give me two bags of coins, that's all I can carry. You can keep the rest. You see, things aren't so bad! I'll take two or three brooches too." She pinned one to her blouse.

"What will I do without you?" Sparkla wailed.

"Oh, you've plenty to do," Emily smiled sweetly, "like winning back all your old friends, who brought you their repairs when times were hard. You have quite a backlog, you know!"

Sparkla flushed and hung his head. He knew Emily was right. When he raised his head, they were gone.

"Never mind, Nova," the crafty elf chuckled. "We won't be poor again, so you can stay and help in the shop. Emily was right," he reflected, "friends are precious. Maybe I've been a blinded by greed. But now I'm rich, I can spend my time winning back my old friends." But, even if he had reached one-hundred-and-forty-four elfyears, in that time, Sparkla had learned nothing about true friendship. One day, much later, he died rich and friendless.

*Success* took Emily out of Aldebaran into the countryside, where they met up with Adam. His smile was friendly, and he said the right words of greeting, but Emily could tell that he wasn't himself. His eyes were glazed, still beguiled by *Success*, not the old Adam that she knew and loved. Emily would have to try to break the spell. For her own part, she wasn't going to fall prey to *Success's* false charms a second time. This time, she would keep her wits about her and not trust the maiden of the all-promising eyes and of the silken alluring voice.

Now *Success* used that voice: "Adam and

Emily," she said with an entrancing smile, "you are both so charming, I have decided to take you to meet some important people. I'm going to lead you to the *Citadel of Wealth*."

"Oh ay," Adam breathed, excitedly, "I'd like that!"

"Mmm," Emily pursed her lips, "we can hardly present ourselves like this. What about our servants?"

"Servants?" *Success* opened her turquoise eyes wide.

"Ay, my dwarf and his pixy," Adam said, his quick wits sharp as ever. "I left them at the artist's studio. I really must insist!"

"Very well, of course, I can arrange that." It pleased *Success* when people had servants.

They headed away from the city, towards the sunset, each holding *Success* by the hand, one in a dizzy trance and the other coolly level-headed.

# IV

## THE CITADEL OF WEALTH

---

$\mathcal{G}$ ilded roofs, golden towers and gilt turrets circled the brow of the hill like a splendid crown; from there they blazed sunlight in a boastful message to everyone outside their massive walls. A plaque gracing those walls proclaimed:

*"This Citadel, Poor World, was built topped by a crown*
*to display the wealth within."*

*Success* brought them right under these walls for the four friends to gaze up in wonder. They had no idea of the splendour inside where each window ledge and door frame was carved in jade. Bulls' heads, pouncing jaguars and arched scorpions menaced coiled serpents, demons and dragons across the narrow jade-green streets. Way above them, blazoned banners, worked in gold and silver thread, unfurled lazily in the breeze at every pinnacle. Wherever the eye rested in the Citadel, it was struck by rich detail, charm and beauty.

Adam was the first to take his gaze from the Citadel. When he turned around, he found a member of their party gone.

"Where's *Success?*"

The others dragged their eyes from the Citadel and blinked around them. There was no sign of the elf.

"She's pretty good at disappearing," Emily muttered. "In fact, she makes a habit of it."

For the first time in several days, Adam addressed his three companions: Lar, Palustric and Emily.

"There's no point in standing around here; we might as well go into the Citadel."

Emily smiled happily because Adam was back to his old self. With *Success* around, he'd not even looked their way, never mind spoken to them. In the elf's presence, her brother was no more than a marionette.

"*Success* wanted us to come here, so let's explore," the till-devoted Adam set off towards the fortified gateway which guarded the drawbridge across the moat.

In the gateway, two guards barred their way with crossed pikes and two others came out of a small room in a corner tower. Across the chest, their burgundy silk uniforms bore the emblem of a golden fist clenching a laden purse.

A guard told Emily that no-one was permitted into the Citadel unless he could demonstrate *sufficient means*. Emily held up her bags of gold while Adam pulled out his bag of coins too.

"We're not beggars," he said, trying not to sound rude.

"Quite so," one of the guards smiled, pressing his hands, heavy with gold rings, together in a gesture of apology.

"He's a goblin," Lar whispered to Emily, nervously. "They're all goblins, Mistress."

Emily knew that from their ugliness, but their friendliness made her feel more at ease. The sumptuous goblin guards' uniforms, deep burgundy velvet embroidered with lions in gold thread, also helped to soften their appearance.

"Come this way," the heavy-ringed guard spoke with authority, "to the Weighing Chamber."

"A kind of *Weighting Room*," Adam said, but

the others were too curious to take any notice of his weak pun.

They entered a bare, circular stone room, where at once they were met by a piteous plea: "I've got three gold teeth! Pull them out! Won't you pull them out, *please?*"

The four friends stared in amazement at a finely dressed goblin who was swinging inside a cage suspended from a beam made of the same heavy brass. Red in the (ugly) face, he was trying to convince two guards, who were consulting a chart on the wall. They shook their heads, at which the goblin in the cage became more agitated. He began to jump up and down, pulling at something inside his mouth. Finally, with a yelp of pain mixed with triumph, he thrust a hairy hand through the bars of the cage.

"Here, here," he spoke with difficulty, like one whose mouth is causing him considerable pain. He held out a gold tooth in his open palm. "Add this to the bag...and there are two more!"

One of the guards came across slowly and took the tooth from the caged goblin; he inspected it carefully.

"Well, that seems to be in order," he said at last. The caged goblin nodded and pointed eagerly to a bag hanging from the other end of the beam. No sooner had the guard dropped the tooth into the bag than the elegantly-dressed goblin began tugging inside his mouth again. The cage swung wildly as the goblin fell to the floor where, kicking and twisting, he grunted and pulled until, with an agonised howl of delight, he jumped to his feet brandishing another gold tooth.

"Put it in the bag!" His words were difficult to understand now. "There's another—" Both hands were inside his poor mouth. Goblins already had very wide mouths, but this one seriously risked making a barn door of his, Adam thought.

The guard, having added the second tooth to the bag, was now glaring at the writhing goblin. "Hold still! I can't read the scale. Won't you hold still, I say!"

The goblin ignored the command. Or rather, in the frenzy to pull out his last gold tooth, he didn't hear it. By now he was an extraction expert and out came the third gold tooth, along with a howl of tortured glee. Its swollen-mouthed owner finally stood still, holding the tooth out through the bars. With a sniff, the guard ignored the offering and studied a dial on the enormous balance. He looked back at the anxious goblin.

"That won't be necessary," he said with obvious disdain. There was a pause, then finally he added, "You may enter the Citadel."

At these words, the elegant, gap-toothed goblin flung open the cage door with a whoop of joy. His gold tooth flew unheeded through the air and landed at Lar's feet. The fat goblin clasped his hands above his head and jumped up and down several times while grinning a hideous swollen-lipped grin of triumph at the shocked friends. Victorious, he was led off, with his treasure bag, by the same contemptuous guard. With difficulty, Lar understood the words: "Keep it, *do!*" as the goblin brushed past him, pointing to the tooth on the floor. Lar picked it up and slipped it into his pocket.

The other guard, who had finished writing an entry in a leather-bound ledger, turned to the travellers. "Next," he called in a loud voice.

"Go on," urged their guard, pointing with his heavily-ringed hand towards the cage. One by one, the little band entered the cage until their guard closed the brass-barred door with a clang behind them.

They watched as he sorted their coins into two piles, one of gold and one of silver. Then he carefully hung them from two different hooks at the other side of the balance. He was joined by the guard with the pen. Together they studied the dial, while the four companions looked on curiously. Over to the chart they went and, as with the goblin earlier, they shook their heads. The one with the pen pointed to a column and shrugged. They whispered together, still shrugging, occasionally looking over their shoulders at the caged band. Finally, their guard came over. "You," he said, pointing to Adam, "out!"

Adam looked at his friends. He shrugged and left the cage without a word. Again, the guards consulted the dial and the chart.

"Fine!" said the guard with the pen. "You may enter the Citadel." The friends smiled with relief, but he turned to Adam and added, "*You* may not."

"I'm very sorry," said their guard kindly. "You see, there are *insufficient means* for you all to enter the Citadel—as body weight against precious metal will have it, the young lady, the dwarf and the pixy may enter, but sadly—"

The others refused to enter without Adam, but all Emily's pleading and charm made no difference, the guards were resolute. Under escort, they trudged heads down to the gateway and out beyond the massive walls.

"*Success* wanted us *all* to enter the Citadel," Emily said to Adam in a tone of voice meant to stop him from suggesting otherwise. "For some reason, I'm not sure why, I feel we have to go in there if we want to get home to our parents." She looked apologetically at Lar and Palustric, who, as far as they were concerned, were on an adventure. They didn't seem bothered by her words, so Emily looked up at the turrets of the Citadel that seemed so rich and distant, truly part of another world.

They sat down on the outer bank of the moat, proportionately as small as ants, under the immense walls which enclosed the Citadel, each deep in thought. How could they find more money quickly; enough for Adam to pass with them through the guarded gateway?

The smallest of the company stood up after a while and wandered off. The pixy hadn't gone far before he came across an old woman wearing a grey habit. Her face was hidden deep within her hood and her feet were bare. The old woman leant on a stick and greeted Lar, "Good day, little fellow. What brings a hoer of land to a place of feather beds?"

Something most unusual in the hooded stranger's voice stopped Lar in his tracks; despite her twinkling, knowing eyes, she seemed *as old as the earth*. Before long, they were sitting together on the ground, and Lar poured out his tale. The old woman sat with chin on her chest, so that Lar could only see her hood, but he felt more and more compelled to tell his tale to the very end.

When he had finished the tale, the old woman raised her head, saying, "Here are your friends, who have missed you." Surely, she could not have seen them coming, Lar thought, puzzled. The others joined the pixy and stared with curiosity at the stranger.

"My name is Sapiens," that strange disturbing voice came again. "I know your tale." The three newcomers, like Lar before them, were awed in the old woman's presence. There was a long silence.

At last, Emily asked haltingly, "I don't suppose you could give us some advice, madam?"

The hood nodded.

"How can we get the money to enter the Citadel?"

"Had I not heard your tale," the old woman began slowly, "I should tell you not to enter that place. As things are, you must enter; otherwise, you shall not have what you desire most."

"Well, I don't want to be rich," Adam said, sharply.

"I know your desire," Sapiens said with a steadiness which made Adam wish he hadn't spoken.

"You share it with your sister, but you have a hard road to travel and many dangers to face."

She sighed sadly and lowered her head in thought for a moment.

Palustric, who was the least patient of the group, could wait no longer: "But how can we get the money to get Adam into the Citadel?"

The old woman raised her head, and her eyes flashed. Then she laughed, *"Money,* young dwarf, *arrives walking slowly, but leaves running fast."*

Even Palustric smiled at this, while Lar clapped his hands in delight at another gem for his collection of sayings. The old woman seemed to address Palustric, but they weren't sure whom she was looking at because of the hood. "There is a way for one of you who is bold enough." She pointed away from the Citadel. "Down there is a plain, where you will find—" she smiled approvingly at Lar, who was repeating the saying about money in a low voice to memorise it. Lar stopped and paid attention at once. "Where you will find a lonely white rock. About the rock, there is a legend here, which is passed down from father to son. The legend is true, for I was here at the time." She smiled mysteriously. "A long time ago, hereabouts, lived a wicked hobgoblin, who was extremely rich." Sapiens looked up at the

Citadel. "He died in there, you know. He was even more wicked than most of his race."

Lar and Palustric exchanged glances because they both knew about the wickedness of hobgoblins.

She continued, "When he was dying, wishing to conserve his old habit of harming everyone, he summoned a fairy and entrusted all his treasure to her. He told her to enclose a broody hen made of gold and thirteen golden chicks in the white rock. She enchanted them so that they come out on the last Friday of every month and, invisible, run through the grass and thorns around the rock—"

Palustric was counting on his fingers. "It's only the third Wednesday," he muttered gloomily.

"Anyone can possess the golden fowl," the old woman looked around the expectant faces.

"How?" Emily asked.

"You must follow these steps: first, you must get up an hour before cockcrow and before sunrise take enough flax to make a napkin; then, you must tease it, spin it and bleach it, weave it and having finished, place a piece of maize bread in it which you must eat as the sun rises. If you have done well—"

"What?"

"The rock will slowly crack open and dissolve away like chalk in the sea, leaving the golden birds—"

"Are they solid gold?" Palustric asked.

The hood nodded.

"It doesn't sound easy," Adam said slowly. "There must be a catch."

"Pixies can work flax into linen, Master," Lar said, thoughtfully, in his fluting voice, "but it's a question of time—"

"You could do it, Lar!" Palustric urged, but the little pixy shook his head.

Emily had been thinking. "You said he was a wicked hobgoblin." She looked at Sapiens, searching for the old woman's eyes deep inside the hood. "What happens if you don't finish the linen in time?"

The old woman nodded. "That's why I spoke of boldness before. Whoever fails falls under the fairy spell and is doomed to rise every morning to crow the dawn, like a cockerel!"

They all laughed, but Sapiens raised a crooked finger. "It's not funny, you know. You wouldn't like it at all!"

"I suppose not," Emily smiled, "but it seems so ridiculous." She frowned and then added, "But you said that the hobgoblin entrusted all his treasure to the fairy. What happened to the rest?"

Once again, Sapiens nodded slowly. "*So you want turnips for one hundred pigs?*" she said in her curious way. "You can have all the treasure of course, but that's far harder. You must mount a fast horse and draw near the rock. Then, split a pomegranate into seven pieces and spur the horse. As you gallop around the rock, you must eat all the pomegranate seeds, without letting even one fall or leaving one. Then, you must jump from the saddle and sit on the rock—"

Palustric jumped up. "That's impossible!" he boomed.

Once more, the eyes flashed from deep within the hood.

"What happens if you fail?" Adam asked quietly.

"Your head will spin with dizziness until the day death gives you relief," Sapiens finished. She raised herself with difficulty to her feet, leaning heavily on her stick.

"I'm going to try then," Adam said in a determined voice, but followed this by adding less certainly, "I like pomegranates, after all."

"I knew you'd try," Sapiens said, and as if everything had all been decided in advance, she reached into her grey habit and pulled out a creamy-orange fruit. "Take this," she said, "it might help." She held the pomegranate out in her old and shaking hand.

"Thank you," Adam said and looked at the old woman with curiosity and with puzzled eyes.

She smiled kindly at him. "There is so much you don't know," she placed a gnarled hand on the boy's arm, "but it's enough to stay true to yourself and be brave. Oh, one other thing," she added as if she'd almost forgotten, "learn to wield a sword, my boy." She let go of Adam's arm and turned to hobble away.

In silence, they watched her go until she was quite a way down the road.

Adam turned to the others and frowned. "Did she say a sword? I wonder who she is?"

"She's as old as the earth, Master," Lar said, which seemed to be enough.

They fell silent again and watched the stranger disappear from sight.

"She's a wizard!" Palustric suddenly burst out. "She's one of the *Wizards of Enlightenment*, that's who she is! I never thought I'd meet one," he added in awe. "I didn't realise till now, but I'm sure. She's the Wizard of *Wisdom*." His voice trembled with excitement and admiration.

"But I don't understand, why should I learn to use a sword?" Adam said. "After talking to her,

I don't understand anything any better." He looked at the pomegranate in his hand and shrugged.

"Exactly," Palustric nodded. "You...we...*we* don't understand what we are doing or what lies ahead. For understanding, we would have needed to speak with a different wizard. As it is, we are wiser. We know what we have to do, where and how and, what's more, she gave you advice for the future."

Adam looked from the dwarf's sincere eyes to the pomegranate and shrugged again. "I don't feel very wise," he said. Then he took a decision. "Let's go! But where?" he ended, lamely.

"To buy a horse?" Palustric suggested.

"Do you believe all that legend stuff?" Adam looked from one to the other, but he didn't see any doubt on their faces.

"Let's go and buy a horse, then!" he said, convinced.

They found a fine black horse in a village not far from the Citadel. The goblins there were not rich, but neither were they poor. *Hard-working* was how Palustric described them, and that, coming from a dwarf, was praise indeed. They paid an honest price for the horse, which seemed young, healthy and too lively. Adam had his first doubts at the sight of it. He had been riding a few times with Emily at the stables near his home, but there, they gave children the calm, old mounts. This one was a snorting stallion that stomped and frisked as Emily led him along by his bridle. Adam fell so silent that his friends noticed. In his heart, Adam wanted Emily to take over the task. She was a much better rider than he because she had many more hours' experience in the saddle. The wizard, though, had given him the pomegranate, he thought, as he glanced unhappily at the magnificent beast next to him.

They entered the plain below the Citadel. Emily was having trouble keeping the stallion under control. Adam, pale as the chalky rock they were nearing, broke out in a cold sweat. He imagined what a life would be like with one's head constantly spinning.

The rock stood on its own, about the size of a truck from His World. Fearfully, Adam looked from it to the black stallion. He looked at Emily and was about to ask her if she'd take over when he remembered the wizard's words: *stay true to yourself and be brave.* He tried to control his trembling knees.

Suddenly, Lar spoke, "Lift me onto your shoulders, Master."

At that moment, Adam was happy to do anything that didn't involve mounting the stallion. He didn't even ask the pixy the reason but took him under the arms and did as asked, marvelling at how little his friend weighed and how he seemed bony, like a cat.

"Go to the horse, Master, I must speak with him."

Again, Adam obeyed silently so that the pixy whispered into the champing horse's ear. The stallion's ear twitched, and it tossed its great head. It neighed mightily, scaring Adam, but then, for the first time, stood still. So did Adam, who stared in surprise at the motionless animal.

"You can put me down, Master," Lar reminded Adam.

The stallion remained perfectly still and looked more or less like a riding-school horse. Adam's knees felt firmer, and the colour slowly returned to his cheeks.

"Thanks, Lar!" he breathed.

"'Twas nothing," the pixy beamed. *"One hand washes the other and both together wash the face,* is it not so, Master?"

"I'm sure that's right, Lar," Adam said, he didn't feel like working out the saying just then.

Emily felt in her pocket and fetched out a beautiful, jewel-encrusted dragonfly brooch which she had made. She unclipped the pin of the brooch and handed it to her brother. "I made this, and I know fairy magic it helped me. So, use it to eat the pomegranate seeds—it will help." She smiled encouragingly at her brother, who looked into her silver eyes and a strange warmth came over him. Strange how much closer he felt to his sister in this world. He took the brooch and handed it with the fruit to Palustric.

"Pass them up to me," he ordered as he mounted the stallion.

Irritated, Palustric gave them to Emily. "I'm not tall enough," he said, shortly.

Once he had them in his hands, Adam realised another awful truth. With his hands full, he couldn't hold the reins. He said as much, in a defeated voice.

"Fear not, Master," Lar's voice fluted up to him. "Hold tight with your knees. The horse knows what to do. Split the pomegranate, Master, and may Good Fortune be with us all!"

"Don't drop any seeds, Adam," Emily warned.

"And don't leave any," Palustric added. "Eat them all!"

Adam studied the pomegranate. He wondered just how to break it into seven equal parts. First, he tested the fruit with his hands, applying just a little pressure, certainly not enough to split it. To his amazement and joy, the fruit divided perfectly in his hands.

"Sapiens!" Adam breathed, at whose name, as if spurred, the stallion leapt forward in a gallop around the rock. With the shock of the charge, Adam was almost thrown, but somehow, he managed to grip with his knees and stay on. The horse galloped smoothly, and Adam felt like he was riding on a carousel at a fairground. He picked at the blood-red seeds. He'd always made a mess digging out pomegranate seeds at home where he'd been sitting at a table, not whirling around on a mighty steed. But the brooch pin spiked the seeds as cleanly as an arrow passing through a straw man, so Adam was able to carry them safely to his mouth.

The black horse sped around the white rock. Adam began to feel desperately dizzy. Time and again, he saw his friends' anxious faces, static markers of his gyrations. He felt sick but gritted his teeth and swallowed hard. Three pieces left. He was dizzy, his sense of balance was going, but he mustn't fail. He began to work as quickly as possible on the fourth piece. His stomach heaved. Swallowing again, he gripped the horse tighter with his knees; meanwhile, nausea gripped his stomach. Adam gulped several times. It would never do to be sick; otherwise, he'd vomit the seeds and lose the challenge. Then he'd be condemned to life with a spinning head. Several times he was almost sick, but with great determination, he mechanically spiked and swallowed the seeds, despite the whirling trap.

At first, Emily, Lar and Palustric were excited. They clapped their hands and cheered Adam, who passed in a black blur against a background of white rock. But soon they fell into anxious silence as they became aware of the difficulty and the danger.

Time passed, but the whirling blur continued. Just watching, Emily felt dizzy and queasy. With the passing minutes, she became convinced that Adam would fail. Although she hadn't met one, she began to hate hobgoblins with all her being. She turned away, unable to watch any longer. Palustric came up to her while she sat on the thorn-littered grass and placed his hand on her shoulder to comfort her.

"We shouldn't have let him, Palustric," Emily sobbed. "He'll never be well again. I should have done it. I'm the better rider!"

Tears coursed down her beautiful face. Deep down, the dwarf knew she was right; his heart felt as heavy as stone.

Only Lar knew that Adam would succeed

and only he, therefore, was watching when the stallion dug his hooves into the dusty ground.

"Look!" he cried to the other two, who turned just in time to see Adam rise unsteadily to his feet on the saddle of the motionless horse, nearly fall off, and then throw himself with a thump on to the top of the rock, where he sat quite still.

Nothing happened.

Emily looked with tear-filled eyes at Palustric, who clenched his fists and shook his head. Still, nothing happened. Palustric stamped his foot angrily. He didn't want to believe that his friend had been through that torture for nothing. Even Lar was losing faith, when suddenly with a crash, a great crack speared across the side of the rock like a fork of lightning.

Instantly, the rock was hidden in a cloud of fine white dust. It filled the air around them and then began to settle like snow on the ground. Where the rock had been, lay the boy—like a dragon on its treasure hoard. Except that the boy looked more like a mummy because white dust covered him from head to toe.

When he opened his eyes, Adam could see wisps of cloud whirling around the sky. Suddenly, much closer, his friends' spinning faces peering down at him. He groaned and closed his eyes, only to see spinning stars. So, he had failed. Now he realised his terrible fate: a whole lifetime of dizziness stretched ahead of him. He groaned again and, to his surprise, clutched two handfuls of gold coins as he needed something to cling on to, to fight the sickening sensation.

*Gold coins!* Adam sat up suddenly, giving Palustric a terrible crack on the head with his own. Now, the two friends saw spinning stars!

Adam staggered around unsteadily like a drunken man, while Palustric held his head and groaned, swaying backwards and forwards on his heels. Meanwhile, Lar and Emily were throwing gold coins into the air, ignoring their friends' distress.

At the height of her joy, Emily suddenly remembered her brother. Going over to him, she put her arm around him and made him sit down. "You did it, Adam! You did it!"

Adam groaned and closed his eyes tightly for a minute or two. When he opened them, the world had stopped spinning; instead, he found himself grinning at a huge heap of jewels and golden coins.

"Phew! I wouldn't want to go through that again. What's up with Palustric?" he asked suddenly and frowned when the other two burst out laughing.

"We'll have no trouble getting into the Citadel now," Emily said. She eyed the pile of coins and jewels doubtfully. "The only thing is, how are we going to carry them all?"

They soon decided that Emily would ride the stallion back to the village and buy two big packs and two small ones.

"I must speak with him first, Mistress," Lar insisted and, again, Adam lifted him to the horse's ear.

Lar, Palustric and Adam sat down next to the pile of coins and watched Emily expertly ride off towards the village.

"While we're waiting for Emily," Adam said to Lar, "tell me about the horse."

Lar grinned happily and looked from Palustric to Adam. "Humans are like dwarves," he said with a superior air. "They have forgotten how to talk with animals, but we pixies haven't."

"Like when you heard the stream singing?"

"Exactly, Master. I told the horse that it could have his freedom after it had done its duty. It is happy to get away from the goblins." Lar's strange, slightly squinting yellow eyes opened wider, and he stared at Adam. "There's one thing you should know, Master—"

"Eh?"

"Horses are afraid of pixies."

"Why?"

"There's a belief among horses that they can be ridden to death by a pixy."

"And is it true, Lar?" Adam studied the pixy's leathery face and, therefore, didn't miss the odd look that came into his slatted eyes.

"Better I don't twine my fingers in its mane, Master. I threatened the horse I'd ride it if it didn't help us." Lar surprised them with a sudden wild-pitched laugh. Then he became serious and added, "When I spoke to the horse this time, I promised that we would ask it no more favours and that it would go free."

"That's fair enough," Adam said. "I'd never have broken the fairy's spell if it hadn't been for its help."

He looked at Lar and noticed that the strange light still burnt in his eyes. What on earth was it with pixies and horses?

Emily returned before long. She threw four bags at their feet, dismounted lightly and hugged the horse's neck. Palustric inspected the bags.

"Goblin work," he sniffed, "crude, but stout enough, I suppose."

They loaded coins and jewels into the four packs. "Look!" Palustric shouted. Among the coins, he had found a golden egg—the first of thirteen. Then a golden hen appeared, but it wouldn't enter any of the packs.

"I'll carry it," Emily said firmly. "It's cute!" Apart from the hen, there were too many coins for the packs. Emily wanted to return for more, but the others disagreed.

"We only have to enter the Citadel," Adam said, "and we won't need all this money. We're already rich, so let's find some poor goblins in the village and send them here." Emily agreed reluctantly and began to tie the packs together.

"What are you doing, Em?" Adam asked.

"They'll be easier to load on to the horse."

"We can't." Adam explained what Lar had told him. Emily looked very unhappy; even the leftover gold lost its importance for her. She walked over to the stallion, spoke gently and kissed its great head before turning bright-eyed back to her friends, too upset to say anything.

The great horse tossed its head, snorted, stamped the ground and cantered off. Then it began to gallop backwards and forwards wildly like a young colt.

"It's enjoying its new freedom, Mistress," said Lar who received a weak smile from the girl.

Since Palustric and Adam were stronger than the other two, they carried heavy, white stones and placed them all around the remaining gold. Lar and Emily helped to put smaller stones over the top until a white cairn marked and hid the rest of the treasure trove. When they had finished, they heaved the packs onto their backs and tramped towards the Citadel. They had only been walking for a few minutes when they heard hoofbeats behind them; the stallion brushed past the girl at breakneck speed, almost knocking Emily off her feet. The horse suddenly spun round in a cloud of dust and trotted up to her, where it pressed its head against her arm. When Lar called out in a strange tongue, the horse pricked up its ears and neighed several times. Lar looked at Emily and grinned. "The horse wants the packs on its back. It will stay with you, Mistress!"

"Oh, thank you, horse," and tears of happiness shone in her silver eyes. "Lar, ask its...I mean...*his* name."

Again, Lar spoke in the strange tongue, and the horse whinnied.

"*Blitz*, Mistress."

"Blitz!" Adam laughed. "It suits him!"

"Blitz!" Emily echoed. "I love you, Blitz!"

When they arrived at the village, they couldn't find any poverty, perhaps because it was a place of honest (ugly) workers. These highland goblins weren't particularly bad-natured, even if their looks were off-putting. They grew their food and brewed beer, keeping themselves to themselves. Palustric warned that no race of goblins was ever to be trusted. They noticed nervously that many of them carried swords at their sides, and there must be a reason for that. Yet, when the friends decided to look for the oldest goblin in the village (Adam suggested that such a goblin should be the wisest), they were treated politely. Of course, they were stared at, studied and thoroughly weighed up, as happens to strangers in any village anywhere. Afterwards, they were led to a small house of solid stone walls.

Emily found a pail near a water pump, and so she stayed outside to give Blitz a drink, but the others went into a room where a tiny, spotlessly clean window let in just enough light for them to see. They made out a small, hunched figure with unmistakably wide-mouthed, flat-nosed goblin features, sitting in the corner on a chair by the fire. The goblin's white tufts of hair sprouted around his head and his skin was so wrinkled that the creature reminded Adam of a dead leaf, half-covered in snow and swept by the wind into this stony corner.

They introduced themselves and politely refused their host's offer of food and drink, wishing to get their business settled quickly and be on their way. Adam explained about the gold and ended by saying that with the wisdom of years, their host would know best how to use the treasure.

The wizened goblin had followed the boy's every word. His wasted little body was perfectly still, but when Adam finished, he suddenly threw out his thin arms and nodded violently: "I know exactly what to do with it," he said, his voice frail but harsh. "*Leave* it where it is, that's what!" Adam hadn't expected this. "You look surprised," the goblin shook his head sadly, "but if you're sensible, you'll go back and bury what you've taken."

"Why?" Adam was shaken by the shrunken goblin's ferocity.

"Because that's hobgoblin gold, that's why, and each piece can be weighed in misery and misfortune," the old goblin toned solemnly. He raised a crooked finger and waved it under Adam's nose. "It can only bring sorrow and suffering. None of us here will touch it, that's for sure. Take my advice, put it back!" The goblin sank back wearily into his chair.

"I can't do that," Adam said, "not after what I went through to get it. Besides, we need gold to enter the Citadel."

"I wouldn't go there," the old goblin muttered almost inaudibly and looked even more unconvinced. "My great-grandfather helped build the place—" His words fell away, and his head sank onto his chest. They got no more out of him because he was fast asleep. Outside his door, the friends decided to forget about the other half of the treasure and to head straight for the Citadel.

# 20

*B*ack at the gatehouse, everything proceeded smoothly. The guards recalculated their body weights in terms of gold on the chart; then, they informed the visitors that they would have to pay one-tenth of this figure as an entry toll. The travellers paid with seven golden eggs which the guards took into a strongroom opposite the weighing chamber. The heavy-ringed guard informed them that their horse had to be stabled outside the walls as animals were not allowed into the Citadel. They paid another golden egg for stabling, saying a see-you-soon to Blitz, shouldered their packs and, at last, stepped through the gatehouse into the lower square of the Citadel.

At first sight, it seemed that the square was snow-covered because it stretched white and glistening before them.

"It's paved with metal," Palustric said puzzled.

"With silver cobbles, friend Palustric," Lar squeaked.

"Real silver?" Emily gasped.

"Ay."

Adam passed his foot over the pavement and found that Lar was right. "They can afford it with all the taxes they collect at the gatehouse," he said before they crossed the busy square towards the magnificent silver fountain in the centre. Goblins came and went all around them, mostly wearing velvet suits and dresses, each exquisitely tailored to measure. The male goblins all carried swords at their sides.

"Have you seen the lace on those dresses?" Emily said enviously. She lowered her voice, "But the goblins inside them are so ugly!"

They stood before the fountain and admired solid, silver dolphins leaping in front of the silver mermaid that sat on a silver rock under the silver spray sparkling in the sunlight. Their eyes followed the mermaid's lovely form up to her ugly goblin face.

"Ugh! Why have they made her so hideous?"

Emily toned down and stifled her cry into a whisper.

"To the goblin eye she's probably beautiful," Palustric reasoned.

Lar studied the silver statue and thought about what the dwarf had said. He began to think about beauty and art, mermaids and goblins, ugliness and reality. His pixy mind sifted through its vast store of sayings and finally selected: "*Call it by any other name, but it remains a marrow,* is it not so, Master?"

Adam had also been thinking about beauty and art, but even if he lived to be a hundred years old, he would never have linked a marrow to a mermaid! He looked at the curious little pixy and shook his head with a smile. "Ay, you're right there, Lar—*er,* I suppose."

The pixy gazed in confusion at Adam's bafflement.

They left the fountain behind and entered a steep, narrow street which looked as if it led up to the golden roofs. Carvings, statuettes in niches, mosaics, complicated clocks, sundials and columns, lined the street. Blaring down, full of detail, all were crafted in semi-precious stone such as amber, onyx, jade and jet. They would have been beautiful to the friends' eyes, except that the wealth of detail often included grotesque goblins.

The narrow, green street wound up the hillside. Elegantly dressed (ugly) goblins hurried about their business, showing no interest whatsoever in the four visitors. Finally, the street opened onto another square. Being at the top of the hill and full of imposing buildings, they supposed it to be the main square. They gazed in wonder at the solid gold cobblestones and the gold obelisk in the centre. A fortune had gone into simple construction!

On one side of the square, fronted by a magnificent portico stood THE BULGING PURSE HOTEL. They crossed the square to its entrance, where they hesitated, but reminding each other that they were rich now, they entered. Inside, they continued to marvel. Adam saw his open mouth reflected over and over again in the numerous reception hall mirrors and promptly closed it. The mirrors multiplied tapestries, damask curtains and upholstery until the travellers felt they were in an endless meadow of flowered softness.

"Can I help you?" a polite voice asked.

They turned to face a goblin (ugly) in a black velvet suit who was eyeing them with disapproval. Their clothes were dirty from travel and dusty from the plain below. They didn't fit at all into their luxurious surroundings.

"We'd like two rooms, please, a single and a triple."

The goblin's eye moved to Emily's dragonfly brooch, sparkling so enchantingly in the soft, re-flected light. His eye never moved as he replied, "We have no rooms, madam; we have only suites."

"Well, two suites then, one for me and one for my friends. How much will it cost us to stay here?"

"Uh?" the goblin finally looked away from the brooch. "I'm so sorry...?" He tried to recover.

"I said, how much?"

"Ah!" the goblin's eyes returned to the brooch. A hairy, long-nailed finger pointed with a tremble. "May I ask where madam obtained such a magnificent piece?"

"I made it."

"Really?" The goblin's eyes widened, and in a shaky voice, heavy with desire, he managed: "Such a brooch would pay for...for a very long stay indeed."

"Would it?" Emily frowned. "But it's not for sale."

The goblin looked anguished. "You could stay for as long as you liked..."

"For as long as we like?"

"Yes, yes." The goblin was hopping from foot to foot, rubbing his hands together; his eyes were pleading.

Lar, Adam and Palustric looked from the goblin at each other in astonishment.

"Well, I don't know..." Emily watched the look of hope change back to anguish. "Well, perhaps..." and back again to hope. "As long as we like?"

"Yes, yes, *as long as you like!*" The goblin nodded furiously.

Emily unclipped the brooch; without a word, the goblin snatched it from her hand and dashed behind the reception counter. They watched him seize a bunch of keys with which he frantically opened a wall safe. Thrusting the brooch deep inside, he slammed the door and locked it, all at whirlwind speed. Pleased, he turned to face them with a repugnant wide-mouthed grin.

"May I show you to your suites, madam and gentlemen?"

Clean and refreshed, they passed several idle days enjoying the comfort and food of the hotel. They explored the fascinating streets of the Citadel as sightseers. Soon the novelty wore off, and they became restless. An emergency meeting was held in the sitting-room of Emily's suite.

"Nothing's happening," Adam said gloomily. "We're just wasting time here."

"Shall we leave the Citadel?" The enthusiasm in Palustric's voice was impossible to miss.

Emily shook her head. "*Success* brought us here, so there must be a reason."

"I say we go." Adam looked at Palustric, who nodded his agreement.

"You always agree with Adam." Emily's silver eyes blazed at the dwarf. "Even if we go, where do we go, eh?"

"Anywhere," Adam said defiantly, "anything is better than wasting time here."

"At least we're comfortable, and as I said, I'm sure we're here for a reason."

"What reason?"

"We've *got* to get home, or have you forgotten?" Emily said angrily.

There was a long silence in which Adam felt that there was something wrong, but try as he might, he couldn't think what it was. All three looked at Lar, who hadn't said a word.

"Why do you look at me?" the pixy squeaked.

"*You* decide, Lar," Emily's voice was gentler.

The pixy's slatted eyes squinted from one to

the other. "Of course, pixies would never argue over something so obvious—"

"Obvious?" Emily said, just as Palustric growled, "What's obvious?"

"It's obvious...at least, we pixies believe that *the wintering bird never flies into the teeth of the wind,* is it not so?" He spread his hands and opened his eyes wider.

"The wind brought us, so we'll let it take us too," Emily latched onto the saying and looked straight at her brother.

Adam stood up and crossed over to the window and, looking out, bored, said, "Speaking of wind, I think we're in the doldrums, but I suppose pixy lore must be right." Secretly, he was thinking about Sapiens but chose not to mention the wizard's advice for the moment.

After another couple of days, when Adam's boredom and frustration were becoming unbearable, something happened. They were crossing the entrance hall to go out when one of the goblin waiters politely asked them into the owner's office. Dimly lit, behind his dark, oak desk and dressed in his usual black velvet, the goblin looked like a crow in its nest.

"Oh, do come in! I'm so sorry," he said, "*so very sorry.* I had *no* idea, of course!"

The four friends looked at each other.

"I'm mortified; if I'd known that such a *famous* person was gracing my poor hotel—" He stood up and, with an exaggerated bow towards Emily, addressed the luxurious carpet, "I'd certainly have offered our best suite!" He straightened up. "But how was I to know? I have so little time to read *The Investor and Accumulator's Gazette.*"

"But we're not famous," Emily objected.

The goblin grinned wider with certainty. "You're *Emily Dragonfly*, that's who you are! And what's more, the Archgoblin *himself* wants to see you." He lowered his voice to a confidential tone, "Modestly speaking, I, myself, personally showed your brooch to the Archgoblin, himself, in person! Now the brooch is his, I'm honoured to say," although the goblin's expression was more regretful than honoured. "Take this card. With this, you will be admitted into the Archgoblin's presence." He continued with a reverential explanation about the Archgoblin's wealth, power and importance. Only after a long, patient wait were they given directions to arrive at his magnificent palace.

Nothing the goblin had said had prepared them for that place or the Archgoblin. Although entering through gates of wrought gold gave an idea of the wealth that lay within. They passed through an ornamental garden, where a heated waterfall splashed into an inviting pool, along an avenue where numerous goblin gardeners tended fruit trees laden with every kind of fruit and nut.

Green velvet uniformed servants admitted them through a hall into a visitors' ante-chamber. A series of gilt-framed portraits hung on the wood-panelled walls. They were all of goblins: goblins wearing lace ruffs, goblins in silk dresses and goblins in armour. And all of them singularly ugly.

"Our host's ancestors," Palustric said.

Emily gazed along the walls. "Aren't they *ugly?*"

"Hush!" Adam looked anxiously towards the door at the silent, unmoving goblin footman.

When a bell rang on the wall above the door, the footman nodded towards them, gliding over to the double door, which he threw open with a white-gloved flourish. He stood aside and bowed, indicating the way with his right hand. Feeling smaller than usual, the four friends entered the Archgoblin's reception chamber.

The Honourable Forty-Fourth Archgoblin stood, hands clasped behind him, in front of a marble fireplace where a log fire crackled cheerfully.

He was particularly ugly, even for a goblin, and stood out among Highland Goblins for his greater height and girth. The Archgoblin was nearly as tall as Adam and at least five times fatter. He stood out, moreover, for the richness of his well-tailored clothes. Under a red hunting jacket, the gold buttons of his yellow waistcoat fought a desperate battle to keep his stomach in check. Each button bore the family crest. A crest which was repeated on the hilt of his sword and on some of the fifteen heavy gold rings which crowded his fingers. *I wonder how he ever manages to lift his hands with all that weight,* thought the intrigued Emily.

Goblin eyes are always black, but the Archgoblin's were also small and crafty, lost in a heavy face, where whiskers sprouted from the flat goblin nose above a wide mouth. The whole was made more grotesque by its permanently curled upper lip. Indeed, the Archgoblin's wobbly jowls with their silver sideburn-tufts under a domed brow gave the idea of a boar without tusks.

The Archgoblin raised a hand in a golden arc of greeting, and his lip curled even more in an intended pleasant smile.

"Welcome, dearest friends. Welcome to my humble home. It doesn't reflect my..." he coughed modestly— "...*ahem*...standing in society, but it's been the family home for so long, I'm very fond of it. I hope you understand."

"B-but it's lovely!" Emily gazed around the richly furnished room.

"You are far...*infinitely*...too kind, my dear." The Archgoblin bowed.

Adam and Palustric exchanged a glance which said that they weren't going to like their host. Emily, on the other hand, was charmed by the Archgoblin, and it showed in her smile.

The Archgoblin reached across to a bell-pull, and a servant entered at once. His master whispered something in his ear; the servant bowed out of the room.

"I've sent for my tailor," the Archgoblin announced. He smiled at the little group. "A little lace, a little velvet..." his hand traced another golden arc, "...wouldn't go amiss. I really can't let you remain..." he sniffed, "...in that state."

Adam's pride was hurt. "I don't need new clothes, thank you. These will do fine!"

"Oh, Adam!" Emily gasped.

The Archgoblin smiled an oily smile. "As you please, dear boy. But you must allow a gracious lady such as your sister to dress *in style*."

The day passed in the Archgoblin's company, during which time Adam lost his sister.

The more Emily liked the Archgoblin, the more Adam's dislike for him grew. Until, after what Adam took to be yet another insult, the boy stormed out of the house. He led Palustric and Lar right out of the Citadel to the goblin village outside the walls, where to their relief, they found a simple inn for their lodgings.

Emily was shocked and hurt by what she considered Adam's boorish behaviour. *Of course,* she thought, *I have always had superior manners.* In reality, the Archgoblin's promises had seduced her. Over a splendid dinner, they struck a deal. Her host agreed to set up Emily with the best workshop, forge and workers, with no expense spared. There she would make her dragonfly brooches. She would also have her own house, servants and coat-of-arms. In exchange, the Archgoblin would have the right to choose and take one in every three brooches created by Emily.

Emily returned to THE BULGING PURSE HOTEL and discovered that the others had gone. She wasn't particularly upset because she had so much to think about. Tomorrow, she had an appointment to have elegant clothes fitted and another to choose her house and furnishings. It was all so exciting; she could have the best of everything that money could buy. She dreamt on for a while and distractedly thought how badly Adam had behaved. Just wait till she saw him again! He had nearly spoilt everything with his bad manners. She frowned and returned to her thoughts of wealth and power.

## 21

*E*mily and Adam used the next few months apart in very different ways.

"By my black blood!" cried Malrog the Goblin as he failed to parry Adam's thrust. "If the sword hadn't had a button, I would have had at least three inches of your blade in my chest. There's no doubt at all, the student has surpassed his master! Now, I've nothing left to teach you." Saluting his young adversary, the bow-legged goblin laid down his practice sword and sat on a rock to get his breath back.

Of course, it hadn't been so easy at the start. Adam smiled wryly at the memory of his first few days. He was mortified time and again; he felt clumsy and leaden-footed, body mottled with bruises and ego badly mauled. Slowly, slowly, and then, ever faster, he'd improved until now he was excellent.

Malrog hadn't exaggerated when he said that he had nothing left to teach Adam. In only a few months, the long-legged boy had become a really fearsome swordsman. For some time now, to tell the truth, Adam had continued practising and listening closely to his master, letting the goblin occasionally touch him with his sword not to hurt his feelings. Of course, before long, Malrog realised but wasn't offended because he had grown fond of the boy.

Malrog stood up slowly and, shaking his long, goblin arm, picked up his sword once more. "Well, you *almost* know more than me. I'm sure you can rid yourself of any adversary, but just in case one proves more difficult, I'll teach you a move that is my secret alone."

"Your secret?" Adam repeated with great interest but didn't have time to think about it.

"On guard!" Malrog shouted, crossing swords with a clash. For a while, they fenced as usual, but suddenly Malrog brought his sword from a high defensive position in a series of feints, then crossed swords from an angle which disarmed Adam and left Malrog's sword at his throat. "Again!" the goblin cried, and once more,

Adam's sword hit the ground while Malrog's pressed at his throat.

"Now I see!" Adam exclaimed and, to prove his words, repeated the move several times.

"Now I really have nothing left to teach you, Adam," Malrog said, "except to tell you that you should only draw your sword in anger when you have no other choice. By the way, promise to keep our secret! You know, you're the best student I've ever had the honour of teaching."

During his apprenticeship as a swordsman, word occasionally reached Adam about his sister. Sometimes Lar or Palustric, chatting with goblins, heard something about Emily. It wasn't so difficult because she was already the wonder of the Citadel. Her dragonfly brooches were more magnificent than ever. Thanks to the Archgoblin, Emily could use any material she desired, her tools were the best that money could buy, and the results were breathtakingly beautiful. Her prices were high, but there was no shortage of buyers, not just among the Highland Goblins, but now THE BULGING PURSE HOTEL was no longer the empty place they had stayed in some months ago. A new NO VACANCIES sign appeared in reception for the many wealthy would-be buyers arriving from the Elven lands, from Brownie hamlets and from the Dwarfish towns. Among the well-to-do, to pin an *Emily Dragonfly* brooch to one's evening gown was not only desirable but also essential. Anyone of standing could not be seen without one.

From the village below, goblins had pointed out to Adam his sister's golden-turreted house. This had not been necessary because the banner which fluttered there bore her coat-of-arms: a pale blue dragonfly on a silver ground. Adam shrugged on these occasions and thought bitterly how his sister had changed. She really seemed to fit perfectly into Citadel life. It just showed, no matter how well you thought you knew a person, you could always get a shock. Emily hadn't even tried to get in touch with them, as if she had shut them out of her life.

The months dragged on in this way. The three friends only heard about Emily and her successes second-hand. One morning, things changed; the day began with frantic hammering on the inn door.

"What is it, what is it?" their landlord hurried to the door. "Anybody would think the Citadel's about to fall on our heads!" he grumbled.

"Where's Adam?" the agitated goblins demanded of the landlord as he opened the door. "Quick! Fetch him!"

Curious goblins began to gather outside the inn until, by the time Adam came downstairs, tucking in his shirt and rubbing the sleep out of his eyes, quite a crowd had gathered.

"Come with us, quickly!" the goblins urged so that Adam found himself jostled in a procession, hurrying through the village towards the Citadel. When Adam asked questions, the goblins hurried him on, saying that there was no time to lose. They came to a little hut on the road to the Citadel, where they stopped and pushed Adam inside.

In the corner of the little hut, lying on a straw bed, was a uniformed goblin. At once, Adam saw that he was wounded. Black blood seeped from his chest, darkening the emblem there. He recognised the blood-stained dragonfly and hurried to kneel by the dying soldier's side.

"My mistress—" the goblin croaked in a voice so weak that Adam had to put his ear near his sickly face.

"Ay? Tell me!"

"Taken...in prison—" the goblin groaned and closed his eyes.

"Who, why?"

"Arch...goblin—" the soldier gasped, opened his eyes while Adam watched them grow dull.

With his dying breath, he sighed one word—
*"masterpiece."*

Adam stood up and gazed vaguely around
him. *"Masterpiece?"* he muttered, then in a clear
voice: "Bury him!" He pushed his way out of the
hut. There was something in the boy's face
which warned the goblins not to speak to him.
None of the goblins followed him.

Adam pondered as he hurried to the inn.
Emily was in danger. He had never trusted the
Archgoblin; that loathsome creature had thrown
his sister in prison. But why? Her guard had said
*masterpiece* with his dying breath. What did that
mean?

Adam found Lar and Palustric up and
dressed, waiting anxiously for him. He rushed
his explanation and, seizing Lar by the arm, told
him to speak to the horse. "Tell him Emily's in
danger," Adam said, "and that I'll need his help.
I'm off upstairs for my sword."

A few minutes later, from the saddle, he ordered the dwarf and the pixy to wait for him at
the inn. Their protests were choked by a cloud of
dust as Adam galloped Blitz towards the Citadel.

He was in luck because the drawbridge was
down. The goblin guards only had time to cross
their pikes to bar his way, but the black stallion
leapt over them smoothly without any command

from Adam. The horse was worried about his mistress; no guard was going to block his way. Two or three arrows flew past Adam's head, but now Blitz was past the fountain and speeding up the hill towards the Archgoblin's palace. Adam didn't care a fig that animals were not allowed into the Citadel: his sister was in danger.

The wrought gold gates were closed, so Adam was just considering halting Blitz when the stallion increased his speed.

"Aw, no!" Adam dropped the reins and flung his arms around Blitz's neck as the stallion took off into an impossible leap. Adam closed his eyes and they flew. When he opened them again, they were inside and speeding along the avenue towards the courtyard.

"Steady on, Blitz," Adam begged in his ear, but the horse put his head forward and went even faster. His mistress was in danger, and there was no time to waste.

Blitz skidded to a halt in front of the ornamental steps leading to the main entrance. Nobody had ever dismounted a horse as quickly or with as much relief as Adam at that moment. Even so, as he drew his sword, he thanked the stallion. His words were lost in the loud clanging of the alarm bell.

Two guards with drawn swords ran towards

him while others were coming. Adam took in the situation with the eye of an expert, if inexperienced-in-real-combat, swordsman. He would have to put these two out of action quickly so that he could hold the steps and avoid being surrounded.

Adam blessed Malrog for his secret as two swords went arcing through the air. The two guards ran to retrieve their swords, and Adam realised with regret that he would have to hurt them if he wanted to reach the Archgoblin.

There were about twenty goblin guards in the grounds, but only two at a time could attack him on the steps. Two at a time were therefore disarmed and wounded in the sword arm, always in the same place: in the upper-arm muscle so that they could fight no more.

Adam kicked open the door and strode into the Archgoblin's palace. At the sight of his bloodied sword, the uniformed servants scattered in all directions. Adam kicked open the antechamber's double door with a great crash and came face to face with a shocked footman who made the mistake of turning and reaching for a heavy candlestick. Adam pounced and hit him with his sword hilt between two spiky tufts at the back of his head.

"No need for candlelight when you're

asleep," Adam muttered as the goblin fell unconscious at his feet.

Adam entered the Archgoblin's chamber.

"I could give you a little push onto that fire," Adam said as he placed the point of his sword under the Archgoblin's double chin.

Even with the unpleasant feeling of cold steel at his throat, the Archgoblin's small, black eyes shone with craftiness, not fear.

"My dear boy," he forced a smile, "this is not the way to present oneself in another's home."

"What have you done with my sister? Where is she?"

The Archgoblin slowly spread his hands in a gesture of apology. "My dear boy, I don't know."

Adam pressed the sword just a little more. "Take me to her," he ordered.

Beads of sweat appeared on the Archgoblin's brow; he spoke very quickly, "The sword isn't necessary. It's not a civil way to converse at all!"

Adam was losing patience. "Tell that to Emily's guards!" he snapped. "Now, lead the way."

"I'm afraid I can't," the Archgoblin said slowly. "You see, I don't know where she is." The sword point pricked into his flabby throat. "Please, believe me, I don't!" he squealed.

Adam looked into the Archgoblin's eyes, but they were too small and crafty to be believed.

"Dear boy, lower your sword, I'll tell you everything you wish to know."

"You'll tell me anyway because if you don't, I won't bother much about your miserable life," Adam said in a hard voice, meaning the threat because, apart from the Hag, he had never disliked anyone so much as he loathed the Archgoblin.

Adam's eyes were only too believable, so the Archgoblin came out with a torrent of words. "It's true! I had her arrested. But it was her fault. She didn't keep her promise, you see."

Sweat poured down the domed brow. He could see that the miserable boy was serious. "We had a clear agreement. I kept my side of the bargain, but she didn't keep hers...That brooch was *mine* by rights...but she called it her '*masterpiece*' and hid it from me." He fished in his pocket for a handkerchief and, raising it around the sword with difficulty, mopped his brow. His voice rose in resentment. "*Ungrateful!*" he spat out the word. "Ungrateful and deceitful..." Then he remembered who he was talking to and, taking a calmer tone, added, "I mean, dear boy, one should always honour one's word, shouldn't one?"

Adam lowered his sword, half-convinced. He

let the point rest on the Archgoblin's ample stomach. "Why should I believe you?"

"If you will permit it, dear boy, I'll show you why."

Adam nodded and stood aside. The Archgoblin took a key out of his waistcoat pocket. Going over to a large cabinet, he unlocked its heavy, wooden door. He lifted three trays, one by one, onto the table. Each velvet-covered tray contained five brooches. The jewelled dragonfly wings caught the candlelight and dazzled with the fifteen fairy crowns twinkling gaily.

"There!" The Archgoblin pointed. "That's why you must believe me. Only a fool would harm the person capable of making jewels of such...such exquisite beauty. I only wanted to scare her, to make her keep to our bargain." His voice rose again, "Her masterpiece is *mine!* It's mine by rights." His voice broke, turning into sobs of frustration and rage. "And now she's gone —vanished!" he choked the words out.

"Vanished? What do you mean?"

"I don't *know!*" the Archgoblin shouted. "Six dead guards and an empty cell. Nobody knows what happened to your sister or her masterpiece. Earlier this morning, she *disappeared!* And I don't know where she hid her masterpiece!" he wailed. "I've had her house turned upside down, but to no avail."

Adam put his sword back in its sheath; it was clear that the Archgoblin was telling the truth.

"Ay, they've disappeared," the Archgoblin repeated spitefully, leering into the boy's face.

"In any case, I'll find her," Adam said, "and lucky for you, I believe you!"

He turned on his heel and marched out of the Archgoblin's palace, hoping never to see that grotesque creature again. Maybe word had spread about his skill with a sword because nobody tried to stop him. He mounted Blitz and told the horse that there was no hurry. He hoped that the stallion had understood because he didn't want to repeat his earlier experience.

Blitz understood. Guards opened the golden gates, only too glad to see the back of the ferocious warrior. They rode slowly down the hill while he thought about his sister and the Citadel of Wealth. He also thought about Sapiens and how she would have preferred them not to enter that place because accruing wealth caused many problems.

# V

## THE THEATRE OF PRIDE

## 2 2

---

$\mathcal{A}$dam was mid-sentence when his gaze, passing over Palustric's shoulder, met a stranger's eye. The eye was pale grey and belonged to an old man seated in the corner of the quiet inn. He was entirely grey—hair, beard, hooded cloak and clothes. Maybe that was why Adam hadn't noticed him before, but it was clear that the Stranger was listening as the boy told of his adventure in the Citadel. His stare never wavered as Adam met his eye; instead, he stood up and crossed to their table, where he sat down without a word.

The old man slowly drew back his hood and smiled at Adam. The boy studied the long, thin, wrinkled face and had the feeling that he already knew him. But it wasn't the Stranger that he knew; rather, he recognised the feeling. The Stranger seemed old, *as old as the hills* or the plain.

Without asking, the Stranger reached across, helping himself to their bread and cheese. He tore hungrily at a chunk of bread, saying indistinctly, "Please forgive my forwardness, but I have travelled so far." They had difficulty understanding his words, spoken with a full mouth. Adam leant back in his chair, studying their uninvited guest while the log-fire pleasantly warmed his back. He marvelled at the cleverness in the grey eyes; nothing was hidden from those eyes, he thought.

Before the Stranger bit off a large piece of cheese, he mentioned, "My name is Deductio," and went on munching. Lar looked startled while Palustric gasped: *"The Wizard of Reason."* So that was why he seemed familiar; Adam understood now: that was how he had felt in Sapiens's presence before ever entering the Citadel.

"This cheese is delicious," Deductio said, sitting back. He looked at each of them with those steady grey eyes, then placed his hands wide on the table. "Dear friends," he said indistinctly with a bulging mouth, "the world is in danger."

Adam wasn't sure he had heard correctly,

but the wizard went on, "The hobgoblin, *Pride*, has taken Emily to himself; he wants to use her to arrive at you. *Pride* is the evillest of the hobgoblins—if not stopped, his dark forces will crush us all, like flowers in a mailed fist." Deductio brought his fist down with a crash on the table to better make his point. He studied Adam's face with sad eyes, kind but troubled.

The three shocked friends waited for him to continue, but the wizard calmly helped himself to another piece of cheese. "This is heavenly." He waved it appreciatively before it disappeared into his mouth. He munched away in silence. Lar tilted his head and raised an eyebrow at Palustric, who shrugged at him, confused. Adam was struggling to understand anything. After a while, he said, "But why does this person, *Pride,* want to reach us?"

The wizard frowned and swallowed his cheese. "*Pride* has learned about the Key of Ingenuity." Deductio smiled thinly at Palustric stiffening in his chair. He addressed the dwarf directly. "He knows that your people have built an impenetrable fortress to house the Key. *Pride* is blind, but his eyes are everywhere. He is well-informed; thus, he knows that the Key is just as unattainable as it was when with Lentor. How-

ever, there is one difference, one important difference—"

They waited, but Deductio remained silent
as before.

"We're the difference, aren't we?" Adam said
suddenly.

Deductio nodded. "You reason well, my
boy." He placed a hand on Adam's arm. "Only
reason can save us all now—" He broke off as the
inn door opened and watched through narrowed
eyes as a goblin entered. He waited until the
goblin had gone to the bar, then continued in a
lower voice, "That is why the *Council of Wizards*
has sent me to warn and advise you. *Pride* knows
that the only way he can gain the Key is to draw
you to himself to take possession of your souls.
*Pride* is an expert in corruption; he has countless
misguided souls in his power. Once in his grasp,
he will use you to arrive at the Key, and the re-
sult for the world—for us all—will be unthinkable." The wizard sat back in his chair again.
"Act quickly! Return to the Citadel!"

"Oh no," Adam groaned, "that's the last
place I want to go."

"My boy," Deductio said gently, "where
would you expect to find *Pride* if not in the
Citadel of Wealth? There you will find the *Theatre of Pride*."

"The Theatre?"

"Ay." Deductio tore off another piece of bread and munched thoughtfully while the three companions studied his face impatiently. "It is a Theatre of Illusion," he said in a muffled voice. "You should know that *Pride* has a seven-fold nature. Each aspect of his nature is deadly and on its own is enough to corrode any man's soul. Alone in *Pride* are the seven united. That's why, as I said earlier, he is the evillest. The door of his Theatre is open to everyone. Admittance is free, but the final cost is incalculable." Deductio's eyes glittered fiercely, and he went on, "*Pride* uses his Theatre to draw souls to himself, you see. By nature, he is too proud to present himself. Others must go to him. Emily is an exception; she was taken to him by force and is lost inside the Theatre. Even if Emily's soul was already open to *Pride*; find her and bring her out. The risk is greater than you can possibly imagine, my friends—" he looked around the anxious little group, "not only for your souls, but I repeat, for us all, myself included."

The old grey wizard's eyes stared into Adam's. They seemed to penetrate the soul he had just been talking about. Adam shuddered. A long silence followed. Each of the four was lost in his gloomy thoughts.

"Have you any idea what a hobgoblin could do with the Key!" Palustric burst out.

Deductio's eyes bored deeper into Adam's.

"He's not just *any* hobgoblin; there would be no limit to his evil inventions," Palustric added, half to himself.

"Then, I have no choice," Adam said slowly. "In any case, Emily is in danger. I have to save my sister. I must go to the Theatre alone."

"Not without me!" Palustric objected.

"This is my affair," Adam refused to discuss the matter and half-rose.

Palustric grabbed his sleeve. "You can't stop me coming!" he said, red in the face.

Deductio tapped on the table impatiently. "Neither of you is using a grain of reason," he said disapprovingly, looking at the silent pixy, who grinned at him.

*"Knowledge and reason speak; ignorance and wrong shout,* is it not so, wise wizard?"

"Exactly!" Deductio rapped on the table with his knuckles and stared at Adam again, who sat down again slowly. "Without our little friend, your mission will fail." The wizard smiled at the pixy. "Now you can put all your sayings to a greater purpose, Lar. Use them to unmask each of the seven natures of *Pride*. The only way to make him ineffective is to tear away his disguise; without it he cannot convince—"

"Why can't you come with us, Deductio, wouldn't it be simpler and safer?" Adam interrupted.

"Impossible," the wizard said. "*Pride* does not open his door to Reason. Nay, my friend, sadly, without me, you must risk more than death: your very souls. I can only advise you of the danger and how to proceed."

Adam nodded. The grey wizard went on: "Once inside the Theatre, you will find seven closed doors. Choose one and enter. The Theatre is all illusion, and *Pride* will present one of his natures to you. Unmask him because *Pride* cannot bear to be exposed for what he is. Exposure weakens him, and total exposure will weaken him severely, perhaps enough to nullify him for a long time. On the other hand, if you cannot see through his disguise, he will slowly possess you with that aspect of his nature, then we are lost, all of us. You must not fail! Once you realise his true nature, our little friend here will know what to say to wound him most effectively."

Lar nodded solemnly, pleased to be of such importance.

"If you have not erred and you are lucky, you

will find Emily in that room. Her soul is possessed by one of the natures of *Pride*. As yet, we do not know which, even if I suspect. The fact remains that she will be a slave to that vice until you unmask it before her eyes, then you can escape and—well, that comes later." Deductio paused and wrinkled his brow. "I feel sure that *Pride* will hold back that part of his nature which has taken Emily until last. In that way, dear friends," Deductio shook his head sadly, "I fear you will have to face an awesome seven-fold task. May Reason be on your side!"

The wizard took each of them by the hand in turn. Adam felt a tremor pass through him in that instant. Could it be that he was thinking with a clearer head, or was it just a momentary impression? Deductio didn't shake hands but held each one firm while looking its owner straight in the eye. The wizard held the pixy's hands longer than the rest.

When he let go, Adam stood up. "We might as well start at once."

"No!" the wizard cried, surprisingly. "The Archgoblin has given orders for your capture should you re-enter the Citadel. Where, no doubt, Pride would subject you to an ordeal to weaken you mentally before having you taken to his accursed Theatre. They have strengthened the guard, so you must be very careful."

"But the Theatre is in the Citadel. How can I get there?" Adam looked at Deductio.

The grey wizard stood up. "My friend, my task is complete for the moment. Lose no time, neither throw yourself heedlessly into danger. I know that in the end, reason solves every problem. So, it is reason that you must use. Farewell!" He pulled his hood close to his face. He called the goblin landlord and recommended him not to tell anyone of his visit. Then he slipped out of the inn.

# 23

The morning passed without inspiration. The three friends ate lunch in dismal silence, which contrasted with their heated arguments before the meal. The Citadel boasted massive stone walls, a drawbridge and many armed guards at the gate. There didn't seem to be any way in; after all, in a Citadel of goblins, a boy, a pixy and a dwarf would stand out, even in disguise. The afternoon was passing in the same way as the morning when Adam, who was sitting with his head in his hands by the fire, leapt up with a cry.

"Let's go!" and was out of the door before Lar or Palustric had time to say a word. They chased after him towards the centre of the village. By the time they caught up with their long-legged friend, they didn't have the breath to ask questions. In any case, they recognised the small, dark house with solid stone walls and clean, little window which Adam entered. Lar and Palustric followed him inside, where the wizened goblin sat in his usual place by the hearth, just as they had left him weeks before.

"I told you it'd bring you no good, *heh, heh!*" The withered goblin shook his white-tufted head at Adam's tale. "Bad gold that! But if you want to get into that place again, you've come to the right goblin! *Heh, heh, heh!*" He chuckled like a child.

He raised his thin arm, causing his blanket to fall aside as he pointed to the corner of the room. "In the chest," he said. "Go on, go on, open it! What're ye waiting for? There's a plan, but be careful! It's fragile. My great grandfather drew it, you know. He won the Forty-first Archgoblin's Public Competition to design the Citadel! *Heh, heh!* Very clever, he was, you know, *heh, heh!*"

It was already evening by the time Adam had finished studying the map. He made some notes on a sheet of paper and, after thanking the old goblin and warning him not to tell anyone of their visit, returned with his companions to the inn.

They waited for nightfall, and Adam

breathed a word of thanks for the clouds above as they set off under a particularly dark sky. Before long, they came to the moat which circled the Citadel. They crept along, doubled up, making themselves as small as possible (which was easy for Lar).

Adam peered into the gloom of the opposite bank. "It must be here somewhere," he repeated to himself. He grumbled about the high reeds at the water's edge but, at a certain point, he indicated a small opening, like a dark stain, under the wall on the other side. "Here it is!" he breathed excitedly. "It's a culvert, a part of the drainage system," Adam said. "We've to swim across to it and squeeze through, it'll take us under the walls and into the Citadel."

"Master!" Lar whispered urgently, tugging at Adam's sleeve.

"What's up, Lar?"

"I can't swim!"

"Can you swim, Palustric?" Adam asked anxiously because he hadn't thought of this important detail in his planning.

"Ay, that I can!"

Adam breathed a sigh of relief. He lowered himself into the water of the moat and gasped at its iciness. Good job the moat wasn't wide, he thought.

"Hurry up, Lar, climb on my back," he ordered. The pixy was afraid but tried not to show it and obeyed his master. They were soon across to where Adam helped Lar into the black hole, before squeezing in after him. They heard the scuffling of tiny feet running away through the concrete tube, which was slimy and stank, but they were through in no time, with Palustric on their heels. The rusted hinges of an old iron grating at the far end surrendered at once to their combined forces.

Before long, they stood dripping and shivering in a dark corner of a back street in the Citadel. Their wet clothes clung to their bodies. "Let's go!" Adam said. "Before we freeze to death here."

Twice, the cobbles rang under the boots of the goblin night-watch; so, they slipped into an alleyway where the darkness kept them hidden from the goblin lanterns. Adam had pored over the plan of the Citadel so that he didn't once lose his way in the maze of narrow streets. Only when he arrived at the large portal which he expected to be the Theatre did he have a doubt. He saw no posters or lettering there. At the very least, he had expected a sign over the door because theatres always have signs of some kind there. He was about to say as much to Lar when clouds of different colour began to swirl in the glass of the main door until they formed into letters and then into words:

## THE MOST MAGNIFICENT THEATRE
## ADMISSION FREE
## AT ANY TIME OF DAY OR NIGHT

The three companions gazed in astonishment at the lettered pane, then Adam looked at Lar, who was trembling. Adam wasn't sure whether from cold or fear, but it helped him to decide. He pushed the door open and led his friends into a sumptuous entrance hall. Red and gold velvet covered the semi-circular wall that contained a series of doors.

"Seven doors!" Palustric exclaimed.

"Look!" Lar pointed to one of the doors where golden letters flashed out the words:

## 'WELCOME. PLEASE ENTER'

"There was no writing a minute ago," Lar said, his squeaky voice even squeakier with fear.

Palustric looked sternly at his friend. "There's no use being afraid. We've got to defend our souls, save—"

"Hush!" Adam warned him. "*Pride* will be

listening. This is the Theatre of Illusion, I'm sure he can hear every word. I don't want him to have an advantage. He mustn't know who we met this morning." He raised his voice, *"You would like to know, wouldn't you?"*

There was a moment's silence, then the walls began to ring with horrible laughter. There was something chilling and malign in the sound, so Lar gripped Palustric's arm, but the dwarf shook him off angrily as the hideous noise died away in its echo.

"So, I was right," Adam said in a shocked whisper. "We must be careful with our words."

Palustric's face was dark with suppressed rage. He hadn't appreciated the mocking laughter; indeed, he was quite willing to give his own life to save the dwarves' beloved Key.

"Come on, Adam," he growled and strode towards the door with the golden letters.

"No, Palustric!" Lar squeaked. "Not that door! Don't you see, that's where *he* wants us to go."

Palustric halted. "Which then?" and as he spoke, the letters flitted derisively from one door to another.

"You choose, Palustric," Adam said quietly because he could see that his friend was almost beside himself with rage.

"This one." Palustric kicked open the door and was inside so quickly that it forced the other two to dash after him. They crashed into his back because the dwarf had stopped, astonished, in his tracks.

They were inside a cave: a Dwarfish cave such as from the *Old Days*. The smooth, white floor cupped them like the palm of a hand, whose fingers rose about them in alabaster stalagmites. The cave roof domed over them, and its stalactite fingers seemed ready to come alive to pick one of them up. The three friends looked around in wonder since each stalagmite and stalactite ended in a carving, where a dwarf's head was worked in the alabaster, its white face always with the same smug smile.

Lanterns spluttered smokily on the walls while the weak light cast from their flames caused bright yellow gemstones and veins of precious ores to glitter and sparkle in the rock. They formed a recurring pattern around the cave wall. When Adam looked carefully, he noticed that they formed letters—a word—which, at different angles and heights, repeatedly spelt the word F-L-A-U-N-T-R-I-C. Armour stood under every lantern, each with fine jewelled weapons. The three friends went over to inspect the workmanship.

"Magnificent," Palustric's voice was full of respect.

Adam drew the sword, at once noticing the incised letters along the blade. He read the scrolled writing with difficulty - F-L-A-U-N-T-R-I-C. Adam's eye passed to the pommel where the same carved face of the stalagmites smiled smugly up at him. Slightly irritated, Adam thrust the sword back in its sheath and went to check the others, which sure enough were all the same. In some places, tapestries and banners draped the walls and, of course, stitched into the design in various colours was the image of the same smug dwarf and the same scrolled name.

Palustric felt the quality of the cloth, and his eyes lit up with admiration at the craftsmanship. He knew that only dwarves, indeed, only dwarves from the *Old Days* were capable of such perfect creation. He, too, was a dwarf, and at moments like this, he was proud to be so. His chest swelled as he repeatedly muttered, "Magnificent, truly magnificent!"

Adam read the same name for the hundredth time and burst out, "But who *is* this Flauntric?"

"I!" boomed a voice.

The three friends spun round.

"He wasn't there before!" Lar squeaked.

The flickering flames lit the smug face of a

dwarf who made an exaggerated bow; he straightened up, so the friends got a good look at him, shifting their gaze from his face to the nearest sculpted stalagmite. The face and smile were identical.

"Welcome to Flauntric's cave," the dwarf boomed.

"It-it's magnificent!" Palustric enthused and offered his hand to the stranger, adding, "I'm a dwarf too."

"So, I see, my friend!"

"But is this all your work?" Palustric waved a hand.

"Of course."

"But-but...it's magnificent!"

"It is, isn't it?"

"Only a *dwarf* could craft such wonders! I wish I were as skilled as you, Flauntric." Palustric's eyes shone with a strange new glow.

"Ay, but you aren't," the dwarf smiled even more smugly. "There's only *one* Flauntric. I'm unique, you see. Now if you like..." the creature studied Palustric's eager face, "I might consider taking you on as my apprentice—"

Palustric's heart beat furiously, and his eyes widened. Gladly, he was about to accept this offer when Lar stepped forward.

The pixy stared up into Flauntric's smug,

bearded face: *"The lowest chimneys make the most smoke,* is it not so, dwarf?" he said as fiercely as his squeaky pixy voice would allow.

Flauntric looked as if he'd been slapped hard across the face and faded away before their eyes, along with all his cave and trappings. They found themselves once more in a simple, empty room of the theatre.

Adam, delighted, squeezed his friend's bony shoulder, and they both looked at Palustric. The dwarf's eyes had lost their fanatical glow; indeed, he seemed to be waking from a deep sleep.

"Where are we, what's happened?"

"You were about to be taken by Pride, Palustric," Adam said gently. "Luckily, Lar saw through him."

"His real name isn't Flauntric at all," Lar said. "That was *Ostentation*, Master, one of the vices of *Pride*."

Adam laughed and patted Palustric on the back. "You wanted to be ostentatious, too, Palustric! Better watch out in future!"

Palustric looked confused and scowled. He wasn't sure whether Adam was serious or not. He felt as if he'd been sleepwalking and, what's more, he was oversensitive to criticism.

"In any case," Adam added, "Emily isn't guilty of ostentation because she isn't in this room. And we've survived the first test. Just six to go, but we're going to have to keep our wits about us, and above all, we have to use reason, just like our friend *who can't be named* said. Let's go!" and he led them back into the red and gold, half-moon entrance hall to try another door.

Palustric was the first to notice. "Look," he counted the doors aloud: "one-two-three-four-five-six! There are only six doors now, we've got rid of one of them!"

# 2 4

"And we'll get rid of all the others, too," Lar said half under his breath, but in a very determined, if squeaky, tone.

"Yes, well, we'll have to be on our guard," Adam warned. "See how easy it is for *Pride* to take hold of one of us."

They looked doubtfully from one door to another. Once more, the gold letters flashed:

WELCOME. PLEASE ENTER

on one of the doors.

"Not that one then," Palustric growled.

"Yes, *that* one!" Adam said. "*Pride* is bluffing."

They opened the door and slipped inside, at once finding themselves deep in a beechwood. Orange and russet leaves that crackled under their feet littered the ground. As Adam spoke, a startled jay flew off calling *skaaak, skaaak* in alarm between the trunks which reached up tall towards the almost completely hidden sky. "Strange, you wouldn't expect to find *Pride* in a place like this," Adam said. They walked over a carpet of crackling leaves, which with the occasional snapping twig, were the only sounds to break the woodland silence. Lar stiffened.

"A horse, Master," he said, head cocked with a pointed ear turned to where Adam was staring at the empty wood.

"Are you sure, Lar?" Palustric asked.

"Dwarves are hard of hearing, Master!"

Palustric snorted.

"I can't hear anything, either, Lar," Adam strained his ears. They moved on, trying to be light-footed (difficult for Palustric). As usual, Adam's eyes served him better than his ears as glimpsed the rider through the trees in the distance.

Before long, the horseman reined in just ahead of them. He was a human figure with a lordly air, finely dressed in a quilted jacket, richly worked with gold thread. A broad leather strap bound his left wrist, protecting it from the talons of a hooded hawk perched there. With his other hand, the rider flicked his blue cloak away from the sword which hung at his side. He tossed back his blond hair, his black eyes boring into them down his straight nose.

The travellers searched in vain for any kindness there, finding only harshness and unfriendliness.

His white stallion stamped the ground restlessly with a hoof as its rider snapped: "How dare you cross my land, villeins?"

The three friends stared at him in shocked silence.

"Idiots! Have you lost your tongues? Or are you so stupid you can't string two words together?" he sneered.

His rudeness was too much for Adam, who stood up straight and put his hand to his sword-hilt. "Not at all!" he said boldly. "We aren't villeins or idiots, and we're not simple either. But one thing we are, which you *aren't*, is good-mannered!"

"Ha!" the rider's black eyes flashed. "I shall take great pleasure in having your tongue torn from your peasant's mouth before I watch you hang! Worm! Nobody insults Lord Hubris and lives!"

"And nobody speaks to Lord Adam in that way..."

"Ha!" The rider's lip curled, he laughed scornfully. "Now, I see I am wasting my time with a half-wit." He took his hand from his sword and gathered his reins. "On your way, poor crazed vermin!"

"Come on, Adam." Palustric anxiously took his friend's arm, but Adam shook him off angrily.

"Leave it be, Master!" Lar squeaked urgently. "We should go!"

"No!" Adam drew his sword, his eyes flashed. "Lord Adam is going to teach Lord Hubris a lesson—"

"Ha! *Lord* Adam," the other sneered, "but what a fine *lord*, dressed in rags and *on foot!*"

"I have a horse."

"Oh, ay?"

"Blitz!" Adam called as Lar and Palustric gaped in astonishment, which was nothing compared to their amazement when the black stallion galloped into the clearing and halted in a swirl of leaves. Adam climbed lightly into his saddle and turned Blitz to face Lord Hubris, who was commanding Palustric to hold his hawk.

Lar looked dismayed as Lord Hubris drew

his sword. He realised he would have to intervene quickly; otherwise, his master's soul would be lost. The little pixy bravely threw himself between the two horses and, pointing at Lord Hubris, at the top of his squeaky voice, yelled, *"The less noble the heart, the higher the head,* is it not so, my lord?"

Lord Hubris's eyes closed, and a frown creased his noble brow; the last they saw of his horse and he was his curled, mocking mouth trying to make a reply before it, too, faded away.

Adam was sitting on the floor of a bare room, looking stunned. Of course, Blitz wasn't there any longer because, in reality, he'd never been with them: just another part of the illusion.

"W-what happened?" Adam asked, looking around in confusion.

"You were haughtier than Lord Hubris himself, Adam," Palustric told his friend.

"Who?"

"Master, *Pride* sent *Haughtiness* to you. It's his most terrible vice, ay, haughtiness almost took your soul. I'm afraid I was a little slow to recognise him."

Adam scratched his head. "Well, I don't remember any of that, in any case," he said proudly. "I don't think I'm—" He stopped himself. "Oh dear," he smiled ruefully, "now I see!" He smiled sheepishly.

Palustric slapped his friend on the back. "I like you like this, Adam. I didn't recognise you in the woods! Come on, let's risk another door!"

## 25

They moved through the hall without even stopping to notice that there were only five doors, but rushed straight in through another, into a very small room where a dwarf was painting at an easel. He put his brush down as they came in and wiped his hands. His thick black beard and bushy eyebrows, his hair which stuck out in all directions, all made him look crazy.

"Good day! Good day! What brings you to Bragtric's Studio? Of course, I know!" He smiled slyly. "After all, my reputation is worldwide. I'll bet you've travelled a long way to see me, am I right? Yes, of course, I am! This portrait is my latest masterpiece. What a portrait! Come a little closer, look! Admire the superfine technique. Magnificent, don't you think? Nobody in the universe can match my command of colour and perfection of line. Wouldn't you almost think he was breathing? He's so lifelike, isn't he? Naturally, it all depends on preparation, even if a talent like mine is inborn." Bragtric took a deep breath and moved to a stool behind the easel, where he sat down and began again: "You see, only a truly-deep knowledge of art, I mean, a total understanding—an absolute mastery of method—allows one to become *the greatest living artist* in the world. Unfortunately, many artists are so scarce in preparation. I, for example, know the name of every colour that exists. There are 7,542 colours in the world. One hundred fifty-eight are hues of red: there are scarlet, burgundy, vermilion, poppy, cochineal..." his voice droned on and on, as Lar and Adam politely followed the artist's lesson in red.

Palustric, meanwhile, moved stealthily to the easel, where picking up a brush, he added a perfectly detailed teardrop to the portrait's eye. Then he made his way silently back to Lar's side.

Bragtric was just finishing reds: "...magenta, that's 157 and CRIMSON makes 158!" He stood up. "Now, if you look closely at the portrait, how many reds can you see?" He crossed over. "Go on! Guess! I'll bet you'll come up with a ridiculous number. Only a real artist, a true master of his craft, would be able to discern reality from art. There are so many subtleties in it – that's why it's called *art*, you see, it's *art*ful!"

He glanced at the portrait and brushed away the *teardrop* from the subject's eye. But of course, he smeared the wet paint over its nose. His jaw dropped while the three friends burst out laughing.

Bragtric's face turned red with anger. "Steady on, Bragtric," Adam chuckled. "You'll create the 159$^{th}$ shade of red like that!"

Tears of mirth ran down Palustric's cheeks while Lar stepped forward: *"The man who is full of himself is empty of all else,* is it not so, foolish dwarf?"

Bragtric was just crossing the boundary between red with rage and purple with fury when he disappeared and the friends found themselves laughing in an empty room.

"Ah!" sighed Adam, "Emily wasn't victim of that vice, either."

"None of us got caught by it," Palustric said triumphantly, "but which vice was it? Boastfulness?"

"Ay," Lar nodded, "it was *Conceit*."

"But how did you manage to paint such a

perfect teardrop, Palustric? I didn't know you were an artist!" Adam said.

Palustric puffed up his chest and was about to say something, but then he stopped and looked ashamed, his chest lowered noticeably. "Oh dear," he said, "I was about to say something worthy of Bragtric! I'll bet *Pride* would have snaffled my soul if I'd said it! I'm not such a good artist, Adam, you know!"

The three friends laughed together, and then Adam added thoughtfully, "I'm not sure I would recognise these vices without you, Lar. Keep your head clear; otherwise, we'll become enslaved by one of them."

## 26

"Let's take the first one," Adam said wearily. "In any case, we can't hope to find Emily until we've got rid of another three."

As they opened the door, a bell tinkled since they were inside a hat shop. The walls were lined with shelves piled with hats of every colour, shape and style. Lar's slightly squinting, yellow eyes shone at the sight of so much leather and felt headwear.

A small figure emerged from a back room and stood smiling behind a low counter. He was a shaggy, brown-skinned person, dressed all in brown, too. Adam noticed with surprise that the little wrinkled person's hands had no fingers, as this was the first time that he had been close to a brownie.

"Hello," the brownie said in a very friendly voice. "Allow me to show you some hats. They're all of the finest quality, I assure you."

Those peculiar hands nimbly took a hat from a shelf and put it on.

"There, how do I look?" he asked, eyeing them expectantly. Since none of them answered, he picked up a mirror with a handle from the counter and studied himself, turning his head this way and that, adjusting the leather hat over his pointed ears, patting it better into place. "Mm! Perhaps it's not quite *me* – is that it?" His brown, slatted eyes moved anxiously from face to face. "I know!" He snatched off the hat and exchanged it for another flatter type. "There, how about this? What's it like in profile?" He turned his head.

"It quite suits you," Lar said uncertainly.

"I'm sure they all suit me well," the brownie said touchily. "Look, this one is rather comely!" The little brownie pulled a wide-brimmed, floppy hat over his head, adjusting it carefully. Adam smiled as the little shopkeeper pulled his pointed ears through the holes in the brim at either side, specially created for the purpose. The brownie looked apprehensively at the boy.

"Why are you smiling, doesn't it flatter me?" He rushed over to a full-length mirror and studied himself from various angles. "Oh, dear!" For the next five minutes, he kept changing hats and posing.

Adam and Palustric were so absorbed by the brownie's performance that they hadn't noticed Lar trying on several hats behind them. When the brownie looked in the pixy's direction and said: "Oh, ay, *that* one suits you, or my name isn't Fopp!" Adam and Palustric realised from Lar's sparkling eyes and strange posturing that he was steadily being drawn by *Pride*. Pixies wear hats all the time. Come to think of it, Adam had never seen Lar without his little brown skullcap.

The dwarf and the boy stared at each other. The same worrying thought struck them at the same instant. *Pride* was tempting Lar, the very person who had thwarted him up to now.

Adam thought quickly as the brownie came with a hand-mirror from behind the counter towards his victim. Then he smiled; of course, he knew which aspect of *Pride's* character this was! It wasn't that difficult; only, they had been distracted. The problem was he needed a saying when he didn't have many to draw on. But then he remembered what his father always told him: "Excuse me, Fopp," he said quietly, "but, you know, as my father often says, 'The peacock forgets how well the sparrow can fly.'"

The brownie's slatted eyes glared at Adam with so much hatred that the boy shivered, but then, to his great satisfaction, Fopp disappeared and the walls were bare. Lar stood hatless looking puzzled at his cap at his feet.

"Put your cap on, little fellow," Palustric boomed. "It makes you look less ugly!" and the dwarf, who wasn't likely to win (even) a goblin beauty contest, burst out laughing.

"Don't take any notice of him," Adam nodded towards Palustric. "It's just that *Vanity* was getting the better of you, Lar. I didn't know you were so vain. Watch out in the next room, because it was pure luck that this was an easy vice for me to recognise this time. And I've used up about a third of all the wise sayings I know!"

"It's certain *Pride's* holding Emily back till last," Palustric said gloomily. "It probably doesn't matter which door we choose. We'll have to outwit him twice more before we get to your sister, Adam."

"In that case, that's what we'll do," Adam growled.

# 27

The next door led straight to a bridge which spanned a deep narrow chasm. The three friends stepped fearfully onto the dizzy-making bridge.

"Back off the bridge!" a rough voice commanded.

"He wasn't there a moment ago," Lar squeaked, his voice quavering.

A stocky, muscular figure, holding an ash staff in his hands, blocked their way. The man was dressed in ragged clothes, but it was his eyes which disturbed the three companions. They were small, but the menace and hatred there burnt like coals.

"Back off, I said!"

"But we want to cross the bridge," Adam said. *It's like Robin Hood and Little John,* Adam thought, *except it's not a shallow stream, it's an abyss!* He trembled at the thought of the fall that would follow being pushed off the bridge.

"Well, you can't," the swarthy man sneered, "not unless you pay for the privilege."

"Why, is it your bridge?"

"No, but it's my staff!" the ruffian mocked. "Let's see, I'll have the small fellow's hat and the dwarf's jerkin." He pointed the heavy, wooden weapon at Adam's belt. "And that horn'll do nicely. Come on, lay them all at my feet."

"What's your name?" Adam asked suddenly.

"The name's Strutt. And don't you forget it because he's the fellow who'll have taken your horn. An' that information'll cost you your sword too, my fine fellow. Now get on with it!"

"My name's Adam the *Dragonteaser*," Adam said proudly. "It's written on the horn, which is staying right where it is. I think, rather, that you can lay your staff at my feet." He drew his sword and stepped on the bridge.

"No, Master," Lar whispered urgently, "come back off the bridge!" He tugged at Adam's belt. "Palustric, help me!" They tugged together, in vain, for Adam broke free and leapt toward Strutt.

Backwards and forward they parried and thrust with staff and sword. Adam took a ferocious blow to the shoulder and staggered. Strutt seized his opportunity and smote the boy a stunning blow to the side of the head. Adam's senses reeled and he tottered into the ropes making up the side of the bridge. With a mocking crow-like laugh, Strutt stuck his staff under Adam's armpit and heaved him off the bridge into the void. Palustric rushed to the edge of the bridge and watched aghast as his friend tumbled over and over to his doom.

The ruffian turned to face them and asked for the next to challenge him. Lar darted forward without hesitation and without stepping onto the bridge. *"The crushed flower still keeps its scent! Is it not so, vile one?"*

Immediately, the bridge vanished in a puff and shocked, Strutt plunged with a cry into the chasm, but as he fell, he, too, disappeared along with the chasm and all that surrounded him, while Adam landed with a thump at Lar's feet on a level floor in an empty room.

"Are you all right, Master?" Lar peered at the boy anxiously.

Adam felt his head first with a puzzled look and then touched his shoulder. "Strange," he said slowly, "they don't hurt at all, but at the time I was half-dead."

"Because, Master, 'twas all an illusion. You wouldn't have died, but you would have lost your soul to *Pride* – quite uselessly, I may add."

Adam still had an angry look on his face as if he were spoiling for a fight. Palustric turned towards Lar. "What was all that about flowers, Lar? And who was that Strutt fellow?"

"Verily," Lar's yellow eyes studied the dwarf, "dwarves are fine craftsmen, but don't know much about the nature of anything!" The pixy grinned, happy to get even with his friend.

"Which vice was I about to get drawn into, Lar?" Adam asked contritely.

"That which takes the rights of others, Master—*Arrogance.*"

"I hate this place," Adam said in a low voice. "It brings out the worst in my character. I never thought I was the arrogant type, but it just goes to show how weaknesses come out when you're stressed. The more I have to do with *Pride,* the more I know that Deductio wasn't exaggerating. Thank you, Lar, that was too close for comfort. You saved me from the clutches of *Pride.* Well, well, *me* arrogant!" He hung his head and Lar's tiny hand took his and squeezed it.

"Pick up your sword, Master, I fear you may

still need it, but I beg you, Master," and his yellow eyes were imploring and at the same time full of friendship. "Only use it in the service of humility!"

Adam nodded, feeling truly humbled, picked up, sheathed his sword, and said, "On to the next room, men, and I pray that I do much better there!"

## 28

"Oh, dear," Palustric said to Lar, "Adam's head is in a state if he can't tell dwarves and pixies from men!"

They returned to the hall where the sight of two doors left heartened them, but Adam wasn't deluded. After failing miserably in the last room, he didn't doubt that their adversary had something far worse in store for them. He knew that it was all illusion and that his physical well-being wasn't at risk, but worse, far worse, would be to lose one's soul and be taken once and for all by *Pride*. He hesitated before the two remaining doors, and it seemed to him that the room had a life of its own: that the room itself was sneering at them. Adam fought back his angry reaction and swallowed his pride – *humility* – he told himself, so he turned to Lar, saying in a humbled voice, "You choose, Lar, please."

The yellow eyes looked at him, and Lar's head tilted to one side, but the pixy pointed to a door and they entered with a smile as Palustric repeated: "He can't tell pixies from dwarves!" with a deep rumbling chuckle; he found it very amusing.

Their smiles grew broader as they stepped into beautiful mountain scenery. The only sign of life was a goat that bleated and sprang away up the mountainside, alarmed by their voices. Bright sunlight bathed the magnificent land-scape and picked out the tiny wildflowers that sparkled like gems among the rocks. Breathing the pure mountain air sent a feeling of well-being through their bodies as they sat on some flat rocks to admire the snow-capped peaks all around them. The clear blue sky and the splashing of a waterfall nearby completed the delightfulness of their surroundings.

Adam lay back with his hands behind his head and soaked in the warm sun. He sighed contentedly; such was the power of the illusion. He forgot the danger they were in as his body began to relax. Lar examined a small, yellow flower near Adam's feet and Palustric took a deep breath and let out: *A-YO-DIDDLEY-AY-OH-DEE!* causing Adam to leap up, spin around and stare at his friend. Before the boy could say anything: *A-YO-DIDDLEY-AY-OH-DIDDLEY-DAY!* boomed and echoed around the mountains and valleys in Palustric's deep voice.

"What a voice, eh?" Palustric grinned. "You didn't know I had such a deep, mellow, baritone voice, eh?" *YO-DIDDLEY-OH-DOH-DID-DLEY-AY!* he boomed again. The noise was deafening, insupportable. Lar covered his ears in pain, while Adam stared at Palustric as if the dwarf had lost his wits.

"What do you think, then?"

"Very nice, Palustric," Adam said hurriedly, hoping to forestall another refrain.

"Nice?" Palustric repeated, looking rather hurt. "You mean *glorious*, surely?"

"Well—"

*DOH-DIDDLEY-DOH-DIDDLEY-DOH-DIDDLEY-AY!* boomed and echoed around them, drowning Adam's words.

Just as Adam copied Lar to protect his ears, another person jumped out from behind a rock. Dressed all in grey, with long, golden hair, her hands were not over her ears, but clapping enthusiastically.

"A mountain elf!" Lar shouted to make Adam hear over the dying echoes of Palustric's booms.

As welcome silence returned, the elfin maiden cried, "Bravo, bravo! What a superb voice!"

Palustric smiled at his two friends. "There you are, I told you," he said. "This young elf-*er*- excuse me, what's your name?"

The elf smiled and curtseyed. "Coy," she said.

"Well, Coy," Palustric smiled, "you certainly recognise talent when you hear it. You must be very musical yourself."

"There is a little music in my veins," she said in a lilting voice while the upland breeze ruffled her hair.

"Mm!" Palustric scratched his chin. "Perhaps you would care to join me in a duet?"

The elf smiled. "It would be wrong. I'm unworthy of such an honour. My poor voice is more fitted to a little cave than to mountain peaks."

"You are too modest, Coy; I'm sure you have a lovely voice, won't you change your mind?"

"Well, if you can put up with it, I would be proud to—"

Adam groaned and covered his ears just in time as they both began:

*YO-DIDDLEY-OH-AY-OOOOOOH!*

*HEE-OH-YEE-DOH-ee-OH-*

*EEEEOOOOH!* The elf's piercing voice joined in.

The first stones began to bounce down the mountain side, dislodging others. The din of voices and thumping rocks echoed and rumbled around them. Adam dragged Lar against the mountainside. "Avalanche!" he yelled. His ears were hurting him as he stared helplessly at Lar, whose face was a mask of panic. For the pixy, indeed, also for Adam, there was a grave risk of deafness, but Palustric was in mortal peril. Huge stones missed him by a miracle, yet he went on yodelling heedless of the danger.

A sharp stone pinged off a rock and flew at Adam's face. He put his hand out to protect his eyes; the stone sliced the back of his hand. "Ouch!" Adam yelled and *"Ouch, ouch, ouch!"* echoed all around them mingling with another piercing *HEE-OH-YEE-DOH-ee-OH-EEEEOOOOH!*

Adam stared down at his hand. It was dripping blood at an alarming rate and throbbing painfully.

"Do something, Lar!" he shouted, pressing

himself against the rock face as sharp pieces of rock showered down on them. "Do something, or Palustric is dead! And we'll soon join him."

"I cannot, Master," the pixy looked anguished.

"Why not?"

"Because I do not know which vice Coy represents."

Another giant boulder thundered down, hitting the ground in front of Adam and Lar, where it bounced and spun directly at Palustric and Coy. Adam closed his eyes, sickened, sure of his friend's terrible end. Lar opened his wider and watched the boulder pass over the two possessed singers by a hair's breadth. They carried on, oblivious of any danger.

*HOH-DODELY-HOY!*

*HAY-EEEH!*

"Please, Lar!" Adam begged.

"Ay," Lar nodded, "I must risk, Master."

The pixy ran up to the elf, Coy, tugged at her sleeve, crying, *"The donkey's bray does not reach the stars,* is it not so, fair deceiver?"

The elf cried out, clutched her throat, and disappeared before another boulder could fall.

They were back in the blessed silence of an empty room. Lar's hands were still over his ears, but Adam's ears that were ringing and humming a moment ago were perfectly all right while his hand, he was relieved to see, bore not the slightest scratch. It was all illusion in this Theatre, but frighteningly real while you were living it.

Adam removed Lar's hands from his ears. He could imagine how the poor pixy had suffered with his acute hearing. It must have been torture. "It's all right, Lar," he said to the shaken pixy. "It's over now!" and hugged him off his feet. "Well-done, Lar, well-done!" He put the pixy down gently, "How did you get it right?"

"Master, what gave me trouble is that I forgot this vice can also hide itself in the very good and lead them astray, too: 'twas *Vainglory*, Master. Palustric showed it by boasting about his gifts and Coy by being falsely modest."

Palustric looked at Adam with a sleepwalker's eyes.

"Promise me you won't sing, Palustric."

"Sing? Why should I? I've got an awful voice!"

Once again, Adam and Lar left one of the rooms laughing, but their laughter had a very strained note to it. Palustric was puzzled by his friends and declared: "I don't know what you two are laughing at, but we've got our severest test now." He shrugged his heavy shoulders.

"This is the seventh door. It's through here that we'll find Emily or meet our doom."

As if in answer to Palustric's words, golden letters flashed on the last door:

GAME OVER
DEPOSIT YOUR SOULS WITHIN

## 29

"We'll see about that!" Adam pushed the door open so forcefully that a cloud of golden feathers flew into the air. They were in a workshop where tools and benches lay under the mass of golden feathers. A fat goblin stood knee-deep in them in the middle of the workshop. He was glueing another feather into place on a giant wing he was making.

The goblin smiled at them and, fitting the wing on to one arm, declared, "You have arrived at a historic moment. Just in time to witness the first flying goblin!"

"It won't work," Adam said.

The goblin looked as if the stranger had

slapped him across the face. "You realise that you are speaking to Snook the Inventor?"

"Well," Adam said firmly, "it still won't work. The concept's wrong."

Snook took off the wing and laid it on a bed of golden feathers. "These are *bird* feathers," he said, "and with these two wings, I'll soar into the sky."

"Just like Icarus," Adam said.

"Who? Has someone else had my idea?" the inventor asked anxiously.

"Oh yes, many centuries ago. A Greek named Icarus made two wings from swans' feathers held together with wax. But he flew too close to the sun. The wax melted and he fell to his death."

"There you are then...this Icapus—"

"Icarus!"

"*Icarus* wasn't a genius like me. You see, I'm using *eagle* feathers. The Golden Eagle is King of the Birds, I'm using glue, not wax and—"

"It *won't* work! You see, the tale of Icarus is only a legend and there are scientific reasons, biological reasons why not. You haven't got a bird's chest muscles and you haven't got a bird's heart rate, just look at you...you're fat! Not in the least aerodynamic!"

"Mm," the inventor patted his stomach, "you have a point. I am a little overweight!"

He eyed Lar. "Now, your friend here, he's a real featherweight!" The goblin leapt to his feet with surprising agility. "Here, try this on and this!"

Little Lar stood there, a tiny green figure with enormous golden wings.

"Try flapping them, they're very light," the goblin urged.

Lar flapped half-heartedly a couple of times.

"Come on, we'll go to the cliff, it's not far!"

Adam's eye flashed a warning, but Lar was already taking the wings off.

*"An ass is still an ass, even with a golden saddle,* is it not so, inexpert goblin?" the pixy fluted.

Snook and his workshop began to fade away and in one corner was a screen that also faded. Behind the screen slumped in a corner was a girl with long silver hair.

"Emily!" Adam darted forward across the bare room to his sister.

He stared into Emily's startled silver eyes and hurried over to catch her as she stood up. She was weak and looked on the point of fainting.

"W-where am I?" she mumbled.

"*Presumption* took you, Mistress," Lar squinted happily at her. "Welcome back."

"What?"

"Come on quickly!" Adam said urgently. "We're in danger. We've got to get out of here." he dragged his sister towards the door. "There'll be time for explanations later."

He was too late, even as he put out a hand to open the door, it faded away and left Adam staring at a white wall. Palustric leapt forward and thumped the wall where the door had been. There was no doubt: the wall was solid, there was no way through.

## 30

They looked around desperately at the four blank walls surrounding them; they were prisoners.

Rather needlessly, Lar said, "*Pride* has trapped us, Master."

At these words, the plaster on one wall began to bulge and ripple. As they watched, it formed into two enormous lips; it formed a mouth that spread into an evil leer. Suddenly, the room was filled with mocking laughter. Palustric leapt forward and kicked at the lower lip with all his strength. In an instant, the mouth snapped open and sucked in the dwarf's leg to the knee. The plaster mouth smoothed out and disappeared, leaving Palustric standing on one leg, with the other embedded in the wall. The dwarf tugged, struggled and swore, becoming very red in the face, but all in vain, his leg wouldn't budge.

Emily's strength had returned, so she was the first across to Palustric. Taking him by the waist, she began to tug with him. Adam sprang across and seized his sister's waist to pull, too, but nothing could shift Palustric.

"It's no use," Adam panted. "We're getting nowhere like this. We'll have to think of something else." He started unloading objects from his pocket, with the vague idea of digging into the wall plaster.

"Think of something!" Palustric grumbled. "The leg I'm standing on is aching like mad!"

Adam took *Cari* out of his pocket and laid it on the floor with the other assorted items: damp string, bottle-opener, soggy matches and so on. Three pairs of hopeful eyes studied the orb; sure enough, it grew paler.

"Look!" Emily cried. "*Cari's* going to help us!" Slowly, steadily, *Cari* grew transparent, "Like a crystal ball!" the girl breathed.

They looked into the orb and suddenly a face appeared. It was a face Emily had never seen. "Look, there's an old man," she whispered. The old man smiled as if he could hear her.

"Deductio!" Adam said. "Look, he wants—"

"Hurry up, will you, get me out of here!" Palustric called over his shoulder, ignorant of what was happening.

Adam continued, "...to tell us something." He ignored Palustric and turned to Lar, "But I can't hear him, can you hear him, Lar?" The pixy shook his head. Adam looked at the wizard's lips, which were moving, forming a word over and over again.

"Reason!" Lar squeaked. "He's telling us to reason."

At the pixy's words, Deductio nodded and the orb instantly became silver again.

Adam snorted: *Huh! That's a fat lot of use! Reason! That won't get us out of here!"* He dug at the wall plaster near Palustric's leg with his pocket knife. The plaster seemed as hard as stone and the knife made little impression. Palustric urged him to try again, but Adam knew it was no use. The dwarf began to suffer now. To torment him more, mocking sniggers came to their ears.

Emily, who had never met Deductio, was the only one thinking about his message. Suddenly, she said, "We're in the Theatre!" Adam and Lar looked at her blankly. "What do people do in a theatre? They act!" She looked hopefully at the others, but their faces remained blank. "What I mean is," she said, "is that we have to reason our way out of here. It's no use digging at the wall. It must have something to do with the Theatre."

Adam would have scoffed at Emily's suggestion, but he'd learnt too much in this place. He tried hard to find a solution, as did the others; but it was Emily who spoke first, in a voice so low that only Lar could hear her easily. "We're in the Theatre of *Pride*," she whispered. "The only way out of here is to fight him with the weapon he fears most...*modesty*. Now, follow my example." She moved to the centre of the room and, putting her hands on her hips, tilting her head back like an actress, she declared in a ringing voice, "My name's Emily. I'm not really as beautiful as this in real life, but I'm not ugly either. I'm not very good at school, because I daydream a lot, but I'm not stupid. I used to spend too long in front of the mirror, but I'm not going to be so vain in future." She waved silently to Adam, who joined her. He had understood.

"My name's Adam," he said quickly in a strong voice. "I fooled the dragon, Lentor, but I couldn't have managed it without *Cari's* help and I used to show off about being clever, but I'm not going to anymore."

Lar joined them. "My name's Lar," he

squeaked. "I'm a pixy who knows a lot of wise sayings. None of them is mine. I promise to invent my own sayings in future." Adam groaned at the thought, just as Palustric began to boom from his plaster prison.

"Palustric's the name. I've always been so proud of being a dwarf, but now I know I've a lot to learn from other folk and I'm sure I'll do that in future."

"Aaagh!" a cry of frustrated rage filled the room as the door reappeared and flew off its hinges into the hall with a great crash. Palustric fell to the floor with a thump and rubbed his suffering leg frantically. Adam dragged him to his feet without ceremony, and the dwarf half-limped, half-stumbled out of the room on Adam's arm as a hate-filled voice screamed, "Vengeance! Revenge! Revenge!" The word rang in their ears. Emily and Lar dashed after the other two while they all kept hurrying until the Theatre was well behind them.

In the dark backstreets, as their chests heaved for breath, Lar piped: *"Now Pride has lowered his wings,* is it not so, Master?

"Shut up, Lar!" Adam hissed.

"But I thought it up myself—" the pixy began to protest as Adam's arm swept him off his feet and into a dark corner between two houses. Palustric tugged Emily after them. "Hide!"

For the first time, Lar's hearing had let him down. Maybe he had been concentrating too hard on his new saying—they were just in time.

Goblin soldiers with fiery torches held above their heads passed the end of the narrow street. Their harsh voices boomed in the stillness of the night; their firelit faces modelled by shifting shadows from the flames meant they reached new levels of ugliness.

"*Pride* has sent his troops after us," Emily whispered.

"I don't think so," Adam breathed. "Didn't you see their uniforms? I reckon they belong to the Archgoblin and that they are still searching for you, Emily. We can't risk going back to the inn; they'll be watching it."

"I'm sorry," Emily whispered sincerely. "It's all my stupid fault. I behaved very badly up there. I should have given the Archgoblin my masterpiece. It was his by rights. I don't know what came over me..."

"Don't think about it anymore. It's the place —the Citadel of Wealth—it has a corrupting effect on people. What did you do with your masterpiece, by the way?" Adam wanted to know.

"I threw it in the moat."

"A pity!"

They made their way downhill by back-streets and sticking to the shadows as much as possible. On three occasions, they had to hide as patrols passed them, their torches lighting up alleyways and dark corners. More by good luck than skill, they were not found. So, they left the Citadel with great stealth, the way they had come in. Even if soaked from the moat and cold and uncomfortable, they didn't stop till they had left the village far behind them.

# VI

## ON THE ROAD OF
## STRIFE

# 31

The moon cast a disturbing red glow over the earth and didn't help to relieve the gloom of the four friends as they sat on rocks under the stars. They were without a plan, cold and miserable and couldn't decide what to do. It was in this state that the two shadowy hooded figures found them.

"Sheath your sword, Adam," a friendly voice greeted him.

"Deductio!" Adam said with relief. Now they would know what to do with two wizards for advice.

The wizards sat down on the rocks with them. "There's no time to lose," Deductio began.

"The storm clouds are gathering. We must slumber no longer!"

The other hooded figure nodded in agreement, and in the gloom they recognised Sapiens.

"The balance has been disturbed," the old wizard went on, looking at Adam. "The winning back of the Key of Ingenuity has stirred up the forces of evil. Long ago, *Pride* lost all sense of good, corrupted by power to devote himself to evil-doing. Now the Key is away from Lentor, he senses the opportunity to seize the absolute power he craves. The Key alone can give him that."

Sapiens nodded again. "Time is on his side, already he has mobilised the hobgoblins while the goblins are in foment," she said. "In the West, the Hag is rubbing her hands at the prospect of suffering and destruction. Her spriggan columns have crossed her frontiers with orders to unite with the Marshland goblins, who even now await them in arms."

"My friends, the peril is grave," Deductio took up the theme, which Emily felt was just right for such a spooky night. She shivered violently. "We are in the shadow of death, but we must not bend the knee. There is no choice—unless we wish to live as slaves."

"What shall we do?" Emily asked, shivering all the more. Deductio took her hand gently and looked into her eyes, which were wide with fear.

"You were fortunate, my child: *Pride* had you in his clutches, yet, here you are. *Pride* is merciless when crossed. He will seek revenge. To avenge himself on you is now one of his fondest desires. Therefore, your peril is great. You have no choice; be willing to meet danger, even to court it." He gazed even deeper into the girl's frightened eyes. "This is a question of absolutes —only the power of love and truth can defeat evil. You possess the power to fight with these weapons without reward."

"We're *too young!*" Emily protested. "We're weak and—"

Sapiens pulled her hood back from her face and took Emily's other hand. She fixed Emily with her cool, blue eyes. "It has always been so," she said firmly. "You are young and, as such, weak. The weak are not equal to the challenge. They are without expectations, except the hope of their own making: a struggle to be worthy. Do you understand, my dear?"

Emily looked at the wizard's stern face and nodded feebly. Sapiens was right, even though the only thing she wanted was to be back home with her parents and her Jasmine. She bit her trembling lip to hold back the threatened tears.

"What shall we do?" Emily repeated, this time almost under her breath.

"Each of us must move at once," Deductio said, snapping his fingers. "There's no time to lose. Sapiens," he let go of Emily's hand, "leave at once for the Council of Elves. Warn them and lead the Elven forces directly to the Dwarfish lands."

Sapiens nodded, stood up and pulled her grey hood over her head. She squeezed Emily's shoulder, "Be brave and may fortune be with you." Without another word, she turned and left.

"As for me," Deductio reclaimed their attention, "I shall seek the two most powerful of our order: Valens and Veritas.

"Wizards," Palustric whispered unnecessarily to Adam.

"Lar," Deductio ordered, "take a horse and summon the pixies and brownies to arms, we'll meet in the Dwarfish lands."

"O Wise One, I cannot!" Lar squeaked, squinting more than usual.

Deductio's eyes flashed from within his hood. "Why not?"

"*A horse?*" Lar spread his hands and

hunched his little shoulders by way of explanation.

"Ah! You're right!" Deductio smiled thinly and stood up "Come, come out of these rocks." The little band obeyed, climbing down to the level ground, where, to their surprise, the wizard whistled a high-pitched series of notes. Out of the darkness came a flash of brown and white fur. A large, shaggy dog skidded to a halt at Deductio's feet, sat down and stared up with adoring eyes into the wizard's face. The tip of its tail gently beat on the dusty ground.

"Oh, he's lovely!" Emily cried. "What's his name?"

"Guess," the wizard smiled.

"Fido?"

"No, Guess!" Deductio's smile widened.

"Ben?"

"No, Guess!"

"Patch?" Emily frowned

"No, he's called *Guess*," the old wizard chuckled. "My sense of humour!"

"Aw!"

Adam, Palustric and Lar laughed, momentarily forgetting the danger they were all in. Emily stroked one of Guess's floppy ears and laughed too.

"Guess, this is Lar," Deductio presented the pixy to his dog. "Take him to the pixy lands. Serve him well and defend him, with your life if need be, my canine friend," Deductio said sternly.

The dog leapt up, he was as tall as Lar, and, tail wagging furiously, licked the pixy full in the face.

"Eeh!" Lar squeaked, jumping backwards, spitting and wiping his face with his tattered sleeve as the others burst out laughing again.

"Lar, it looks like you've got a new friend," Adam grinned.

The pixy scowled, but Guess wagged his tail even more fervidly. *"Friends get on better from a distance,* is it not so, O Wise One?"

Deductio smiled and shook his head. "You know that this is not the true meaning of the saying, Lar. Come on, up you get!" He lifted Lar onto Guess's back, and Lar grasped the leather collar at the dog's neck. Then Deductio stooped and spoke into the dog's ear, warning him of the hazards they would have to steer clear of on the road.

When he had finished, Emily stepped over to Lar and put her arm around his thin shoulders. "Take care, Lar, and good luck!"

Adam hardly glanced at his friend. "Bye," he

said trying to sound casual, but his heart was heavy. Even though he'd known Lar only a short time, it seemed like a lifetime after what they'd been through together. Lar was more than a friend and Adam would miss him sorely.

Palustric went over to the pixy and squeezed his hand, but didn't say anything.

The two youngsters and the dwarf watched sadly as their friend waved from the dog's back and disappeared into the night. Their mood was not helped by Deductio, who sighed: "He has a long, dangerous road ahead of him."

"I hope he'll be all right," Palustric said with feeling.

"At least we'll have some peace from his sayings," Adam said gruffly, but they could tell he had a lump in his throat.

Deductio wanted no further waste of time. "You three must warn the dwarves. Palustric, it is your land that is under immediate threat. *Pride* means to have the Key—"

"Never! He'll never get into the sanctuary!" Palustric said hotly.

Deductio sighed wearily, "Not by direct assault, friend. Do not underestimate the enemy; he has many devious arts. Even now the word is spreading among the goblins. They are uniting. Goblins only need the slightest encouragement to harm—as you know. They're wicked by nature, no matter how civil they might pretend to be."

Palustric knew that Deductio was right; you couldn't argue with a wizard, they were always right.

"Then we'd better be going," he growled.

"Don't trust anyone, friends. These are dangerous times in which you must cross hostile lands." The wizard gave them a tired smile and began to walk away. They watched his back wordlessly for a few seconds until Adam spoke.

"Why are we waiting? Let's go!"

Hesitating only the instant required to glance from Adam to the gloomy road, Deductio vanished.

"He's gone!" Emily gasped.

"He *is* a wizard," Palustric said in a matter-of-fact voice.

"Come on!" Adam wanted to be off.

"No!"

He looked at his sister. "Why not?"

"We can't just leave Blitz," Emily said, "and in any case, our journey will be much quicker and easier on horseback. Remember how far it is and...and, I don't mind telling you, I'm tired out as it is."

Adam had forgotten about Blitz in his understandable desire to escape from the Citadel. It was true; life would be much easier with the great stallion.

"There's no way I'm leaving him with those horrid goblins," Emily added. "Blitz is the best horse in the world."

"All right, all right," Adam said, "message received, but we can't just walk back to the inn and collect Blitz. It's too dangerous. The Arch-goblin's soldiers have probably taken him into the Citadel."

There was a long, depressed silence. Then Palustric suddenly said, "No!"

"Eh?"

"No. Think about it," the dwarf said. "The Archgoblin wants Emily, not a horse. He'll know that Emily wants her horse back."

"So, he'll have set a guard to watch Blitz," Adam reasoned.

"Exactly!"

"So, how do we get Blitz?" Emily asked desperately.

Adam pursed his lips. "Not by daylight."

Unlike the previous night, there were no clouds; the stars twinkled in defiance of the gloomy old moon. Since the old moon throws little light, it often witnesses secretive deeds; therefore, it was just right to cloak the three friends' silent approach through the goblin village to the rear of the inn. The inn yard, enclosed by a high wall and a large gate, was flanked by two old stables with double wooden doors. From the shadow between two houses across the street facing the yard gate, they could see two goblin guards.

"Remember," Emily whispered, "the stables have got barred windows at the back to let air in?"

Adam and Palustric nodded.

"When I get those two guards to follow me, you two go down the side behind the stables and look through the windows. Find out where Blitz is."

"But how...?"

"Give me some gold coins," Emily whispered, "about twenty."

"That's about all the money we have left," Adam said reluctantly but passed them to his sister.

She took them and handed three back to him to spend later.

"Now go around the back of this house and watch from the next alleyway," Emily said. She waited just long enough to give them time, then tossed a gold coin onto the cobbled street in front of the guards. It fell with two loud clinks, making both guards spin round.

"What's that?" one grunted.

The other pointed to the ground. "It's a coin!" he cried.

"Hush!" the first goblin said, leaning his pike against the wall. "You'll wake the others: this is *ours!*"

"Right!" the other grinned craftily, leaning his pike too and joining his companion as he straightened up.

"It's gold!" he said, holding it out on his palm and closing it quickly as the other reached for it. Their greed for gold was so great that neither goblin asked himself where the coin had come from.

This was the moment. Emily tossed another coin much nearer the alley entrance. The goblins shoved each other roughly as they scrambled for it while, in the next alleyway, Adam nudged Palustric and grinned. Emily led the goblins deep into the alley with another three coins, but one goblin was faster and stronger than the other; so, as he pounced on his fourth coin (to the other's single coin), the weaker goblin slid a knife into his ribs before prising the coins from his dying companion's hand. Emily shuddered but lured the killer on with another coin.

Meanwhile, Adam and Palustric were collecting the two abandoned pikes at the gate. They had already checked the stable at the left of the yard. It was full of sleeping goblin soldiers in burgundy uniforms.

The boy and the dwarf went down the alley to the back of the stable on the right. Under the barred window, they laid the pikes on the ground. The window was higher than that of the other stable. Even if the dwarf stood on his shoulders as before, Adam judged that his eyes wouldn't quite reach window level. He looked around and found two large stones, one flat and one round; placing the latter on the flat one, he climbed up. "Quick, Palustric, on to my shoulders!" he whispered, holding out cupped hands to help his friend up. As Palustric placed a foot in Adam's hands and pulled himself up on to his friend's shoulders, the rounded stone began to move. Adam wobbled, and Palustric lost his balance.

"Aaagh!" the dwarf cried and crashed to the ground.

"Are you all right?" Adam knelt over him anxiously.

"Urgh!"

"Palustric?!"

"Urgh!" The dwarf sat up.

"Quick, get up!" Adam hauled his friend roughly to his feet and, just in time, tugged him into the nearby warren of alleyways.

Alerted, two goblin guards came running around the corner, swords in one hand and flaming torches in the other. They stopped when they saw the pikes on the ground and looked around in all directions.

"Raise the alarm!" one said to the other. Even as he turned, Adam's sword finished him. The other's torch flew out of his hand as Palustric's tackle knocked him off his feet. As he fell, his head crashed against the stable wall, and he crumpled senseless to the ground.

Palustric struggled to his feet.

"Hush!" Adam warned.

Silence reigned. They listened for a good minute, but nothing disturbed the peace. Adam trembled violently; he, who was a pacifist, had killed a living creature. It was true, goblins were ugly, evil creatures, but apart from some insects in his *Own World*, Adam had never harmed anyone. Now, here he was, only a boy and having to play a soldier's role. His feelings were getting the better of him; he loathed himself for what he had done.

Palustric looked at him strangely. "Are you all right, Adam?" he whispered.

"No, I killed that goblin!" he answered in such a low, shaky voice that Palustric had trouble hearing him.

"Thank goodness you did!"

"But it's wrong to kill!"

Palustric grabbed Adam by his shirt sleeve. "Adam, remember what Deductio said, this is a war and the world is in danger, and you're upset about a filthy goblin! He'd have killed you without a second thought!"

Adam sighed and thought about it, nodding his head. "You're right, Palustric. I'm sorry, I'll have to learn to be a soldier in double-quick time!" The urgency of their situation flooded back to him. "They must be the guards from this stable," Adam indicated with his head. "Probably they were guarding Blitz," he whispered. "In any case, we mustn't lose time. I say we go in there."

Palustric nodded, and with that, they were on their way into the yard. Adam pointed silently at the left-hand stable. On the wooden doors were two big, iron brackets and leaning against the wall was a sturdy wooden bar for keeping the heavy doors closed when required.

Some distance from the yard, Emily stepped out of the shadows, face to face with the goblin guard who held ten gold coins in his hand.

"There are another ten," Emily said to the

startled goblin, who still hadn't taken the trouble to ask himself where the coins had come from, just as long as they kept coming. She showed him the remaining coins in her outstretched hand. "You can have them if you like."

The goblin rushed forward, but Emily threw the coins high into the air.

"No!" cried the goblin as a shower of coins hit the ground and began to roll in all directions in the darkness of the alleyway. Emily paused just long enough to see the goblin throw himself to his knees, crawling and groping on the cobbles in a frantic search.

"Have fun!" Emily chuckled and ran back towards the yard, where she found Adam and Palustric leading Blitz into the street.

"Quick!" she called. "I think we'd better disappear!"

Palustric in front, Emily with the reins, and Adam behind on Blitz's back, they set off out of the village as quietly as possible before galloping away across the dark, open plain under the stars.

They rode for several hours until they and the horse were exhausted. By now they had reached a hilly region. Judging that they were far enough from the Citadel to concede themselves a pause, they found a comfortable spot by a shallow, rocky stream, where Blitz could drink and they could sleep. Emily took the first watch.

Before falling asleep, Adam whispered to the dwarf, "What is it with pixies and horses?"

But Palustric was already snoring.

## 32

She couldn't see very far in the weak light cast by the waning moon. Deep shadows endowed disturbing forms to the rocks and shrubs. She quelled her imagination because it was too vivid and scary in these conditions. The deafening splash of the stream in the stillness of the night worried her, too. Its noise might cover the sounds of an approaching foe. She knew that they needed rest; meanwhile, her uneasiness grew. Eyes stinging with tiredness and from repeated rubbing, she had to keep alert. Emily's head began to nod despite herself because she had almost surrendered to sleep when a sixth-sense made her suddenly sit up and stiffen.

Straining to listen, she wished that she had Lar's hearing, grumbled at the noise of the stream and jumped to her feet. Running a short distance from the stream, she stopped to cock her head: there was no doubt now, she could hear hoofbeats. The Archgoblin's troops were on their trail.

Emily hurried back to the others, waking Adam in an instant, but they couldn't wake Palustric even by shaking him. Between them, they heaved the sleeping dwarf onto the stallion's back like a sack of flour. Adam marvelled at how such a short person could be so hefty, the opposite of Lar. Mounting behind Emily, Adam shook her shoulder. "Quick, into the stream! They won't know which way to go; I'll bet they've been following our tracks."

"We'll go upstream," Emily decided, urging Blitz into the brook. "Let's hope they'll think we've taken the easier way."

She kept Blitz in the shallow water for almost three-quarters of an hour. He slipped a few times, but he was a princely horse, tireless and agile. When Emily headed him out of the stream, the horse reacted as if he had been freed, galloping off with an easy, flowing movement, which soon put a great distance between them and the brook. When dawn broke, at last, Emily reined in Blitz to scan the fresh horizon, but there was no sign of pursuers.

After some time, Adam and Emily noticed a flickering, red glow in the distance.

"It looks like a fire," Emily called over her shoulder. Before long they could smell the smoke, and it was not much further before Palustric spluttered awake and would have fallen off the horse if Emily hadn't grabbed him.

"What's burning?" the dwarf coughed.

Emily nudged Blitz in that direction.

There was a heavy pall of smoke rolling over the hill. They continued upwards to its brow, where the road led down towards a village. The whole place was in flames, the bodies of dwarves lay bloodied in the road. Emily gasped and looked away from the sight. There was no sign of the attackers and no movement in the village except for the dancing flames and parts of buildings occasionally collapsing in a shower of sparks as the flames greedily devoured everything.

"Who's done this and why?" Adam asked.

Emily shook her head and bit her lip; she had no idea.

The dwarf provided an answer. "Either the Archgoblin's men who were following us or, more likely, *Pride's* goblins. Remember Deductio's words, the war is in the offing, and these poor dwarves probably lived here among the goblins. Their only offence," he said bitterly, "was to be dwarves."

"Well, they didn't deserve this!" Emily protested, outraged.

"Yes, well," Palustric said gruffly, "goblins don't exactly need a reason to massacre anyone, even their own kind." He spat on the ground to show his dislike for accursed goblin-kind.

Blitz was getting skittery; he could smell dwarf blood while the flames frightened him, so Emily headed him along the road, away from the village. In any case, their direction through the Goblin Highlands took them up that way.

They followed the road for at least an hour before Adam pointed out a little group ahead in the distance. Since the group was on foot, it wasn't long before Blitz caught up with them. At the sound of hoofs, the travellers scattered in all directions into the bushes lining the road.

Emily could have kept on, but she chose to stop. At first, there was no movement, then a deep voice boomed: "Look, there's one of our kind!" At once, the bushes parted and, from all around them, out stepped dwarves.

"Dwarves!" Palustric cried out, pleased.

One of the dwarves, over fifty dwarf-years-old, going by his beard, grinned at Palustric.

"My name's Cloutric, I'm a smith, son of Rodric, he was a smith too." The dwarf continued with his family tree for quite a while, going into considerable detail over various blood-ties.

"We're related!" Palustric slapped his thigh. "Very distantly, but we are—" and to Adam and Emily's horror, related his family tree as, fascinated, the twenty or so dwarves crowded round to follow the complicated list of births and marriages.

Adam drew Emily aside. "We'll be here all day if they carry on with this dwarf behaviour."

"I wonder why they were so scared before?" Emily frowned. She pushed aside a couple of dwarves and interrupted Palustric, "Look here," she said, "I don't mean to be rude, but there's danger—" She didn't expect her interruption to have such an effect. At the word *danger* the dwarves stared up and down the road with frightened faces, all thoughts of family trees driven from their minds. Emily took Cloutric by the arm. "Tell me what happened," she said.

The dwarf folded his muscular arms across his broad chest and snarled, "Marshland goblins. They came last night," his swarthy face darkened even more, "killing and looting. They put our homes to the torch. We're the lucky ones who got away. At least ten of our friends and family were less fortunate." Cloutric unfolded his arms and clenched his fists. "But why? Why?" He shook his head, "They didn't torch the goblin homes, only ours. They only killed dwarves and burnt dwarf homes. Why? We've lived peacefully alongside the Hill goblins for many years, without any trouble. Keeping on good terms, that sort of thing." Cloutric looked from one to the other of the newcomers. "Do you know why?"

"We're all in danger," Emily said. "But I can't explain now. It's a long story. Keep away from goblins of any kind. Make your way as quickly as you can back to your homeland and, I beg you, remember you didn't see us three. The safety of the Dwarfish lands may depend on your silence."

Cloutric and the other dwarves studied Emily's face. Seeing her so sincere troubled them even more. But they nodded in agreement.

"There's no time to lose," Emily said. "You'll find out soon enough what's going on. Good-bye and good luck."

They mounted Blitz and galloped off without looking back. As they rode, Emily said, "That explains why the Archgoblin's troops followed us so far. They wouldn't have if it had just been for my brooch. No, they wanted to capture us on *Pride's* orders. I believe he's mustering a vast goblin army and is preparing to invade the dwarves."

"That's what the wizards said was happening," Adam reminded her.

They rode on for a long time in thoughtful silence until, by mid-afternoon, they came to crossroads with a fingerpost.

"Straight on," Palustric said without a hint of doubt.

But Emily was curious. "Trow Town, 10 miles," she read. "It's not so far."

"We should keep straight on. We mustn't waste time," the dwarf repeated.

"Blitz needs to eat and rest and, so do I!" Emily said in a tone that meant she wasn't going to argue about it.

"Do you know Trow Town, Palustric?" Adam asked quickly.

When Palustric was cross, his brown eyes seemed to become darker like pieces of coal. He turned them on Adam now. "There's nothing there for us!"

Adam persisted, "Who lives there, Palustric?"

"Highland *goblins*," he growled the second word.

"They're usually friendly, aren't they? Like

the innkeeper at The Traveller's Rest, remember?"

Palustric didn't answer. With his land was in grave danger, his friends wanted to make a dangerous twenty-mile detour.

Emily understood the dwarf's angry silence, but they couldn't keep on along the road until Blitz dropped of hunger and fatigue. She turned in the saddle and looked deeply into Palustric's smouldering eyes, smiling and opening her lovely eyes wider, watching as the dwarf's turned back to dark brown. "Is it a big town?" she asked sweetly.

"It's the capital," Palustric's voice softened because, despite himself, he couldn't resist Emily's charm.

"All the more reason then. We must convince the Highland goblins not to join the Marshland goblins. They are better folk. I'm sure we can persuade them not to take up arms."

"They're still goblins," Palustric said mistrustfully.

"It's our duty to try," Emily nudged Blitz forward towards Trow Town.

By late afternoon, they had finished their meal in an inn half-way along the High Street of Trow Town. The inn, like all the domed buildings of the town (except for three), was circular and made of flat stones. After speaking with the landlord for a long time, Emily rejoined the other two at the table and explained: "The Highland goblins are controlled by three important families. They do whatever the heads of these families decide together. That's why the buildings are such a strange shape. It seems they are built with a special keystone. If a goblin family doesn't pay its rent in time, the chief or head of the powerful family sends a gang of goblins to pull out the keystone. Then the house collapses, like a house of cards."

"That's not very kind, is it?" Adam gasped.

"Since when have goblins been kind?" Palustric spat on the ground again.

"Anyway, their word is law in these parts, so we have to speak with them. The landlord says that one of them lives in a big house not far away. He's given me directions. We can't miss it because it isn't round and domed—nobody can pull it down."

The splendid ebony door had an iron ring for a knocker and was opened slightly by a goblin servant dressed in black. The servant stared at them with a mixture of suspicion and hostility. They were forced to wait outside on the steps as he closed the door in their faces while he went off for instructions. Before long, he returned with the same unfriendly expression, admitting them into a huge hall which seemed to be the only downstairs room in the house.

Under a gallery, the walls were lined with shields and mounted on each an animal's head. Foxes, badgers, wolves and bears stared sightlessly at each other across the vast room. Emily shuddered; she hated hunting of any kind.

By an open fire, in a deep, hide armchair, sat the owner of the house. He reminded Emily of a toad. This squat goblin, ugly as a whiskered bat, didn't rise as they entered, but sat back, crossed his legs and stared at them.

"What do you want?" he growled.

Emily approached and stopped a couple of yards in front of the goblin's chair. Just looking at the repulsive creature made her wish that she had continued along the road as Palustric had wanted. At her back, Palustric did not doubt that he had been right all along. Still, she took a deep breath, looked the goblin in his small, crafty eyes and explained what she wanted. From time to time, the goblin stopped her to clear up the odd point, but followed her words with great interest when she spoke about the Citadel of Wealth.

Adam studied the goblin's face with just about the same suspicion as the servant had shown to them. Above all, he didn't like the way the goblin brushed aside the threat to peace from *Pride*.

The goblin eased himself out of his armchair to stand in front of the fire with his back to them. Staring into the fire without turning towards his visitors, he growled, "Suppose the Highland Goblins help you against *Pride*, what's in it for us?"

Emily had no hesitation. "*Pride* won't stop at conquering the dwarves," she paused, not to sound threatening, "but he'll take over the whole world so that your people will have to obey him, too." Emily stopped because she wasn't at ease speaking to a person's back. She couldn't tell what impact her words had on him. She waited. Still, he stared into the fire. Emily exchanged glances with Adam and Palustric, who just frowned and shrugged. "Perhaps you don't re-alise what a menace *Pride* is. The wise wizards told us that he wants absolute power—"

The goblin turned to face her with a strange expression on his face, which confused her even more.

"Of course," the goblin said thoughtfully, "I can't decide on my own. I shall have to speak with certain other people. What you have told me is grave." The goblin's crafty eyes darted from face to face, but when he spoke, he looked no-one in the eye. "Most certainly, a decision will have to be reached."

"There's no time to waste," Emily interrupted. "The Marshland Goblins are already on the move and..."

"Where are you staying?"

"At The Fell Top Inn in the High Street."

"Well, stay the night," the goblin said. "Tomorrow I will give you our decision.

Emily smiled and stepped forward to thank the goblin, but he ignored the hand she offered. "Grum," he called to the sour servant, "show these people out." He turned to Emily, "I'll find you at the inn tomorrow morning." He nodded dismissively, turning toward the fire, once more showing them his back.

At the inn, Adam tried to convince his sister to leave Trow Town at once. "You can't be serious, you don't mean to trust that...that *creature!* Didn't you see his eyes? And why was he so interested in the Citadel?"

Emily didn't reply.

"Come on! A famished crocodile would be more trustworthy!" He couldn't believe how stubborn his sister could be. Adam turned in frustration to his friend, who was following the discussion anxiously. "What do you think?"

"I don't know," Palustric said.

Adam hadn't expected this reply. "What do you mean?" he snapped.

The dwarf hung his head. "I don't know what a *crocodile* is."

Brother and sister looked at each other and started to laugh while Palustric scratched his head. But it broke the tension. "Look, Adam," Emily said softly, "I didn't like that horrid goblin, either. But goblins aren't likeable. Everybody knows that. If we want his help, we have to trust him, I'm afraid. Don't you think it would be a good thing, Palustric, if we convince the Highland Goblins not to join *Pride*?"

Palustric sat down on the edge of his bed. He sighed heavily. "Well, it would mean one less frontier to defend."

"There you are," Emily said, seizing the opportunity. "If we don't try, we won't gain anything, while if they refuse to help, we'll have only lost half a day, but we'll have gained a rest for Blitz and a night's sleep in a comfortable bed." She yawned at the thought and yawned again, her words difficult to understand. "We'll travel faster tomorrow."

Her last words convinced Adam finally to give in. Emily could be right and, in any case, they were tired. He yawned, too, soon lying in bed, thinking what a horrible smell freshly put out candles make, before falling into a deep re-freshing sleep.

In the darkness, Palustric whispered, "Adam, what's a crocodile?" There was no reply. He never did find out.

Palustric's deep-chested snores were inter-rupted before dawn when their door was flung open and steel blades pressed to their throats. The intruders dragged them out of bed and chained their hands behind their backs.

## 33

By the light of smoky lanterns, they recognised their captors' burgundy uniforms. The Archgoblin's men had caught up with them. They also recognised another uglier goblin in the doorway. Adam looked accusingly at Emily. "I told you a crocodile was more trustworthy," he said even as the Highland goblin chief snatched his payment, a sizeable bag of gold, from the Archgoblin's captain.

They didn't have time to insult the treacherous goblin, for they were bundled roughly downstairs and out onto the street. Hoisted onto a horse in front of a guard, they left Trow Town just as the first cocks began to crow and daylight broke. Each of them weighed up the situation:

twenty mounted guards with swords and Blitz's reins in a goblin rider's hands. They were heading back to the Citadel across country, not by road. On the whole, their situation seemed hopeless. Before long they would be in *Pride's* grip and their mission failed.

Uncomfortable and sore, they travelled for two hours. When one tried to look around or call to the other, their captors slapped and pinched them cruelly. They stopped at another moorland stream, where the goblins flung them to the ground like sacks of potatoes. The goblins watered their horses and Blitz. They sat in a circle around their prisoners, occasionally tormenting them with jibes or offering the bread and cheese they were devouring, only to snatch it away again. The goblins soon finished off what food they had with them. Adam, who always had an appetite, began to worry. It was a long way to the Citadel. With this thought in mind, he noticed a guard staring at his belt. The goblin looked up and sneered as their eyes met, then leapt to his feet and tore the horn from the boy's belt. With his hands chained behind him, Adam could do nothing.

The goblin turned the horn over in his hands and grinned, admiring his prize. He didn't have much time to do so because another goblin jumped to his feet and ran his sword into the un-suspecting guard's back. Before he could bend to pick up the horn, all the guards were on their feet. Only with difficulty and thanks to his greater strength did the captain restore order.

Two guards clung to the killer's arms, and his captain stood in front of him. The goblin's eyes were wide with terror under his sweated brow. The captain drew his sword slowly. Emily turned her face away as Adam and Palustric watched the captain coldly run his sword into the guard's stomach.

When the goblin fell dying at his feet, the captain grinned and kicked his body. Then he reached down for Adam's horn. Like the other goblin, he turned the prize in his hand, but not without warning glances at the other goblins. Slowly he raised the horn to his lips.

Adam was going to say, "Go on, then we'll soon be free!" as a kind of bluff but then thought of a better idea. He put a pleased expression on his face. It was enough. The captain had been watching the boy for his reaction. When he saw that blowing the horn would please the boy, he lowered it at once and grinned slyly. He clipped the horn to his belt and set about cutting the dead guards' purses, instead. Adam breathed a sigh of relief. No-one must blow the horn except himself. He remembered Balom's warning, only to blow it as a last resort.

The goblins left their dead unburied and gave their horses to Emily and Palustric. So, only Adam was pinched and slapped from time to time. They travelled on until the sun was high in the sky. It was clear from their faces and their grumbling that the goblins were suffering the heat under their uniforms.

As soon as they saw woodland, their captain gave orders to enter. Under the broad-leaved trees, the air was cooler and fresher. For a while, they followed a track in single-file with the captain in front. He was the first to see the clearing with a giant oak stump in the centre. The stump was a living tree because at its edges were many new shoots that formed a coppice of young oaks. To everyone's surprise, inside the circle of trees, on the old stump, was an irresistible spread of food. Adam's mouth watered and his stomach rumbled at the sight of roast meats, bread, vegetables and fruit. The goblins were off their horses in a trice. Adam, Emily and Palustric could only watch enviously from their horses as the goblins threw themselves on the feast like a pack of starved wolves. Adam thought about escaping while the goblins were busy at their feast, but they wouldn't get far with chained hands. It was no use.

Palustric nudged his horse over to Adam. "Look!"

One by one, the goblin guards were clutching their stomachs and toppling over, green in the face. Not one of them was left alive.

"They've been poisoned," Emily said. She dismounted with great difficulty and went over to the captain. She poked him with her foot. He was dead.

"But who could have put poisoned food here?" Adam asked.

"I think I know," Emily said and looked at Palustric, but he had no idea. "I'll tell you, but I think you should get down off your horses."

This was easier said than done, as neither Adam nor Palustric were horsemen. Both crashed heavily onto the hard, woodland ground.

"Are you all right?" Emily asked.

"Never felt better," Adam groaned.

"Turn sideways, Ad," Emily ordered, "I'll try to get my hand into your pocket. Let's see if *Cari* can help." It took her a long time because she needed to be a contortionist to put a chained hand into her brother's pocket. In the end, she managed it and pulled out the orb with a cry of triumph. She held the sphere in her open hands behind her. "Come on, *Cari!*" she pleaded. "Get these chains off my wrists!" She waited, but nothing happened.

Adam stood, groaning because of his bruised, aching body. It hadn't been a good day, so far. "Give it here," he said roughly and turned his back to his sister, who let the elven orb roll into her brother's hand.

No sooner was the orb in his hands than he felt his wrists move apart. He held his hands out in front of him and was astonished to see that there was no trace of the heavy goblin chains. It was as if they had dissolved away.

"*Cari*, you're fantastic!" he cried. "Now Emily's," he ordered, dropping the orb into his sister's hands. The elven sphere glowed brightly and Emily's chains vanished.

"I wonder why *Cari* doesn't work for me?" Emily said touchily as she stroked Blitz's flank.

"I know why."

"Why?"

"I'm not telling you until you've told me who put the poisoned food there," Adam laughed.

"Hey!" Palustric boomed. "What about me?"

Adam looked at Emily and chuckled. "I quite like Palustric like this. I think I'll leave him chained up!"

"Hey!" Palustric boomed menacingly, and Adam released him with a laugh.

Meanwhile, Emily ran across the clearing to a grassy bank where wildflowers grew between the trees. There she picked pale yellow blooms until she had quite a bunch in her hand. Adam and Palustric strode over to join her.

"Primroses?" Adam asked.

"Here, two-four-six, seven," she passed seven to her brother and another seven to Palustric. She remained with seven in her hand.

They turned back to the centre of the clearing. In the oak coppice, growing among the bodies of the goblins were toadstools: poisonous toadstools.

Adam gasped. "It's impossible! I saw it with my own eyes. There was food there, not toadstools."

"Give me your flowers," Emily said.

Adam passed her the primroses, and as he did so, the toadstools became food to his eyes.

"It's an illusion," his sister told him.

Palustric nodded. "Now I understand, *Glamour!* — magic made by the spirit of the felled oak."

At these words, from behind the oak coppice stepped a curious, brown figure about as tall as Lar, but much older and even more wrinkled. He wore a large acorn cup for a hat. His bare chest and his long arms with oversized hands were gnarled; at his waist he wore a skirt of beaten bark. The strange creature bowed: "Good day," he said in a gruff voice, "the Oakman, at your service."

Emily and Palustric stared in surprise, but Emily remembered her manners. "Hello," she said, "we're Emily, Adam, and this is Palustric."

"Who are you talking to?" Adam asked, puzzled. Emily passed back his primroses.

"Yes, I know who you are," the Oakman replied, "a jay told me, and unless I'm wrong, a magpie told him."

"What gossips birds are!" Emily laughed. "But how did they know?"

"A wizard asked them to spread the word, just in case you needed help. At your service," the Oakman bowed again. "I really can't stand goblins." The strange creature waved at the bodies littering the oak stump. "They're always cutting down trees and never planting them, for one thing..." He went on with a long speech about the nature of goblins. Then he explained how when he'd seen the goblin riders approaching with their captives, he'd *glamourised* the toadstools.

When he'd finished, Adam and Palustric

dragged the dead goblins out of the Oakman's clearing. Adam took his horn from the captain's belt and gathered all the swords and money bags from the bodies.

"These could come in useful," he said. In this practical spirit, he tied all the horses' reins together. "The horses might be useful, too, it's a shame to leave them behind."

He looked round to say good-bye to the Oakman but couldn't see him.

"Where's he gone?"

"I'm here," said the Oakman.

"Where?"

"Adam, you can't see the Oakman without seven primroses," Emily said, "but he's still here." She pointed to an apparently empty space. "Don't worry, I'll say good-bye for all of us. Good-bye, Oakman, and thank you for your help."

Emily mounted Blitz while Adam and Palustric mounted two others, Adam leading all the other horses in a line. Adam's horse was a chestnut. "I'll call him *Oakman*, it's a good name," Adam said.

## 34

They came out of the wood and headed uphill, knowing they would come to the road sooner or later. They had been travelling for half an hour when Emily remembered *Cari*. She rode up to Adam's side. "Why doesn't *Cari* work for me?"

"It's obvious," Adam smiled, "you're not pure in heart like me!"

Emily gave her brother an impure glare and rode for an hour in wounded silence.

They finally regained the road which they had left for Trow Town the day before. By mid-afternoon, Emily broke her silence to complain about her hunger. She was right, of course, because they hadn't eaten that day. She described her idea of a perfect meal to Palustric as they passed over the brow of a hill. Ahead of them, they saw travellers.

"Look, it's Cloutric and the others!" Adam shouted.

This time the dwarves didn't hide because they recognised the three horsemen. Instead, they waved and grinned at the newcomers.

Palustric was first to jump off his horse to shake Cloutric's hand. Before long, all the sore-footed dwarves were on horseback, gratefully riding with them towards their homeland. Each had a goblin sword at his or her side, provided by Adam, whose providence had paid off. They rode along chatting, even Emily because she had eaten some excellent honey biscuits that Inga, a dwarfess, had given her.

It was perhaps an hour later, as they passed through a rocky defile, when fortune turned its back on them. Though the sides of the narrow valley seemed empty, the deep, raucous cawing of the raven suddenly filled the air: *pruk, pruk, pruk.*

"Spriggans!" Cloutric yelled as he drew his sword.

Even as the dwarf shouted his warning, a

hail of blistering hot stones pelted down on them. Agony where they touched bare skin, the dwarves roared in anger and pain. Their horses reared in the commotion, and the air filled with dust as huge rocks rolled down upon them, leaving two riders and their horses lifeless beneath them.

The boulders crashed down in front of and behind them, sealing the defile and trapping them. Suddenly, the hillside was thick with spriggans, who launched their hairy, brown bodies down upon the riders. Their cruel, long-nailed fingers tore into the dwarves' flesh or twisted in their hair. The hideous creatures pulled them off their horses and sent them crashing to the ground in a desperate struggle to free themselves. Outnumbered at least four-to-one, with Palustric completely buried under a mass of coarse-haired bodies, their situation was dire. The dwarves' screams filled the air as teeth and claws dug home.

Much bigger than the dwarves and spriggans, Adam and Emily were not unsaddled in the ambush. Quick of reflexes, Adam had run one flying spriggan through with his sword and knocked another to the ground with his other fist. So, he was free to move from the start. Horrified at the number of writhing spriggans, he turned

Oakman quickly and charged towards Blitz. Emily, who hadn't been so sharp of reflexes, struggled to shake off two clawing spriggans.

Blood pounding in his head, Adam charged and hacked the spriggans from his sister. Leaping off his horse, his sword scythed through the enemies, freeing those dwarves who were still alive.

Already, a band of spriggans was escaping up the hillside as Emily dismounted and began helping her brother with her undamaged arm. The remaining spriggans fled, scrambling after their fellows over the rocks. Adam followed a little way like an avenging giant, but the spriggans were much faster and more agile over the rocky terrain. He turned back to look in dismay at the grim scene. Dead bodies sprawled on the ground. Thanks to him, there were many more spriggans than dwarves, but, in any case, it was a disaster.

Emily was clutching her bloodied arm while Cloutric was sitting on a rock sobbing. A wave of useless anger passed over Adam. Poor Cloutric had lost many friends and family. Two or three dwarves struggled to their feet, inspecting their wounds. They were the only survivors. Adam looked around desperately for his friend.

"Palustric! Palustric!" he called. The rocky hills echoed to his voice: the only reply. Adam rushed over to the heaped bodies, frantically heaving dead spriggans from their victims. Eleven dwarves lay on the ground, four others and Cloutric were on their feet, but Palustric was nowhere to be seen.

"No!" Adam groaned and sank to his knees, understanding the reason for the attack. Cloutric came over to him, wiping his eyes, his face a mask of misery.

"They've taken Palustric," Adam said.

"That's who they came for, but if *Pride* thinks he can use Palustric to get the Key," Cloutric said stony-eyed, "he knows nothing about dwarves! Balom will never trade the Key for his nephew." Cloutric shook his head sadly. "Poor Palustric!"

"I'm going after them!" Adam spat out. But Cloutric grabbed his arm as he turned. "No, it's no use. You'll never catch them over this ground. Even if you did, they'd kill Palustric first, sooner than surrender him." He squeezed the boy's arm. "Palustric would want you to complete your task. We must hurry to warn our people, so they will have time to prepare for war."

Adam nodded without a word. They began the sad business of burying their dead. The best they could do was cover them with a stone cairn, but they left the spriggans to the carrion. They used their fallen companions' drinking water to rinse the cuts of their wounded. Luckily, none of the survivors had serious injuries. A sad and silent group made its way into the Dwarfish lands.

# VII

## THE WAR OF THE KEY

## 35

*A*s Cloutric had foretold, Balom the Black did not waste time grieving for his nephew. Instead, he threw himself at once into organising preparations for war. For this reason, a steady procession of grim-faced individuals entered the sanctum where the dwarves kept the Key of Ingenuity. The same dwarves and dwarfesses, too—in their odd long, grey dresses—came out, faces aglow with inspiration. Wheelwrights made extra-sturdy cartwheels, smiths tempered and honed unmatchable battle-axes and needle-dwarves stitched brilliant-coloured war banners. The dwarves worked everything to the highest standard, as in the *Old Days*.

Emily received armour made of white iron,

so cleverly worked that it was light but could turn any blade or point. On her head, she wore a helm of the same metal crested with a dragonfly, whose wings were two long, blue plumes. She worried that she wouldn't learn in time how to use the sword at her side or her shield (emblazoned with a flying dragonfly).

Adam wore blue chain mail as light as Emily's armour and just as strong. A rampant dragon with ferocious teeth crested his helm, its tail draped loosely behind the helm and between Adam's shoulders. He preferred to keep his goblin sword, which, at first, irritated Balom. But as Adam pointed out, he was used to it now, and it had served him well, accounting for goblins and spriggans. He accepted his new shield with pleasure, proud to see that the dwarves had given him a recumbent dragon as an emblem.

On Blitz and Oakman, they rode either side of Balom the Black's pony at the head of the Dwarfish army. Since news had reached Balom that the river border with the Marshland Goblins was under threat, they were on their way to the Twin Towers, which held the bridge over the river. It was a race against time because whoever held the towers also held the future of the Dwarfish lands.

An anxious, enthusiastic army of young and

not-quite-so-young dwarves left the cheering crowds of women, children and decidedly ancient dwarves behind. The enthusiasm for armour, banners and weapons and the great adventure was not shared by Adam, Emily or Balom, who understood and feared the price to be paid if they were to thwart *Pride*.

The dwarves, who had not fought for many dwarf lifetimes, had no warfare experience, and it showed. Adam suggested to Balom that the columns were getting ragged and strung out. But Balom's eagerness to press on to the Twin Towers with his way of not taking advice was to cost them dearly.

Too late, Adam burst out, "I'm not going any farther, Balom!" Adam grabbed the angry dwarf's reins. "Until we've regrouped. Strung out like this, we're easy prey for the enemy."

"What *enemy?*" Balom boomed, snatching back his reins. "There is no foe in Dwarfish lands! We have to get to the towers as quickly as possible—or else there will be!" The dwarf's thick eyebrows met menacingly.

"Look back," Adam was worried, "can you see all of our army?" He answered his question, "No! Are you sure the rear-guard and the supply carts are safe? No!" Adam watched doubt replace the stubbornness in Balom's eyes. "Balom," he added quickly, "our enemy is terrible; we must take care."

"Adam's right," Emily said, drawing near to lend her support, but just how right, Balom was to find out all too soon. For the moment, he agreed to call a halt for the main body of the army to regroup. Time passed, but there was no sign of the rear-guard or their carts.

Before long, it was clear that something was wrong. With heavy heart, Balom ordered his troops to retrace their steps.

After an hour, they came upon a frightful scene. Horror replaced the dwarves' early morning enthusiasm for adventure. The bloodied bodies of friends and relations lay broken on the ground. Many of the dwarves covered their faces while others wept openly. Balom supervised the grim task of burying their dead. There was no trace of the enemy, so they could only guess who was responsible for the slaughter. Whoever they were, they weren't experts in warfare because they had left the laden supply carts untouched: without them, the Dwarfish army would have had to turn back. When they had finished their work, Balom drew his sword and boomed out: "I, Balom the Black, swear to avenge the death of our comrades! As the first step towards the glorious victory, I charge Adam the *Dragonteaser* with the rank of *Supreme Commander of the Dwarfish Forces!*" He turned to Adam with tears in his eyes. "I beg you to accept," he said in a low voice, "you are more worthy."

Adam nodded without a word, and the dragon-tail of his helm beat against his mailed shoulders as if in encouragement. At his nod, a gruff, angry cheer burst from the dwarves, who now bore no resemblance to that morning's host. They set off in a tight, orderly formation with fury burning in their breasts and fierce loyalty to their new commander in their hearts.

Towards mid-afternoon, Adam halted his columns. Pointing away to the east, he drew Emily and Balom's attention to a dark, moving mass against the skyline. Peering hard, they could see a halo of dust around the dark form.

"Danger!" Adam said. "They are moving fast in this direction, but this time we'll be ready for them."

Since dwarves fight with the battle-axe, they need room to swing the double-headed weapon. Adam divided them into three well-spaced groups: Emily to the left and Balom to the right. The dwarves waited silently and tense, each with legs apart and battle-axe head down between his feet. All eyes were on the approaching force in the distance, with every dwarf promising himself vengeance for his fallen companions.

The first sounds reached them before their eyes could make out any detail of the distant moving mass. A sound they hadn't expected carried to them: the barking of dogs.

Hundreds of hounds of every shape and size bounded towards them, yapping and barking. On their backs were two and sometimes three little riders armed with slings. The leading dog had one rider only. It was a big, brown and white, shaggy dog with Lar on its back.

With some difficulty, Lar managed to stop the headlong gallop of four hundred dogs carrying eight hundred pixies and four hundred brownies. Or rather, Guess was in charge of the hounds, growling his orders here and there, according to what Lar wanted.

It was only after four hundred mixed mongrels, hounds and mastiffs were finally stretched out on the ground, tongues lolling and chests heaving, that Adam, Emily, and Lar were joyfully reunited in front of an army of astonished dwarves.

"Where is Palustric?" Lar's eyes searched among countless dwarves in vain.

After exchanging only vital news, the Dwarfish columns moved off again, this time flanked by the hound-riders from Halewood and Elm-dale. Balom the Black led them to the nearest stream, where at last, the dogs could have a well-deserved drink. Here, they made their night camp, lit fires and ate together.

As they dined, they caught up on their other news. Lar explained how he had travelled quickly and *almost* safely across the goblin marshlands on Guess's back to Halewood. There, Guess had gathered all these hounds that had come to war as pixy and brownie steeds. Pixies, he told Adam and Emily solemnly, could ride dogs quite happily. Horses were a different matter, he didn't know why, but horses brought out something primitive and uncontrollable in pixy nature. Lar glanced over to where the horses were tethered and began to tremble, a wild look coming into his squinting eyes. "But I've made my pixies promise not to go near the horses; the brownies know they've got to keep an eye on things as far as that's concerned."

"What did you mean when you said *almost* safely?" Emily asked, thinking it better to change the subject.

Lar stopped trembling while his eyes slowly lost their wild look.

"Ay, *almost* safely, Mistress," he smiled, his yellow eyes gentle now as he looked at Guess.

We travelled quickly, and, with my hearing and his nose, there was no danger of meeting up with goblins."

"Do marshland goblins smell, Lar?"

"All goblins stink, Mistress. They are not the cleanest of creatures!" Lar smiled at Lupp's high fluting laughter. Lex held his nose with his long-nailed fingers and winked at Adam.

"That Highland innkeeper didn't smell," Adam said in an attempt at fairness.

"The Marshland ones are the worst!" Lupp said quickly, causing the pixies and brownies around the campfire to burst into high, tinkling laughter until tears rolled down their cheeks.

Adam looked at Emily and shrugged. They waited until the little creatures had calmed. Then, Emily said, "Tell us about your journey, Lar."

"Ah, Mistress, the marshlands are foul-smelling places." Several pixies began to snigger at this. "There's a criss-cross of path-ways, and it's easy to lose your way. If you lose the path, you can sink into the bog and drown. That's where hounds are so useful." Lar looked gratefully at Guess. "They never put a paw wrong."

"Guess!" Emily called the shaggy hound, which slowly rose and crossed over to sit by her.

Emily stroked him behind his ear. "Tell him he's a very smart hound, Lar."

Lar said something in a low, growling voice; Guess beat his tail on the ground and licked Emily's hand.

"Oh, Lar, will you teach me to speak to animals?" she gasped eagerly.

The little pixy smiled and shook his head. "That would take many moon-risings, Mistress; there is a war to be fought."

"When we've won the war," Emily insisted. She had Jasmine in mind.

"Ay, when we've won the war," Lar said slowly, but his voice held the sudden, heavy weariness which had come over the group at the thought of what faced them.

Everyone sat in gloomy thought, but then Balom broke the silence. "Come on pixy!" he boomed. "Cheer us with the tale of your adventures!"

"Ay!" Lex urged.

"Go on, Lar!" Adam encouraged his little friend.

"Well, the worst moment came on our third day in the Black Mire, the worst part of the marshlands."

Lex's mouth dropped open. "He crossed the Black Mire!" he said to Lupp, next to him.

"Ay," nodded Lar, "to go around it takes many days, we did not wish to lose time. But 'tis a place of stinking ponds and ditches or slime and quag. One false step and you are lost, sucked under. 'Tis a land worthy of the Hag herself." Lar paused and sipped from a cup of honeyed water. "In this vile place, we came to a hummock of land, where reeds marked the limits of a soft, grassy island. We thought well to eat there and snatch what rest the bothersome insects would allow. 'Twas here that I saw her...a pixy maiden so fair of face, with long, cascading hair and the deepest, greenest eyes." Lar shuddered as he recalled every detail, "She smiled so sweetly that I forgot to ask myself where she had come from or what she was doing in such a hateful place. *Dear sir*, said she, *please help me, for I have hurt my leg and cannot walk farther.* Oh, her voice was clear as a meadowlark," Lar had a faraway look as he spoke, "how could I resist one so fair? I stepped over to her and took her in my arms, where she pressed her lovely self against my chest. Ah, my friends, at that moment I was lost, believe me. When she whispered, *take me down to the reeds, I live that way*, like a fool, I began to walk towards the treacherous ground—had it not been for Guess—"

The great dog's ears pricked up at his name,

his tail beat the ground, while Emily hugged him around his neck.

"My foot touched the first soft ground, and I would have been lost forever, but Guess's furious barking snapped me out of my trance. My right leg was already up to the knee in ooze and..." a look of disgust came across Lar's face, "and in my arms was no pixy beauty, but a foul bog hag. A green-faced, whiskery hag with weedy hair and sharp teeth, ready to drag me down to a watery end." Lar shuddered, his face wrinkling even more in revulsion.

"You were lucky, Lar," Adam smiled, "that Guess made you hear."

"Ay, *the lucky man has bread and a friend,* is it not so, Master?"

"I knew you couldn't tell us a whole tale without one of your sayings, Lar!" Adam laughed while Lar went on to tell of his other adventures so that the company's mood was much lighter as they prepared to settle down for the night.

The Dwarfish army rose with the sun, setting off in a tight formation. As before, Lar's pixies and brownies rode at their flank. The morning passed uneventfully with them covering a lot of ground. Over lunch, Balom told Adam and Emily that, at this rate, they would reach the Twin Towers before sunset.

It wasn't long after lunch that the first warning sign of opposition appeared. Where there once had been a lovely, wooded valley along the river on the Dwarfish bank was a sorry sight. Blackness replaced the greenery because all the trees were charred and felled.

"Goblin handiwork," Balom growled through clenched teeth.

Before long, his words were proven true: there had been fighting. Balom rode across to a dead goblin, whose black blood was dry on his chest.

"Dead a couple of days, I'd say," boomed Balom. "But I don't understand."

They rode on in silence, with Balom frowning and looking even more confused. As they rode, they passed over other fallen goblins.

"What's the matter, Balom?" Emily asked.

The dwarf shook his great, black head. "The Marshland goblins have crossed the river past the towers, but there were no dwarves to meet them. Who, then, killed them? And why have the woods been put to the torch?" Emily could see the problem. The borderland dwarves had retreated days ago; many were now marching in this army, so there should have been no defenders to halt the goblin advance.

"Unless..." Emily hesitated.

"Ay?"

"You know what goblins are like. I'll bet they fought among themselves." She warmed to her idea. "They'd quarrel with their own shadow, they burnt the woods because they love destroying things."

Balom tugged at his bushy beard. "You may be right," he growled, "it would be in their nature. In any case, the goblins are here in our lands," he boomed. "Yet," he shook his shaggy head, "it was not their work yesterday morning, for they leave their dead where they fall."

"You mean the rear-guard?" Emily asked.

Balom nodded. "Goblins would have destroyed the carts, too." He reined in his pony, and the others also halted. Balom squinted against the strong sunlight and pointed to a curve in the river: "Not far, around the bend in the river stand the two towers which guard the bridge. We now know they are in goblin hands." He took Adam's mailed arm. "Do you propose a headlong assault?"

"The trees are down, there's no cover. We can't hide our numbers or take them by surprise." Adam stroked Oakman's ear as he thought. He remembered his history lessons at school, which weren't much help since he hadn't taken interest in siege warfare. "I don't know," he said lamely.

"Perhaps we should go and have a look. How strong are the walls?" he asked, hoping to sound convincing.

"Impenetrable." Balom nudged his grey pony forward, unconvinced.

The Twin Towers lay below them, impressive bastions on the river bank. They were joined by a gateway whose iron portcullis blocked the entrance and exit to a fine stone bridge which spanned the river on five arches. Everything was silent, but they knew that the towers were full of eyes, watching and waiting.

"Built in the *Old Days*," Balom said with the tone of a dwarf proudly asserting that there was no way to break down the towers.

"Now what?" Emily said with the tone of a sister challenging her brother.

"Why don't you think of something?" Adam snapped grumpily.

"You're the *Supreme Commander of the Dwarfish Forces*," Emily said sarcastically.

"That's true," Adam said in a determined voice, ignoring his sister's tone. "So, we should build ladders and siege towers...on wheels," he added.

"What with?"

"Wood."

"What wood?"

"From the trees," Adam waved his arm behind him.

"Which trees?" Emily stepped up the sarcasm. "They're all burnt, or haven't you noticed?"

Balom, Lar, Lex and Lupp and others near enough to hear their leader's difficulty looked at Adam anxiously. Adam had forgotten this essential fact, and looking at the massive walls of the towers, he panicked. Without thinking, he blurted out: "We'll build a battering ram."

Groans greeted his words.

"What *with?*" Emily tormented her brother, who hadn't got a clue. "*Fine* Supreme Commander!" she hissed under her breath. She had resented Balom's decision from the start because she was older than Adam and in this white armour, she fancied herself as a Joan of Arc figure. She'd forgotten the lesson learnt only a few days ago in the Theatre of Pride and that she couldn't use a sword. She was as brave as Adam though and as bright, even if she daydreamed more than her brother.

"We'll have to undermine the walls," she said with an air of command. "We've got spades on the carts."

"They'll throw things down on us while we're digging," Adam objected.

411

"Of course," Emily replied coldly, "that's normal in warfare. You don't think we can take those towers without losses, do you, *Supreme Commander?*"

Luckily, just before Adam could lose his temper, Lar's high voice put an end to the matter.

"Look, Mistress!" the pixy's sharp ears had noted the squeal of a winch. The heavy portcullis slowly raised.

"They've decided to attack us." Balom couldn't believe their good luck. He looked to Adam for orders; at least he hadn't lost all faith in the *Dragonteaser.*

"That solves our problem," Adam said, re-lieved. He quickly gave orders to spread their forces as before, but this time he split the dog-riders and placed them on each flank to encircle the enemy. They were ready for battle. Their banners fluttered proudly in the breeze, the sun flashing off their sharp battle-axes. Some time passed, but the enemy did not come out of the open gate.

When at last, there was movement, only one small figure emerged from the gateway: the figure of a woman walking with difficulty and leaning on a stick. Her grey cloak had a hood.

# 36

"*S*apiens!" Adam shouted joyfully and spurred Oakman down the hill to meet her.

Once the dwarves, pixies, brownies, dogs, ponies, horses and carts were all safely inside the towers, there was time for explanation. Sapiens presented Xylor, the leader of the forest elves, and Montor of the mountain elves. Both almost as tall as Adam, they were slim with long, golden hair. The light seemed to shine in their faces while their voices were sweet to the ear. No wonder, thought Emily, that legend related that elves taught the other races the art of speech and song. She looked at Xylor, who smiled at her, causing her heart to beat faster and her face redden; she looked quickly at the floor.

Sapiens led them to a bare room with wooden chairs around an oak table. There wasn't much comfort in the twin towers. The eight of them sat around the table: Adam and Emily, Balom, Xylor and Montor, Lar and Tann, the leader of the brownies, with Sapiens.

The elderly wizard explained how she had arrived swiftly in the Elven lands. Her wise eyes didn't miss Adam's little smile.

"You are asking yourself how one so old and slow could arrive swiftly at her destination, is it not so, Adam?" She looked piercingly into his eyes, and Adam's lips formed a perfect circle as he gazed open-mouthed at Sapiens's seat, where now, one unblinking eye fixed him from the tilted grey and black feathered face of a peregrine falcon.

"*Gyak, kee, kee-a!*" the falcon called, and before Adam had time to say anything, there was Sapiens sitting and smiling mischievously where the falcon had been.

"*Who goes out in the world sees everything, he who stays at home doesn't believe it,* is it not so, Master?" Lar laughed at Adam's amazement.

"Wizards are always transforming their shape," Tann whispered to Emily, who was sitting next to him with her mouth open, too. His little, brown face became serious. "That's why I never harm any creature. It might turn out to be a wizard! Then there'd be trouble."

"Mm, yes," Emily agreed with wide eyes, "I see what you mean!"

Sapiens took up her explanation again. On the wing, in her falcon form, she had seen the Marshland goblins marching towards the Dwarfish Lands. She knew that the elves could not arrive at the towers before the goblins, so her forces crossed the river by raft at night, and Xylor's forest elves vanished into the woods. With Montor and the mountain elves, she had formed a decoy, marching brazenly past the goblin-held towers.

As they had hoped, at this provocation, the goblins stormed out of the towers after them. A hail of arrows from the forest elves in the woods met them. Since goblins are ill-disciplined, they plunged into the woods after the elves. There they met with even greater losses. Unable to catch or even see their enemy, the surviving goblins set fire to the woods, but by this time, the mountain elves had taken and closed the towers. The Marshland goblins were furious, but as Sapiens explained, they are not such stupid creatures that they would charge the walls and risk great losses to the elfin archers. They simply marched off into the Dwarfish lands, leaving the woods ablaze and their dead unburied.

"About their dead," Balom said, "I didn't see arrows in their bodies, or we would have realised that the elves had arrived."

"I can explain that," Xylor smiled. "We are going to need all the arrows we possess in the dark days ahead. No sense in leaving good arrows in bad meat!"

Emily shuddered at Xylor's choice of words, and the handsome elf smiled apologetically at her, but Emily didn't meet his gaze.

"The enemy will not be so easily outwitted in future," Sapiens said, "once the hobgoblins take charge. They are more astute than goblins and much stronger."

Balom was on his feet and pacing backwards and forwards, something clearly bothering him: "The marshland goblins are freely roaming our lands, pillaging and plundering, while we are here making small talk!" He bellowed like a wounded bull, "We are wasting time!"

Sapiens eyed him coldly. "What do you propose, Balom the Black?"

"Let's get after them!" Balom boomed, smashing his fist down on the table to back up his words.

"Leaving the towers unguarded and the road open to the enemy?"

"The elves can hold the towers. The dwarves will hunt the goblins. Adam shall lead us!"

"Why do you think the Marshland goblins have gone off?" Sapiens asked patiently. "They want to tempt you after them. They are the least of our problems. By splitting our defences, they'll make the barrier weaker for the advancing tide. The enemy is mighty, Balom. Just think, *Pride* commands the hobgoblins, Highland goblins, the Archgoblin's forces, the spriggans, the Elves of Adversity..."

"Vermin!" Montor spat out at mention of their treacherous cousins.

"...we are already outnumbered and must resist at all costs," Sapiens concluded, "even if, dear Balom, other dwarves must pay the price to avoid Universal Death. Each of us must be prepared to face death to save what we love from Pride. Not even wizards are immortal, my friend."

Balom sat down slowly, tight-lipped. He didn't say anything, but he had accepted Sapiens's words. Adam suddenly leapt up and snatched *Cari* out of his pocket with a cry. He looked suspiciously at the orb.

"What's the matter, Adam?" his sister asked.

"It burnt my leg!" Adam said incredulously. "Through my pocket." He looked at the orb, perhaps expecting it to tell him something. Instead, he dropped it to the floor, more in shock than in pain. "It did it again!" he cried.

"Maybe you're no longer pure in heart," Emily said sarcastically.

Everyone looked at the orb lying on the floor. Sapiens was the first to offer an explanation: "Adam, you have carried the lost orb worthily, but now it has returned home among the elves."

Adam smiled; he was quite happy about handing the elven orb to a worthy elf. "*Cari* might have found a politer way of telling me," Adam said sorely, "after what we've been through together."

Sapiens smiled. "It's an elven orb; even in this company, I'm not afraid to say that even the best elves have peculiar characters!" She looked at the two elves, who smiled mischievously. "Mmm!" Sapiens nodded. "They know what I mean, look!" She indicated the orb with her head and looked at Xylor.

The forest elf stepped forward nimbly and bent over the silver sphere. He reached to pick *Cari* up, but stopped, reading the runes. "Ah no," he smiled at Montor, "this is a mountain orb. Come, my friend, the orb is yours!"

Montor joined the forest elf, and his face couldn't conceal his curiosity. "Why, 'tis so!" he said, surprised, and took *Cari* into his hand where suddenly the orb joyfully burst into song —melodious elven music and cast multi-coloured stars into the air, which hung there, only very slowly sinking to the floor.

Adam and Emily laughed till their sides ached, and even Balom managed a smile. Adam wiped his eye, and when he'd got his breath back, said, "You can tell when *Cari's* happy!"

Montor smiled at the boy. "Adam the *Dragonteaser*: I name you *Honorary Mountain Elf*, for you are truly worthy of our people's friendship if *Cari* has let you carry it."

Adam grinned. "I've parted with *Cari*, but I've gained lots of new friends." He spent the rest of the evening talking to Montor. They chatted until late before retiring to uncomfortable straw beds. Everyone except Adam because Sapiens drew him to one side, leading him into an empty corridor.

"Adam," the ancient wizard said, "the dwarves have made you their *Supreme Commander*; now you are an *Honorary Mountain Elf*."

Adam looked sheepish and searched for irony in the wizard's face or voice but could find none.

"Nay, my dear boy, I have no need to mock. You have earned your honours through your bravery and good-sense. However, one so young has little or no knowledge that serves for a military commander, am I right?"

Adam looked in the grey eyes of the wizard and saw only compassion and understanding there. He hung his head and said, "I'm not worthy of being their leader."

"No, but you will be," Sapiens said and pressed a hand to either side of Adam's head. "Empty your mind of thoughts," she said. "Nay, try harder! Good, that's good!"

Adam felt a tingling in his head as if energy were flowing into his brain from the wizard's hands. Then the feeling passed, and he felt extremely tired.

"That's done," said Sapiens. "You may now possess unrivalled military knowledge, but your body needs its rest. Go to bed, Adam. Get a good night's sleep. You will need it before you lead your troops into battle."

Adam looked at the wizard with a new-born awareness that no living foe could match his soldier's grasp of strategy and tactics. "Thank you, Sapiens. I'll sleep easier now I know I'm equal to the task." It wasn't until he'd pulled the blanket up to his chin that he had an unworthy thought:

'I'll show Emily how *Supreme* I am as a *Commander*,' but he immediately felt ashamed. If there were any credit to be taken, it belonged to Sapiens. How could he defeat *Pride* if he was vain and arrogant? The young warrior fell into a deep and untroubled sleep.

# 3 7

$\mathcal{D}$aylight brought with it an unwelcome sight. The opposite river bank was crawling with goblins, hobgoblins and spriggans. Adam and Emily joined Sapiens and the others on the outer wall. The enemy's ranks were so full that they seemed to have no end. Adam groaned, "We can't possibly beat so many."

"Why not?" Balom boomed defiantly.

"Look!" Sapiens pointed across the river. "Can you see that hobgoblin with the hounds?"

They all followed the line of Sapiens's finger to an iron-clad figure hauling five ferocious hounds back on their leashes. "That's Fray," the wizard said, "Captain of the enemy forces. He's cold-blooded and merciless. Over there," she said, moving her finger, "is a pavilion. Do you see it? Purple and black stripes? Inside will be *Pride*, the Archgoblin and other goblin commanders."

"Perhaps we should raise a banner," Emily said suddenly, "just to let *Pride* see that we're not afraid of him."

Sapiens linked arms with Emily. "*Pride's forces* maybe, but not *Pride*."

"Why not?"

"Didn't you know? He can't see: *Pride* is blind."

"Blind!" Adam exclaimed. "So why does he want to rule the world?"

"All the more reason, I'd say," Sapiens invited Adam to think.

"Do you think they'll come on to the bridge," Tann asked, "or will they cross on rafts?"

Adam looked at the brownie's anxious, little face and back at Fray, the hobgoblin captain. At that moment, the war seemed to him as good as lost.

"We must wait and see," Sapiens answered the brownie. "Only when they move can we react."

Time passed with no movement from the enemy. When it came, it was a surprise. Fray strode on to the bridge, his five leashed hounds straining furiously at their leashes. Behind him, some twenty goblins pushed a strange, wheeled machine. The rest of the enemy army stayed where it was.

Fray's iron shoes rang on the cobbled stone bridge as he drew near. He stopped and tugged on the five leashes. The vicious hounds bared their teeth and barked up at the defenders on the wall high above them. They strained, but Fray displayed his great strength by the ease with which he restrained the slobbering beasts.

Xylor unslung his bow and took an arrow from his quiver. "I can rid the world of that monster," he said fiercely, eyeing Fray's bare throat. Sapiens held up her hand. "No, Xylor! The enemy wouldn't expose himself without reason. Let's see what he intends."

As if on cue, Fray raised his free hand, bringing the machine to a halt. The hobgoblin's cruel face slashed into a malign grin. It reminded Emily of one of those demons carved in stone on church walls in her *Own World*. He waved his hand. In response, the goblins snatched away a cover from the machine.

"Palustric!" gasped four or five of them on the high wall. Their friend lay stretched and bound with rope on a rack.

"Let me show you how this toy works," Fray shouted up, gloating. "I pull this lever to start the sand in this container trickling out through the bottleneck." Grinning gleefully at the taut faces above, he pulled the lever. One of his hounds tugged him slightly off balance. With an ugly expression, Fray kicked it violently in the ribs with his iron boot. The creature howled and turned viciously on its attacker. Fray hit the savage creature repeatedly with his mailed glove until the beast lay whimpering, bloodied and twitching at his feet. The others sat cowering next to it, watching Fray from lowered eyes. "That's better," Fray growled, baring his yellow teeth. "Now, where was I? Ah yes, the sand counterbalances these four extremely sharp weighted blades." The hobgoblin let the leashes fall to his feet and pointed out the blades. "One here, above the dwarf's right arm; one here, above his left arm; one here, above his left leg; and I'm sure you've worked it out by now," he sneered, "one above his right leg! Of course, after a certain amount of time," he sneered again at the horrified onlookers, "there won't be enough sand left in the container, and the blades will fall..."

He looked up at the pale, strained faces. "A little demonstration, perhaps...?" The monster turned quickly and grabbed the nearest goblin soldier. His mighty arms hauled the wretch off his feet and up towards the blade above Palustric's right leg. "Now, as I was saying," the hob-goblin effortlessly held the wriggling goblin's neck close to the blade, "these blades are *extremely sharp*. I'll lop off this soldier's head to prove my point."

The goblin screamed and thrashed. "Please!" he wailed a desperate plea. Fray was enjoying himself. He put the goblin closer and laughed, snatched him away and then put him closer again. The goblin's pitiful cries echoed around the towers. Fray lowered the goblin slowly and leered into his white, sweating face. "I think they believe me, don't you?"

The goblin nodded furiously.

"Careful," Fray grinned fiendishly, "you'll nod your head off like that!" He guffawed at his joke and let the goblin drop. The soldier scrambled to his feet and scuttled off to lose himself among his companions. Fray watched him and laughed. "These blades are for *Dwarfish* blood." He stared up at the tower. "Unless, of course, we make a deal. The dwarf," he pointed at Palustric, "in exchange for the Key. You have exactly two hours to decide—well, less than two hours, to be precise, the sand has been running for a while now!" Fray laughed unpleasantly. "I think I've made myself clear." With that, he whistled, setting off the four hounds bounding to his side. He picked up their leashes and strode off noisily, un-caringly leaving the senseless hound where it lay while the goblins wheeled the machine back to the other end of the bridge. There they left it to stand, in front of the enemy forces and under the gaze of the distraught defenders.

Adam already had his sword at Balom's throat to prevent the maddened dwarf from rushing across the bridge to certain death for himself and his nephew. When Balom the Black had calmed down, they went to their meeting room to discuss what to do.

The only thing all eight could agree on was that the Key would never be handed to the en-emy, for that would be the end for all of them. None of them wanted to leave Palustric to such an appalling fate, but what could they do?

"They've given us about an hour and a half," Sapiens said, "just long enough to break our re-sistance."

"Never!" Balom repeated. "Not even for Palustric. If I ever get my hands on *Pride*..." he boomed uselessly.

At that moment, three swallows flew through the open window and circled the room. Sapiens leapt to her feet with a cry of joy. "Here's help!" she laughed.

In an instant, the swallows became three

wizards, one of whom Adam, Emily and Lar recognised.

"Deductio!" Emily cried.

"In person," the wizard smiled, "with Valens and Veritas. Now, first things first," he looked at Lar, "did you take good care of Guess?"

Lar's little face lit up. *"Grain and gratitude only grow in good soil,* is it not so?" He looked around undecided who to ask, with all these wizards and his master too.

"It's quite true, Lar," Sapiens smiled, "even if I suspect that Guess took good care of you! But now we must explain our predicament to our friends."

"It's unnecessary," Deductio said, "because we've been flying around the towers for some time. We heard and saw everything. Did you not see us?"

"Huh! With all the other birds and with more important things than bird watching on our minds?" Sapiens clicked her tongue.

Deductio sat down at the table and indicated the two chairs next to him for Valens and Veritas. "Every problem has a logical solution," he said. "This one is no exception—the answer lies with Emily."

"With me!" Emily wasn't expecting this.

"I'm sure of it. And not by chance, I have my two friends with me. Sit opposite us, Emily."

The girl moved to obey and found herself looking into three wonderful, ageless faces. Veritas had the most honest eyes; at once, she felt she could trust him with her life. Without thinking, she held out her left hand to him across the table. Veritas took it, his sincere smile making lines around his eyes.

Valens, the youngest and strongest of the wizards said, "Emily, give me your other hand." She obeyed, losing her tiny hand locked in his great one. Her eyes strayed to his steely gaze; she could feel courage flowing into her.

Deductio asked, "Emily, who is our enemy?" Emily couldn't take her eyes from Valens but answered without turning, "*Pride* is our enemy."

"Emily," the wizard insisted, "what is the opposite of *Pride*?"

She hesitated. "Humility, I suppose, or simplicity."

"Good, how can *Pride* be defeated?"

Emily's face suddenly brightened. "Yes, I know!" she cried, and the wizards let go of her hand. She stood up and smiled at the other anxious faces in the room.

"I'm sorry, Adam," she said to her brother.

"What for, Em?"

"I'm sorry about this morning. I shouldn't have been sarcastic."

"That's true," Adam was surprised. Why the sudden change of heart? It wasn't like his sister to be so sincere, but Veritas had an odd smile on his face.

Emily unbuckled her sword and took off her white armour. "I won't need these," she said. "Now, I need a sharp knife, who's got one?"

Balom pulled a knife from its sheath at his belt. "Be careful," he boomed, "it's very sharp; it's the best blade in all the Dwarfish Lands."

"Thank you, Balom," Emily said and kissed him on the cheek. The dwarf beamed with pleasure because he couldn't resist a pretty face. "Now, I'll bring you your nephew!" she added.

"What!" Adam snatched at her arm. "You're crazy! You can't go out there. You've seen the enemy. You've taken your armour off..." he ended weakly, in a state of shock.

"Exactly!" Emily smiled and walked out of the door, down the stone, spiral staircase to the courtyard.

"Don't worry, Adam." Deductio put his arm around the boy's shoulder. "Emily will be all right." There was something so reassuring in Deductio's words that Adam allowed himself to be led with the others to their observation post on the tower. From there, they all watched Emily in her blue jeans and red shirt, knife in hand, walk alone across the bridge towards the enemy and their infernal machine.

Emily was so sure about what she was doing that even the sight of the shouting, swearing, gesturing goblins didn't bother her. She looked at the enemy rather like she would have looked at slugs or snails, with distaste, but not with fear, meaning that she walked head high, without hesitation towards the machine.

The girl's state was the exact opposite of her brother's. Adam stared with knotted stomach as Emily drew nearer Palustric. He watched the goblins turn in confusion for orders, and he heard Fray give them. In a sickened daze, he registered the enemy shouts and saw the first arrows winging towards his sister. Even as he supposed her death, he saw the air around Emily wobble and distort, like a heat haze over a road on a hot summer's day. The arrows, spears and stones just seemed to pass through his sister as if she didn't exist. Adam's mind couldn't take in the information his eyes provided.

"What's going on?" he asked Deductio. The wizard only nodded and smiled.

"Is it magic?" he asked Sapiens.

"Nay," replied the wise wizard, "it's just the opposite."

Adam rubbed his eyes. He watched Emily climb up onto the machine and hack at the ropes binding their friend, even if it was like watching a reflection in a pool disturbed by a lobbed stone. She seemed to ripple across to the other side of the machine and back again. As if in slow motion, he saw Fray and his hounds, with other hobgoblins clatter onto the bridge, and his heart sank.

Emily helped Palustric down from the machine and put her left arm under his. They turned towards the towers and ambled back; far too slowly, for Adam's liking. Fray unleashed his hounds, which bounded past the machine towards them. Even from as far away as the top of the tower could be seen the bared, white fangs of the snarling beasts. Adam turned away, so he didn't see the hounds leap completely through Emily and Palustric, skid and slither on the stone in angry confusion, before turning and leaping uselessly through them again and again. When he looked back, Fray and other hobgoblins were stabbing and hacking his sister and the dwarf to pieces—except that their blows seemed to be slicing through thin air. Emily and Palustric walked unconcernedly arm-in-arm along the bridge as if on a Sunday afternoon stroll.

Adam turned to Balom the Black. "I think I'm going completely out of my mind," he said. "Is what's happening *real,* or am I dreaming?"

"Then we share the same dream," Balom boomed, "but so long as Palustric gets back safely—"

"Lar?"

"I haven't a saying for this, Master!" His squinting eyes were puzzled.

Emily and Palustric walked through the Twin Towers gateway with the cheers of the defenders ringing in their ears. Fray and his hobgoblins didn't come too close to the walls, the first few elven arrows enough to keep them at bay.

Palustric was the centre of attention. To have him safe and in one piece was more than they could have hoped for. He told his story, though, in truth, he didn't have much to tell: a tale of illtreatment and discomfort in goblin hands. Indeed, his sunken cheeks and baggy eyes told the tale for him. He went off to clean up, eat wholesome food and rest so that their attention moved to Emily.

"I saw arrows pass through you as if you were made of air, or, at least, I thought...that is...

well, I *don't know* what I thought!" Adam's face was the very portrait of confusion because his brain still couldn't accept what his eyes had seen. Besides, Sapiens had told him that there had been no magic; therefore, the impossible had happened, which he knew was impossible!

"It's difficult, Adam," Emily said, "but I'll try to explain. You see, life is like a film in the cinema. It's made up of a lot of illusions. What we believe is what we see. *Pride* knows that better than anyone else: that's what he plays on. The only person *Pride* can't deceive is a *simple* person: the person armed with the truth and courage that only truth provides. That person sees reality and *not* an illusion. Are you with me so far?" She looked around at Adam, Balom, Lar and Tann and saw that they were all having trouble understanding. On the other hand, Xylor and Montor were nodding and smiling, while the four wizards were chatting among themselves, because they understood everything in the world, anyway. Emily sighed at this thought—how wonderful to have so much knowledge! She tried again. "What happened out there was that I challenged *Pride* on his preferred ground. The wizards gave me the truth and courage to cut Palustric loose. This was the last thing *Pride* expected, and he couldn't cope with it. His world of illusions went into tilt. So, his soldiers couldn't harm me; let's say that they weren't in the same reality. Clear?" She smiled happily at her brother.

Adam frowned. It was no use; he didn't have a clue. He struggled to make sense of what his sister was saying, "Do you mean that the goblins and all can't hurt us?"

"I wish that were true," Emily said. "I'm afraid we're going to have to fight them."

"Well, I don't understand then." Adam shook his head.

Emily smiled at him again, a very sweet smile. "Don't worry, Adam, I know you will one day."

Deductio caught Adam's eye and nodded reassuringly. "You will," he promised.

Adam scratched his head in his usual way. "Well, in any case, the important thing is that Palustric is safely back here."

"None of us is *safe*," Sapiens said quietly.

"Ah!" Lar squeaked suddenly, startling everyone, "*Truth is a torch which flickers in the fog, without dispelling it,* is it not so, Mistress?"

Emily, the wizards and the two elves laughed. "You have understood, Lar." Veritas's kind eyes looked gently at the pixy. "Now all your sayings will hold much more sense for you, is it not so, Lar?"

The little, greenish face spread into a huge grin. "Ay, 'tis just so, oh truthful one."

"*Pfffffh!*" Adam blew out his cheeks in exasperation and stomped across to the window. It seemed that he was the only person who didn't understand anything: first, arrows which passed through people and, now, a pixy who talked mysteriously about torches in fog. He couldn't take any more!

# 38

---

*J*ust as he reached the window, agonised screams from the walls above filled the room. Xylor joined him at the window but leapt back, dragging Adam with him. *"The Spitfire!"* he cried as smoke wafted into the room and more screams reached them. Suddenly, there came loud hammering at the door, and when they opened it, a band of excited dwarves burst in. They all waved their arms and shouted at the same time. One black-faced dwarf, his clothes charred and still smouldering, was pushed forward as living proof. In all the shouting, Adam heard the word *dragon* repeated several times. At the same time, he heard the beating of huge wings outside. Just in time, he turned to see Lentor circling the tower and blowing fire at the battlements above, from where the occasional arrow bounced harmlessly off his armoured scales.

"Oh, no!" Adam groaned and thought out loud. "Lentor! If only I'd known, I'd never have told you the solution to the riddle, then you wouldn't be here now. You've come for the Key! Now what?"

As if in answer to his murmured question, for the second time in the space of a day, he saw a wizard transform into a falcon: this time, it was Deductio. With a screech, the falcon took off and passed Adam at the window like an arrow. Out into the open, the falcon wheeled and, in an instant, transformed into another dragon, whose great talons latched on to Lentor and dragged him screeching down to the river bank.

There the two dragons faced each other. Even from high on the battlements, they could sense Lentor's great fury and hatred. Deductio's strangely dragon-like, hissing voice drifted up to them too: "So, you seek the Key? You shall not have it till you have defeated me in riddling:

"In the morning he has four legs,
At midday, he has two
And in the evening, he has three!"

"What is it, Lentor? Tell me if you can!"

"Oh, no! Here we go again," Adam thought. "At least that'll keep Lentor quiet. I've no idea, myself. I'll work on it, though!" He looked down and saw the two dragons glaring at each other in hostile silence. Lentor was working on it, too.

"Thank goodness we've got the wizards on our side," Emily said, who had joined him at the window. She was wearing her white armour again. "Lentor had already killed about twenty of our men. He would have roasted the lot of us if Deductio hadn't been here."

"Maybe not," Adam said proudly, but Emily gave him such a look that he at once felt ashamed of his boastfulness: "Em, we're changing, aren't we?" he said, abashed.

"Yes," she took his hand and squeezed it, "we are – I don't think we'll ever be quite the same again."

That night, the defenders in the towers slept uneasily. With the dawn, the guards reported that Lentor and Deductio were on their fifth riddle.

"On their *fifth!*" Adam gasped. "I still haven't worked out the *first!*"

"Don't you know that one, Adam?" Emily said, "I do!"

"You do?"

"Yes, it's *Man,* first when he's an infant on all fours, finally, when he's old with a walking stick."

"Brilliant!" Adam said. "Well done!"

"Not really," Emily smiled. "You see, it's a famous riddle, the Sphinx asked Oedipus—"

Adam looked at his sister with appreciation. He'd always been close to her, but she had hidden depths. He'd always thought she took no notice of learning, and now there was this new, modest version of Emily, too—he liked her this way.

The other news was that the enemy was very active on the opposite bank. By mid-morning, the reason was clear. The foe began to cross the river on hundreds of rafts. The fateful moment had arrived to fight the battle. In counsel, Adam persuaded the ten leaders that it was better to fight on the open ground than to lose their strength undergoing a long siege, even if they were outnumbered. They had two advantages, he said: they could choose their ground and formation, and no-one had finer armour or weapons than the dwarves. He decided that only the mountain elves with Sapiens should remain in the towers, while the dwarves would try to drive the enemy back under the towers so that the elfin archers could shoot down on them. The pixies and brownies were to take the flanks, moving quickly on their dogs to harry the enemy with slingshots. Valens would lead the central column of dwarves, Adam the right, Emily and Balom, the left.

Emily gaped in amazement at her brother. Only yesterday he didn't seem to have a clue how to be a Supreme Commander; now he was convincing even the wizards that he knew what to do!

Xylor and his forest elves opened the battle, loosing arrows into the goblins as their rafts approached the river bank, and many goblins took no further part in the battle. But their numbers were enormous; like a black tide, they swamped over the bank and against the Dwarfish axe-men.

The dark-skinned hobgoblins in their iron armour, swinging poison-spiked maces on chains were so strong that the dwarves were forced steadily backwards. The hobgoblins wore domed, riveted helms with side-plates that protected but also covered most of their hideous faces. Yellow fangs lined a wide mouth around a thick red tongue. In battle, they frothed at the mouth at the joy of killing, and their broad flat nostrils flared open, while their eyes were small, red slits that burned like embers in a grate.

The battle raged all day and did not go according to that morning's plan. At first, with their speed, the pixies and brownies on their dogs had great success. Using their slings, they drove the spriggans, on the goblin flanks, back into the river, where the forest elves picked them off with arrows. No spriggans survived the battle, but the pixies could make no impression on the goblin flanks. When the enemy sent the Elves of Adversity in support, they had to retreat because the elfin arrows picked off too many dogs.

At the centre of the battlefield, the hobgoblins and goblins pressed the dwarves hard. The steady retreat would have been a rout if it hadn't been for the quality of the dwarfish armour. The stoutest Dwarfish resistance was around Valens, where the hobgoblins could make no inroads. Sensing this, Fray led an assault on the left. Here, with his four hell-hounds, he came face to face with Balom the Black. Gleefully, the foul hobgoblin captain unleashed his savage beasts on the dwarf. Balom's axe smashed between the eyes of the leading hound, but he had no time to repeat the blow. In an instant, he disappeared below the other snarling fangs.

Horrified, Emily spun Blitz round so that the mighty stallion reared up, crashing his hooves down time and again on the dodging hounds. Palustric, who had been fighting near his uncle, finished off a goblin and rushed to meet Fray.

Laughing horribly, the hobgoblin swung his mace around his head with his knotted, ape-like arm. With his first blow, Fray dashed the battle-axe from Palustric's grip. With his second blow, he sent the dwarf crashing to the ground. But for the skill of the dwarfish smiths in the making of his armour, the poisoned spikes would have already pierced Palustric's flesh. Fray leapt forward for the kill, but blinded by his bloodlust, his desire to finish the dwarf that had escaped their fiendish machine. He didn't see the flash of Emily's sword. Arcing down from Blitz's back, the keen, Dwarfish blade sliced into the small gap between the cheek-plate of Fray's helm and his breastplate. Black blood spurted from his neck, and with a surprised, agonised cry, Fray turned his hate-filled, red eyes up to Emily, who coldly watched the burning embers spend their life-flame.

At the sight of their fallen leader, the hobgoblins lost heart and, turning, ran in disorder towards the river. Palustric, though dazed, was on his feet. Frantically, he pulled the heavy bodies of the hounds from his uncle and, tears in his eyes, gently took the helmet from the elderly dwarf's head, which he cradled against his chest. In the fading daylight, Palustric kissed his uncle for the last time.

Over on the right flank, it was the dwarves who were in full retreat. On Oakman, despite his own valour with the sword, Adam believed that the battle was being lost right at the end of the day. All around him, dwarves' bodies littered the ground. He was exhausted after a long day's fighting, in which there had hardly been any time to rest.

The dwarves around him finally broke rank, fleeing in the face of another goblin assault. Adam, left alone on Oakman, was surrounded by so many goblins that it would be only a matter of time before he was dragged off his horse and hacked to death. So, Adam thought, *now is the time!* He reached for the Dwarfish horn that Balom had given him, hanging at his belt. The moment had come. He raised it to his lips and blew with all his might. A long, deep vibrating note of great beauty came from the horn, causing the goblins pressing around him to drop their swords and cover their tufted ears with their hands.

Adam let the horn fall to his side and looked around. Nothing had changed. The goblins were scrambling around on the ground for their swords to hack at him again. Adam was bitterly disappointed. He had only blown the horn in a moment of grave danger as Balom had instructed him. He hadn't known what to expect, but he hadn't expected *nothing*. He urged Oakman forward and started stabbing and parrying with his sword again. At least, he would take as many of the goblins with him if he had to die. He didn't want to die. He was too young! He was only thirteen, after all! The thought drove him into a frenzy of hacking and parrying as if he weren't tired at all. Some minutes passed, in which he fought desperately for his life when, suddenly, he became aware of great agitation among the goblins. Some were grabbing their comrades and pointing up at the sky.

A black triangle, growing ever larger, was coming from the east. Adam, who was momentarily no longer under attack, gazed up, too. He wasn't sure what the triangle was, but it was coming his way very quickly. Soon enough, he realised that the triangle was a vast formation of birds. As they drew closer, their cry *Kveck, kveck* became deafening. Only to be matched by the ringing cheers of the dwarves, who were regrouping behind Adam.

With cruel talons thrust out in front of them, hundreds of eagle owls plunged from the sky. They tore the helms from the frantic goblins and swooped again for their eyes. The goblins slashed futilely at the air with their swords, but soon they fled in desperation, shedding armour and throwing themselves in the river to get away from the vengeful birds.

Adam took the horn in his hand, looking at the metal birds with the same flat face and ear tufts as the owls swooping in the dusk around him. He remembered Balom's lesson in Dwarfish history. With a great cheer, Adam stood up in his stirrups and shook the horn aloft in one hand and his sword in the other: *"Victory!"* he shouted at the top of his voice out of the sheer joy of still being alive.

## 39

*A*nd victory it was! But at a cost: apart from Balom, Xylor and Tann and, most surprisingly, the wizard, Valens, all lay dead on the battlefield. The exhausted victors buried the dead by torchlight, tramping silently along the river, past Lentor's huge body (riddled to death), back to the Twin Towers.

They sat in sombre mood around the usual candlelit table, reduced from ten to six, plus Palustric. Emily had used the word victory, but Sapiens shook her grey head. "It's not so much a victory," she said, "as time gained before the next inevitable clash. Things are always the same: the wheel whirls and the world changes, but, in reality, it never changes. Take the elves, for instance;

they were already a dwindling folk. Today many forest elves have lost their lives. We have lost our brother, Valens, while the goblins grow ever stronger."

When daylight came, Adam had another shock. Below the towers stretched a too-familiar landscape. Gone was the previous day's scenery; gone, even the river. In its place was the wilderness of stagnant pools and tangled gorse. Adam dashed from the window and found Deductio. "Quick!" he said, "Come to the window. There's something wrong."

"Of course, it's wrong," Deductio smiled, "but what did you expect?"

"We're in the Land of Poverty," Adam said.

The old wizard nodded. "After War comes Poverty," he said grimly.

"What about the Hag?" Adam asked anxiously.

"I think you'd better go out and face her," Deductio said flatly. "I have an idea that the time has come."

"Meet her?" Adam felt a cold grip on his heart. "That's about the last thing I was planning to do!"

"And, yet," said Deductio with a thin smile, "there is a time and a place for everything. Good-bye, Adam." The old wizard turned away from the boy and vanished from the room.

Adam went after him, but there was no sign of him on the stairs, either. In fact, there was a silence which struck him as odd. He dashed down to Emily's room, throwing the door open, shocking her into wakefulness.

"What's the matter?"

"Em! We're in the Land of Poverty!"

"Eh?" Emily sat up in bed and pulled her silver hair out of her face.

"And we've got to face the Hag—Deductio said so!"

"What!"

"Get up, look out of the window!"

Emily stood looking out of the window for a long time. She turned to Adam. "Of course," she smiled, "this world is governed by the same laws and principles as ours; it's what you'd expect."

"Is it? Well, I'm glad you understand." Adam shrugged and, frustrated, gave up trying.

Some minutes later, they had checked both Towers and found no-one. There was no sign of Lar nor Palustric, nor the wizards. They were alone.

"It's what you'd expect," Emily repeated.

Adam gritted his teeth and refused to ask why. "Yeah. Of course!" he said.

They set off once more into the wilderness, Emily shivering in the cold air. She looked back longingly at the Towers, where she thought of her warm bed, but, of course, the Towers, too, were gone. Emily nodded, smiled and kept on walking—it was only to be expected.

Soon, the Hag, in her weeds, was standing in front of them. Her colourless eyes glistened with evil as she bared her white, pointed teeth.

"So, we meet again, my lovelies, I knew we would—"

Adam had fought hobgoblins to the death, but he hadn't been so afraid as at this moment. He cringed behind Emily, his heart thumping wildly.

"I see there's no fairy magic to save you this time, the Hag hissed maliciously, pointing a long-nailed, curved finger at Emily's wrist. She cackled at the thought of turning them into ghouls, taking a menacing step towards them.

Emily turned to Adam and smiled sweetly, without the slightest trace of fear. She smiled wider at his pale face. Taking his hand, she said, "I think it's time to leave."

Adam and Emily saw themselves as if from the outside. The girl watched one of her hands take her brother's and the other point to a dragonfly circling their heads so that its wings almost touched Adam's nose. Seated on the dragonfly was a woman dressed in white. Tiny and perfectly formed with a golden crown above her long, silver hair; she smiled at Emily.

This time, Emily waved back and smiled. She clutched Adam's hand tightly, and her words came in their own tongue. Adam wished to tell her that he preferred the tongue of the *Other World*, but the air vibrated and whirled. It felt as though they would be swept off their feet and into the air while the grip of Emily's hand became painful. The Hag and the wilderness in front of them blurred as they spun, and the air became opaque like a steamed-up mirror. The mirror cracked across while the gap widened, all else spinning and whirling around it. The scene within the crack was firm and well-defined while the outer, opaque part swirled like an impenetrable fog. Adam and Emily found themselves inside the gap as if sucked in, but Emily swore she hadn't taken a step. There was no sign of the dragonfly, but they were standing on a green in the middle of familiar woodland. Behind them stood a copse in which was their secret den.

The most bewildering thing for them was that nobody had missed them. Whereas they'd passed several years in the *Other World*, only a few hours had passed in theirs. Adam pestered

Emily for several days, but she wouldn't explain. She smiled secretly, saying, "You'll work it out, then you'll have a lovely surprise!"

Adam was growing more and more frustrated by the day, but one night, as he lay in bed, an answer came.

He understood, as Deductio promised he would. Everything fell into place easily. The secret lay in being a simple person; the humble soul is free to fly where it will, to pass through barriers of time and space. That was why he saw Lar's hat on his chair and how he found the pixy waiting patiently with Palustric. Simple really! They were not an illusion; Emily was with them, too, because she already knew. What a welcome they gave him! Silver-eyed Emily kissed him, telling him that he could go whenever and do whatever he wanted as long as he kept his guard up against the deceitfulness of Pride. Who knew what new adventures awaited? The whirligig keeps on spinning.

# EPILOGUE

*E*mily gazed admiringly at Jayne's black leggings sculpting her long legs. Previously, those legs were a source of envy, but Emily now knew better than to succumb to the green-eyed monster.

"I've spoken to Miss Harrington, Jayney. I told her you should represent the school in the high jump. You're much better than me; remember, you had tummy-ache on the day of the trials."

Jayne stared in amazement at her former best friend, her eyes uncertain and hopeful.

"Did you honestly speak to her, Em?"

"I told you. She agreed and said you can

compete. It's better for the school, isn't it? You're sure to win, Jayney."

"Oh, Em! You did that for me!"

"We're best friends, aren't we? It's only right."

"Oh, Em!" Jayne threw herself into her best friend's arms. When their heads came together, Emily whispered in her ear, *"Friendship is worth more than treasure, isn't it so, Jayne?"*

To the taller girl, it seemed a curious way of speaking but sincere. When Jayne stood back, just for an illusionary moment, it seemed to her that Emily's eyes changed from silver to their normal blue. Jayne put it down to a trick of the light or her indescribable happiness.

The euphoria of regaining her best friend was surpassed only by winning the high jump competition and raising the cup with her, whose gritty performances had won the sprint and the long jump. When Emily played down her part in the school's victory and praised Jayne to all and sundry, the girl wondered if she was living in an alternative and better world.

## THE END

A World's Whirligig

An appeal to readers: please help me out—

I sincerely hope you enjoyed *Whirligig*. I would greatly appreciate your feedback with an honest review.

First and foremost, I'm always looking to grow and improve as a writer. It is reassuring to hear what works, as well as receive constructive feedback on what should improve. Second, starting out as an unknown author is exceedingly difficult, and reviews go a long way toward making the journey out of anonymity possible. Please take a few minutes to write an honest review.

Best regards,

John Broughton

Dear reader,

We hope you enjoyed reading *Whirligig*. Please take a moment to leave a review, even if it's a short one. Your opinion is important to us.

Discover more books by John Broughton at
    https://www.nextchapter.pub/authors/john-broughton

Want to know when one of our books is free or discounted? Join the newsletter at
    http://eepurl.com/bqqB3H

Best regards,
    John Broughton and the Next Chapter Team

# ABOUT THE AUTHOR

John Broughton was born in Cleethorpes, Lincolnshire, UK in 1948: just one of the many post-war babies. After attending grammar school and studying to the sound of Bob Dylan, he went to Nottingham University and studied Medieval and Modern History (Archaeology subsidiary). The subsidiary course led to one of his greatest academic achievements: tipping the soil content of a wheelbarrow from the summit of a spoil heap on an old lady hobbling past the dig. He did many different jobs while living in Radcliffe-on-Trent, Leamington, Glossop, the Scilly Isles, Puglia and Calabria. They include teaching English and History, managing a Day Care Centre, being a Director of a Trade Institute and teaching university students English. He even tried being a fisherman and a flower picker when he was on St. Agnes Island, Scilly. He has lived in Calabria since 1992, where he settled into a long-term job at the University of Calabria teaching English. No doubt his lovely Calabrian wife, Maria, stopped him being restless. His two kids are grown up now, but he wrote books for them when they were little. Hamish Hamilton and then Thomas Nelson published 6 of these in England in the 1980s. They are now out of print. He's a granddad, and happily, the parents wisely named his grandson Dylan. He decided to take up writing again late in his career. When teaching and working as a translator, you don't really have time for writing. As soon as he stopped the translation work, he resumed writing in 2014. The fruit of that decision was his first historical novel, *The Purple Thread,* followed by *Wyrd of the Wolf.* Both are set in his favourite Anglo-Saxon period. His writing is now divided between straight historical novels set in that period and writing incorporating fantasy, such as the Jake Conley psychic Investigator series of seven novels or Angenga, a time travel novel linking the ninth century to the twenty-first.

HISTORICAL NOVELS:

- *The Purple Thread*
- *Wyrd of the Wolf* and *In the Name of the Mother* (2-book set)

- *Saints and Sinners* and *Mixed Blessings* (2-book set)
- *Sward and Sword*
- *Heaven in a Wild Flower, The Horse Thegn* and *The Master of the Chevron* (St Cuthbert trilogy)
- *The Rebel Scribes*
- *John the Old Saxon* (soon to be published)

JAKE CONLEY NOVELS:

- *Elfrid's Hole*
- *Red Horse Vale*
- *Memory of a Falcon*
- *The Snape Ring*
- *Pinions of Gold*
- *The Serpent Wand*
- *The Beast of Exmoor* (soon to be published)

FANTASY NOVELS

- *Angenga*
- *Whirligig*